THREE LIVES

THREE LIVES

JOE WASHINGTON

To Mom.

I think I said once, when I was eighteen or so, that had I grown up without you, I probably would have turned out the same, maybe a little different. In order of ascension, least to most, there is just plain stupid, then *remarkably* ignorant, then me at eighteen years old.

Thank you.

NOW

I looked down at Mrs. Sanborne from the pulpit. I was so pleased by what I saw, I experienced something that was very rare for me. A chill ran through my body. I was finally getting through to her and it gave me the chills.

Her son had died a month earlier. Since she'd come to me and told me that her only son had been killed, I'd yet to see her shed one single tear. I hadn't been able to do much for her except to marvel at how composed she was. But something I'd done, perhaps something I'd said, perhaps because I'd stopped talking altogether . . . I'd finally gotten through. Lisa Sanborne had always been a special kind of strong.

Her husband left her when Evan, the boy who died, was born. It was their third child together, and apparently the straw that broke the camel's back. The child wasn't alive for two full days before she got the note. She walked in the door of the house they had lived in for sixteen years, newborn baby in her arms, looked down at the kitchen table, saw the envelope that said "Lisa-kids" — and ignored it. She took the newborn into her bedroom and placed him in his crib, then called her mother and asked her to move in. Just like that. No great spectacle of despair, as would have many women. Not a single complaint, despite the fact that the man hadn't even bothered to take her home from the hospital before he disappeared.

She told me she never opened the letter. "The words," she'd say. Words pleading for atonement, consideration of the no longer tolerable position he'd been put in. Perhaps he thought he was to be allowed some leniency; he had, after all, cared enough to stick it out through the pregnancy. That was the last thing she would ever do, allow him to feel as if his act of cowardice was . . .

ok. It wasn't ok. And I allowed her the sentiment. Most ministers wouldn't. They would tell their members to always at least try and forgive others their wrongdoings.

I know what the book of Mark says about forgiveness, chapter eleven, verse twenty-five. But I knew better. Some things are just unforgivable. Some things stay with you your entire life. No matter how hard you try to expunge the effect left upon you by an experience, sometimes the hole that is created just doesn't go away. And you're left minus a part of yourself. I describe it so well because I have been there. Time and time again I have been there.

Now that son was dead. Eighteen years old. He grew up fine thanks to his mother. Joined the army first chance he got. Almost immediately after, he had been sent to the new base in Russia. He was assigned to a recently created, specialized unit that focused, among other things, on the unending nearby Middle Eastern threat. What were once called extremists were now more accurately described by the general term of "anarchists" — factioned, splintered groups of terrorizers that roamed the countryside and assaulted anyone, including other Muslims that didn't immediately promulgate loyalty to the old ways. In an attempt to convey a particular message to Westerners and Europeans, they enjoyed slipping into Orgun, Khowst, Jalalabad, or any other city along the border and attacking tourists and journalists. In recent years, over thirty English, French, and American citizens had been killed. Message received.

He was one of those that walked the line, as they say, patrolling the border between Afghanistan and Pakistan, preventing these groups from being able to enter the former. The U.S., by treaty, not allowed to enter the latter. As always, they sympathized with these clans, though they denied it.

Still a boot, just barely out of basic and his initial training, Evan was sent to the area. Not long after he'd arrived, checked in and been sent to his post, he had promptly been killed by one of the intermittent potshots fired from a position situated only 800 meters away. Apparently, this happened a lot - instigatory shots fired over the border at the other side. These shots seldom actually hit anything but the barricades. Per their orders, the soldiers usually just sat them out and let the rounds come downrange. The logic was that a firefight with a four or five person gang of bandits, when they couldn't pursue, was pointless. So you just had to let the enemy shoot at you and you could do nothing about it. A nerve-racking post to walk, without doubt.

But this time was different. I believe the report was that not even a full minute passed before the rest of Evan's unit could no longer quell their anger over their FNG being hit and returned fire. With patient, systematic precision, they picked off the entire unit on the other side of the border. Without leaving their positions, they drove them out of their hastily constructed foxholes with LGGs, laser guided grenades. Then their resident sniper brought them down individually as they made for better cover. Their fucking new guy was avenged. All against orders.

Of course, no one was ever actually court-martialled, or for that matter even reprimanded. I think perhaps an NCO or two that looked the other way were "dismissed" from duty and re-assigned. But it would have been a nightmare domestically, to have to explain how these heroes who'd simply returned fire on the evil terrorist extremists that had just taken the life of a young, artless and well meaning United States serviceman were being persecuted for doing what was the only right and just and American thing to do. Sarcasm aside, I did think they were heroes. And so was he.

The bullet ricocheted inside him like a firefly inside a glass jar and tore his diaphragm and intestines to hell. He died a few days later. I looked up at his picture, enlarged to three feet across, hanging up on the wall to my left in front of one of the stained glass windows. I liked for the photos of the deceased to hang there, just beneath the ceramic display of the crucifix, as if Jesus, on the cross, was looking down upon the person and watching over him. Evan had been a handsome boy. A handsome man. He died a man, truly.

In the middle of my eulogy, I'd suddenly felt compelled to stop speaking and look at his mother. Still, as I spoke of him, not a tear. Her two older children, both young women, one on each side of her, were in pieces. All three in the front row where the family always was during these services. I had witnessed scenes like this many times, looking down upon a family, as I preached how God would welcome this person into his greater kingdom and how their loss was but a transition for the one they loved so much. It struck me as just a little awesome how this woman seemed to be exempt from the pain. Of course, I knew it wasn't that simple. But how could someone who had fostered so much love in her household, who had striven at every turn to give these children so much, many times even at the cost of her own happiness, not be destroyed by what happened and let the whole world know it? I had never been good at hiding how I felt. Even now, having lived my life and seen so much, how other people manage it is still a mystery to me.

When I stopped speaking she looked up and our gazes connected. And that's when I finally saw it. Since she had come to me and told me that her son died, I had tried and tried to access her pain. But she just wouldn't let it come through. Ever since her husband left, that part of her, that mechanism that allows the heartbreak to maneuver its way from the acknowledgment of an event to internal anguish and finally to external anguish, it had stopped working. And eventually that same mechanism shriveled up from disuse. But now, as we looked into each other's eyes, across my pulpit, the deceased's coffin, and the walkway in front of the first row, I finally got through.

No, that's not right. I didn't get through to her. It was that she was seeing right through me. The moment I stopped speaking and looked at her, and really, for the first time, thought about this young man and all he would now never have the opportunity to experience, she had seen, in my expression, my own quiet disappointment in life's cruelties. She finally saw how in awe I was of her and all she had accomplished, and this recognition endeared me to her in a way I had sought after for years. She saw how much I cared about her and her son, that it wasn't duty that drew me to her, that it was something more.

So finally she began to cry. Her daughters looked at her, surprised. They had never seen their mother cry. I probably shouldn't have, but I smiled. The looks on their faces were almost comical. They had no idea what to do. They had just never seen their mother cry.

I knew that finally she was releasing all the emotional phlegm that was sticking to the inside of her. The tears would help her cleanse. All the years I had known her, I'd felt that was one thing I might be able to help her do. And perhaps, something as horrific as her son's death was the only thing that could cause the floodgates to reopen.

I liked Lisa Sanborne. She reminded me of my mother. Of course, my mother was black, Mrs. Sanborne white. I remembered my mother as much younger, more vibrant. But they both had that selfless quality about them that only certain people have. That quality that not even all mothers have. I think that might have been why I had tried for nearly eight years to get her to let me inside her sadness. But it was foolish to presume I had the dexterity to guide that sadness out of her once I finally made my way there. She had done most of the work.

Never in my wildest dreams did I think I might become a preacher. I love it mostly. Sometimes I help people, though I am not your typical preacher. This, I would guess, has already become evident about me. I suppose I've never been your typical anything. I think perhaps, especially lately, my choice of vocation is more about the opportunity to be a positive influence, rather than my own connection with God.

Sixty-four years old now. An old man. And happy about it. I can sit on my rear and spend most of my time reading, helping people and repaying a rather large debt not just to society, but to some rather varied and often times magnetic individuals whom you will come to know as I tell the first part of my story. Even so, a large part of my time is spent just reflecting. And in this, my third life, I certainly have plenty of time to do exactly that, contemplate my doings. In the course of that contemplation, something finally struck me as odd, and somewhat sad.

In my first life, growing up in a Kansas City ghetto, societal expectations for someone like me were minimal. I was expected to kill and eventually be killed, a mere product of my environment. In my second life, where I achieved some sort of purpose guided by covert government, I had killed many times and in a way, eventually been killed. And in this, my third life, I minister to others in how they should live their lives and preach to them to never do the things I have done in my own clandestine presence on earth. When I think of it, I can't help but laugh at the irony. The ultimate hypocrite, I am. Three times over.

CHAPTER 1

Throughout my life, whenever something significant was going to happen to me, right before it did, I got this feeling. It was like something was brushing up against my insides. It felt . . . different than love, not nearly as painful as hate, and like every other emotion wrapped up into one. I felt it before my father was killed. I felt it when I was nine years old immediately before I was sideswiped by a car and left in a coma for seven days. But despite all the unhappy occurrences this feeling had preceded I didn't regard it as an omen of bad things to come. I could feel that it was more than that. It was just an indication that change was on its way. I felt that feeling before Raymond Smalls and I fought. I barely remember why. Over a girl I think. That was forty years ago. Around the turn of the century. The year was 2002.

When I was twenty-four I could take a punch, that's for sure. I had been in my share of fights already. And I was . . . competent would be the word I think. Anyone with any technical skill would have demolished me, but I could fight a good street fight. But Raymond Smalls wasn't bad either. And oh, was he trying to prove how much of a man he was with me. I didn't want to be in the fight. As a matter of fact, I had tried to walk away when he started calling me names like bitch-ass and disrespecting house nigger. The last one, I guess, because everybody in the neighborhood knew I was going to college and probably wouldn't be around much longer after I graduated. It didn't make much sense to me either. But Smalls wasn't exactly known for his intelligence.

He was as famous in the neighborhood for selling drugs as I was for being smart. And ugly. He had been cut a couple of times already. Slashed right down the side of his face. A scar on the left side of his face had healed badly and was raised and jagged from his eyebrow all the way down to his jaw. They said he got weird when he smoked and that he liked to inflict wounds upon himself too, and that's where the gash above his eye came from. Abnormally big lips, a pointy nose like you'd expect from an Indian, and eyebrows that angled at forty-five degrees made him look like an African devil. He had hated me since the day we met each other in junior high, and don't ask why because I couldn't tell you.

Whenever he'd see me with a girl, he'd claim her as his and try to start something. The one he'd seen me with this time he actually did like. Plus, he was high. There was no way he was gonna let me walk away from this one.

He was only a little bigger than me. My metabolism had just started to slow some and I was finally putting on some weight, coming up on 170. My arms and legs were beginning to develop well and though I was lean, I was more muscle than fat even then; when I threw and connected, it hurt him. I could see it in his eyes and the way he moved; he was beginning to recognize he was going to lose.

Any seasoned fighter will tell you that every punch your opponent throws, if you're perceptive enough to heed it, carries with it a great deal of information. I was no seasoned fighter, but in the course of our small battle, even I had noticed he was heavy-handed on the left. Every combination he tried started with that left. So when one of them came, somehow I managed to get close to him, inside the cross as it came and went right behind my head, and jabbed him as hard as I could in the ribcage. I could hear the sound of air being forced out of his lungs painfully - an "Aihh!" I swiveled my hips, the right side of my body moving back one step so I'd have room for the uppercut with my right fist, and threw it. He made no sound this time when I connected. Just a sick kind of bone to lips noise emanated. And finally he went down. The whole thing had probably only lasted two minutes, but felt like twenty.

I watched him fall, still charged. Still scared. The adrenaline was making my ears ring. I silently pleaded with him not to get up. But I needed to make sure. I looked back down at him, his face up, his eyes rolled back in his head. If he was conscious, he wasn't cognizant. But still, I needed to make sure. I took two quick steps towards him and kicked him in the head as hard as I could. His head whipped away from me. This time two rapid sounds. The contact of my Timberlands on his forehead, then the sound that was made as his face twisted away and hit the pavement, blood shooting from the gash above his eye when my boot hit. The sight of it made me sick. "What am I doing?" I asked myself. It was over. Oh thank God it was over.

Quickly, my mind unclouded and the noise in my ears went away. I looked up from him and a new noise was discovered. Cheering. A sea of people jumping up and down, surrounding us, screaming like they were at some kind of prize fight. We were in the middle of the street in the middle of the inner city in the middle of the day and I had been completely oblivious to the crowd that had been attracted.

"Nigga, you whooped his ass! Oh, shit!"

"Damn, mufuckin' Roy Jones Jr. in this motherfucker."

"Raymond Smalls you ain't nothin but a worthless drug dealer, nigga! I'm glad he whooped yo ass!"

They had been there the whole time, I guess. Fistfights were so rare anymore that they attracted the whole neighborhood. Everybody always handled things with guns those days.

I put my hand to my face and winced from the sharp pain that came from my lip. He'd connected a couple of times and there was my proof. I looked down at my shirt to see if there was blood on it and saw that the top two buttons had been martyred as well.

I looked around and began to worry that I'd never make it out of the man-made arena I was enclosed in. Smalls was a gang-banger and a drug dealer. Which meant he had his click at close proximity at all times. Just because he hadn't pulled his piece didn't mean his boys wouldn't.

"Yo, man."

I turned and looked at the man who had stepped through the crowd and spoken. My heart and the noise in my ears started back up again. Only this time, my eyes began to water as well. I didn't know him, and the colored bandana he wore around his neck and the matching blue color of his shirt further supported my fears. He was flanked by four other men.

"Yo, I suggest you finish him man."

"Yeah. Finish the punk motherfucker," said someone in the crowd.

I looked back down at Smalls. My heart slowed just a little.

"He's finished," I said.

Someone else in the crowd chimed in. "You need to pump one in that mufucker."

I turned in the direction of the voice. "No! No." I started to push through the crowd. Now assured this new group wasn't interested in harming *me*, I just wanted out of there. One of the men, wearing the same blue colors, obviously there with the other man that had spoken, grabbed me by the arm as I passed.

"Finish his punk ass, man."

I pulled my arm from him, turned back around, and looked him straight in the eyes.

"That's y'alls answer to everything, ain't it? Look at him," I gestured towards Smalls, writhing still on the ground. "It's over with. We're square."

"Square?" he said, shutting his eyes at me contemptibly. "Nigga, where you from?"

The leader spoke again. "Let him be, playa. That's actually one brave motherfucker."

I don't know why exactly, but for some reason I chose then to be offended.

"Man, he stepped to me. I didn't have any choice but to handle him. This had nothing to do with bravery."

He smiled. "I was talking about defying me, brother. That's some brave shit."

A brother in the crowd, his tattered and soiled clothes and dirty, nappy hair distinguishing him as one of those homeless people that always have the wrong thing to say at the right time, "Ooooh, ain't dis mufucker carrying some *shit*?"

The man and his whole crew turned, drew, and pointed their guns at the brother's head.

"Man, shut the fuck up!"

The homeless brother gulped hard.

I took this as a perfect time to make my escape. I pushed my way through the now dispersing crowd and made for the sidewalk. The leader and his boys came right out behind me, but didn't pursue. But he did speak.

"Pretty fucking brave, nigga!" Then more to himself, but audibly, he said, "Pretty fucking brave."

Though my back was turned to him, and I couldn't see the smile that I've always imagined must have been there, I could sense it in his voice. He was very pleased with something.

I didn't know it then, but halfway across the world, at that very moment, another person's life was taking a drastic turn just as was mine, and it was she who would recount to me, though much, much later in our lives, her own experiences that so closely mirrored my own.

CHAPTER 2

Maximilian Bergosi walked into the palace security control room and looked around. Multiple alarm systems and camera feeds from throughout the estate linked to monitors in the small room that served as situation room, observation post, and security headquarters. Cele, seated at the main control desk, heard him come in, stood, turned and popped a salute. Bergosi returned the salute.

"At ease."

"Thank you, sir."

Bergosi liked Cele. He liked all his men. All so eager to please. But capable, every single one of them. He had done his best to train them well. He had tried to impart upon them as much of his own knowledge as he could. Still, though good men, they were no more than second-rate soldiers in a second-rate African country. They'd be torn to pieces by any highly trained unit that they came up against in combat. A shame. Because that was exactly what was about to happen.

Cele moved to take his seat again but Bergosi touched him on the shoulder before he could do so.

"Cele, why don't you take a break? I'll watch your post."

"Thank you, sir. But, no need. I am wide awake. See?" He widened his eyes for effect.

Cele's African accent had long since become commonplace to Bergosi, an American. He had lived in this country many, many years now and even had a slight accent himself. His men would affectionately joke that he had become an Afrikaner. Bergosi smiled at the face Cele made now.

"Cele. You're a good man. You deserve the break. You should know generosity like this doesn't occur often with me. I won't offer again. Go."

A bit hurt by the admonishment, Cele conceded. "Yessir. Thank you."

Cele left the room and closed the door behind him. Bergosi locked the door, then sat in the chair in front of the control board and got started.

Systematically, he began to disengage all three levels of the palace alarm system and its connections to every security measure under the computer's control. Red switches were toggled to downward positions. He pulled up a screen, at the top of which read "ambulatories", and entered his password, "ChuckE." As in Chuck E. Cheese, his son's favorite place to eat. Then, with an obvious reluctance, a negligible amount of determination, he scrolled down the screen and changed every box from active to inactive. One by one, each monitor in front of him went to static, no longer receiving any signals from the state of the art video and countermeasure security system. In a matter of minutes, the entire system had been disabled.

The lead weight that had lodged itself inside Bergosi now felt like it weighed tons. He fought with the notion of just reinitializing the security system, knowing that no one would question him for it. But he knew he couldn't. It was too late to try and be a hero. His old life was over. Suddenly, a voice startled him.

"Cele!"

Bergosi located the c.b. on the desk and picked it up.

Outside, on the other end of the c.b., Jelani, one of the soldiers patrolling the palace perimeter, stood a few feet away from the previously electrified fence. On top of the fence, a once red light now registered green. Also, just to the right of the status light, the surveillance camera no longer moved to and fro, surveying the grounds.

"Yes, go ahead," Bergosi said.

"Sir, this is Jelani. I have noticed several of the systems have been powered down. Were you aware of this sir?"

"I'm running a diagnostics check that requires all the systems to be turned off while the program runs. It'll only be a few more minutes. I'm glad you're keeping your wits about you out there. Good job. Bergosi out."

A big smile appeared on Jelani's face. "Thank you, sir."

He turned around to resume his pace, pleased that he had passed this most recent test of his soldiering skills and that all was well. Then, inexplicably, his body lurched and the right side of him seized. Before he could get his hand to his side to investigate the searing pain, he was hit four more times in rapid succession, and was thrown to the ground landing hard on his face. There was not enough time to grab his radio before he died. His face, turned towards the fence, watched with blank and lifeless eyes as a squad of men climbed over the fence and then descended it on his side. The first man to him checked to make sure he was dead, then motioned to the others to continue.

Maximilian Bergosi stood up and exited the control room. He looked down the hallway and was relieved to see no one. Then, with much regret, he realized he would still have to kill anyone that might see him leaving the palace grounds. He pulled his weapon from its holster. His burden was an unenviable one. His compassion for those he'd just condemned was genuine.

"These are good people. God help them," he said. Calmly, he walked down the hallway, distancing himself from the carnage that was about to take place.

CHAPTER 3

Even unconscious, Chelsea Matawae could not get away from the impending sense of doom that had occupied her thoughts for the past three days. Her sleep was severely troubled, her mind, almost feverish. But the reason for her state of mind was still inaccessible. And the more she slept, if it could be called that, the more distraught she became. And then. Something horrific.

Awakened by some unknown event, Chelsea lurched forward in her seat violently, as if someone had attacked her in her sleep. She had felt a pain unlike anything she had felt before. Unfathomable pain. Or loss? She tried to catch her breath. Finally, with difficulty, she managed to regain her composure. And immediately, she was embarrassed, aware of those seated close to her who also would have been startled, but by her sudden, exaggerated awakening and not some weak-minded nightmare as she had been.

"Are you alright, madam? Princess?"

"I just felt . . . yes, I'm alright." Chelsea looked at Jonathan Nihe, the man in the seat beside her who had spoken. She didn't know him well. Their relationship could be described as acquainted at best. But she most certainly did not trust him. Odd, but significant, she thought, that that would be one of the first things to occur to her upon looking at this man. Not five years prior that would have been a totally foreign way of thinking for her. But her training had changed all that. They had stripped her of all optimism when it came to people's loyalty. As far as she was now concerned, true altruism was a dead notion. Anyone who had not proven themselves to her previously was suspect. Actually, everyone was suspect. Some just more likely to be the enemy than others. Her instructors would have been proud.

She had lied to him. The truth was she felt like she had been punched in the stomach — with a bag of ball bearings. She had fallen asleep as soon as the plane had departed the runway. The now airborne DC-10 commercial airliner was only 30 minutes outside U.S. airspace and cruising across the Atlantic back to her home. The entire ride out from the East Coast, she had been sleeping without sleeping. And then that terrible feeling hit her.

"Nonsense. You're being a nonsensical little girl like always Chelsea," she told herself. "Stop it."

She *was* still young. She had looked at herself in a mirror in the hotel room before she left and had smiled, unapologetically pleased by her own countenance. The traits that inspired that smile were abundant: the kind of intelligence that shone through her eyes; flawless, mocha skin; full lips that men were always drawn to and observed a few seconds longer than they intended; the way her features told of her heritage. All contributed to a beauty that was rare and exceptional. Her braids made her look even younger than her twenty-seven years. What had pleased her most when she looked in the mirror was that at twenty-seven, she knew her looks had yet to plateau. She was at an incredible place to be, but yet nowhere near her prime.

The beauty that enveloped her was more than just about her looks, her mother had always told her; it came not just from within, but emanated from all around her. Effortlessly, it could often be used to ensnare those she came into contact with. It was now a fact of life for her that her sexuality was an immense instrument at her disposal. Early on, it was the boys she came in contact with. Those boys became men. Lately even some women were immediately smitten.

Chelsea had learned, over the past several years, to use many tools to accomplish her goals, her looks being only one of the many. But now, she could not find one single lesson to apply to and erase the feeling that now overcame her. "Something is wrong," a voice whispered internally. "So very wrong."

"Do you need medical attention?" Jonathan asked.

"Don't be absurd," she thought. "No," she said, "I just want to get home."

She felt a hand on her shoulder reaching over from the seat behind her and knew who it was immediately. And for just a moment, she felt better. Her longtime protector's touch had always brought with it a reassurance that everything would at least be manageable. Caleb had been her guard since she was a child and had come to the U.S. to escort her back to her homeland.

Fondly, she remembered him, throughout her childhood. She'd needed only to gesture, or look in his direction pleadingly, and he would come to her rescue. Plucking her out of boring situations like policy dinners and political appointment dinners and succession dinners time and time again to whisk her away to freedom. Smiling all the way, he was. Always smiling down at her with his pleasant yet weathered face with its dark skin and big, hawk like nose.

When she was six years old, her father's chief of staff had attempted a coup. Really, contrary to his own wishful thinking, he had very insubstantial backing in his own military, and was killed within days of the pitiful operation he initiated against his king. But for those days preceding the man's death, Caleb had always been there with her, to keep her from harm should he make a last ditch attempt on the king's family.

She remembered waking one night and sitting up in her bed to see the silhouette of a man sitting across from her in the darkness.

"Caleb?" she'd said hushedly.

"Princess," was his only reply. And that was all the little girl had needed. Her protector was there and she'd gone back to sleep. Protector. An accurate term for the odd connection they shared. As she grew older she realized her view of their relationship as a friendship was romanticized and unrealizable. He saw their relationship as purely a working one. They had never had any contact outside of his duties and he chose not to speak to her of or about any other matters. He'd simply smile down at her again and that served as the most substantive communication between the two on most occasions. Truth be told, she knew nothing of the man except that he had been there for her when she really needed him, her entire life. But for her there was no greater reason to trust someone. Her years in America had been the only time they had been away from each other for any extended length of time.

"Your parents have missed you sorely, Chelsea."

That was it. It was her parents. She didn't know why, but it was her parents that she longed for. Or hurt for? But why?

"I miss them very much also, Caleb."

Indeed she did. Missed them more now that she was on her way back to them than she had the entire time she had been separated from them in America. "This is too odd," she thought. "Something is very wrong. Trouble is ahead." Good thing she had Caleb with her. She might very well need his help soon.

CHAPTER 4

It had been a couple of days since the fight. Two whole days had passed and nothing happened, so I became optimistic that it was all over. That morning I actually woke up without a dark cloud of dread looming over me. The fear was dissipating, which I interpreted as freedom. Maybe I could finally begin to operate without constantly looking over my shoulder? And then I walked into Willy's shop.

Willy was one of those white people that just fit into the hood scene so well people didn't even notice he was white. He had one of those little shops on The Paseo, a long stretch of city street that ran almost 85 blocks and took you right through the middle of the city. He had everything you'd need if you were trying to avoid actually going to the Pic and Save and doing some real shopping — snacks, drinks, liquor and smokes. He had been there forever, at least as far back as I could remember, probably before the neighborhood was even mostly black. And he just never left, like all the others. Or at least that was my theory. Never really asked him. He was a crotchety old bastard. But we did get along great, nonetheless.

Sometimes I'd walk into his place and wouldn't leave for hours. We'd play checkers like it was chess. He'd lean in over the board and plot moves as if we were participants in some kind of national championship. That was the most fun of it, watching his brow furrow and his temper flare when I'd beat him. Upon losing he'd jump up and stomp around his shop as if he'd lost the deed to the place. He'd raise one of his seventy-plus-old fingers, point it at me and dare me to play him another game. Sometimes I'd say no just to see his reaction.

"You little fucking bastard! When I was a pool shark in Atlanta, if I beat a man fair and square, I'd give him a chance to come even. The only ones that didn't accept a second game were the cheats who didn't have another game in 'em. Now you give me another game or I'll kick your black ass out of my store for good this time!"

And so I'd throw up my arms in defeat and let him beat me the second time around just so I could go home.

"You cocksucker, you let me win that game!"

I nodded in shame. "Yes I did Willy. I'm sorry man. But I gotta go."

He would throw his eyes up towards the ceiling and feign disapproval at my deception, but I knew that he was just disappointed that I had to go.

"Ok, be careful going home. Tell your mother I'll be over later."

"Watch it."

"Heh, heh, hee, hee. Kidding! Kidding. I know how you black people are about your mothers."

"You can be an ass sometimes Willy, you know that?"

"Better an ass than a jackass."

"What's the difference?"

"A jackass has absolutely no redeeming qualities whatsoever my boy."

"Of course. I'll see you later . . . jackass." And I'd run out the door. It was always a game between us to see who could get in the last word. The only time I ever saw him smile was when we'd bicker.

When I walked in this time he wasn't smiling. He stood behind his counter and had his hands placed upon the register desk. He just watched me as I entered and walked to the back of the store to grab a soda. I could tell something was wrong with him immediately. A definite look of concern present on his face.

"Willy One Blood, what's up?"

"Nicholas. Uh, how you doin' son?"

"I'm good." I walked up to the counter and set down the soda. He was a few inches taller than me so I looked up at him and searched his face.

"Is everything ok?" he asked.

I pulled out some change and laid it on the counter. "Yeah, as far as I know. Why?"

He pushed the money back towards me. "You know your money's no good here." He ducked underneath the counter and reappeared quickly and placed something in front of me.

I looked down at it. A gun. A revolver. A really old revolver. A really old Smith and Wesson revolver. A .45. I didn't like guns. I never had. Guns meant death. A simple rationalization, but a fair one I thought. I was nearing my mid-twenties and had seen enough death to last a lifetime already.

"Here," he said, pushing it towards me.

I looked back up at him. "What's that for?"

"Take it. I heard you had some trouble the other day."

Suddenly, I understood. "Oh, aw, man that's done with."

"Oh, yeah?"

"Yeah, man I'm good. Really."

"You sure? Here take it just in case. You're a good kid Nicholas. I don't want to see you get hurt. And from what I hear you might need it."

"Naw, man. I don't need it, put it away. Please. I'm fine. Ain't nothing happened since then. Don't sweat it."

"Ok." He put the gun back underneath the counter, almost dejectedly.

"But thanks." Suddenly I felt kind of ungrateful. "I do appreciate it. But Willy, take some of that valium you always taking man, dag. You gotta chill on the high-powered weaponry, dude."

"I'm just trying to help you out. I don't tell you, but I really do like you. Don't find many like you around here anymore."

His face said it all. I could see the desperation more around his eyes than anywhere else. Willy was scared for me. I had never seen him scared, not even for himself, despite the dangerous circumstances that we lived in. I felt the bond I had with this man I had known all my life was suddenly made more special. It occurred to me that I needed to stay and calm his fears, but now my own fears were renewed and I had to get somewhere to think.

"I know," I said. "And I appreciate it. I'm gonna go. I'll see you later?"

"Be careful Nicholas Gambit."

"Yeah. I will." I walked out the door, rounded the corner and stopped where I knew he couldn't see me. Suddenly, my heart was going again, as if the fight with Smalls had just ended. And I felt the same fear I had seen in Willy's face. Fear for my own immediate future.

CHAPTER 5

I went straight home from Willy's. I didn't have any classes so I didn't have anywhere to be and really, all I wanted to do after being scared by Willy and his gun was to just go home and sit in safety for a while.

The Victoriano brothers and their family lived two houses down from mine. My mother and I had been in our house for fifteen years and the Victoriano family had been in theirs for almost as long. They were a real Castilian family from Alcorcon, Spain. When they moved in, the three sons and I had immediately bonded. They were always very sociable those three, but tough. They enjoyed cutting on each other, good banter. Sometimes it was just plain mean but they were always fun to be around. I liked them and the way they would often draw me into their lives, like I was part of the family.

They were outside practicing soccer and saw me as I neared my house. Alejandro picked up the ball, yelled out my name, and came running over. Emilio and Diego followed. This was their way; Alejandro, the oldest, always in the lead, Diego and Emilio never far away. It was, I had realized, a means of protection as well. The safety in numbers approach in our neighborhood was always a good idea.

"Qué onda cabrones?" I yelled, trying to jump right into our usual roguish exchange. But it must have been immediately obvious to these guys who had known me for so long how distracted I was. Alejandro looked at me with searching eyes, attempting to identify what was wrong.

"Nicholas. Cómo estas?"

"Qué tal amigo?" Emilio asked.

"Yeah, what's up, bro?" Diego said.

I gave up the charade. "My day was just fine until a few minutes ago."

"What happened?" asked Emilio.

"Willy . . . was wigging. Got me thinking about some things, that's all."

"Raymond Smalls, huh?" asked Diego. "You alright?"

"Yeah." I decided it wasn't healthy to let this get to me any more than it already had. So I changed the subject to a favorite topic of ours.

"You know what? I don't even want to deal with this anymore. So wuz up fellas? Where's all the señoritas at?"

Diego, the youngest and probably the most handsome of the three, was quite the ladies man. He was well known as the neighborhood Latin Lover. But when it came to girls, there was so much Latin self-assurance and aggressiveness, there was absolutely no room left for love itself. More than a few hearts had been broken by that kid over the years. And he was damn proud of it too.

"Well, you know I gets mines," he said.

I figured I'd take him down some. Sometimes his arrogance became a little too much to bear. I held up my forefinger and thumb only a very small distance from each other. "Yeah, and I heard Spaniards have little dicks."

He opened his mouth in surprise and then smiled. He threw a mock punch at me and I pretended to block it. Then we slapped hands.

"And when was the last time you were with a girl, Nicholas?" Alejandro asked.

I almost said, "I don't know, ask your momma," but thought better of it considering they were even more sensitive about their family than most black folks I knew. So instead, I just said, "Why so interested in my love life all of a sudden, Alejandro? You trying to get wit me or something? Man, you gone sweet on me or what?"

"Eww. Naw, I want to know. Qué piensas de nuestra hermana, eh?"

"What do I think of your sister? She's fine. Why?"

"She likes you, you know," said Diego, a big smile on his face.

"Really? Can you hook me up?"

"Un negro in our familia. I don't know," Emilio said playfully.

"I just said hook me up. I ain't trying to marry her or nothin."

Whoops. Suddenly the three began to close in on me. Like I said, very sensitive about their family, and you never knew what particular would set them off.

"Why not, she's not good enough for you?" Diego said, completely serious.

"Man step off me. C'mon, you know me. I ain't gonna treat her wrong. C'mon."

This relaxed them.

"Yeah, we know. You're the only nigger we'd ever allow her to see."

"Say what!" It was kind of childish, but I figured if they were gonna get mad at me for saying something completely innocent like I had, I wasn't gonna let them get away with calling me a nigger.

"Oh, sorry. Where we come from that doesn't mean the same thing," Emilio apologized.

"Well you in America now fool! Think you need to get that green card booklet out and do some catching up."

"Alright, alright, I'm sorry."

"Hey, who's that?" Diego interrupted.

We all turned to look towards the street. Coming down the street were four men in a green Cutlass, moving very slowly. Everyone in the car was staring directly at me and the Spaniards. As my mind began to bewilder itself with all the dangers seeing a car like that full of young black men, focusing on your position held, I could feel the brothers tensing up beside me. We knew this scenario well enough. Each one of us individually was planning which direction to run if anyone in that car made a move.

Then I saw him and my heart dropped. Raymond Smalls. In the passenger seat, looking at me like he was looking right through me. Very slowly, he extended his arm outside the window. My eyes went to his hand and saw no weapon. But I knew the rest of his boys could have something or it could just be some kind of trick. I watched him as he pointed at me, then raised his thumb, pulled back his trigger finger and simultaneously motioned with his mouth the sound of a gun going off. Then he smiled that ugly smile of his and made a point to look me in the eyes until he had to turn away. I didn't lower my head or breathe until his eyes left mine.

"Ohhh, tienes un problema grande, hombre," Alejandro warned.

"Yeah, man, what are you gonna do?" asked Emilio.

"Voy a casa," I said simply. I'm going home.

"Be careful, black," Diego said in Spanish.

"Tu también. Hasta luego."

"Hasta luego. Adiós," they said.

CHAPTER 6

There are times in the telling of my story, as you will see, when I yield to the omnipotent third person. Events that I know occurred, some of it by way of research done in preparation to write my story, some of it from firsthand accounts from someone that was present and deeply involved in the incident. Sometimes I *was* there, but not in eye or earshot. Still, I know they happened.

The following is one of those events. I especially feel that I need to include this one, because without it, brief as was this exchange, one might not see the role my mother played and why and how it is that she shaped my destiny forever.

Leslie sat on Gina Gambit's desk, watching over her as she worked. Furiously, methodically, Gina worked to pull the info from the disk that Leslie had given her. She stared at the computer screen and tried to block out Leslie's whispered cries for her to finish.

"C'mon Gina. Hurry up. C'mon, please, hurry, hurry!"

"I'm going as fast as I can. Leslie, hold on a second."

"Oh, god, I'm gonna eat this one big time. Please, god. C'mon Gina, please hurry."

"Leslie, shut-up!"

At this everyone that surrounded them in the office looked up from their own work. Almost too pretty for her skinny frame, Leslie looked around and smiled sheepishly. Then she looked back down at her friend Gina. Her friend Gina. Her friend Gina who held her career in her hands at this very moment. If she didn't get the information the disk held sent by e-mail to one of her bosses in New York by the time he walked into his office, that career of hers would be no more. This man was well known for firing people, by phone, for not making deadlines just like this one. Luckily for her, he was a total hypocrite and never showed his face before 11am. Not long after coming into the office, she had realized her blunder and gone to her one true, only, special friend Gina. Giving them almost two and a half hours to fix it before he entered his office on the east coast.

She noticed Gina was slowing down. "Wha . . . Gina . . . ?"

Gina glared at her in a way that stopped her cold. "Right," she thought. "She knows what she's doing."

Gina finished a few inputs, then slowly, intentionally torturing her friend, pulled the disk out of the computer and handed it over to her. Leslie thought she was gonna cry.

"Bless you." She ran over to her desk, inserted the disk into her own computer and a few clicks later absolutely marveled at the graphic showing a file being sent from one source to another. "File sent, download complete." It was the most pleasing combination of words she had ever seen. She wiped the symbolic sweat from her brow and looked upward. "Thank you."

Leslie walked back to Gina's desk and sat down again.

"And thank you. You just saved my butt. I love you like no woman has ever loved another. If I wasn't a chronic heterosexual we'd be getting it on right now."

Gina laughed. It was Leslie's sense of humor that had brought the two of them together as friends originally, and she just couldn't keep from laughing when they were around each other.

"Leslie, you've got to devise some sort of system to help you remember your passwords. Breaking into a disk like that is a lot of hard work and it would all be unnecessary if you'd write something down for once. And I'm not doing it anymore."

"Oh, come on. You talk like you've had to do it a bunch of times or something."

"Four, Leslie. Four times."

"Really?"

"Umh-hmh."

"Well, geez, you're some kind of sap. Why would you let somebody take advantage of you like that?"

Gina's mouth fell open.

"I'm kidding! Kidding. Won't happen again. And anyway, this is nothing for a computer genius like yourself."

"I'm no genius."

"Sure you are. Gina, how many people do you know that can do what you just did who haven't spent their entire adult life in college? Face it. You're a genius. You even passed it along to Nicholas."

"He may be a genius but I'm not."

"Well, maybe you're right." She looked over her shoulder at a very well built and handsome black man at his desk across the room. "There you have a perfectly good man with probably a perfectly good . . . you know what, who wants to take you out and you're having no part of it, him, it. Whatever."

"You're sick."

"And you're lonely. Who's the worse off, hmh?"

"Shut up. Don't you have some files to botch?"

"Oh, that hurts. Fine." She stood up and looked away as if she didn't care anyway.

"I'm just not ready."

Leslie looked at her poor disillusioned friend, not completely misunderstanding what she really meant. "You're not ready or Nicholas isn't?"

"What are you today . . . ?"

"Well, sorry, but isn't it a valid question?"

"What does he have to do with this? And him?" motioning to the man at his desk. "He is quite handsome," she thought to herself. But that was beside the point. "I don't know. Maybe neither of us," she said out loud.

"No, Gina. I think it's him. You're there for him. You always have been. Stop holding yourself back from being happy because you think Nicholas won't be able to handle it. For once, follow what you feel. He's grown now. It's your life."

Leslie thought she had pestered her friend for long enough, so she gave her a "think about it" look and walked away.

Gina Gambit wasn't the least little bit unsure about the role her son played in her life. There was no question in her mind that all she wanted out of life was to see him get out of that miserable living situation she had gotten them into and make a life for himself. She did more than just live vicariously through Nicholas. When he excelled, she flew higher than she could ever have done with some man. She thought of Leslie's good intentions and smiled. "It's your life," she had said.

To herself, but out loud she said, "Not for twenty-four years it hasn't been. And I wouldn't have it any other way."

CHAPTER 7

The night had fallen. Finally. Boy was I scared. I hated that. I hated that he made me scared. I hadn't left the house since Smalls had ridden by. The thing was that I had beaten his ass and he was the one making me look like some kind of chump. I realized there was no reason to even look at things in that way, that I was just being macho, but I couldn't help but feel like I had bitched up when I should've been out there looking for him or just . . . doing something, something constructive. I had to formulate some kind of plan.

You know, I knew I was different since the very first day I started public school and seen so many faces that just didn't care. I didn't look at things the way other people in my neighborhood did. Logic and reason always played a part in how I dealt with problems and people. Emotion had its place; emotion *ruled* at times even. But, put simply, I sought after more, in all things. This life that people like Smalls had taken for themselves was just not enough for me. Not that I thought I was in any way better than those in my neighborhood, just different. And because of this, I had to think different. Outsmart those that were bigger, stronger, faster, or had guns when I didn't. This was my dilemma and I knew it. How do I outthink Smalls and his gang of half-wit Negroes? I groaned out loud. I was twenty-four years old, a post-graduate, and too busy and too old to be dealing with this shit. How come life couldn't ever be easy?

So I sat in my living room and watched a television that wasn't turned on. I barely noticed my mother come in the door.

"Hey boy."

And didn't notice her greeting.

"Nicholas."

Even the second time she spoke barely registered. "Hi momma."

She looked at me questioningly, and then at the turned off television I seemed to be entranced by.

"You feeling ok?"

Now this was an interesting decision of mine, to not tell her about my situation - one I still often wonder about. I think I may have just not wanted to give her any bad news when lately it had all been so good. The best news being that we were almost out of there. I was six months away from a master's degree. Her job was going well and she was soon to be promoted to a better-paying position. A better life was right around the corner. We were almost there. Almost. Too many things just yet accomplished. I would soon learn to never be satisfied with almost. Being close to your goal sometimes serves only to amplify the disappointment when you don't reach it.

"Yeah, I'm ok," I said, glumly.

"What are you doing?"

"Nothing."

I could tell she was perplexed. She knew. She knew there was something going on with me. I'm sure she thought a girl was involved somehow. When it came to being sullen and distracted, my track record would have proven it likely.

"What are you thinking about?" she asked. "Your father?"

But. Whenever I didn't want to talk about something she always thought it was my father that was on my mind.

"No. Why? Have you been thinking about him?"

"Yeah."

"I do sometimes," I said. "I really wish he was still . . . here. Sometimes."

She sat down beside me and looked at me. I looked back at her. And my mother was lovely. At forty-five she barely showed her age. She'd told me that she had modeled before she met my father and I could believe it. High cheekbones, straight, long eyelashes but still very soft features combined for a real beauty that I'd noticed more than a few men double take at. She had just recently highlighted her short, dark hair that came down and swooped in around her neck the way the old-time movie starlets had done, and that made her look even younger. She had a mother's figure but was still quite womanly. I was proud of how pretty she was. And I was glad that she had passed on some of her looks to me. I was sure she must have had plenty of men who wanted to be with her though I never met any of them — and didn't want to for that matter. Me and her against the world. That was how it was supposed to be.

"I bet there's a lot of things he could help you with that I can't."

"Yeah . . . I mean, uh . . . no . . . ."

She smiled and put her arm around me and pulled me in close. "I know. I understand. When he died that's kind of how I felt too. Just know that you can come to me about anything."

I couldn't think of anything else to say so I just nodded my head.

"You know what the best thing about your father was?"

"Hmh?"

"He gave me you."

I couldn't help but smile. She could be so sweet to me. One of the toughest people I knew, yet she had always been incredibly loving. And those days I enjoyed every minute of it.

"I am so tired. I'm going to bed." She stood up and walked into the hallway towards her bedroom.

I called after her. "You taking me to school in the morning?"

"What kind of question is that, you dummy, don't I always?" she said, laughing.

I stood up and walked into my bedroom, pulled off my shirt, and plopped down onto the bed. I rolled over and looked up at the ceiling, put my hands behind my head and thought about my situation again. I'd had all day to think myself a way out of my situation and hadn't figured out one single thing. I could be dead soon if I didn't work something out.

When I woke that next morning, I felt no better than I had when I'd finally gone to sleep the night before. It was more just being unconscious than sleep. To say that I was still troubled by everything would have been a massive understatement. But I had achieved one mental milestone. I wasn't going to overburden myself with worry so much that I locked up and couldn't function. When Smalls made his move, whatever it would be, I'd deal with him then. Until that time came, all I could do was behave as near to normal as possible. Just . . . live. Though at the time, I thought the end to my story might very well be right around the corner, it seemed to be the only choice that made sense.

I showered and dressed, grabbed my backpack then went in the living room and sat down in the same spot I had occupied the night before. On the way, I passed my mother's room and heard an unfamiliar noise. It was her shower going. I had awoken an hour before my alarm went off so I was uncharacteristically early. So I turned on the television and watched cartoons for the first time in five years. I didn't recognize any of them until after about the fifth channel change the Power Rangers came on. I immediately shut off the television. I hated the Power Rangers.

A few minutes later, I heard my mother come out of her room. She didn't even look down the hallway in my direction. Why would she? I was never there before her in the mornings. I let her walk to my room and bang on the door.

"Nicholas? Time to get up."

"Ok," I called.

She turned and walked towards the living room and gave me a surprised look. "Since when do you get up this early?"

"I'm turning over a new leaf."

She nodded her head. I don't think she believed me. "Right. You ready then?" she said as she walked back to her room.

"Yeah, actually, I gotta hurry. I think I may have to sub for Professor Gilliam today. I forgot all about it with everything going . . ." I grimaced. I was going to have to lie again.

She came out of her room and walked up to me. "What's going on?"

"Aw, oh . . . well, just, you know, school stuff."

"You're a horrible liar, Nicholas Gambit."

"Yes I am."

"Well, you just tell me when you feel right about it."

I was relieved. "I will." I got up and started for the door.

"Hey, hold on a second," she said.

I thought maybe she had changed her mind. "Momma."

"Sit down," she said.

I just stood there. I did not want to lay this on her right then.

"Sit down, c'mon," she said.

I sat back down on the couch and she sat beside me.

"I want to tell you something. I want you to know that I'm very proud of you for doing so well at school. I don't get to tell you enough how proud of you I am. And I am."

"Oh," I said. "I know." I never knew how to tell her how good it made me feel when she said things like that to me. But I think she knew.

"You doing so well in senior high and getting all those scholarships, it was the only way. And you did it. Not many kids from around here go to University, most of them don't even consider it an option. I've always regretted never getting a university degree. A city school degree's just not the same."

"Momma I've already heard all this."

"Thank you. For being a good son, for taking care of me when I should have been taking care of you."

"Momma." Sometimes she'd get on a roll and it'd be an hour before the therapy session was over with. I wanted to avoid that this time. I had other things to deal with.

"For getting such good grades there. I can't believe you're a graduate student. And for not being like all those hoodlums out there. Nicholas, no matter how bad things might get you'll always have family . . . and righteousness, like I told you before. They're both very strong in you."

"Mom-ma."

She looked at me in a way that showed she meant business this time, so I figured I'd better just ride this one out.

"You are so special. Never ever forget that. You have something very one-of-a-kind within you, Nicholas. It's a, well, I don't really know how to describe it, but don't ever let anybody take that from you. Ok boy?

"Ok, and I understand and you're right and can we please go now?"

"Don't patronize me Nicholas Gambit."

I put my head down and smiled. I was a grown man and she could still stop me on a dime by using my full name.

"God gave you brains, use 'em. I beg you, don't get careless and get caught up in all this mess." She waved her hand, inferring all the hard ways our people had adopted in this environment. Oh, if only she knew what was going on in my life at that very moment. That last statement had reaffirmed my decision to not get her involved.

"I promise, okay?" I hoped I wasn't lying to her.

"I mean it."

"I know. And I promise. Now can we go?"

"Ok." She cradled my face in her hand like I was still three years old. "Hey, you know I love you don't you?"

I smiled and nodded my head.

"Ok." She slapped me on the cheek. Then the doorbell rang.

"Get that." She walked back to her bedroom to gather her things.

I thought to myself as I walked to the door, "Man, the Huxtables ain't got nuttin on you woman." I opened the door and looked out the screen.

"What's up, dog?"

It was the brother from the day I'd fought Smalls. The man who had suggested I kill him. This was the first chance I had to really look him over. At the fight I had been too occupied with whether someone near me was thinking of taking a shot at me to pay attention to his physical characteristics. He was smiling. He looked to be in his mid-thirties. Older than most of the thugs that ran around town. They didn't tend to live that long. At first he appeared to have short hair, then I looked more closely and noticed tight cornrows. He wore a stripped down thug outfit. Jeans and a long white t-shirt. I could see the bulges underneath the shirt at his waist where his piece was probably located.

"Who is it Nicholas?" my mother asked, calling from inside her room.

"Nobody Momma," I yelled back. Then to him, more quietly, "What you want, man?"

The man looked me up and down through the locked screen. If he made a move I didn't like I figured I'd have time to shut the door, but I didn't get the impression he was there to do me harm.

"I just want to talk to you, brother," he said.

"What about?"

"Your future," he said, smiling.

I didn't know what to make of him. But something still told me he didn't want to hurt me. The smile on his face, it was genuine. He didn't do it to take me off guard, but because he found something amusing. Now I was more curious than worried by his presence on my doorstep.

"Momma, I'm gonna be outside for a second."

She looked around the corner of her doorway and I gathered she was changing again. My mother was like any other woman, at least in that respect. And as I have since found to be their way, she would sometimes just give up on one outfit and change into another for no discernible, compelling reason.

"Nicholas, who is that?"

"Just a friend. I'll be right out front." I stepped outside and closed the door behind me. I looked at him, attentive to what he did with his hands. "What's up?" I said bravely, raising my head and looking down at him.

"Fame and fortune, changes and rearranges. But all that's up to you."

I just grunted and kept looking at him.

"I saw something in you the other day. That's why I'm here. To invite you to the brotherhood. Be all you can be in KC, playa."

I was a bit taken aback by his disposition, considering what it was he was asking.

"So what, you came here to ask me to join yo' crew?" I smiled. "Look, man, I ain't really down with that brotherhood bull, man. I mean that's cool if ya'll want to kill yourselves but I ain't wit it and never have been. My time is too precious to be walking around worrying about whose turf I'm on."

"I don't really see how you got a choice. That mufucker you beat down the other day has been busy for yo ass since the day after it went down. And he ain't alone, my brotha. And every single one of em got heat, wit about a dozen slugs wit yo name on em. You need me. And e'ebody that comes with. Man, check this out. Nigga, if I could find you, don't know you from a black piece of shit in the road, he could find you. And he ain't gonna just talk to you in front of yo momma's house. I hope you agree."

I lowered my head and thought. Clarity of mind came quickly. He was right. "Yeah, I do. I agree. But what do you get in return?"

"We'll talk about that later. I'm Kato." He handed me a piece of paper and I opened it up and looked at it. It was an address.

"I know you a big college man and everything, so meet us there tonight, after you're done."

It must have registered that I was a little curious how he knew so much about me because he smiled again.

"Yeah, I know all about you Nicholas Gambit. True 411 is the key to survival. And it's all about survival or so people tell me." He walked towards a car parked across the street, three other men inside. I berated myself for not having noticed them as soon as I left the house.

"Watch yo ass, nigga. From now on, paranoia is your very best friend." He got in the passenger side of the car and they drove off.

This thing was getting thicker by the moment, but I realized if I needed something more than any other, it was an ally. Kato. Like the Green Hornet's Kato. Bruce Lee's Kato. I laughed. What kind of G'd up, thug life nigga would name himself that?

CHAPTER 8

Later that day, I sat on campus outside my first class. I had tried to locate Professor Gilliam to find out if he still needed me to cover for him in his ethics class, but he hadn't made it into his office yet. So I decided to refresh myself on the lesson that he had provided just in case, but that only took a few minutes because I had already taught the lesson twice before in the past two weeks. If I had been awarding a grade, professor Gilliam would have received a D for attendance. He was taking advantage of the fact that he knew I was comfortable and capable as a student-instructor and sometimes it seemed like I was teaching his class for him. But I liked being in front of that class, sharing *my* knowledge; so I guess I didn't mind so much. After looking over the lesson twice, I soon realized the only advantage being early that day provided was a chance to sit and ruminate about everything that was going down.

I watched all the young people walk by. Usually, I took pleasure in sitting and counting how many girls I could get to smile at me, maybe look twice in my direction. But not that day. Instead, I thought of how easy life must be for them, in comparison to my own. Sure, they had all the same issues as most students, trying to find some sort of balance among many conflicts. Conflicts like money, their studies, friends, a love life, money, entertainment, family, an often insubstantial attempt at expanding their minds, and of course money. A pressure and a desire to do well that sometimes was more defeating than inspiring. Uncertainty about one's future, both short term and long term, could make things hard. I had experienced all those same mental sufferings. Now I yearned for them, for that to be all that I worried about.

If Kato knew I went to school and probably where, then so could Smalls; which meant I wasn't even safe there. Everybody in our neighborhood knew Smalls had killed people. He was even beginning to gain notoriety for it. Maybe I could just be patient and wait until the police caught up to him for his past transgressions? Yeah, that was likely. Maybe I should've taken the gun from Willy, stopped being so high minded, did what anybody else in our neighborhood would've done and gone after him and capped him first. Desperate measures for desperate times, right?

"But I was no killer", I kept telling myself. I didn't want to start down that path then, when I was so close to getting away from it all. All I wanted was to take a teaching position somewhere, make some money, maybe have a family and just live a normal life away from the sirens every night and the bullets that you could hear flying through the air, making that "phhttt" sound. That's all I wanted. And now Raymond Smalls wanted to take that all away from me. I began to feel sick to my stomach. If I ever got out of that situation, oh how nice it would be to worry only about whether my scholarship check came or if I got an A or a B+ on an exam.

"Hey."

I excused myself from the well of worry I had lowered my subconscious into, one that had momentarily blocked out everything going on around me and looked up from where I sat and saw one of the sexiest girls I had seen in a very, very long time. The first thing I noticed, from my vantage, were her legs. She wore a very short mini skirt that I think must have stopped just below the point of no return. Not light skinned, but a lighter tone of brown that would have best been described as creamy. As I looked up her body, I only hoped her torso and face could match the feeling of intoxication her bare, well-proportioned calves and thighs imprinted upon me.

I wasn't disappointed. She was very pretty. Maybe twenty, at first guess. However, her face - as attractive as it was with its somewhat round, almost Asian features and very pouty, lipsticked red lips - lost the competition for attention with the ample breasts that pushed against the far too tight half-sweater she wore. A man's eyes were powerless against that kind of imagery. This sister knew exactly what she was doing. She might as well have had the word "Sex" written all over her in big, glittery letters.

Thinking it in my mind, unintentionally, I might have actually quietly said, "Wow." She smiled and for a second all my troubles just floated away. But her smile was gone as quickly as it appeared, as if it had been unintentional and there we were, complete strangers again. No, not complete strangers. I had seen her before somewhere but I couldn't place the location. But there was something moderately familiar about her. So I spoke again, this time intentionally.

"Hi. Do I know you?"

"I hear you got some trouble with Raymond Smalls. That means you're a dangerous person to be around."

"Oh, really," I said, suddenly becoming very suspicious of this sex dream in front of me who had completely avoided my question.

"Uh huh," she said.

"What's he to you?"

"Nuttin."

"Then wh . . . ."

"Just curious." She turned and almost bolted away without actually running.

Great. The one thing that might manage to pull me back from the piteous, depressed entity I was slowly becoming and she turns out to be a complete mystery that may or may not be connected to my worst enemy. Life was just getting better and better.

I pulled myself together and decided I'd go to my first class a little early and get a decent seat somewhere in the back corner. I walked three buildings across campus and entered the sociology hall, took the flight of stairs up to the third floor and walked into my class that didn't start for another twenty minutes. This was an intro sociology class that I didn't need to graduate. I'd taken it mostly for scholarship purposes. It gave me a full time semester schedule, which fulfilled full-time scholarship requirements. And I had a vague interest in the subject. Usually, it was populated with undergrads who were still trying to decide what they wanted to do with themselves. At the moment, it was empty.

I looked around. It was one of the smaller, stadium-seated rooms where the rows inclined upwards as you moved to the back of the room. I pointed myself directly for the stairs at one side of the room, and headed for the farthest up and most secluded chair.

I owned up to the impulse to get a seat with a good view of the door as paranoia but after being approached by someone that made parts of me grow just by looking at her and then finding out she had some kind of affiliation with *the* resident evil in my life, I thought it best to let paranoia rule, as Kato had suggested. So I sat down, pulled out a book and tried to catch up on some reading. Soon, other students began to enter the room and I made sure to get a good look at all of them.

It was after the class was half-full when I saw her. So did all the other guys. There was a collective rising of men's heads all at once. Amusingly, many of the girls simultaneously emitted a collective groan, I assumed as a remark to how sheep-like we were.

"Of course," I thought, "that's where I've seen her before." Once a week for the past couple of weeks I had seen her right here. She must have transferred from another class because she had joined this one a few weeks into the semester. She saw me immediately and locked gazes with me from across the room. Then she turned and proceeded to climb the stairs. As she walked, along with every other guy there, I couldn't help but watch and was reminded of previous weeks. This was now evident to me as a very familiar experience. When she had come in before, the two-thirds of the class that worked up a great deal more blood flow than usual when she appeared, had secretly prayed she wouldn't take a seat up front and would take the stairs just so we could witness the blessed event. And she loved it and we all knew it. She loved to flaunt her sexuality and made sure everybody was getting a good show. As far as the guys were concerned it was a win-win.

"My God," I thought, "she looked . . . wow. Kind of trashy but, still."

She made her way up to my row and I assumed would have sat directly next to me, but because the seats between us were occupied, took a seat four down from me. She leaned forward, looked down the row at me and made sure I looked back. No expression on her face. She looked right at me for just a moment, as if to reaffirm she had some kind of interest in me and me in her, then sat back in her chair. Now I was really clueless. The ambiguity of the situation was dazzling. What this girl had in store for me was so unclear. This was either the beginning to one of the best experiences in my life . . . or perhaps I was just deluded as usual.

"Here. For you, I think." The girl beside me handed me a piece of paper, folded in two. I took it from her and unfolded it. It read:

"I don't mind danger so much."

I looked back down at the girl who had been the only thing I had thought about for the past half hour. She was leaning out again so I could see her. She wanted to make sure I knew the note had come from her. I smiled. This time she smiled back and it held. Hmh, or maybe I wasn't so deluded after all.

CHAPTER 9

Her name was Shanay. That was all she'd tell me after I met up with her after class. The way she brushed off further questions with a sly, yet still inviting smile did clarify at least one thing for me. She was using me to amuse herself. I figured she was just one of those girls. It had been her intention all along, from the minute she came up to me, to keep me puzzled. She wanted me overcome with excitement, shrouding herself in mystery so much that I just couldn't resist her — a well-shaped, large-breasted perplexity. That was her game. The sad thing? As profoundly obvious as it was, having quickly seen right through her tawdry enticement . . . it was working.

Still, there were some questions of timing that bothered me, so I suggested we get lunch. I thought it might be a good chance for me to get more specifics about what exactly this girl wanted with me and why at this particularly heavy time in my life. Also, I tried to remind myself to not let my guard down completely just because she was so fine, and that the reason I was even in this situation was because of some stupid girl.

We pulled our trays down the line without talking and she followed me to a table. Despite cautioning myself seconds before, not to allow this girl to get to me too soon, as soon as she sat down and looked at me everything else went blurry. Though it was filled nearly to capacity, suddenly I would have sworn that there was no one else in the entire room. It was the way she looked at me that did it, as if she was lost in some thick fog and I was the light on the other side of the lake, and how her eyes never left my face but also never stopped scanning it. Then she skillfully licked her lips a few times and I was all hers.

And then I was embarrassed by how easily, without saying a word, she was manipulating me, just as she had probably done to countless guys before me. I checked myself and decided I needed to take control of this right now.

"So how do you know so much about me?"

"I heard some things," she said.

"Like what?"

"I heard about how you supposed to be real smart and I heard that you and Raymond got into a fight and how you kicked the shit out of him . . . and I heard that you was real cute too." The last part she said slowly. Intentionally. I chuckled. She was so good at this.

"We got a class together," I said. "How come you couldn't decide that for yourself, how cute I am?"

She stared at me and gave me a coy smile.

"I did."

She was *so* good at this.

"You know I heard some things about you too."

"Oh, really?"

"Uh, huh."

"Like what?" she said.

"I heard you have a reputation . . ." I said.

"What kind of reputation?" she said abruptly, preparing to be insulted.

"I heard you like to live on the edge."

"Oh," she said, her almost released fury relenting, pleased I hadn't questioned her obvious virtue.

I had told the truth. Thinking about her had triggered a memory from the first day she came to that class, where I overheard a guy next to me talking to another behind us. He said she had come to one of his frat's parties and she had immediately latched herself onto the thugs with the fastest cars and the largest rings and that she was some kind of an adrenaline junkie. I stopped paying attention because you could never believe most of what guys said in situations like that anyway and had redirected my focus to the lesson. Now I wished I had listened to the rest of the conversation.

"Is there some other reputation I should know about?" I asked.

"You'll find out."

"Nicholas."

I turned and looked up to see someone I hadn't seen in a long time. James . . . something or other. We'd gone to high school together a few years prior. He was a sophomore when I was a senior. I remembered him because he was one of the few people that I dealt with in that school and in our neighborhood who was as dedicated to succeeding as I was. He'd asked me to tutor him a couple of times. It had never worked out, and we mainly stayed acquaintances, but we knew each other as academic allies. I stood up and shook his hand.

"What up, man? How you been?"

"Hey man, I'm sorry, I didn't mean to break up your lunch."

"Naw, man, it's cool. What's crackin?"

"Brother, I just wanted you to know." He hesitated, then raised his eyes up to my own. "This is kind of weird but I just felt like I wanted to tell you something."

"Oh, ok," I said. "What's up?"

"In high school man, it was like you were my role model. I wanted to do more than just graduate, like you. I wanted to know I was going somewhere, just like you. I get my degree next year, and it just occurred to me when I saw you just now, that, even though we barely knew each other in high school, watching you and stuff, it had a lot to do wit me sticking with school and making it here eventually. Nobody thought I could do it man. But I saw you do it and I knew I could too. Much respect to you, dog. And good luck." He put his hand up to shake and I took it, genuinely moved.

"Wow, man, thanks. Thanks a lot."

James nodded his head, humbly. "That's it. I'm sorry."

"Naw, man, naw. That's fantastic man, thank you. Wow . . . you know?"

"I'll see you around," he said, turning to walk away. I watched him go, a bit impressed with myself.

"Aw, that's so sweet. Wow, man, thanks a lot," Shanay said, mocking me.

I looked down at her beautiful face, then unapologetically lowered my eyes to take in her just-as-beautiful breasts. She noticed me looking and scooted in her chair back from the table, then wiggled them and smiled gleefully. I smiled back and thought to myself, "This girl is gonna be some trouble, and she's yet to even begin screwing with me."

When I arrived home that night I called her as soon as I got in. Phone to my ear, I lay on my bed and talked to her, wishing I could give her my full attention. But other matters were still heavy on my mind.

"You know I'm beginning to think the only reason you got so interested so quick is so that you can say you knew me before I got killed by Smalls. I mean everybody knows he's planning on killing me, right?

"Man, you wrong," she said.

"Am I?"

"It's not even like that. I want you." She paused. "I want you to want me too."

"I do want you."

"That's all I want. Are you going to fall in love with me?"

"I don't know. I've never been in love."

"Do you think you could fall in love with me?" she asked.

"Maybe."

"Are you going to cry when I break your heart?"

She asked this question seriously and I knew there was some significance to it that I couldn't quite fathom. Now of course, having lived, I would immediately recognize the obvious hint at depravity. But I was still young, and a fool.

"What makes you think we won't live happily ever after?" I asked.

She didn't say anything for several seconds.

"So when you comin over?"

I smiled to myself and decided to let her get away with avoiding the question. "Dang girl, you don't waste no time do you?"

"Most guys like that about me."

"I ain't most guys, Shanay."

"I noticed. So you comin over?"

"I can't tonight."

"You ain't no faggot are you?"

"Oh, girl, hell naw! What's wrong wit you?"

She choked out a devious little giggle.

"Naw, tomorrow I'm gon' tear it up," I said. "I just, I can't tonight. I got to see somebody."

"Who?"

"Hopefully, somebody who can help make me a little less dangerous to be around."

I hung up with her, but didn't move from my bed for a few minutes. This girl was obviously not right for me at all, yet here I was, walking right into some kind of trap that she had laid for me. I no longer thought she was affiliated with Smalls, but that didn't make me feel any better. The truth was, I just didn't know what her plan was. She played dumb and raunchy, but I could see that she was quite intelligent, which made things even more complex.

Why was it I always allowed myself to get so caught up, so lost when women were involved? When it came to them I always managed to turn my good friend common sense into a long lost acquaintance whose name I could barely remember. This time I had to be careful, I told myself. Yeah. I was still a fool.

I got up, put on a shirt and walked out the door into the night and turned down the sidewalk. As soon as possible, I cut into a neighbor's yard and went the long way. A safer route I figured, because it would keep me away from the street and sidewalks and no one could creep up without me noticing. I didn't want one of Small's crew seeing me out alone in the dark. I pulled out Kato's address again. I guessed it would take me around twenty minutes to get there.

I had slipped out of the house quietly without telling my mother I was leaving. She probably thought I was asleep in my bedroom. I had been avoiding her and she could probably tell, but I just didn't want her to know the truth. She had fought so hard, so long, my entire life to provide me with security and a future. She'd overcome bouts of clinical depression after my father died, so many physical ailments I'd lost count, as well as just plain bad luck - to make things good for us. For me. She'd done it all for me. She'd grown and changed and adapted and sacrificed because she refused to not see me succeed. I was her reason for being. And that was no exaggeration. Telling her some gangsta from the neighborhood was trying to kill me was the last thing I wanted for her to deal with. I had to fix this on my own, keep her out of it and not get killed in the process. I knew that somehow that was selfish of me but when I made a mental list of pros and cons, whether or not I should tell her, the cons far outnumbered the pros.

Eventually, I came upon the address. From beside a house located directly across the street, I looked at Kato's house. It was a big place surrounded by a small wire fence that gave it an almost suburban appearance. Older muscle cars sat parked on the street in front of the house; but the Jaguar stood out from the rest. It was a fairly recent model, maybe a ninety-eight, ninety-nine, I guessed. A leader's automobile. I assumed it was Kato's. A drug dealer's show car. But a drug dealer who didn't think like most people in that business because most drug dealers didn't have enough class to appreciate a car like that. It was all Cadillac Escalades and Mercedes-Benz for them.

I looked back at the house and could tell there was a lot of activity inside. The gangsta rap music could be heard from all the way across the street. From outside, I could see a shadow pass in front of the windows every few seconds. There were a lot of people in that house. This wasn't going to be just me and Kato and that bothered me. As soon as I walked into that house I'd be severely outnumbered. But my options at that point were nil. I needed to find out what Kato had to offer.

I walked up to the fence, undid the latch, opened it and walked into the yard, then up to the door and knocked. A very large man opened the door and looked at me. The smell of weed hit me with force.

"Well, well, well, if it ain't Kato's boy. Step on in nigga."

I walked in and looked around. There were people everywhere. All brothas. To my right, in one of the living rooms were a number of men watching an old time karate movie, some on couches, some in chairs, others sitting on the floor. They passed joints back and forth. Two men stood in the corner of the room practicing martial arts moves on each other. Only a few of them even looked at me, and that was momentary. Then they returned their attention to the movie and their weed and their liquor.

I looked to my left and saw five men at a table playing cards. Now all of these men had stopped their game and *were* looking me over. I raised my head and nodded. They just smirked or chuckled and went back to their game. They thought I was bougie. I was dressed in black jeans that didn't hang from my ass, a black shirt that fit me snugly, and Timberlands and they thought I was square.

"Welcome my brother, to the proverbial den of thieves."

I looked forward as Kato walked towards me. His cornrows had been let out now and he wore a gigantic afro. In complete contrast to his hairstyle, he was dressed in a $400 three piece suit and very shiny dress shoes. I smiled.

"What?" he asked.

"I have never met anyone like you. I see that already."

"Very observant. You see it's good to be unique. Different. Different means special in my book." He looked hard at me. "You're different. You remind me of one of them preachers that always be trying to get us to see the error of our ways. I never really agreed with what they wanted to turn us into, but I respected how much they seemed to care about other black folk. That's why I wanted you to come."

He turned his attention to his men in both rooms.

"Hey, y'all, turn that shit off man."

The men did as they were told. One of the men turned off the TV. and another lowered the volume on the stereo so Kato could be heard, then they all looked at us.

"This is Nicholas Gambit. As of right now he is down, he is under our protection. This is that man Raymond Smalls is after. You will take care of him. Because I ask you to. Anybody got a problem with that?"

One of the brothers in the living room, whose lowered eyelids and bloodshot eyes I could see from across the room was the only one to speak up.

"Don't give a fuck," he said.

I took this to mean "ok". "Thanks man," I said, feeling extremely self-conscious.

"Nigga, I don't give a fuck about you either. Only reason I'll do this is because Kato says. Flying fuck if you die or not. Probably gonna get fucked up anyway," he said to me. "Should have just killed that mufucker in the first place when you had the chance."

Kato stepped forward as if to retake control. "You should care. This brother is getting out. He's gonna make something of his life. Maybe even come back and help change things. Nigga, we can't rely on other people to change things for us. We got to do it ourselves. And the only way to do it ourselves is to gain power. And knowledge is power."

Kato grabbed me and pulled me near him and pointed to my head.

"This is power," he said. "And we need to make the most of every chance we get at using that power. Cause think about it. They ain't just gonna give it to us. They don't want us to have shit. They don't give a fuck if we live or die. As long as we ain't in the way."

The weed and liquor stimulating his debating skills, the angry brother spoke again. "Man, fuck you, fuck him and fuck e'ebody else too. I'll do what you say. But I don't know this Negro and I don't owe him DIDDLEY!"

The other men chuckled.

"That's where the problem lies, my brother. As long as you and I are forced to sell drugs to survive and live in a fucking war zone we are not exempt. You're wrong. We owe a lot. We owe all our children a chance to live into old age. We owe him and others like him a chance to make that happen. You want to tell your daughter that she has to live in fear for the rest of her life because you didn't care, cause you didn't owe nobody?"

The brother looked down, silent. Then he looked back up at Kato. "Why'd you have to bring my baby into this, man?"

One of the other men socked him in the arm, laughing. "You high as a mufucker man."

"Yeah, yeah," Kato said. "If you don't care then ain't nothing goin to change. So what's up? Everybody down?"

All of Kato's men were humbled. They nodded or answered in the affirmative. Even the angry brother nodded his head this time. I was suddenly very impressed by this man that stood beside me.

"Good. Now, Nicholas, let me introduce you to the men who will keep you alive. All of us got names from Bruce Lee movies cause that was a baddass mufucker."

His men chimed in on this as well. Kato began to say the names of all his people as we passed them and I either slapped hands with them or just nodded. "This is my dog Master Po."

The man dropped his head and muttered a "Hmh," in a very Chinese way.

"This is Bolo nuts right heah. That nigga over there is just . . . that nigga is just FUCKED up, never mind him." Finally, we came to the last man sitting by himself in the kitchen. He was another big man. I guessed he weighed in at about 250 and a good portion of that was muscle. His head was shaved bald and his face was all round shapes, round nose, round lips, rounded cheeks, circles within a circle. He looked up at me and nodded.

"This is Fook Yoo. That's cause all he ever says is . . . fuck you. I ain't never heard him say anything else. My nigga. Retarded motherfucker," he said, baiting him.

"Fuck you," said Fook Yoo.

"See."

I spent the rest of the night trying to relax and getting to know these men. I had some Hennessey, and when they offered, though I wasn't much of a smoker, I took a couple of tokes and it almost knocked me on my ass. After a couple of hours, I realized that compared to these guys I *was* square. But I was fine with that and they were fine with that and that was all that mattered.

Kato finally rescued me from his boys and motioned for me to follow him, which I did. We went outside and he positioned himself in front of his Jaguar and then looked me over. All night I'd been hoping to get a chance to speak with him more. After the way he'd commanded his men to protect me, the way he'd identified at least one of his motives for doing it as being inspired, unless I was mistaken, by some newfound sense of duty — a desire to take on at least some responsibilities of a reformer, I did not doubt his sincerity in the least. But something told me that there was more to this, that there was something else behind this sudden urge to become my protector and savior.

"So? Are you gonna be everything I'm hoping you'll be?"

"That depends on what you expect of me."

"Good," he said, smiling. His appreciation of me was evident. "Spoken like a real scholar. How much knowledge *is* locked up in there?" He pointed at me. I inferred he meant inside my head.

"Enough to make a difference, I suppose. That is why you're helping me isn't it?"

"C'mon, let's go dog." He stood and walked around to the car door.

I smiled at the second person that day who was avoiding all my questions and jumped into the passenger seat beside him. He turned on the ignition, put it in gear and drove us into the night, but in the opposite direction that we would take to go to my house. He pulled out a box from a storage compartment, opened it and held it up in front of me. I waved my hand, declining. He took a cigar from the box, returned the box to its station, then lit the cigar with a match and puffed and puffed until it was to his liking. I couldn't help but invoke the cliché from the old blaxploitation films. Drug dealer, gang member, leader of black men, mack daddy, puffing away on his cigar, on top of the world. I remember it smelled foul and I was tempted to roll down my window, but thought better of it. I didn't want to offend the one man that stood between me and Small's gang of killers.

He didn't speak for several minutes and the silence was a bit troubling, so I asked the first question that came to mind.

"So how come you're still alive man?"

"Say what?"

"What are you, like in your thirties or sumpthin?"

"Early thirties, thank you very much," he said, half amused.

"Well I'm no professional on the subject, but most guys your age have either already gotten out of the game or are dead. Why aren't you?"

"I'm resilient. And I'm smart. You know I've never been locked up?"

"You lying, for real?"

He looked at me with an intensity I had yet to see from him. "I know how to choose my battles."

I returned his gaze with as sincere a demeanor as I could muster. "I'm glad you chose this one. And I won't let you down."

He nodded and looked away, satisfied.

"I studied up on you, brother," he said.

I figured as much. "Yeah?" was all I said.

"Seems like your whole neighborhood thinks you gon' be the next Martin Luther King."

"What?"

"Yeah, homie, they talk like you gon' save the whole mufuckin planet from itself, dog."

He never stopped talking after that. Taking a circuitous route to my house, that more than quadrupled our travel time, he spoke of what he'd been, what he was, what he intended to be. He talked about his more than meager beginnings, his girl and how she was the only respectable stripper in existence, how he'd turned a ragtag band of hoodlums into more than just a gang, but a unified group of soldiers. But I must confess the truth. I was disinterested and could only half listen as Kato's saga unfolded.

I couldn't think of anything but that singular and altering statement he'd made. The people in my neighborhood, my people, expected me to come back and initiate what . . . reform? Kato had become my savior and now I was supposed to be theirs? Not that it didn't seem an honorable direction in which my expectations were to be led. I guess the truth is I had always envisioned my future self as a professor, a very well paid professor, teaching in a reputable school and coming home every day to my young, nubile, sexually adventurous and abundantly fruitful wife. Most importantly, all of it was to be far, far away from my neighborhood.

"Well", I thought, "there will be plenty of time to worry about the future and who it involves other than myself." For the moment, I was just happy that I had an ally that didn't seem to want anything except for me to follow my path unmolested. That was a heavy weight lifted off my shoulders. But I vowed one thing — I would find a way to pay him back once this was all over.

The next morning, I was up early again. I showered and dressed quickly then made my way to the living room so I could be there again when my mother woke. Only a few minutes after I sat down she came out.

"Hi," she said. "Up early again, huh?"

"Yeah."

"Well, you about ready?"

"Yeah Momma, why?" I said stupidly.

"Do you not have classes today?"

"Yeah, but you don't need to take me to school today. You can go on ahead to work."

"How you going to get to school, son?"

"I got a ride."

"Oh. With who?"

"Some friends of mine."

Her brow furrowed. I could see the suspicion rising in her face.

"Well, who is it?"

"It's just friends of mine."

"Why can't you tell me their names?" she said frustrated, unhappy with whatever it was I was hiding.

"Kato and some of his friends."

"That boy that was here the other day that was obviously in a gang?"

I had hoped she hadn't seen him.

"Nicholas, what's going on? Why are you hanging around with these individuals all of a sudden?

"Momma, you going to just have to trust me. Please." The car horn sounded from outside. It was Kato. "Just trust me. I ain't done nothing wrong."

"I want to talk to you tonight when you get home," she said, desperately.

The horn sounded again. "Ok, we'll talk tonight. I gotta go. Bye." I walked out the door and got in the car. I looked back at the house and saw her standing in the doorway, watching me drive away. I remember her face growing smaller as we pulled off. She was longing for something. For me? There was an almost painful expression on her face.

I hated myself for making her worry like that. She had done so much worrying about me already. I'd been wrong not to tell her. But I could fix that. I knew I would have to just tell her everything and get it all out in the open. I knew this day would be hell for her. As soon as I got home I would have to free her from as many of her suspicions as possible. Years had passed since I'd seen her look the way she did on our doorstep that morning. She had seemed so happy for so long and I had taken away that contentment in five minutes. How could I have let this happen? I promised myself I'd tell her everything as soon as I got home. She'd be upset but that was better than not knowing anything.

CHAPTER 10

Gina Gambit watched her son pull away in a car filled with a number of obvious gang members and felt as if her heart stopped beating. She knew Nicholas was smart, and that he wouldn't involve himself with these hoodlums without some kind of reason. But what could that reason be?

"I love you so much. I don't want to lose you, Nicholas. I can't."

She turned around and walked back towards her bedroom to gather her things and go to work, but something prevented her taking another step. She had walked into a wall of dread that was as tangible as the actual walls of her home. "I mustn't overreact," she thought to herself. "But . . . he just walked out the door. Why do I miss him so much all of a sudden?"

CHAPTER 11

I sat in the back seat. Fook Yoo was driving his Cutlass; Kato sat in the front passenger seat in front of me. In the back seat with me, to my left, sat two of Kato's men. I tried to think of their Bruce Lee names but couldn't remember. The previous night was still kind of hazy. I looked at my immediate neighbor and noticed a formidable looking automatic weapon in his lap. The man next to him rested his hand on a pistol, his forefinger tapping against it. These guys were ready for war.

"So what's up, preacherman? Ain't it nice to have your own personal limousine service?"

"Thanks for coming like this Kato," I said.

"Ain't no thang. Nothing like a gang war to wake up to in the morning."

"Say what?"

"Fuck yeah, man," said the man next to me. "That nigga Smalls is trippin' boy. Got all his homies trippin' too."

"A gang war? Damn. I'm responsible for all this?"

"Bullshit," said Kato. "That fucking pussy got a grade-A ass whoopin and now he wants revenge, it's as simple as that. This ain't even got that much to do wit you anymore. It's all about him and the respect he lost when you put yo foot up his ass," he said, chuckling. "That nigga done lost his mind. He wants your head on a stick and I ain't talking about the head on your shoulders. Told you should've killed the trick when you had the chance."

"His boys would have been after me anyway."

"Yeah, I guess that's true. But at least then he'd be dead and he wouldn't be able to stir up all these other people he got involved to come after you. There's a hell of a lot more of 'em after you now than there would have been if you'd just killed the bitch. At least then it would have been just a few of his boys."

My neighbor spoke again. "He's fucking stupid. He made a fucking agreement with Ray Ray's click just so he could use them to help find you. But now he's gon catch beef wit anybody don't like Ray Ray. He's playing war games like a motherfucker. He wants you worse than he wants to nut, man."

"Aw hell I'm gonna die," I said. "I mean up till now I just thought this whole thing was gonna somehow just blow over without anything really happening. This brother is really going to kill me, or try at least."

Kato turned in his seat and looked at me. "Don't sweat it man. Just watch your back at all times. We can't protect you in school so there it's on you, naw mean?"

"Alright."

What frustrated me the most was that we were waiting on Smalls and his people to come to us, not the other way around. I didn't like the idea of having to constantly look over my shoulder until they decided to make their move. I was learning that being on the defensive was not my style.

We arrived at my school and I rushed to climb the steps that led to the entrance to the main streets on campus, as if there might be a sniper positioned somewhere waiting to pick me off. I'm sure Kato and his boys got a good laugh watching me go inside in such a hurry.

My day went by . . . slowly. I couldn't concentrate on anything else. I knew I was just torturing myself, but every time I thought about it I wanted desperately to go somewhere and do some . . . thing. Anything. I wanted to actively affect things or somehow prepare for what I had finally accepted as being inevitable. I knew I couldn't talk to Smalls and change things. It was too late for that. I knew that if we even came into view of each other, people would start dying and that was unacceptable too. I had no options except to just wait. But the uncertainty regarding when or how it would all go down was beginning to overpower me and I felt imprisoned by it.

Finally, I just couldn't take it anymore. I found a hallway somewhere near my next class, then found a wall and put my back to it, the symbolism not escaping me at all. I sat down, closed my eyes, and tried to clear my mind.

Ten seconds later I heard a scream. Jumping up to face my attackers, I was relieved to see that ten feet away, two guys were fighting — each other. One of the girls nearby had screamed. The two pugilists were anything but. They were both exhausted after a few seconds of throwing punches that never connected and ended up rolling around on the ground groaning like they were making love to each other. That's when I lost interest. I started to sit back down when I felt someone behind me. I whipped around as if someone was trying to put a knife in my back and met with another surprise. It was Shanay. I guess what I said was kind of rude, the stress I was feeling clearly evident.

"What do you want from me, girl!"

She looked at me like I was crazy. "The fuck kind of greeting is that?"

"You know what Shanay, you don't want to be around me right now."

"Well, somebody's got a canoe paddle stuck up their ass today," she said, pulling her head and not her body away from me in that way that they do. "And how do you know I don't want to be around you right now? Why don't you let me decide about that?"

"I don't understand you girl."

"Ain't really nothing to understand. You want pussy, I want dick. Ain't nothing to understand."

Now to this I could only lower my head and smile.

"You want to come over tonight?" she asked. She moved in closer and looked up into my eyes. I looked her over and was impressed with her ability to wear clothes that so effectively demonstrated her form. She wore another short midriff t-shirt that said "love" on it and tight form-fitting pants that were of a sleek material I couldn't place. The pants stopped just above her ankles. The running shoes she wore were the only thing keeping her from looking like a stripper from head to toe. I raised my head to look at her face and had to stop myself from kissing her very sexy pink lips.

"Shanay, I want to but I don't know if I can."

Her closeness was intoxicating.

"I know why you so stressed out. I can help you with that."

She moved even closer and this time I felt her breath on my neck, her breasts pushing against me. I felt myself begin to grow hard and I knew she could feel it too, but I didn't want to move away.

"Come over right after school," she said. "Please?"

"Ok." I had lost that battle as soon as it began.

"Damn! For a second I thought I was gonna have to offer you money to come. Usually all I have to do is say the word pussy and guys have to change they drawls."

I said nothing and looked at her and smiled.

"See, it's working already. Here's my address." She handed me a piece of paper. She'd already had it written down. She'd known all along what the answer would be. "What time?" she asked.

"I'll meet you there at three."

"Alright, baby." She kissed me, very pleased with herself.

I watched her walk away, marveling at how well built she was, imagining how she would look naked and what it would feel like to pull her into me and touch her in the few places that were, at the moment, still covered by clothing. I hesitated to move at all for several moments, fearing my crotch might betray my thoughts to anyone who was looking.

A friend of Shanay's, who had been watching us, met up with her as she walked. I think they wanted me to hear.

"That boy is about to get killed and he still made time for you?" she said.

Shanay looked at her as if it was a given, then offered her hand. "If the world was about to come to an end they'd still find time for the na-na, girl."

Her friend nodded her head in agreement, then placed her hand on Shanay's and slid it away. "True."

Let's face it, they were right.

I went to that next class but did no more than occupy a seat. When the class was over, I tried not to hurry out to the car, and when I jumped in the back seat I asked Kato to take me to

Shanay's house. He smiled and said something I didn't pay attention to and before I knew it we were at the address.

She lived in a very large house in a very nice neighborhood, which was not what I expected since she knew so much about my situation with Smalls. This helped me come to another conclusion about her. I decided she was one of those girls that was exhilarated by involving herself with those of lesser means and more dangerous lifestyle because it lent some intrigue to the life of someone like her, that came from an environment like that. She probably thought of her upbringing as mundane. A rich girl trying to live the thug life. But to be honest, at that point, I couldn't have cared less about her motives.

I had struggled for the past several days to find a way to end the conflict before it began. But I now realized that it was too late for that. The only way to end it all was by finally allowing things to come to a head somehow. A battle was coming, whether I liked it or not. And I could only wait for it and do no more. The epiphany in a nutshell — I was slave to my situation and slave to my need to surrender to it; and her - surrender there too. For all her game playing and hidden agenda, I needed me some of that girl, right then and there.

I rang the doorbell and she opened it immediately. She'd changed from the outfit she wore earlier. She stood before me in nothing more than a bra, panties and a robe. I didn't even say hello. I rushed in and attacked her. I closed the door behind me as I moved to kiss her. She welcomed me with her tongue and wrapped her arms around my neck. We moved backwards until we hit a wall and I kissed her with a ferocity no other girl had been able to bring out of me before. Suddenly a thought occurred to me and I grabbed her by the shoulders and held her away.

"Where are your parents?"

She looked at me like I was stupid, then threw a surprise jab into my stomach that actually hurt a little. "Don't interrupt me again. They're out of town. Don't worry about it. You're here for a reason."

"Damn," I thought to myself. Suddenly, I went flying backwards and landed on my back. I looked up at her and saw an odd, almost cold look of determination in her eyes. I realized she had just stuck her foot behind mine and pushed me, on purpose. She stood looking down at me, smirking, her tongue literally planted into her cheek, enjoying seeing me upended. Then she jumped on top of me and began to kiss me. I held her head in my hands and kissed her back, then moved my hands to her bra, undid the clasps, pulled it from her arms and threw it. I lowered my head to look at her bare breasts and before I got a good look, she pushed on my forehead with her palm, bending my neck back violently.

"Girl, what is wrong wit you!"

"Upstairs," was all she said.

Carrying her up the stairwell, her legs wrapped around my waist, we kissed all the way. Periodically, I'd pull away to crane around her and look where I was going, despite her protests, and eventually found her room. I threw her on the bed and began to remove my clothes. She watched with enthusiasm as I disrobed. I took my shirt off and smiled at her reaction to the six-pack I was very proud of. Then my shoes, socks, pants and finally boxer-briefs. Pleased by the way she licked her lips at the sight of me naked, I said, "Come here."

"No, you come here," she said from the bed. She curled her forefinger at me and smiled.

I joined her on the bed and began to kiss her neck, then moved downwards and kissed the bottom of her breast, meaning to kiss and caress her entire body. But her body language told me something was wrong. She moved her head away and breathed slowly as if impatient.

"No. Put it in."

I looked up at her, not understanding what was wrong.

"Put it in. I want it in me."

I got up, walked over to my jeans on the floor and pulled a package of condoms from the pocket. When I looked at her from across the room, her face registered a fair amount of disappointment at that choice. I ignored her disappointment because I didn't see any other option, slipped the condom on, then went back to her and tried to kiss her. She looked down and waited for me to enter her and so I did. Her whole body spasmed.

She gasped, then grit her teeth in anticipation of my next thrust, looking up at me now. Every time I pushed inside her she cried out, but her gaze never wavered from mine.

She looked at me defiantly, daring me with her eyes to do it again. Vigorously, she scraped her nails up and down my back, at times digging them in. Soon, she pushed against me simultaneously with each thrust of my own, then raised her legs and held them in the air as I pushed inside her. I started to feel myself nearing climax when she grabbed me by the shoulders and pushed me over onto my back.

She sat on top of me, put me inside her and that's when what little sanity she was in possession of was cast aside faster than an ugly retarded child born to a pair of movie stars. She bounced up and down on me, flailing around wildly, screaming at the top of her lungs. Her eyes and the look on her face advertised a complete loss of control. I began to pray I'd orgasm soon, and when I finally did, I immediately pushed her off for fear she'd break me in half. Then I just tried to catch my breath.

I lay there for a few seconds and didn't know if I had a second time in me with this girl. I turned my head and looked at her, lying next to me. She stared at the ceiling intently. I looked up and tried to discern what was so interesting. I didn't see anything so I looked back at her and this time she turned her head as well and looked at me.

"Ain't it about time for you to go?"

I looked at her, incredulous. By that point, it was already very clear that when it came to mental stability, she was equivalent to being poised on a precipice, exposed to heavy windage. So I thought I'd give her the benefit of the doubt and maybe somehow, some way in her fucked up world, she hadn't meant to be rude.

"Yeah, I guess they will be here pretty soon." I got up and dressed. "What you doin tomorrow night, maybe you can ride with us . . . "

"I'm busy tomorrow night. Shawn is coming over."

"I am one of the dumbest Negroes of all time," I thought to myself. It had never occurred to me that she wouldn't want to see *me* again. I mean, that was the guy's role. The guy was supposed to be the asshole, right? I just stood there and looked at her, dumbfounded. I finished dressing and tried to get her to look at me, but she wouldn't.

"So . . . you played me. I just got played, huh?"

"Yep," she said, now looking in some far away corner of the room.

"I can't believe I just got played." I said *I* like it was just unheard of, someone like me being duped in such a way.

"You sure fucking did."

"Why? Wait a minute, let me guess. What, is this about revenge? Do unto others maybe, huh?"

She had no reply and continued focusing her attention on the corner.

"Yeah," I said. "I'm not as stupid as you thought I was am I?" I said, talking only for the sake of having words to spew out of my mouth and to be indignant. I walked to the door and spoke as I walked out. "I go blind when I smell pussy but I'm not as stupid as you thought I was. You . . . sneaky-ass trick." I stopped at the stairwell, thought for a second, then turned around and reentered her room. This time she looked up at me standing in her doorway.

"Ok, I *don't* understand." I said. "Why? What did I do to you, Shanay?"

Her eyes closed momentarily and when they reopened, were downcast. But before she spoke again she looked me straight in the eyes.

"I play niggaz before niggaz play me. Nigga. Get out."

She looked away again. I turned around and left. Really, I couldn't blame her. It was more my fault than hers. All the indicators were there and I had ignored every single one of them. Subconsciously, I had known I shouldn't involve myself with a girl like that, but it hadn't been my subconscious that had guided me to that house that day.

I shut her front door behind me and walked down the short stairway in the front yard of the enormous house. Kato had been waiting on me. I got into the car and tried not to be too obvious, but as soon as he turned around and looked at me, he saw that something was wrong.

"What the fuck happened to you? Couldn't get your shit up?" His boys laughed and I said nothing. "Gambit. I'm just messing wit you, man. What's wrong wit you?"

"I am stupid," I said.

A look of understanding came to his face and he turned back around in his seat.

"Ain't we all, my brother? Ain't we all?"

CHAPTER 12

Inside her bedroom, still on her bed and looking up at the ceiling, Shanay heard the car door shut outside. She stood, looked through her window and watched as the car with Nicholas drove down the street in front of her house. A familiar feeling overcame her. Shame. She began to cry and thought, "Why does it hurt like this after?"

She sat down on her bed, wiped her face with her hand and thought of Nicholas. He wasn't so bad. He tried to be gentle with her. When she told him to leave he wasn't near as angry as some of the others. There was something different about him. He didn't seem as bad. Maybe she had made a mistake not to trust him. Maybe he wouldn't try and hurt her like they always did. Maybe she'd call him later and apologize.

CHAPTER 13

Princess Chelsea Matawae was finally home. From the rear of the limo, she looked out the window into the grasslands she'd missed for so long and watched as the wall of transplanted acacia trees that enveloped the road on both sides sped by. She had spent much of her time, the past three years, longing for this very sight - so many nights remembering the happiest moments of her life, many of them on this very road. It had been paved since she left. It was no longer the sandy dirt road she would ride her horses on when she needed to be alone. No longer where, if you left the road and passed through the trees, you would immediately encounter Africa's finest. Beyond that wall of trees, wildebeests, leechwes and cheetahs had roamed. If you turned your head to the skies, it wouldn't take long to spot an eagle. At least the savanna still belonged to the beasts. In her opinion, which she realized many would categorize as uninventive romanticism, that was how it should be.

She looked at this newly paved road again. Because of the road, the animals would have been driven back by the construction and the heavier automobile traffic. Chelsea remembered how once, when she was riding her favorite mare, a lioness had entered the road and stood before them as if claiming the road for herself, preventing all others from passing. Her mare had spooked, then tried to throw her and run from the animal, but Chelsea stayed calm. She'd leaned down, rubbed her horse and spoken soothingly in her ear, telling her quietly that she would handle this, never taking her eye off the lioness.

Finally, the mare calmed enough for Chelsea to conclude she would no longer try to bolt, though she still occasionally snorted and pranced lightly to show she did not feel safe this close to the beast. Chelsea pulled her rifle from its pouch, chambered a round, then pointed it at the animal and aimed. The lioness, in return, looked directly at Chelsea and cocked her head, unaffected by the presence of the weapon.

Chelsea lowered her rifle and studied her. Had she meant to attack she would have done so already. No, she was smallish and wore an inquisitive look common to the young, probably barely into her first year. She had approached them out of curiosity, not hunger. So there they stood, each in mild appreciation of the other, for many minutes.

Chelsea revered the beasts for their prowess and strength. A lioness, she would become the primary hunter and provider for her family, not the male lion who did little save fulfilling his procreative duties. No, it was she who would nurture and kill, in the same breath. It was she who made all the other animals cower. Her mere presence instilled fear, an admirable quality in any being. It was she who was truly the king of the beasts.

After a few minutes, it occurred to Chelsea that she should be getting back. She took one last look at the lion, raised the rifle again and fired a shot that struck the ground, creating a cloud of dust a foot away from the lion. Instantly, she shot off back in the direction she came from and was never seen by Chelsea again. It would be nice to see that lion again, to see how it had grown in the years since she'd been gone. Perhaps she had a family now and young pups of her own.

Chelsea's father had probably commanded that the road be paved. She smiled. He would have decreed it, so that when she returned she would have a smooth ride, on her favorite road in all their kingdom, on her way back to their estate. He tended to spend his money in this way — liberally, nonsensically at times. Even she knew this. And he occasionally took heat from those in the government for it.

Still, there were few that were openly unhappy with the way he ruled, and they had very little say on the matter. But they did have certain resources and connections, these dissenters. Her training the past three years told her men with those kinds of resumes were extreme liabilities. She made a mental note to discuss this with her father. But there would be plenty of time for business. First, she would allow herself a chance to enjoy just being home. It felt good and filled her with cheerfulness just thinking about it.

She looked at Caleb, who sat beside her, then forward at Jonathan, who focused intently on the road ahead. He trailed a black Lincoln that held two more guards. They moved at a good clip. As a matter of fact, it seemed as if they were moving at an unnecessary pace and Chelsea wondered at the significance.

"Nonsense, Chelsea. The Americans have made you unnecessarily paranoid," she thought. But, maybe not. One of her lessons had been that paranoia, when supported by evidence, is no longer paranoia; it then becomes theory. And that was just it. Some component relevant to her training, what had become near instinct, had been triggered when she'd looked at Caleb, her protector for so long. Subtly, she turned her head back in his direction again to verify something was not right. Despite her attempt to feign nonchalance when she looked at him, he'd known immediately that she was observing him and now looked back at her squarely.

Their eyes locked and in that moment, Chelsea observed what she could only describe as . . . preoccupation. He was conflicted about something. Chelsea had never seen that look on his face. He was conflicted about nothing. But then, as they looked at each other, the expression on his face morphed into something else she could only describe as anticipation. The corners of his mouth twisted into a smile unlike any she had ever seen him wear before; he opened his mouth to speak but was cut off by Jonathan.

"Caleb! We're being followed!"

Chelsea and Caleb turned in their seats to look through their rear window. A jeep had just emerged from the tree line behind them and begun to follow. A man dressed in fatigues stood in the back and manned a 50. caliber machine gun attached to the roll bar. Chelsea prepared to duck down, but her training told her to watch the assailant until the last possible second. All of her father's automobiles were well armored, including bullet proof windows that could withstand weapons fire, even from a .50 cal. Still, there was a limit to how many direct hits those windows could take from such a high caliber weapon. The soldier took aim, then fired. A "ddd-ddd-ing" emanating, a steady stream of bullets tore into the ground, shooting up dust immediately behind the speeding limo. Chelsea remained calm, watching him through the window. The sound of bullets impacting the ground generated a negligible response in her. What did draw her attention was the fact that the men in the jeep were only twenty meters behind the limo, on a paved road with nothing to cause difficulty aiming, and the gunner was consistently missing their vehicle. He wasn't trying to hit the car. He was firing behind it. They were being corralled.

"It's a trap! We're being ambushed!" she yelled.

It was too late.

"There is something happening ahead!" said Jonathan, as he hit the brakes. The car ahead of them had come to a stop as well.

Chelsea and Caleb moved forward in the compartment to look through the partition between driver and passenger. Ahead of the point car, the trees were bulldozed. This had occurred very recently, apparent from the fallen tree trunks and branches still lying about in some areas. A circular clearing, intersected by the road, had been created in order to widen the space in which to surround the two cars. A force of men, measuring at about a dozen as best as she could tell, holding automatic rifles that Chelsea identified as AK-47s and British SA-80's, stood directly in their path.

To the left and right of the car, from inside the tree line where they had been waiting, emerged three more jeeps, each carrying another .50 cal. One took up a position behind the line of gun-toting soldiers in order to prevent the limos from trying to break through. The other two simply parked on each side of Chelsea's vehicle and leveled their weapons on the limo that was now surrounded.

Chelsea reflexively reached into a compartment near one of the television sets, stuck her hand into it, and it emerged holding a pistol, which drew Caleb's attention. She'd been a bit surprised to find a weapon was still kept in that secret compartment she'd seen Caleb reach into on occasion years before. Apparently, he'd forgotten himself, that he'd left a pistol inside. He was a changed man, indeed. The Caleb she had known was obsessive, especially over the location of his weapons. He looked at her, holding that pistol, and seemed bothered by the notion of her having a means with which to protect herself. She took note, again, of how oddly he was acting. Reluctantly, he returned his attention to what was unfolding ahead of their car. He picked up a communicator and spoke to the men in the point car.

"We must break through."

"Understood."

The men in the point car opened their doors, using the bulletproof doors and windows as shields, and fired at their attackers over the doors. They were immediately hit with a barrage of return fire that seemed to come from everywhere. A volley of bullets assaulted them from forwards, backwards, and to their sides, ricocheting off bullet-proof windows made useless by the sheer amount of weapons fire coming at them from all directions. Both men were shredded by rounds that measured in the hundreds and easily hit their targets. The driver was cut down immediately; the passenger, wounded and moments from losing consciousness, somehow managed to make it back inside the vehicle, closing the door behind him.

"That was pointless," said Chelsea. She looked at Caleb. "Try and contact the palace. We need backup."

"Communications are . . . impossible."

"What do you mean . . .?" Chelsea stopped herself. Caleb had turned. The less he thought she was aware of this, the more advantageous for her. But he wasn't with the men that had ambushed them. He was as surprised by this turn of events as was she. She would have to find a way to use this to her advantage as well. She looked back through the windshield of the limo to see what was happening.

A man stepped forward from the clearing. He moved in a confident, unhurried manner. It was easy to deduce that he was in charge. He looked at one of the men holding rifles and that man turned on his heels and ran into the trees. Then the leader motioned in the direction of two men who sat in one of the jeeps. They pulled their pistols, pointed them forward, then jumped down and ran at the limos. Just as they reached the vehicles, each man reached into waist pouches and quickly pulled out square shaped plastique charges and placed them on the windshields of both cars. Chelsea watched as the soldier then stuck a receiver pin into the charge on her windshield, enabling a remote detonation.

Realizing what they meant to do, Caleb moved to exit the vehicle. Chelsea grabbed his arm.

"Wait."

He looked at her, unsure, then relented. Chelsea reprimanded herself; she had acted impulsively, instinctively protecting someone who had protected her for so long. She knew had he left the vehicle, Caleb would have been cut down in the same manner as the other two. Possibly, one of the motives to placing the charges had been to accomplish just that - flushing out more of the individuals inside. However, now that she was relatively certain he had turned, it might have been a tactical mistake to not allow him to go to his death, therefore removing one dangerous variable from an equation that was becoming more complex by the minute. But she had trained for this for years. She would find a way to survive.

The men then ran back to their positions. The leader pulled out the remote, looked at the wounded man in the point car and pushed a button. The man's eyes went wide. The explosion split the car in half and sent a wall of fire in both directions. The line of soldiers, standing a full fifty paces away from the explosion, had to throw their arms up and shield their faces from the searing heat and flying debris. In seconds, the vehicle was reduced to a burning heap of metal, folded in on itself and disintegrated. A staggering demonstration of his might now completed, the leader stepped to the fore.

"Everyone but the royalty will get out of the car or we will blow the charge! Do you comply?"

Caleb looked at Chelsea and she looked back at him. So, it was her they wanted. But for what reason?

Jonathan rolled down his window a crack and yelled to the leader.

"What do you want?"

"I just want the princess."

Jonathan turned in his seat and looked through the partition. "What do we do?"

Chelsea looked at Jonathan and started to speak, but was stopped by the gun barrel that was put to her temple. She moved her head just enough that she could look Caleb in the eyes.

"Ah, ah, ah," he said. "Careful."

Slowly, Caleb removed the gun from Chelsea's hand. "We have our money. We give her to them."

Jonathan nodded his head. Chelsea closed her eyes upon final affirmation of Caleb's betrayal.

"Know what this means, Caleb," she said.

"This is not an impulsive decision. I've been paid already to kill you, princess. What matter is it if I let these men do my work for me? Get out of the vehicle, please."

He moved out of the way, pointed the gun at her and allowed her to reach for the door. She released the latch and stepped out. He immediately followed her and put the gun to the back of her head. Jonathan opened his door and stood as well, then almost as an afterthought, pulled his weapon and aimed it at her.

The leader spoke again. "Release her."

Chelsea noticed now that he had an English accent — UK, which explained the British assault rifles some of the men held. He was of medium build, and though he was in all black and white fatigues, the muscles in his legs and arms pushed against the material and showed he was quite fit. A cocky, arrogant manner showed even through his straight-backed military posturing. The square jaw, small, tight reddish lips, and the straw colored hair completed the profile for her. He was without doubt English. She had seen many like him in the past. She'd even had an affinity for them once. But those men never had her at their mercy as did this one.

"You can have her after we've been guaranteed safe passage," said Caleb. He pushed the gun further into Chelsea's temple for effect. The leader looked impatient. He picked up a communicator and held it up in front of his mouth, hiding what he was saying. A moment passed, then Chelsea heard two very distinct, short whining sounds followed by the gross sound of flesh being impacted by bullets at close proximity. She knew the sound well. It no longer bothered her either. She turned her head and watched as Caleb fell to the ground, blood spilling from nearly the same spot on his forehead that he had placed the gun on hers not seconds earlier. She watched him fall until he finally hit the ground with a thud, dead already. The second bullet had killed Jonathan just as effectively. She looked up and tried to ascertain where the shots had come from and located one of the men, almost directly in front of them and high up in a tree. Probably the first man the leader had sent away when it all began. There was another located somewhere who had taken one of the shots, but it would take time to locate him, so she instead focused her attention on the leader, who was at that moment walking towards her. She noticed his stride had gained an ounce or two of confidence, for obvious reasons. He stopped just in front of her and looked her over.

She could see that he was intrigued by the way his eyes moved as he looked at her. Aroused. "Good," she thought.

"You may relax. I'm not here to kill you."

"What is your purpose?" she said, being sure to relax and keep her voice flat, confident. He continued to study her, then finally spoke.

"My name is Peter Granton. I guess you could think of me as an investor. I invest my skills, resources and experience in those who can finance my other career as a mercenary for hire. I have certain friends who were privy to the plans of a group of men whom you will come to know well. These friends of mine, they told me that as the sole surviving member of the royal family, you . . . . ."

"I'm not the last of the royal family."

"I'm afraid that's no longer true, madam."

Chelsea Matawae had been taught by her instructors to assume a role in high stress situations. They'd said that the role you played would, not could, but would save your life over and over again. This role, this persona, must flaunt self-control — one whose capability to focus on the task at hand was unwavering no matter the events taking place around them. And to most it was to be just that, a façade; for no one was unaffected by the events they took part in or witnessed, excepting true sociopaths. But that was okay. A jumbled mess of nerves and uncertainty were okay on the inside so long as the exterior belied nothing.

She'd shifted into that mode of emotive impenetrability as soon as this situation had begun to develop. But now, the fear for her parent's well-being that she had experienced aboard the plane was not only lent significance, but could very well have just been confirmed. Losing them would cause the facade, ballasted by all the training she'd received, to crumble, inward and outward, all through her, destroying every fiber of her being.

"Who are you and where are my parents?"

Granton looked at the princess impatiently. "Are you or are you not capable of accessing your family's personal assets outside of your kingdom?"

"I am."

He smiled a brilliant smile that she guessed was one of his most potent tools. "Then I'm your new best friend."

CHAPTER 14

"There's three kinds of female, man. The ones you fuck. The ones you want to fuck. And the ones you want to fuck up. I think you know which one that ho you was wit is. Nigga," he said laughing, "she played you like an accordion. Just forget about her man."

"Already done," I said.

"Good. Cause we got business."

After leaving Shanay's, we had returned to Kato's den just as night fell, with all the nefarious characters and their forty ounces and their weed smoke clouds wafting above us. I was beginning to actually like it there. It felt safe, and thanks to Kato I felt welcomed. And the truth was, I had managed to mostly put her off my mind. The hate in her eyes and the words that felt as if they'd been screamed out at me when she'd said them almost softly, were enough to completely cauterize any emotional ties that might have been established in the few short days she and I knew each other. And when I thought of it like that, I was grateful in a way. The last thing I needed to be worrying about, on top of everything else I was dealing with, was a girlfriend. "I'm a guy," I thought. "I should be happy that I got some sex with no strings attached.'" But no matter how hard I tried, it wasn't that easy and I knew it. Again, I had more important things to deal with.

"Alright, let's do some business," Kato began. "As you know, Smalls homied up wit Ray Ray and his gang just so he could get you. They had plenty of time to prepare so that means we can expect some shit real soon. Now I got too many peoples up and around this neighborhood so I don't expect them to come through with something stupid cause they wouldn't never get out. But like

I told you this morning, I can't help you in school. You got to stop going, at least for now."

"Aw, Kato, man I can't do that. I got quarter reports coming up right now . . . I'll go ahead and take my chances."

"You taking a chance like that is going to get you killed. Man look, that's the only place I can think of where he can touch you. Fuck, man you ain't no fucking superman. You ain't gonna be able to hide from him forever."

"So what you telling me man? I got to punk out like a little bitch and let him dictate where I can and can't go? Uh-uh."

Machismo, and Kato knew it. He grabbed me by the arm and pulled me towards the back of the house where none of the others could see or hear us. He yanked me into an empty room as if I was a child and closed the door behind us, then turned and looked at me.

"Dictate where you can and can't go? Nigga, he already fucking is. It's too late to find your balls now. The only thing you got left is strategy. Listen to me, Nicholas. What you got to do is come out of school. It's only gonna be for a little while. He's gonna make his play real soon. So either way, this is all going to be over before too long. Frankly, my brother, you'll either be back in school or in the ground in a matter of days."

I shook my head in confusion. It was too much. Too many players. Too many reasons to think it was all hopeless.

"How you know all this man?"

"It's just a matter of evaluating the situation. See, Ray Ray is very smart and very dangerous. The second Smalls came to him for help, he figured out a way to use that to his advantage. If he goes through us and everybody willing to back us up and gets you, everybody else he got problems wit is gon gain some respect real quick, know what I'm saying?"

"Yeah, I think I do. I ain't nothing more than just some game piece to him."

Kato smiled. "Yeah, basically." Then he laughed. "Actually, you hit it right on the fucking head."

I stood in that room in awe of this person who was my only link to any kind of possible favorable outcome. "Favorable" equated with me, not dead. With ease he managed to grasp concepts I had never approached. Warfare was something I was beyond unpracticed with and something he immersed himself in every day, and he seemed to enjoy it. A glimmer showed in his eyes, speaking of Ray Ray and Smalls and how best to protect against them. His men rallied behind him, fighting a fight that wasn't theirs, going against their nature to care only for self, only because he said they should, and because of the passion with which he did. It occurred to me that in another life he could have been a leader of men, under much different circumstances - as a general on a battlefield or CEO in some corporate office.

That thought stirred another feeling within me. Guilt. What would be the cost of Kato's determination to fight for his cause, a cause that without him would have been my fight and my fight alone? Should any of these men take a bullet for me just because Kato said so?

"Why you doing this man?" I asked.

"Aw, nigga."

"Naw, for real man. You putting yoself and your homeys on the line for me without good reason. Brother, I'm starting to think that maybe you need to cut yourself loose from me man, cause all I seem to be doing is setting more people up to get hurt. And I'll tell you the truth, dog . . . I'm so scared even my dick aches," I said, half laughing. "For real. My hair, my fingernails and my package all hurt from being scared, man."

At that, we both laughed out loud.

"You a fool, man," he said.

"But what I'm not too scared to realize is this," I said, shedding the comic and embracing the somber. "What's about to happen is gonna be my fault. Amid all this strategy and all the power plays, I see my world crumbling down around me. Ain't no purpose in me taking y'all down with me."

"That's valiant. Pretty fucking valiant," he said. He looked at me, impressed, and it made me feel a little better.

"Yeah," I said.

"You still wrong as fuck. Nigga. Ray Ray don't care about you. Neither do all them other people after you. Yet they've decided killing you is just . . . good business. People die in the hood so much it's become a way of life. Brothers are gonna keep killing other brothers without a hint of regret no matter what." He paused to let it sink in. "Unless people like you change things. Black people who have lived in this shit and have the intelligence and the need, the need nigga, to give our people a better chance. Whether you want it or not my brother, I have made you the chosen one. Which I guess means I'm using you too. So be it. Fuck me."

Damn. In amazement, I sat down on the armrest of a couch. Add orator to that list of things he could have been. I felt the way it must feel to have just been chastised by your older brother.

"How come you didn't do it?" I asked.

"Do what?"

"Make a better life for yourself. Get out of here. How come you didn't get out? Kato, you're smarter than anybody I know. You're better than everything I see you surround yourself with. You could have been a lawyer or something. You could have been a president someday."

He chuckled. "President."

"How come?" I asked.

"I don't know. Lots of reasons." He lowered his eyes, thoughtful.

"Is that one of the reasons you're protecting me?"

"What? Because I see in you what I might have been?"

He looked down momentarily, thinking.

"Maybe," he said. "So fucking what? Don't mean shit to nobody else."

"Means something to me," I said, trying not to sound dull.

"Yeah, because I'm keeping yo ass from getting capped. C'mon, dog."

He opened the door and we walked towards the front of the house where his men were. One of the men saw him coming and yelled in our direction.

"Kato, we need some more fucking drink man."

"Then let's go get some fucking more." Kato turned to me. "C'mon man. I want you to stay wit me at all times."

The same three that accompanied Kato and I earlier jumped up, grabbed their weapons, and joined us. We all piled into Fook Yoo's car, as we had before, and rode out. I guessed we were going to Sam Won Chin's store. It was a favorite in the neighborhood because it was so big and he carried a variety, unlike most of the smaller liquor stores. The only drawback to Chin's was that he was very paranoid. He closed by nine every night and wouldn't let you in if you knocked on the door at 9:01. And if you were still trying to get him to let you in at 9:02, he'd run and grab his cordless, stand in front of the window, and accuse you of being a "Tief! You jus wan steal my booze! My money, my booze!"

He'd hold up the phone, make you watch him dial 9 and then 1, and wait for you to make the next move. And some days he'd close early for no apparent reason, except maybe to keep any potential "tiefs!" planning a robbery guessing.

I looked at my watch. 8:30. My mother would have been home an hour and a half already. After the run, I'd have to ask Kato to drop me at home. I could put off talking to her no longer. And knowing her, she would have been home just waiting for me to come in the door so she could grill me. Of course she had every right to wonder why I was behaving so mysteriously; I knew that I couldn't rightfully keep the truth from her any longer. I'd tell her everything and just hope she didn't overreact.

The entire ride, the man next to me dominated the conversation with Kato and the others. One subject dominated.

"Man, so that bitch looked at me like I was lying, right. . . ."

"So what'd you do then, nigga?" asked his neighbor.

"Shit, I took that ho upstairs and busted a nut right there on the spot, had that bitch crying like a motherfucker, calling my name out and shit. She thought she was going to mother*fucking* heaven.

"Bullshit, you black-ass motherfucker," said Kato. "I'm gonna start calling you Captain Dark As Night. I think your powers will be compulsive lying and jerking off at superhuman speeds."

Everyone except for the man who'd been speaking chuckled. He twisted up his face into what I guess was meant to show how offended he was.

"The fuck is yo problem?" he said.

"Man, you a fucked up liar. Hey, didn't you fuck Babygat's sister Jennifer?"

"Yeah, I laid the pipe on that bitch. Had her crying like a mufucker too."

Kato nodded his head as if he were taking it all in. He simply said, "Hmh." He had something planned.

"Well, that's fucked up cause she told me she couldn't feel nothing. She said yo' dick was all twisted, looked like it had muscular dystrophy or some shit."

In those situations, the mouth is always the first thing to go. A slow, quiet widening that soon morphs into an incredulous smile, and then finally, laughter — painful, body rocking, stomach-aching laughter. Soon the entire car was filled with raucous, cruel, uncompassionate laughter at this man who'd worked so hard to impress us with his sexual prowess. For a full five minutes we cackled. I clutched my stomach and held myself and tried to keep from hyperventilating. The brother looked around at us and watched us laugh at him in distress. Finally, all he could muster was, "Aw, shit."

"Fuck!" said Fook Yoo. And everyone started up again. I felt tears beginning to stream down my face.

My embarrassed neighbor finally regained his boldness and said, "That bitch knows I was the best she ever had. Fuck. She knows I got the longest ass mufuckin ass dick she ever had the pleasure of getting to know. *Shit.* Y'all better recognize."

"I'm just fucking wit you nigga," Kato said, wiping his face of his own tears.

"Yeah, fuck you too."

Fook Yoo decided to jump in and stuttered out, "No . . . n . . . no, fuck you!" and we all started up again. This time I doubled over, barely able to breathe, not just laughing but convulsing with periodic bursts of air escaping my mouth. My neighbor finally realized he was beaten and just shook his head and chewed on his lip.

When I finally regained control of myself, I sat up and rubbed my eyes. When I opened them, I looked out my window into the night and saw the houses and stores and businesses as they passed by. I glimpsed forward through the front windshield, then my eyes caught an image through Kato's rearview mirror that made me look twice. I turned in my seat and looked through the rear window. What I saw left a lump in my throat.

"Kato!"

"What's up?" He turned around, saw me looking behind the car and took a look for himself. Behind us, in a Mustang, were five black men coming up on us fast. And I couldn't tell for sure, but I felt it. Smalls was among them.

"Aw, shit this is it." Kato turned to Fook Yoo. "Hit it yo!"

Fook Yoo floored it. I continued looking through the rear window and watched the other car. We began to pull away from them and I, in turn, began to second-guess my suspicion that they were hostile. That was, until I heard the pings — pings that it took a second for me to identify as bullets ripping into the body of the car. I stole another glance through the window and saw that the other car was now closing the distance between us. And they were shooting at us. It finally occurred to me that I should probably duck, so I threw myself on the floor.

It was the sounds that came next that I remember most. It was like I'd been dropped into a war zone. Ching! Ching! Ching! Ching! Ching!

My neighbor, the one who'd been embarrassed, had reached over my back and was now returning fire through my window. The man beside him stuck his own body out his window and fired over the top of the car, and Kato fired from his window as well. All of them yelling, screaming obscenities, bullet casings ejecting from their guns and falling all around me, stinging my skin where they hit the back of my neck.

A wall of automatic weapons fire erupted from the windows of both speeding cars. I lifted my head a couple of times and looked over the car window ledge just to get an idea as to the location of Small's car and what was happening. They mostly stayed behind and to the right of us, the driver either incapable or unwilling to pull up directly next to us with all the firepower we had.

Suddenly there was a lull in the firing. I lifted my head again just slightly, hoping it was over, and looked out the window again. The city's night landscape shot by at nearly ninety miles an hour. I looked in the direction of where I'd last seen Small's car, desperately hoping it was no longer there. I was disappointed. They were inching closer. I looked to my neighbor and realized why the firing had ended unanimously. Everyone was reloading. The men in both cars had released full clips and magazines and were now preparing to start back up again. Though it felt like minutes, the entire exchange had only taken seconds.

Then I heard a single shot, a pop, and a hissing sound. The car began to convulse. The firing began again and I ducked my head into my lap for what felt like the millionth time. I thought of the car lurching. It was a tire. They had shot out one of our tires, which meant we would be slowing. That was their plan.

Surprisingly, there was a sudden decrease in weapons fire. The men in my car were still firing . . . but they weren't. That's why it wasn't as loud. I raised my head and looked back out the window again, wanting to see what had transpired. Their plan worked. They were easily closing the distance now as our disabled vehicle limped along much more slowly. They had us. They were closing in for the kill. I kept my eye on their car because I knew this might mean the end for us. Pointless as it may have been, I wanted to look Smalls in the eye.

What I saw initially left me confused. Everyone, including the driver, was sunken down in their seats. Quickly, I began to comprehend their intentions. They meant to match our speed, protecting themselves from our own gunfire, then suddenly sit up and blow us all to hell. And it nearly worked.

Just as they came even with us, a left turn presented itself into the downtown part of the city and Fook Yoo took it hard, almost throwing us up onto two wheels. When Smalls and his boys sat up and fired, only a few rounds lodged themselves into the trunk of Fook Yoo's Cutlass as we lurched down the street. I risked a look back through what was left of the rear window and realized it wasn't near over. Smalls and his boys wouldn't take long to turn around and come after us. And we were still handicapped by the blown-out tire. Kato was thinking the same thing I was.

"Yo man, stop the car we sittin ducks in this mufucker man."

"What we gon' do, man?" The man who had stuck himself out of the car to fire on Smalls and his boys had pulled himself back in by this time. When he spoke I looked at him and my eyes were attracted to a large red spot just under his left shoulder blade. He had been shot. Maybe it was the adrenaline but he behaved as if he hadn't noticed yet.

Fook Yoo sped to a position just in front of a deserted outdoor mall and braked violently. One long building that enclosed several shops made up the mall. Luckily, all of them were long since closed and not a soul was to be found this late in this neighborhood. Had I taken the time to allow myself to appreciate the irony, we were exactly where we had planned to go all along. Sam Won Chin's was in this mall. Turned out Sam Won Chin was a smart man. Indeed it did not pay to be open too late in this part of town, especially not tonight.

"C'mon. They'll be on us in a second. Nicholas, you wit' me."

We all opened our doors, stepped out of the car and hit the ground running. On cue, our pursuers came screeching around the last corner we had taken and up to our position. Facing the driver's side of Fook Yoo's car, they pinned everyone on that side of the car in with weapon's fire. Kato and I fled as the sound of automatics behind us erupted. Fook Yoo and the other two men returned fire, but to no avail. The two men were immediately cut down, overwhelmed by the firepower of the **five** men that stepped out of the car. Fook Yoo managed, miraculously, to make his way around the front of the car and follow us, firing back with his two pistols as he ran. But there were just too many rounds coming his way and he took a couple of slugs in the back. Somehow, like an elephant that had been shot with only one tranquilizer, the huge brother kept moving.

Smalls and his four compatriots moved confidently. My heart sunk when I looked over my shoulder as I ran and saw that not one of them had been incapacitated by all the gunfire we sent their way. And now that they had taken out two of our crew and wounded one, they saw no hurry in finishing the job.

Smalls took the lead arrogantly and the others fell in behind him. Smiling that ugly smile of his, he walked towards

Fook Yoo's car where our friends lay dying. Following us into the mall area, he looked down and fired a shot into both of them as he walked past.

"Yeah, who's the fucking man now, fellas? Ya worthless black pieces of shit. Good riddance. Nicholas Gambit! I'm coming for ya. I'm gonna do you like I had your family done. You hear me? Do you? Do you hear me!"

I turned a corner with Kato and we nailed ourselves to a wall. Kato whispered something but my ears were ringing again, from the adrenaline. I didn't recognize a word he said. He looked at me impatiently, then grabbed me by the collar and pulled me after him.

We came up on Chin's store. Kato must've got the same joke I had earlier and snorted. He used his gun to break the glass just beside the door, reached in and opened it from the inside. I was surprised no alarms went off. I thought Chin would have spared no cost to provide security for his place. I hoped that the alarm was silent and the police would be coming soon.

"You go inside and hide," Kato said.

That I heard. "What are you gonna do? Wait a minute, no . . ."

"Nicholas."

"I'm not gonna let you get killed while I'm in here hiding . . ."

"Get the fuck in there Nicholas, it's the only way. I shoulda never brought you out here in the first place, not without twice as many of my men. I ain't got time for this shit, man! Go!" Kato put his gun to my head, apparently to demonstrate his seriousness.

I knew he wasn't going to shoot me. That would sort of defeat the purpose, but the gesture was convincing enough, so I decided to trust his experience. I walked inside and looked around, then looked back through the window and watched Kato move down the sidewalk slowly. I hoped he and Fook Yoo would find each other and make their way back here. Maybe we could all hide here until Smalls and his crew gave up or the police arrived.

CHAPTER 15

After assuring Nicholas was stashed away safely, Kato made his way back the way they had come. First, he wanted to find Fook. He hated having to leave his men like that, but tactically, he knew there had been no way around it. As he and Nicholas ran, they had both seen Fook get hit. But it was Fook. Kato felt there was a chance he might still be alive. That brother had heart. He wouldn't go down that easy.

The other thing that occupied his mind, even now, was how quickly he dove into this situation. Most of the fellas thought he was crazy, putting himself in harm's way for this kid he barely knew. But something told him he had to do it. His understandings of right and wrong, judgments he had long since learned to ignore, had forced their way up from some pit within. They told him he had to act this time; he couldn't sit this one out. The whys weren't all that hard to understand. He knew it was because he was getting older. His conscience was rearing its ugly head more and more these days. He'd begun to feel a real obligation to give back somehow, especially since his daughter had been born. This thing with Nicholas was all a part of that. Plus, he liked the kid. God knows why cause he was boring as shit, but he did really like him.

He shook himself of all the unnecessary thinking and decided he must focus on the task at hand. He had to find Fook, try to somehow kill Smalls and his little squad, and get out of here before the blues got there.

Four of Smalls' crew made their way down the sidewalk, creeping along as quietly as possible. They knew that the big one they hit a few times had made his way in this direction because he'd left a blood trail. Their problem, only a few nearby streetlights worked. Light was scarce, which made the trail hard to follow. And it had become more faint as they progressed. The more they walked, the more insecure they began to feel about being ambushed. The big one, or the other two, could still be close and could come from anywhere with little warning.

All four focused on the sidewalk and the storefronts ahead as they moved. There were too many shadows. They couldn't all be accounted for. This was their disadvantage and Fook Yoo knew it. They didn't notice a narrow spaceway between two of the buildings as they passed it. From that dark space came Fook Yoo.

Limping, he stepped out, raised his guns and aimed for the backs of the bangers. A shot rang out. He looked down at the guns in his hands. It wasn't his weapons that had fired. Fook Yoo convulsed from the surprise pain that ran through his entire body. A click. Another loud retort echoed. He looked up and cried out when he felt the second shot tear into his lower back. Then another shot sounded and on impact he was sent to his knees. A single thought ran through his mind, "Cold." His strength was gone. It flowed out of him, running down his legs, soaking his pants. Darkness. Quiet. Then stars. Stars in the sky. He realized he'd opened his eyes and was now looking up at the night sky. He had passed out, for a moment, and was now lying on the ground looking up.

From the top of Fook's field of vision, Smalls stepped forward and stood over him, looking down at him. Smalls shook his head and looked at the men he'd sent ahead.

"Careless mufuckers."

He looked back down at Fook and pointed his gun at his head contemptuously.

"Yo, man, before you die, where they at, nigga?"

Fook Yoo smiled up at Smalls, who nearly retreated from the unexpected and bold reaction of the man who lay dying before him.

For the first time in his life, he spoke with perfect clarity, an unheralded composure gifted him by the knowledge that his end was near.

"You can't hurt me. What happens to me now is out of your hands." He choked out a laugh, looked directly into Small's eyes, and watched him fire the gun into his face point blank.

CHAPTER 16

I looked up at the sound of a gunshot. I'd heard three more prior to that one, which meant Kato might have found them. But four separate, solitary shots like that? Maybe he was trying to take them out one by one. Then I heard it. The sound I'd been expecting. More gunfire. Rapid fire. Semi and automatics. If the other shots hadn't been Kato, he was definitely in it now. And he was taking on a lot of people. The sound of glass being destroyed, screaming, bullets lodging themselves in metal and brick. The ch, ch, ch, ch, ch! of the automatics sounding, ricocheting throughout the night. Armageddon. Then, as suddenly as it had begun, the calamity ended.

I crouched by one of the shelves on the far end of the store and waited. I looked around. Sam Won Chin's liquor store was large, luxurious by the neighborhood's standards. Six very tall and long rows of shelves filled the floor, loaded with liquors on both sides. Nearly the entire back wall of the store accessed the typical convenience store freezer racks where he kept the various drinks and snacks common to those places. In the front of the store was the checkout desk. It was one long desk halved by a step that allowed the attendant to enter and exit. The entire shop was barely lit. A couple of fluorescent lights, left on after the store closed, flashed on and off. And it was cold. After only a few minutes I already felt myself beginning to shiver. I wrapped my arms around me and rubbed myself, huddling against the shelving, underneath the eerie flickering of the lights.

Waiting like this was killing me. When I was part of the action and bullets were flying, I had no time to do anything but try and survive. I hadn't the time to think about dying. But there in that cold, dark place, all alone, I was more scared than I had been since it all began on that street when I'd fought Smalls. Hiding, shivering, practically on my knees already, the adrenaline that kept me from thinking the worst abandoned me. Adrenaline, my buoy that had served to keep me focused and optimistic, was now exhausted. And so I waited for someone to come and kill me and I began to feel sorry for myself. I was gonna die, all alone, inside a liquor store, and I would never see my mother again.

I looked up at the sound of movement. Kato? I hoped. I raised my head just enough to look through the windows of the store and decided my situation was helpless. Two men that were neither Kato or Fook walked by very slowly, scanning the street in front of them, searching for me. Then another disappointment. Smalls. Smalls was still alive, trailing the others.

"Just walk by," I prayed, hoping they wouldn't notice the busted-through glass panel at the entrance to the doorway. It was small enough to miss, I hoped, and maybe the darkness would work to my advantage.

My heart started to pump out of control, the adrenaline reactivating again. I hadn't run out of it after all, though it made me feel no better as I had hoped it might.

"Just walk right by," I whispered.

And they did! The two men walked by the door. "Oh, thank God!" I thought. Then Smalls came to the doorway and stopped. I suddenly became very tired. He'd noticed the glass. He studied it for a second, then peered inside the shop, thinking.

"Hey. Hey. In here. Look at this."

They turned around, and upon seeing the glass themselves, nodded to him. They pushed open the door and stepped inside.

Now this was one of the moments where everything began to change. Up to this point, I had been Small's quarry, both literally and mentally. Though it had occurred to me a couple of times to take the fight to him, I hadn't. Because Kato had told me not to, or because I was just too afraid, I don't know. But the fact was, he was pursuing me, I was evading him, and therefore, he was the one in control.

At that very moment, on the verge of being caught and killed, of having my life robbed of me by Smalls only because I had embarrassed him in a place where he undeservedly saw himself as king, in a nanosecond-like space of time, I discovered that every notion of future greatness I had for my family and myself, all that I could or would do in my time on this earth, was suddenly made impotent by the prospect of just accepting my fate and dying a victim. Just like the 300 other black people that were killed in my city every year. Another trigger not dissimilar to the one Mrs. Sanborne experienced was activated, and that's when I decided "No . . . not me."

There was a gift that I always knew I possessed but had never fully utilized. It was a unique talent that I could describe as a special kind of intuition. It was an insight that often guided me through dangerous situations and could even tell me what a person was going to do before they did it. I now realize this talent was what made me such a capable fighter when I'd had no real training. Quite often I saw the punch before it came, the plan before it was developed. I had an ability to profile the simplest actions before they happened. Some would have called it a sixth sense, but it wasn't that abnormal. I would come to learn that though the numbers who had this talent were small, there were certainly others like me.

Cognizant, for the first time suddenly, that I did possess it and that it was a talent, I then decided to use it to get myself out of my desperate situation. For the first time, I'd go on the offensive, find a way to put Smalls on the _defensive_ and not have to run anymore.

Small's men entered first, guns up. I decided that I needed to find a way to surprise them. My back was to the wall, literally. From the wall furthest from the entrance, I peeked around a rack and watched them enter. Moving as efficiently as I could without making any noise, I ducked underneath the rack and watched their feet. Because they were moving slowly, I concluded I had time to move again and did, slinking across to the next lane. I positioned myself under the next rack over, all the while eyeing their feet.

Suddenly, I appreciated how dark it was. Had there been any more light they would have seen my every move. Equally as important were the shelves themselves. In the dim light, the part of the shelves that held the goods and liquors appeared to extend completely to the ground when they didn't, further masking my location.

I watched as one of the men walked to the far side of the store, where I had been only moments before, and began to head down the lane. Another took the closest lane to the entrance and another took the middle lane, one aisle over from where I lay. Moving more quickly now, they walked to the end of their respective lanes and signaled to each other that they had seen nothing; I assumed this was accomplished by shaking their heads because no one spoke. Then they each took another lane and began to search it. I held my breath and watched a man's feet pass to my right this time. I knew I would have to act soon; Smalls would be getting edgy and would do something foolish before long.

The lane to my left still hadn't been searched yet and I thought it best to make my way towards the doorway every chance I got. I slid on my belly again, crossing the lane and taking cover underneath the next rack over. Just as I made it, one of Smalls' men turned into the lane I had just crossed and searched it. I looked to my left and saw that another one of them did the same, walking down the next lane over. Then the third man made his way back to the front of the store and held his position there. And though I could only see his feet and the bottom of his legs, I could see impatience in the quiet tapping of his foot. Smalls. I smiled and was surprised at my newfound coolness under pressure.

The two men searched the lanes and came up with nothing. They walked back to the front of the store and met up with Smalls. Again I thanked God for the darkness and the size of the shelves. Had they even thought of checking underneath them, I still would have had to move for them to pick me out.

The silence was finally broken when Smalls could tame his restlessness no longer.

"I know he's in here. Gambit! You fucking pussy. Why don't you just come out here and die like a real man, you piece of shit."

He was fanatical. He wanted me dead so bad he could taste it. He motioned his men to try the farthest lanes again, near each wall. I watched him position himself near the entrance and stand there fidgeting as they headed again to the back of the store.

"Your homies are dead. And here you are hiding like a motherfucking pussy. At least yo friends went out like men, you know I'm saying? Die!"

Small's men reached the end of their lanes and acknowledged each other. One of them dropped his weapon to his side and called to Smalls, still near the entrance on the other side of the store.

"Smalls, he ain't fucking here. Let's get the fuck out of this place."

"He is here! Keep looking."

I chose then to act. I could still see their feet and knew that relative to my position, they would sandwich me if I made myself visible to them. I was counting on that. The darkness and the effect it would have of handicapping their vision, which I knew would make them skittish, gave me the element of surprise.

I slid out from underneath the rack, jumped to my feet, ran to the end of the lane, and jumped out, making myself visible to them just as they were turning to walk back the way they came. "Hey!" I yelled. I stood motionless for only a moment, then dove back into the lane, then to the floor.

Just as I had hoped, they did what anyone in that situation would. As they both turned in the direction of the noise and the shadow I must have projected for that one moment, their trigger fingers constricted and their weapons erupted. In the process, the men were caught in each other's lines of fire. Their bullets that were meant for me, instead ripped into each other and then the ceiling as they fell backwards, taking hits from so many rounds it catapulted them away from each other.

I crawled under the rack again for cover as bullets flew in every direction. But it wasn't the two men's bullets, as their fingers had eased from the triggers after only a second or two; dead, I guessed. It was Smalls. As soon as he'd realized what was happening, he'd begun running the length of the store, between the register and the shelves, firing wildly in the general direction of the action. I felt pieces of bottle and groceries come down around me, liquor splashing in my eyes and burning them. I closed my eyes and waited for the firing to stop.

When it did, I opened my eyes, ready to spring, but thought better of it when I heard the sound of a magazine clattering to the floor and then another click that I took to be the sound of another magazine, a full one taking its place. I had hoped he wouldn't have had the foresight to bring a reload. I looked without moving my head and soon located his feet. I could tell how amped he was by the way he stepped forwards and then backwards nervously, never leaving his general position, waiting for me to make my next move.

I decided to move again but chose to wait a few seconds. I wanted to let him marinate in the juices that were making him feel less and less in control. The more worried I let him get, the more apt he would be to make a mistake when I needed him to.

"You motherfucking sneaky ass nigga. Gambit!"

"Yes," I thought. "Good."

I slipped out from my cover and made my way slowly, quietly up to the front of the lane and peered around the corner. I observed that, despite the size of the store, this was not a very accommodating place to house a gunfight. There wasn't a lot of room to work with. I could use that to my advantage against one person. Smalls stood, frustrated, at the corner of the store, searching for anything to fire at. I don't think he would have moved from his position had it not been for the bottle.

I started running before it hit the ground. Small's firing had of course hit several of the shelves, sending destroyed merchandise everywhere and leaving the shelving in disarray. What bottles were still whole were severely displaced, and this one, I learned too late, was already teetering close to the edge of the shelving where I stood. In the darkness I hadn't seen it, and when I felt my tricep brush against it and realized there was no chance of catching it before it hit the ground, I turned and sprinted for dear life.

It seemed like forever before it did, but when it finally crashed to the ground and exploded, everything behind me disintegrated in a hail of bullets. Smalls first fired at the direction of the crashing bottle, then made his way to the end of the lane. Upon seeing my silhouette in the dark, he stuck his arm out and fired after me as I ran. Seconds passed but I remember it only as mental snapshots and feelings. The shelving speeding by as I ran, the barely visible freezer doors ahead of me, a sharp pain in my arm that hit me like someone had grabbed me. It whipped me around and turned me sideways. The last snapshot was of the freezer, now only inches away. Next thing I knew, I was in the air. I'd reached the freezer doors and leapt at what remained of the glass casing.

The momentum carried me through what had been the glass door that accessed the refrigerated liquors but was now virtually obliterated, either by the two gunmen's undirected gunfire or Small's wild shots that had just missed me and taken out the doors in front of me. Either way, my life was saved by the glass no longer being whole. I went through ungracefully, splintered, broken glass digging into my skin the whole way, bullets missing me by centimeters, ricocheting around me as Smalls tried to cut me off. Sliding across the cold, wiry metal racks, I came to the end of the rack and was thrown off. Landing on the cement floor on the other side hard, I rolled, glass and bullets still flying.

The freezer was unlit, the floor and walls a dark color. Four smaller metal shelves filled the room, parallel to the glass doors. I got up and moved to the back as fast as I could, and while moving, realized I was hurt. As best as I could tell, I had only been hit in the arm by one of Small's bullets, and though it hurt, I could tell it was fixable. The fall into the freezer had done more damage than the bullet. In the same arm, above the bullet wound, was a severe bruise. When I hit the ground, the brunt of the fall had been taken by the shoulder and dislocated something. The pain was becoming dizzying. But I told myself there was no time to do anything but focus on Smalls.

Right on cue he came busting through the entrance to the freezer. I couldn't see him from behind the shelving, but I heard him.

"Gambit," he said, taunting me. He searched the area in front of him, then moved down to search the next lane over. "It's yo time, Gambit. Why don't you go out like a real man, nigga? I got to admit that was quite a little acrobatic show you just put on. All it did though was get you a few more minutes. Why don't we quit playing games? I'm all played out."

I listened and plotted his position every time he spoke, from every sound he made. The room was small enough for him to see across to the other wall in front of him, which meant all he had to do was clear each space between the four shelves to get to me. I had to get to him before he reached the fourth shelf. And when I heard him speak from just one rack over I knew it was time to move. I could hear the smile and an air of victory in his voice and it compelled me to shut him down.

"I got you now, nigga. Here you are hiding like a Got-damn pussy," he said.

I leapt with all I had left in me. The wooden shelf had to have been a good five feet in height. I could see that it was sturdy too. I used that. I jumped, threw my hands up, pulled myself over the top of it, and cleared it. Then I pushed off with my feet as I came over and torpedoed Smalls with a body tackle. He'd never expected an attack from above. The gun slid away as we both hit the ground.

With my now bad right arm I punched down at him and then I hit him with my left. I connected with his face, then aimed for his body. He either kneed or kicked at me and caught me in the stomach, knocking the air out of me again. I fell back and tried to fill my lungs. Smalls got to his knees and moved into the direction his gun had slid. Knowing I couldn't allow him the advantage, I threw myself at him, coming up behind him, ignoring the lack of oxygen in my lungs. He reached the gun, picked it up, turned . . . and I leveled him. I clotheslined him better than I had ever seen anyone do it on any football field. Just as he turned to fire I hit him. He went completely horizontal, then fell on his back. I lifted my foot and kicked him in the head as hard as I could, again and again and didn't stop until I thought he might have been dead. I looked down at him, dazed as if I had been the one to take the beating. I could feel the blood pumping behind my eyes.

"Twice Smalls," I said. "Twice in a week I ***BEAT YO ASS, MAN!***"

I picked up the gun and pointed it at him and decided to kill him. I had every right to do so and it made sense.

But that just wasn't good enough. I felt my chest tighten and a sour feeling suddenly filled up the pit of my stomach. Mere minutes earlier he'd been desperate to shoot me dead and now he was beaten and helpless and lying there freezing on the cold, hard floor, and though I wanted to kill him I couldn't. As I saw it at the time, the threat had been nullified and I no longer needed to. I certainly didn't feel sorry for him, but I simply could not kill in what I viewed as a cold-blooded, cowardly way even if it was the logical thing to do. I just couldn't muster the disregard for life that I needed to pull that trigger. I didn't want to kill anybody. Not even him. Even then it occurred to me that my rationale might be naïve. But I just didn't want to kill him. Maybe it was easier to explain it away as the honorable, ethical choice. That was a long time ago. It would not be long before my thinking changed considerably.

I lowered the weapon to my side. I nudged Smalls with my foot and he didn't move, so I walked through the exit and out of the freezer back into the eerie atmosphere of the store. The destruction that lay throughout was colossal: mutilated bottles and glassware; splintered wood and dented metal; food spread everywhere; the place would soon be accurately described as a war zone. As I passed them, I looked at the two men's bodies surrounded by pools of their own blood. The blood was already beginning to freeze due to the cold. I felt no compassion for them. I walked up an aisle towards the front of the store and that's when I saw Kato through the windows of the store. Hunched over and struggling for air, he propped himself up against the outside of the window and left a blood trail as he moved forward. I ran to meet him at the doorway and pulled him inside. His shirt was soaked through with crimson. Multiple wounds covered his torso and legs. I put his arm around me and helped him take a seat on the floor. I propped his back up against the front of the register desk and kneeled in front of him. He still held his weapon firmly. I placed the automatic in my hands on the desk above us.

"Looks like you didn't need me after all, brother. I got a couple of 'em. Took two of em out. They got Fook though. They didn't have to kill Fook man . . . ."

"I gotta get the ambulance here," I said, looking for a phone.

"They ain't coming down here. For some reason they think it's too dangerous." He laughed and then convulsed, spitting blood.

"Don't you die, man."

"Fuck you. Why not?"

I couldn't help but smile. "Cause you gonna be president someday. First president of the United States with a whack ass-afro."

He laughed again, but this time didn't spit up blood, which I took as a good sign. "You're alright nigga. But you fucking insane. Black President? That shit'll never happen. President ain't got no power anyway. Not down here." Without warning, he grabbed me by the collar and pulled me close to him. "Nicholas. You gotta come back. Go out there and make a name for yourself and then come back and change things. You the one, brother. Be a doctor, be a lawyer, whatever . . . ."

"Kato." I could see his eyes drooping. He was beginning to lose consciousness and was talking from the shock that was overcoming him.

"Hell, you already a preacherman, so . . . like, have your own church. They the only ones I've ever seen really change things around here. Tell me you'll come back Nicholas. Promise."

I saw then that it wasn't just unintelligible, near unconscious chatter, but that he needed to get something across to me before he died. This was about repentance, and I owed him that much, at least.

"I will," I said.

He nodded his head, confident the message had been relayed, then closed his eyes and rested his head against the desk. I knew I wouldn't have much time. I stood up and walked behind the register, picked up a phone and dialed 911.

"911 dispatch. What is the emergency?"

I put on the whitest sounding voice I could muster and started to scream into the receiver at the top of my lungs. "Yeah, there's a bunch of Negroes shooting up my store! Yeah, I'm a white man and I have rights! There's bodies laying everywhere.

The liquor store on ninth street, Sam Won Chin's!" I held the phone away from my mouth, grabbed the automatic in front of me and held it into the air and fired, emptying the magazine into the ceiling. Confident the operator would have been sufficiently distressed, I replaced the receiver. Empty and now useless, I threw the weapon away, happy to be rid of it.

Brought back to consciousness by the noise, Kato opened his eyes and smiled, pleased with my ingenuity. Then something caught his attention. His eyes registered movement, something moving on the other side of the store. He looked again to be sure his eyes weren't playing tricks on him and in the darkness was only able to make out feet and legs moving on the other side of the store. His heart stirred and nearly leapt out of his chest. Someone was back there!

"Nicholas!"

I immediately knew something was wrong but was given no time to investigate. Almost simultaneous to his outburst, Kato's pistol was suddenly twirling in the air in front of me. From my perspective, I'd seen it rise above the counter, not realizing he'd thrown it from his position in front of the desk. Instinctively, I reached out in front of me and grabbed for it, not yet knowing why he'd thrown it. Surprised, I fumbled it first, then finally took a firm grip with both hands and that's when I saw him.

I'd focused all my attention on getting to Kato, helping him inside and stupidly had forgotten all about Smalls. And there he was. His outstretched arm came into view first as he turned the corner of the rack. He leveled one of his downed men's guns in my direction, wearing a grimace that, at the time, I didn't fully understand the motivation behind it. I now know exactly what it was — sadistic satisfaction with himself and what he'd done.

Then a gun went off. Three separate shots. At first I didn't know if it was mine or his. A time delay occurring in my mind's eye, I recalled, after the fact, how the slide of my pistol shot back and forward and the yellow flame that accompanied each bullet as it exited the barrel each time I fired. Before he'd had time to aim, I had put three bullets in him, knocking him back against the refrigerant racks, dead. Kato, by throwing me the gun, had done the only thing that made sense. Because of the way the racks were positioned, he would have never been able to hit Smalls from his location. He'd saved my life again. It was finally all over.

An intense weariness suddenly overtook me and I wanted to go somewhere and lay down for the rest of my life. With all his wounds, I could only have imagined how Kato must have felt. I closed my eyes and put my head down on the desk in front of me. Seconds later, I raised my head again at the sound of sirens wailing as police cruisers pulled up and spotlights shone through the windows, suddenly illuminating the store.

"That was fast," I said, shaking my head. I grabbed Kato and again propped him against me. We walked through the door and stood in front of what must have been an entire squadron of cops, all standing outside their car doors, pointing guns at us. Due to my phone call, they'd come expecting a mob. I raised my unoccupied hand into the air, squinted my eyes and took in the flashing red, white and blue police lights and spotlights that broke through the night and lit up the entire city block.

CHAPTER 17

"Why do we have to do this now, Granton?"

Chelsea didn't look at Peter Granton when she asked the question, but she made sure the tone in her voice was discernible. She wanted him to know she was bothered by this latest hindrance. They seemed, of late, to be never-ending.

"Princess, our goal, our mission, is to stock up on munitions so that we may retake power from the new leadership that currently controls your country, is it not?"

"We should have killed Bergosi as soon as we arrived in America and found out he was alive. We've already allowed a couple of our initial overseas targets time to prepare before we come for them. We should have finished the job and killed them before we came here."

"Is that your training or your impatience speaking?"

Chelsea looked at him this time, raising one side of her face to demonstrate her disdain. "You are unpleasant when you condescend."

Granton chuckled. "Princess, our primary mission, per your orders, was to stock up on munitions, was it not? Our *secondary* mission, again, per your orders, was to eliminate anyone who took part in your parent's death, was . . . it . . . not?"

She turned her head and looked ahead of her, through the windshield of the moving car. It was early evening. The sun was waning. They were on a rugged highway that seemed to be winding around a large hill. Ahead of them, more hills with badly paved, nearly gravel roads that spiked into the horizon.

Chelsea looked to her left, through Granton's window and eyed the landscape. The land itself appeared to be virtual desert except for the occasional patches of sometimes green, but mostly brown grass that popped up from time to time. Small domiciles, shacks that looked as if they'd been dropped onto the ground from on high seemed to litter the hills. Some of the houses had vehicles parked nearby, others had only wreckage: dead cars, trucks or tractors. Some were surrounded by empty dirt roads. Occasionally, an architectural surprise would appear; a well-built house that had obviously been labored over during its construction would seemingly come out of nowhere, but as soon as it passed out of sight another thatched, barely standing cottage would appear and reaffirm the squalor.

"So, this is Mexico," Chelsea thought.

"I understand your desire for revenge," Granton said. "But you know as well as I do that it will take time; and it will require a disciplined, methodical disposition."

Chelsea exhaled slowly. Out of the corner of his eye, Granton noticed her posture changing. He looked ahead and remained silent for a few minutes, allowing her to fume. He was nearly unable to stifle a smirk that he knew would send her off the deep end. After convincing himself he had sufficiently quelled the impulse, he eventually looked at her again.

"I do work for you, Princess. If you disagree then say so and we will go plodding off back to your country and do what we can with what we have now."

"Just shut up Granton! The only person you're entertaining is yourself. Just shut up. Of course I agree. Doesn't mean I have to like it."

He couldn't hold back the laughter this time and let it flow. He half expected her to punch him in the face while he was driving. He was pleasantly surprised to see, when he calmed himself and looked at her, that she was smiling as well.

"You didn't have to come, Princess. I know we've spoken on this issue but I would prefer if you let me deal with men such as these alone or with one of my other men. As I'm sure you're aware, arms dealers are often not the most savory of characters. I know you wanted to be involved on all major purchases and I'm happy to honor that . . ."

"As you've said, we've spoken on this issue already," said Chelsea.

Granton nodded his head submissively, "Very well."

"Do you think I should trust you with my money simply because you saved my life and demonstrated some skill at accomplishing a strategic goal now and then? The men we've terminated so far have all been gluttonous subordinates, nothing like that which is to come. It will take more, I'm afraid, for me to fully trust you."

"I understand. Don't get me wrong, Princess," Granton said, smiling again and looking at her. "I am invigorated by your company. I'm glad you came, after all."

Chelsea looked at him and met his eyes with her own. Granton was a handsome man. He was definitely not unpleasant to look at. Of course, she couldn't let him know that, so she turned away and shook her head, half-smiling. "How sad," she said, chuckling.

"What?"

"Do you honestly think that your occasional, and I do mean *occasional* charm will work on me?"

"Time will tell, Princess," he said, trying to regain eye contact. "As you said, there is much you still do not know about me. I have much to prove. There are many things I want to show you."

"Perhaps we should focus on this op for now," Chelsea said.

"For now? Does that mean there will be a later occasion for us to focus on other matters?"

Chelsea closed her eyes and allowed a smile to come to her face. "Your desire for me is . . . problematic."
She paused and thought for a second. "There is a Swahili phrase that comes to mind right now. Amakweli ni ngumu kutofautisha kati ya mbwa aliyeshikwa na kichaa na umbwa mwenye taki ya kumuingia mbwa mwenzake. I believe it has an adequate English counterpart."

"Which is?"

She cocked her head at an angle and looked him in the eyes again. "The line between a rabid dog and one that is merely *in heat,* is difficult to draw."

A few moments passed before Granton spoke again. When he did speak he didn't look at her, but was clearly annoyed. "Only the female of the species goes into heat, Princess."

"Yes, but it's the male that is the most dangerous when he catches her scent."

"The difference, Chelsea, between the two species is that a man is capable of deciding he no longer craves the bitch," Granton said, smiling angrily.

Chelsea realized her joke had backfired and suddenly felt as if she'd wronged him, "Granton, I didn't mean . . ."

"We should be there shortly, princess," he said abruptly.

Chelsea put her head down and looked at the floor, not in defeat, but because she simply didn't want to spar any more. "Very well."

In actuality, they were half an hour away from their destination. During that time, not a word was spoken between the two. When they did finally encounter the scrub of desert Granton had been looking for, after pulling onto another dirt road so much like the multitude of others they had passed on the way, the sun had set and Granton had already turned on the truck's headlights.

"This is it," Granton said, breaking the silence.

"What is Wagner's position?"

"I don't know. He's gone black, as instructed. But he should be in a position to support us if we need it."

"How much can we trust these men?"

"Not at all, Chelsea. That's why I wanted you to stay home and why I felt it necessary to position sniper support days before the op."

"Let's not start . . ."

"Yes," he said, nodding.

They both recognized that the awkward air from their earlier conversation had not yet dissipated sufficiently.

"Let's just get this over with," Chelsea said.

Chelsea retrieved her pistol from a compartment underneath the seat, where she had stashed it before they crossed the Texas/Mexico border hours earlier, and stuck it in her waist underneath her shirt. Granton pulled his pistol from underneath his seat as well, reached underneath his shirt and placed it in a back holster that fit into the small of his back.

At that moment, headlights originating from two vehicles appeared several hundred feet southeast of their position; two dune buggies that were already moving fast towards the truck where Chelsea and Granton sat had turned on their lights as they drove. The sand and dust they spat up behind them had not been visible in the darkness but was now very clear. The tension inside the truck increased immediately. Chelsea and Granton looked at one another, then opened their doors and stepped out, an intermittent "ding" sounding for a few moments, as Granton had not turned off the truck's lights. They closed the doors and stepped forward.

It took a minute for the buggies to reach them and pull over to where Chelsea and Granton were standing in front of the truck, lit from behind by the headlights. Two Mexicans pulled themselves out of the desert vehicles and walked up to their clients. The first man to near Granton and Chelsea was tall. He had a well-kept beard and wore glasses. His dress was suitable desert wear — boots and tan fatigues. The second man was tall as well and wore similar clothing. His face was closely shaved and as he walked, put on a pair of large, ancient sunglasses that seemed too big for his face. He looked at Granton first, then looked in Chelsea's direction and turned up the corner of his mouth in a way that seemed to indicate disapproval. Chelsea looked up at him for a moment, keeping her face expressionless, then lowered her eyes and looked away.

The man with the beard spoke first, reaching out his hand to Granton.

"Señor. It's been a long time, compadre," he said.

Granton nodded his head. "How are you Abejundio? Who is your friend?"

"Who is yours?" Abejundio asked, smiling and gesturing towards Chelsea.

Granton chuckled. "Let's just get on with it. Where's the material?"

"It's here. Show me the money first. Perhaps your lovely assistant would like to present a suitcase full of cash." Both

Abejundio and his friend found this surprisingly funny and slapped each other on the arms repeatedly. When they realized neither Granton nor Chelsea was as entertained, Abejundio shrugged and reached out his hand, palm up.

Granton reached into his back pocket slowly and pulled out a Blackberry then placed it in Abejundio's hand. Abejundio looked at the screen:

Digital Zealand, Net Transfer . . .
Designation- Account Cypher wire to
Designation- Account Beekeeper
Bank wire pre-authorized amount? _
Please input password: _

"Of course the password changes every time a currency transfer is authorized. I don't even have the password for *this* transaction yet. I won't check my email and get it until I see the merch."

"Yes, yes. Must we do this every time?"

Granton wrinkled his brow. "Somehow I feel we must."

Abejundio smiled and nodded, appreciating Granton's point of view.

"Ok," he said with some sense of satisfaction. "You know I really ought to charge you more. It's a long drive up here from Mexico City. Maybe next time you meet us in the port at La Paz."

"I don't like going too deep in country. Mexico is . . . complex."

At this Abejundio laughed out loud. "Complex. The English. So sophisticated. So adept at leveling insults that don't sound like insults. Why not just call us backwards, thuggish?"

"I don't think of you as a thug, Abejundio," Granton said, slowly putting a smile on his face as well. "Can we just be done with this? I would like that. I intended no insult, my friend."

Abejundio looked at his associate and nodded his head, satisfied. "Yes, you're right. No worries." He turned to his left and waved a hand in the air. A quarter of a mile away, the sound of an engine cranking broke the silence. After a few seconds, the engine turned over, the vehicle was put in gear and headlights were turned on. A large truck surged toward them, illuminating the floor of the desert and sending a number of small creatures scurrying. Granton and Chelsea looked at each other, both a bit surprised by how close the truck had been positioned, yet neither of them had detected it.

The four waited for the vehicle to near them. When it did come to a stop fifteen feet away, Abejundio motioned for them to follow him to the rear of the truck. The driver, a short, older Mexican, opened the driver's door and stepped down to join them. Abejundio undid the latch holding the door closed and pushed it up in one motion. Granton presumed Chelsea was pleased with what she saw, when he heard a very faint "Hmh," accompanied by the slightest hint of a smile on her face.

Inside the storage area of the 24 foot truck, lit by an interior light that turned on when the door had been opened, was a large collection of state of the art assault equipment, ordnance and weaponry, all of which had been packaged in clear plastic on a pallet.

"Ok," Abejundio began, pulling down a clipboard that hung from a nail embedded into the wall. Using the clipboard as reference, he pointed to the appropriate items as he spoke. "As requested, we have the specified numbers of all the following items. Accuracy International AW 50 fifty cal. sniper rifles. The M4 .308 SOPMOD w/ QD Sound Suppressor, AN/PEQ-2 IR Illuminator, rail interface system, and Leopold Mark 4 CQ/T scope. Ok, we have your specified NVG's the AN/PVS 7 Bravos. Ok, thirty sidearms. I have to apologize, we couldn't get the Smith and Wesson's you requested, but we were successful acquiring the Heckler and Koch's, specifically the USP .45 ACP. Because of the failure here we threw in a few extras. Surefire flashlights attachable to the RIS w/blackout caps. We did acquire the throat mics you requested and enough body armor for 20 men." He took a breath, then continued. "Projectile ordnance: The RPG's here are brand new and American made, you'll notice a few updates that make them a little more user friendly. SMAW's over there in the back. And that's it. What do you think?"

"Nice," Granton said, attempting to not sound too impressed

"Oh, and the truck is yours to take as well. Y'all have a nice day." With this, he busted up laughing again as did his companion who was now standing beside Chelsea and Granton.

"Thank you, Abejundio. Well done," Granton said, reaching his hand up and into the truck to shake.

Abejundio moved forward to shake as well but was interrupted. Small dust clouds, accompanied by a phhttt, phhttt, phhttt sound erupted from the ground in front of the three standing outside the truck. Everyone knew what was happening immediately. They were being shot at. They also knew there was no point in running. Three bullets fired in succession in such a way, placed mere inches from one another? They were being warned, so the events that came next did not surprise them.

More headlights came to life, this time from three automobiles that were moving toward them. Two more floodlights, from a stationary position high up in the hills that rose above them, flared up as well. Their position was enveloped by light so bright it seemed to push down upon them and made them wince.

"Hijo de puta. This is not my doing, Señor," Abejundio said, still up in the truck.

Granton looked up at him and scanned his face, then turned back toward the vehicles now nearly upon them.

A man in one of the vehicles moving towards them held a bullhorn out his window and called out to them, his voice amplified. "Do not move from where you stand!"

"No se mueva!" blared another bullhorn, another vehicle.

"Oh no," said the short man who had been driving the truck.

"Federales," said Abejundio.

"That sniper's only going to get one of us if we separate and regroup," Chelsea said to Granton.

"Yes, but which one of us does he have his sights on? It's probably either you or myself. They planned this well. Let's be patient. Our moment will come."

The cars pulled up to the group and two men from each of the three vehicles jumped out, their guns up. As the first two men got out of the first car, one black and the other white, Chelsea's eyes widened.

"Granton, I know him."

"What? How?"

"He's one of the Rougean guard. He's here for me."

"Hmh," Granton muttered. "Then I think we'll have to give you to him."

Suddenly Granton jumped behind Chelsea, obscuring himself behind her, and put his pistol to her head.

"Hey? What are you doing?" Abejundio said as he slowly began climbing down out of the truck.

"No Granton!" It was the white man who had stepped out of the vehicle and was now nearing them. "Don't even think about it!" The man's accent was English, like Granton's. He and the black man wore khakis and t-shirts underneath bulletproof vests fitted for radios and tactical equipment. The other men had stepped out of their cars, guns up as well, and wore similar clothing and gear. Two of those men came from the back seat of the Englishman's car and were white. The two that exited the other vehicle were brown skinned.

Chelsea's face wore a dull, pained expression.

"What are you doing?" she asked quietly.

"I'm sorry, princess."

"Granton, no. Not like this," she pleaded.

"Stop what you're doing, Granton!" called out the black man that stood beside the Englishman. He spoke with an African accent.

All six of the men were now standing shoulder to shoulder, their weapons still pointed at the three men and Chelsea standing behind the truck. The lights from the spotlights above, combined with the competing headlights from all the vehicles, filled up the space between the two sides in an eerie white divide.

"Granton, you're going to get yourself and Chelsea and all of your friends killed," said the white man. "I hope you're not still hoping your sniper is going to pick us apart. We caught him days ago."

Granton lowered his eyes for a moment, but said nothing.

"Okay, my name is Colin Williams. MI-5. These two men are with me," he said, gesturing towards the men to his left. He then gestured in the opposite direction. "These two men are with the AFI, the Mexican security agency. We have two snipers up in those hills. If there's a firefight, it'll be eight versus four. And now that you have the princess hostage it'll be eight versus three. You're no fool."

"That's right, I'm not. Who is he?" gesturing towards the black man.

"I am Nelson Pangani. I am with the Quandry New Republic's Rougean guard. I am here to take the Princess back to stand trial for her crimes."

"No," Granton said.

Williams and Pangani looked at each other, unsure of what to do.

"Actually, well yes, I suppose you can take her," Granton said, correcting himself, shaking his head slightly.

Williams and Pangani looked at each other again, this time clearly confused.

"But I go free."

The two agents understood his motives completely this time.

"And what if we say no, Granton? What makes you think you can get out of here without just being caught later? Wouldn't it just be smarter to give up now, rather than put yourself and the princess in danger of being killed? As I said, I know you're no fool."

Granton leaned in close to the princess's ear and spoke, but did so loudly enough for the agents to hear.

"Take my watch off my wrist."

"What?" Chelsea asked.

"Do it."

Chelsea, confused, reached up and undid the latch to the watch on Granton's left wrist, then pulled it over his hand. Because no overtly aggressive movements were being made, the agents simply watched, attempting to decipher the motive behind such an act.

"Williams, what's happening down there?"

The voice emanated from a radio on Williams' waist. Still watching Granton and Chelsea, weapon still up and pointing at them and the two Mexicans, Williams freed one hand to raise the mic to his mouth slowly to reply, "Standby."

"Now put it on," Granton said to Chelsea.

"Granton?" Chelsea asked, helpless.

"Do as I say, princess."

Chelsea reluctantly put the watch on her wrist as instructed.

Why are we standing here like this?" said Pangani loudly. "We have them."

Williams looked at him disapprovingly, which shut him up for the moment. But he was curious as to what exactly Granton was up to as well.

"What *are* you doing, Granton? We can stand here all night. But neither of us really wants that."

"You're right. We should end this now."

Granton began to slowly reach into his left pocket, which sent the agents into alert. Their posture changed immediately and from each agent a sudden, barely audible exhale accompanied the increase in tension.

"Stop! Stop! We will fire!"

"Watch my hands gentlemen," Granton said calmly.

Still, very slowly, Granton pulled out from his pocket a small black box.

"Now, this is how things will progress, gentlemen. You want the princess more than you want me, and you want her alive. This much I've discovered already from your behavior. If this was not the case, we would be dead already, courtesy of your snipers."

"I'm here for you as well, Granton," Williams said.

"Maybe, but you've been told your priority is the princess, then me perhaps. So this is what we will do. Are you gentlemen familiar with the Reicher Tech Mine Timekeeper?"

"Oh," remarked one of the other agents beside Williams who had not previously spoken.

It was a quiet, unintentional utterance. Granton noticed how the man's eyes had closed slightly when he spoke and couldn't help but smile at his reaction. He'd virtually admitted defeat.

"I'll save you the trouble of explaining to your associates. There is a very large explosive device imbedded into the watch she's just put on."

Without warning, Granton shoved Chelsea hard in the back, pushing her towards the agents, ratcheting up their tension even more. Simultaneously, each agent repositioned his aim, some stepping forward nervously, others sideways. Their unease was obvious, present in their movements as well as in their demeanor. They knew Granton was toying with them, becoming flagrant about it and there was nothing they could do to stop him. All of a sudden *he* was in control. In a matter of moments he'd turned the tables on them.

Upon steadying herself, now standing halfway between the two groups, Chelsea looked down at the watch on her wrist.

"I wouldn't try to take it off Princess. Once you put it back on it was reactivated. If you try to take it off without inputting the correct code . . . Boom!" Granton said, throwing up his hands for effect and smiling yet again. He knew he had them and was beginning to enjoy himself. "I should clarify something actually. The explosive device inside the tech mine is quite small. The area the blast covers is quite large however. And I have in my hands a transmitter that will remotely activate the device as well as disarm it." He held up the small black box.

"Back," Williams ordered.

The agents moved yet again, taking a few steps backwards and putting more space between them and Chelsea.

"May I go now?"

Pangani spoke up. "How do we know you won't just destroy her when you get far enough away?"

"My feelings for Chelsea are no secret. I won't allow myself to be captured for her but I don't want to see her dead. Once I'm sure you can't catch me any longer, I'll call you with the code."

"Granton, please don't do this," Chelsea said, emotionless.

Granton ignored her. "Abejundio, throw them your cell phone."

"Granton, I have some numbers in there . . ."

Granton turned and gave him a look.

Abejundio relented, began to pull his phone out of his pocket, and then looked at his associate, the tall Mexican wearing glasses. He removed an empty hand from his pocket, slapped his associate on the arm and gestured with his head towards the agents. His associate sighed, pulled *his* cell phone from his jacket and threw it towards the agents.

"If I think you have someone tailing us, or you're surveilling us in any way, I will detonate the device, am I clear?"

A few moments passed before Williams spoke again. He knew he had no choice and he knew Granton was fully aware of it.

"Go," Williams said, turning his head away.

Abejundio and his tall friend walked towards their buggies. The other Mexican moved towards the cab of the truck and Granton pulled down the gate then walked towards the passenger door. As he walked, he turned and looked at the group standing helplessly. Then he looked at Chelsea.

"Good luck, Chelsea. It seems you were right not to trust me. "

"I will kill you for this, Granton."

Motioning towards the African, he said, "Something tells me that when he gets you back to your country, they're not going to let you live long enough to do anything, my dear. Goodbye."

He climbed up into the truck and shut the door behind him. The truck's engine came to life and then pulled away.

Chelsea turned to the group of agents, expecting them to secure her. She let out an indiscreet sound of disgust when she realized they were not going to get anywhere near her until the phone call from Granton came. So she just sat down in the dust. She knew it would be at least an hour before the phone rang.

CHAPTER 18

John Wilkes followed his friend Lieutenant James Conaghan into his office and shut the door behind him. He took the chair in front of the lieutenant's desk and his friend sat on top of the desk, at the corner, in his most casual pose. Wilkes knew what was coming. Jim liked to go on about how much he detested his life and his career and his marriage whenever they were together. He thought his own life, just couldn't measure up against the life of dark secrecy he imagined for his usually very scarce friend that worked for the government. Jim was jealous and would say so. Every time they saw each other it was the same thing over and over. But Wilkes knew his friend needed to vent and he didn't mind listening since they saw each other so infrequently.

"You got the fun stuff and I got the family," he would say. "When Connie told me she was pregnant, I didn't have any choice, you know?"

"I know. And you did the right thing, of course."

"Yeah. She hated me even going to the academy. There's no way I could have pulled off getting into one of the schools."

"I know that, Jim. I've always said you did the right thing. How is she by the way?"

"Getting fat."

Wilkes smiled. "Sometimes I wish I'd have settled down and started a family."

"Bullshit! Don't kid a kidder, dude. You were never the settle down type and would have hated it if you tried. It's the hardest thing I've ever done, that's for sure. I mean look at me. I'm a Captain with a lieutenant's rank, or should I say a lieutenant with a Captain's duties? Anyway, I ride a desk my whole shift, every shift. I'm beyond all the dangerous stuff. Yet she's always worried about me getting shot or something. Still. And I keep telling her that even when I did hoof it for a living, we'd hardly ever actually fire our weapons, or for that matter get shot at."

"Well, she's worried about you . . . ."

"Yeah, but she doesn't need to be. And come off it. Like you're not totally laughing at me on the inside."

Wilkes smiled. One of the things he'd always liked about Conaghan, and one of the things that made him such a good policeman, was his insight. But of course he couldn't tell him he was correct.

"I'm not laughing at you."

"Bull . . . shit!" He waved a finger at him radically. This time they both laughed.

"Anyway, I'm beyond that. I'd be laughing at me if I were you. But back to my original point. It's worse now, with Connie, than when we were in the Corps. She told me last night that whenever I'm not home, every time the phone rings she jumps. She thinks it's just a matter of time before some thug leaves her with a minuscule insurance settlement and a cop's pension."

"So what are you going to do?" asked Wilkes.

Conaghan pretended to mull it over in a way that made Wilkes smile again. He knew his friend well. Upon learning that Wilkes was in town and would be dropping by, he'd probably spent the past few days projecting which topics might arise. And, as was his way, would have therefore prepared a loose script for himself to follow. His insistence to remain on the subject until he'd played it out as planned was obvious. Jim Conaghan. Neurosis, coupled with a complete lack of talent for acting, could make him quite comical. His attempt to simulate a person in deep thought almost made Wilkes double over in laughter. His head was craned as far back as it could go, as if the back of it were sitting on his shoulders. His eyes stared straight up at the ceiling. Finally, he lowered his head to signal he'd completed his analysis, turned and looked at his friend quite seriously.

"Honestly, I think she needs professional help," he said, setting himself up. He reached around and into a drawer in his desk and pulled out a tazer. "Maybe a little personalized shock therapy."

Wilkes laughed out loud and Conaghan was pleased.

"Sounds like you're the one that needs professional help. See, that's exactly why I never married when we were in the military. Too much of a burden, on them and me."

"And John, you have always been one to think with your heart first," he said with unmistakable sarcasm.

Wilkes shrugged. "That, my friend, is what has kept me alive all these years."

Conaghan grunted. "How goes the spy business, anyway?"

"If I told you I'd have to kill you."

"Of course, never expected that cliché."

"That, my friend, at least in my case, is a cliché conforme. It's actually true."

"Oh."

"What about you?"

"Gang war. Besides that it's been pretty slow."

"Gang war?"

"Uh-huh. It's one of the reasons I called earlier and told you to come by. I knew you'd want to see this ASAP. C'mon."

Wilkes stood and followed his friend through the squad room and into an interrogation room. An A.V. stand in a corner of the room held a television on one rung and a VCR below it. A number of tapes were on top of the VCR. Conaghan took one of the tapes and inserted it into the VCR. Then he stepped back and sat on the edge of the table near Wilkes.

"Watch this. You are gonna love this."

The picture came alive and presented a view of the inside of a liquor store from the perspective of a surveillance camera. There was no sound. The angle showed the entire store from behind and just to the side of the register desk. Though it is dark, movement is observed on the left side of the picture. An individual hides underneath a rack as three armed men search the store.

"What is this?"

"Apparently this entire situation is centered on that one kid. Somebody wanted him so bad they sent five guys after him. Keep watching. Two of 'em got taken out in the alleyway."

Then the tape showed the two bangers being tricked into shooting each other. Conaghan looked at his friend, smiling, feeling voyeuristic. Wilkes was entranced.

"That's very good," said Wilkes.

"Yeah, he got lucky."

Wilkes said nothing. They watched as a man ran down the front aisle of the store, firing, trying to catch another in his line of fire. Then they see that man run from his pursuer and jump through the refrigerator racks into the back area to escape him. Conaghan jumped up and ejected the tape.

"My God, is that it?"

"No, no, look at this." Conaghan smiled. "I told you, man. Hold on."

He put a second tape in and pushed play. Another image came to life. This time the perspective was that of a camera inside the refrigerator area. Wilkes watched as Nicholas jumps over the racks and levels Smalls, then the fight between them.

"Ok, hold on," Conaghan said. He stood and pushed the fast forward button and held it a few seconds, then allowed it to play at normal speed again. From behind, they watch Smalls wake and exit the refrigerator. Visible through what were the glass refrigerator doors, they see him nearly surprise Nicholas. His back is thrown against the refrigerant racks from the shot Nicholas fires and he falls dead to the ground. Conaghan stood again and stopped the recorder.

"Who is he?" Wilkes asked.

"The kid?"

"Of course the kid," Wilkes thought. "Yeah," was all he said, hurriedly.

"Uh, his name is . . . uh, it's weird . . . uh . . . Gand, Gam, Gambit. Nicholas Gambit."

"Where is he?"

"He's still here. We gotta let him go though. As you can see, it was all self defense. He's real lucky that shop's cameras were still working; the alarm system had been out of commission for months."

"I want to talk to him."

"Just so long as you realize he's been cleared. I can't keep him here and I can't be involved in whatever takes place next."

"I know. I just want to talk to him before you send him home. Please. And thanks for calling me in. Owe you a solid."

Conaghan nodded. "Ok." He reached over to a phone and dialed a number. "Josh, yeah, before you let the Gambit kid go, uh, bring him up here first will ya? Thanks." He looked at Wilkes. "He'll be on his way soon."

Wilkes didn't even look at his friend. His mind was working furiously.

"Thank you. I need to talk to him alone."

Conaghan left the room, sure he didn't want to be a part of whatever was about to happen.

CHAPTER 19

I sat inside a dark office that apparently wasn't used for anything except a waiting room in special cases; there was a couch, a desk with a phone on it and a chair. There was a plant that looked neglected and dying and no pictures on the wall.

When they first brought me in, a paramedic had looked at my arm and said, "Oh, it went clean through, dude. You're lucky. And it's an upper layer too. Barely more than a flesh wound. Just go easy on it for a while, you'll be alright." He'd then put what I guessed was antibiotic cream on it and then covered it with gauze and wrapped it. That and my shoulder, which had been bruised but not dislocated as I'd thought, did hurt pretty good but it was all bearable. So after an hour-long session with a detective who didn't believe a word I said—hell, I almost didn't believe it—they threw me into a holding cell.

It was my first time in jail. The other men didn't look as threatening as I had always imagined; no one spoke to me. They took seats where they could find them and sat sullenly, awaiting their fates quietly. Still, I was relieved when they finally pulled me out of the cell twenty minutes earlier, then led me to this room and told me to wait inside until another detective came to speak to me further.

There was a phone on the desk. I dialed 9 to get an outline, then tried to call my mother since I hadn't been offered a phone call while I was in the holding cell. I called my house twice but the voice mail picked up both times. That meant she was out looking for me. I called back a third time, left a message and told her where I was and that I was ok.

I was so tired, and equally wired and worried at the same time. All those feelings seemed to cancel each other out and kept me from accomplishing any kind of mental progress. I wanted to sleep but couldn't; every time I worried about my mother or how Kato was doing I got impatient and sad. It was this kind of ping-pong, back and forth manner of thinking that ultimately made me more . . . tired. Dead in the water.

I could barely muster the energy to be proud of myself and how I dealt with Smalls. Except for some arm flesh, I'd survived it all and could start over again and live a normal life. It had only been days but it seemed as if everything that happened had occurred over the course of years. My old life seemed that far away.

I chuckled at myself again. I would forevermore look at my boring life of going to school and planning for the future as pure bliss. "Well," I thought, "I did make it through and learned my lesson. Now appreciate how good things really are."

Still, I had some as-yet unfinished business. I wanted to somehow repay Kato immediately, but knew that I might have to be patient for that chance to arise. That would take time. Maybe a lifetime.

My thoughts were interrupted when the door to the office opened. An officer stuck his head in. "You're free to go. C'mon."

I stood and walked out, then followed him down a narrow hallway that looked more like one you'd find in a business office. He turned at a stairwell and began to climb and I followed. No other police personnel were visible anywhere.

"So I can go home?" I asked.

"Yep. But first, there's someone upstairs who wants to see you."

"Ok. Hey, uh, sir, do you know what happened to the guy they picked me up with? He was hurt pretty bad. They took him to the hospital."

He turned his head to speak. When I saw his face, his expression answered my question.

"Oh, yeah, umh, I don't think he made it, kid. As a matter of fact . . . I know he didn't. Sorry. C'mon."

When he'd looked at me in that way, I'd stopped climbing the stairs. It's not that I was surprised that Kato had died. He'd been so close to death when the paramedics took him away from me, I think it would have been more surprising to have learned that he made it. What did surprise me was how I felt. I'd thought that no new development could leave me more empty. I'd been wrong.

"C'mon, son."

I nodded my head and willed myself up the stairs.

At the top of the stairwell, we came to a door that led to the station squad room. We walked in and encountered an obstacle course. We swathed our way around scores of desks. If they were organized in some fashion it was not discernible. Attempting to take as close to a direct route as possible amid the chaos, we cut through the very middle of the room. The officer had done this many times, I realized. I was surprised at how few personnel occupied the room. These few looked up at me as I passed, then returned their attention to their documents and phone calls. I followed the officer all the way across the room, ending up in front of what looked like an interrogation room. Above the threshold was a clock and I finally realized why there were so few people in the building. It was twenty-five minutes after three in the morning. My wearied mind tried to account for the hours that had passed. It didn't seem possible that it was so late.

"Hi Mr. Gambit, come in."

A man inside the room was motioning for me to sit. The officer had disappeared. I walked in. He was taller than me. I guessed at 6"2'. He didn't have the look of a cop. His look was . . . indistinguishable. I didn't know what to make of him, what position he held. His face, however, hid nothing. As a matter of fact, it broadcast a great deal about him. He was very confident, very used to being in command. Intelligence was immediately apparent. His brown hair was slightly longer than the way most men his age wore it. I guessed at 46, maybe a little older. I could see from his build that he kept in shape. He had no beer belly and he wore black jeans and a light blue t-shirt that advertised real definition. This guy was no cop. I began to think he looked more like some business exec to me.

"Sit down, please. Thank you for coming." He moved around me and closed the door as I sat, then walked back and stood before me.

"They told me I was free to go," I said.

"Well. I wanted to speak to you."

"About what?"

"Well, your future."

I think I grunted. That statement immediately demonstrated this man was someone I did not want to deal with. The only future I cared about at the moment was one where I lay fast asleep in my bed. Anything besides that could wait. And after the day I'd had, cordiality too, could wait.

"The last person that said that to me is dead now," I said.

"I'll be okay," he said softly.

I looked him square in the eye. "Take your time. We just met."

He laughed. "You must be too good to be true. I saw your tape."

"My tape?"

He pointed to the tapes on top of the VCR. I guessed those were the surveillance tapes the officer who'd pulled me out of the holding cell had mentioned. His exact words were, "Those tapes saved your ass, kid."

"Oh," was all I said.

"I was . . . awestruck, is the word I think."

"Glad you enjoyed it." By this point, my mind was moving a little more quickly and I came to a conclusion about how I felt about this man. I was sick of him already and becoming more impatient by the minute. "You're a recruiter aren't you?"

"What?"

"A recruiter for the army or the Marines or something."

"That's . . . why do you say that?"

"There's been a lot of them after me lately, talking the way you are right now. Young, black, college educated."

"Athletic. Yes, those things can be invaluable."

"I'm not interested." I started to get up.

"Wait. I'm not . . . what you think. Just keep an open mind about this. Please. You have a ride home?"

"No, I called home but my mom must be out of the house. She's probably out looking for me."

"I'll get you a ride."

"No, that's ok. I'll walk. It's not that far. Thanks." I got up, opened the door, and walked out. The man called out behind me.

"I'll be in touch."

"Whatever," I retorted. I hadn't even bothered to get his name.

CHAPTER 20

"Whew," Wilkes said, as he watched the young man walk away. He was perfect. He watched him cross the very large squad room. Finally, the young man had to stop to ask someone which door of the many would allow him to leave the building. An officer stuck his arm up and pointed without looking at him. He turned, walked to an exit, and disappeared from sight.

Wilkes pulled a cell phone from his pocket and dialed a number. The call was answered on the first ring. "Thirteen."

"Yeah, let me speak to Taylor."

"Very good, sir."

There were a few clicks as he was transferred, then another voice answered.

"Yes."

"Hey, listen, I want everything you can get me on a kid named Nicholas Gambit, a black kid, the Falstaff area of Jackson County, KCMO."

"Gambit . . . Falstaff, Kansas City, MO, ok. If this guy's domestic, CID might pull up a few matches. Any priors to look for?"

"I doubt it, but I'll call you back if there are and I'll let you know for sure. But I want everything. It's for a potential."

"Oh, ok."

"Send it to my phone. I left my pad at home."

"Very good. I'll have it for you in five."

"Good." Wilkes put the phone back in his pocket. He went to the doorway and searched for Conaghan. When he found him he called him over.

"Hey, I'm gonna need to see your file on Gambit. Now, please."

"Where'd he go?"

"He left already."

Conaghan nodded his head, deliberating on whether to tell Wilkes about something. "So you're pretty interested in him, huh?"

"Oh, very much so."

"Well, in that case I think you might want to know about a report that just came in."

CHAPTER 21

What if there were more coming? It hit me as I walked home from the station. Earlier, Kato had mentioned some guy named Ray Ray being involved with Smalls. I had forgotten all about it. Could this guy still be after me even though Smalls was dead? It couldn't be. It couldn't be. I just couldn't take anymore. Any resolve to fight back had been wrung out of me after the night I'd had. God, please let it just end. Kato was dead. I didn't have anyone else to help me anymore. And I'd killed. The fact that I'd killed for the first time hadn't escaped me either. This had been the night to end all others for me. And I couldn't do it again.

I looked up at the stars and tried to shake myself of the dread and guilt that accompanied the two realizations. I looked at the stars and shook my head again, this time in an attempt to wake myself. So tired all the way through. Like I'd run a marathon. I felt drunk and my whole arm was hurting now. And it was getting worse. My eyelids felt heavy and it felt good to shut them. I wanted to just lie down and go to sleep on the sidewalk and keep them shut forever. "I should have taken the ride," I thought. "I'd be home in bed already. Momma would be angry but she'd see how tired I am and would put me to bed like she used to when I was little and let the explanation wait until morning."

I looked to my left and recognized Wardell's house. We were good friends in high school but the most we saw of each other these days was when I drove by his house or he drove by mine. Wardell's house. That meant I was only another half mile or so from home. A few more turns and I'd be home. So I put one leg in front of the other and willed myself to keep moving.

Something out of the corner of my eye. It took too long for my eyes to focus. Lights. In the trees, above the roofs were lights, white lights. And a generator, the sound of a generator. No, they weren't in the trees, the lights were on the ground but illuminated into the trees. No big deal. It was too far to be my house. It had to be. I walked a little more. No need to run. There was no point. It couldn't be my house. I couldn't let it be. I was breathing heavier and my eyelids no longer weighed so much and my eyes began to water. It mustn't be my house. I had seen those types of lights before and assured myself that I would never see them at my house. But as I got closer my legs began moving just a little faster, not running yet just walking a little faster so that I could see she was safe and our home was untouched by what must have happened to one of our neighbors — I saw that it could be my house. No, it might be close, but it couldn't be. I wanted to run but didn't. I refused to run. There was no point. I knew that I would turn that last corner onto my block and see for myself that it was a neighbor's and not mine. Then I could run home and see her. But I started to cry anyway, even though I knew it couldn't be my house and when I did finally turn the corner I . . . lost . . . myself.

Nonononono it can't be no. Now I was running, the lead weights in my legs and eyes now resettled in my chest. Figures in coats and uniforms came into view and I didn't care about them. I had to get inside. Someone yelled and still I didn't care. I accelerated to full speed, made my way to the front door and nearly collided with someone coming out of the doorway.

"Whoa, whoa . . . whoa," and then " . . . oh," softly, was all I heard. Then I saw her.

"I'm sorry, son."

I couldn't move. She lay there with red all around her head. Her legs twisted under her like she'd fallen from the top of a building. And the ugliest thing I had ever seen on her forehead. Like something had busted through her at that spot. I moved to her slowly, as if the ground might fall out from underneath me. I reached her, dropped to my knees and was decimated. I reached down to touch her but couldn't. I couldn't imagine what she would feel like cold. What little energy I had left flowed out. All the pent up frustration, all my feelings, all my will, it just all went away and finally there I knelt, hunched over my dead mother, trembling. I wanted to be angry but didn't have it in me. There was nothing. Nothing left.

I guess I stood and backed away eventually, because two men moved to lay a cloth over her body. I reached out my hand to stop them, then pulled it back and allowed them to finish. A hand was placed on my shoulder. I looked back to find two detectives standing behind me.

"I'm real sorry, son. Can we talk to you for just a moment, please?"

I turned and followed them outside. They stopped on the walkway just in front of the steps to the doorway. I sat on the small brick wall that was built on each side of those steps and stared blankly ahead of them.

"Do you think you can answer a few questions for us, son? You up to it?"

A limo pulled up on the street just outside the police barricade. A window at the rear rolled down and a man looked in the direction of me and the house. It was all a dream. I closed my eyes and lowered my head. I think the minutes registered as seconds.

"Guess not. We'll come back."

I didn't care what happened to them. I didn't want to talk to anyone.

"Nicholas."

I raised my head and stared directly into Wilkes' eyes.

"I can help you, Nicholas." He reached his hand out to me. "Come with me."

I took it and followed him to the car. I climbed into the back seat and looked out the window at what was once my home, my favorite place of retreat, now made ghoulish and dark by what had taken place there. The noise made by the generator overpowered all other sounds, administering a slow motion kind of silence. The tungsten lights that held jurisdiction over a domain that included my house and yard created an incongruous, perverse impression of day where there should only have been night. Everything outside that domain seemed normal and real, as it should be, which exacerbated the accursedness of it all. The spectacle chilled me through to the bone. I could see nothing left of what I had known as my home.

Two men exited the house, holding a stretcher that carried my mother's body. I felt the limo moving and we began to drive away. I watched them carry her down the first couple of steps coming out of the door. The first man reached the steps midway down the walkway and I thought it wrong for him to be moving towards them so quickly. He didn't see them. He tripped and the stretcher was lost. The body bag, with my mother in it, rolled and crashed to the ground sickeningly. I closed my eyes and felt nothing as we pulled away.

"I'm going to help you, Nicholas."

CHAPTER 22

"Where are we going?" Chelsea asked. She found herself, yet again, in the back seat of a moving vehicle that was leading her to a fate she had not chosen. But this time, on each side of her, sat men holding weapons pointed in her direction.

Granton called nearly two hours after he left her with the agents. Just as they were beginning to think they would have to come up with a contingency plan for removing the tech mine watch, the cell phone rang. Williams told her to move away, then walked over and picked up the phone from the ground, where he'd put it after Granton left — in case there was a bomb inside it as well. He took a notepad from his back pocket and listened as Granton gave him the code, as he'd promised. The conversation was over in seconds. When Williams hung up the phone, he walked back to the other agents, turned and looked at Chelsea.

"Do you think you can trust Granton not to blow your head off?" he asked, the English accent not so different than Granton's own.

"Clearly, I caaann't." Chelsea retorted, mimicking his accent contemptuously. The other men were surprised by this and a short burst of laughter ensued. Williams even found himself smiling. The levity subsided quickly.

"Here's the code, Miss Matawae. Six digits. 436564. That's all he gave me."

Chelsea input the code gingerly, breathed in apprehensively, then removed the watch from her wrist and threw it away. The men immediately gathered her up, handcuffed her, threw her into the car and sped off.

Chelsea had not been given a response the first time she asked the question so she asked again, this time more urgently.

"Where are we going!"

"We're going straight to the Monterrey airport, Miss Matawae," answered Williams, who was driving.

"And then what?"

The African turned in the passenger seat and spoke. "Then I take you back to the Republic where you will be tried and executed."

"No," Williams interjected. "As I've told you already, this is a British operation. At this juncture, you are only aiding us in our efforts, Mr. Pangani. Therefore, she will initially be brought before criminal court to stand trial for the murders of the *British* citizens she destroyed. Ultimately, she will be tried by the office of the Home Secretary and the decision to deport will be made. Then and only then will you be allowed to take her back to your country and do with her as you please."

Pangani turned back around in his seat and faced forward, "Either way she will return to my country and be tried for supporting an unjust administration."

"Pangani," Chelsea said. "Do you think I don't know what you are? You betrayed your country and your king. You took part in its destruction when you vowed to defend it to your death. Am I to simply ignore that fact simply because you *do*? Do not lie to these men and try to make them believe you are on some virtuous quest, that you are uncorrupted. You and *your* regime fear me and that is why you are doing what you are. You are nothing to me. You are less than dirt. Less than shit! I will kill you myself. Sooner than you think."

Pangani didn't turn around, but Chelsea could see that his posture was changing, his head and shoulders inclining forward slowly. Without actually seeing his eyes she could tell they were closed. His fury was mounting. This continued for several seconds and Chelsea prepared herself; her instincts told her the man might do something rash, something reckless and violent. But then something changed. The way he moved was suddenly different. Even from behind him she could see that his behavior was no longer fueled by anger. Still, Chelsea was surprised when she heard laughter. It was diametric to what she was expecting.

He coughed out a loud, jolly sort of cackling that made her stomach turn.

"Princess, I see now you possess the same flaws that your father possessed — the same flaws that allowed us to overthrow him. You're both weak. You trust that others perceive morality in the same ways as you do. But no one does. Nowhere in the world, not like that; especially not in modern Africa."

Then in Swahili he said, "He should have never trusted me because I and my brothers were always plotting against him. And you. You are a remnant of a vanished era, a dinosaur just as was your father. And soon, you will join him in the same tar pit we threw his headless carcass into."

It was like a slap in the face. She was shocked. His words felt as if they were tearing at her insides, which she knew was his goal. It took everything she had not to respond. She put her head down and fought back the nearly overwhelming urge to cry her eyes out — and then to try and get to him so she could gouge out his. Of course she knew that because of the handcuffs and the two agents sitting next to her the effort would have been futile. She could not allow him the pleasure of seeing her respond in such a feeble, emotional way. Just as he waited for the right time to butcher her father, she would have to wait for the right time to do the same to him.

Chelsea turned her head, looked out the window and watched again as the landscape changed. The unrefined desert of Northern Mexico slowly morphed into a bustling, contemporary municipality. Soon the things common to any city surrounded them. Citizens walked along the sidewalks and vehicles filled the streets. Progressively, more and more large buildings appeared. It was night-time, but it was not yet late and the city was still active.

True to his word, Williams drove straight to the airport without stopping and parked at the rental car drop-off. They unloaded the trunk of the vehicle, stashing their weapons into cases labeled with government stickers that screamed legitimacy, legal authority. They did not want to be detained for too long by customs. The two agents that sat next to Chelsea in the car each grabbed one of her arms and walked beside her as the five of them entered the terminal check-in.   A man who was sitting in one of the customer lounges stood and was acknowledged by Chelsea's captors. He had been sitting with his federal badge open, placed on top of a large gun case that lay in his lap. Chelsea assumed this was to assuage any fears that he was out of place or that his sniper rifle might be a danger to the other passengers. He'd probably been ordered to display the badge by the Mexican airport police. He fell in behind them as they walked up to the ticket counter.

The three agents, along with Chelsea and Pangani, stood back and waited while Williams walked up to the ticket counter and inquired about the next flight out of the country that would enable them to ultimately reach London Heathrow.

"I need to use the bathroom," Chelsea said.

"Hold it," Pangani said, intentionally avoiding looking at her.

"That's brilliant. Shall I hold it until we reach London, then? Perhaps I should go in my seat once we're on the plane."

Pangani turned around and looked at the three agents, again without looking at her and then nodded, motioning for them to take her. Rolling their eyes, the three men yanked her in the direction of the women's bathroom. Upon reaching the entrance, one of the agents struck an authoritarian pose. Several women approached the entrance, apparently intending to foolishly walk in and use the bathroom despite his domineering. The agent merely gave them a look, raised his hand in the air and shook his head, which was enough to make them choose another location. After a few women who had already been in the bathroom exited, several minutes had passed and it seemed likely there was no one still inside, the agent looked around the corner of the entrance and inside the bathroom. He then walked in and inspected the entire bathroom, confirming there were no plausible exits or potential weapons. When he came back out, he motioned for the others to uncuff her and then signaled for her to proceed.

Chelsea entered and immediately went for a stall. She did actually need to urinate. When she was finished she exited the stall, stopped in the middle of the bathroom and surveyed the room quickly. She needed to slow them down and she knew she likely wouldn't have another opportunity to be alone. She also knew she didn't have long to come up with something.

Quickly, her attention settled on the one thing in the room she could be certain no man would ever focus on for long. She made her way up to the sink and washed her hands, then walked up to the tampon machine. Upon hearing water running, the agent stuck his head around the corner again and watched her. She'd been waiting for him to do so.

"I need twenty-two pesos."

"For what?"

She motioned towards the tampon machine.

He made a face that told his disgust, shook his head then left the entrance. He returned thirty seconds later and handed her the money.

"Thank you," she said, expressionless.

She inserted the money into the machine, retrieved an applicator and looked at him again, then walked back towards the stall. Satisfied, he turned back around and resumed his intimidating. Just before entering the stall, sure that he was no longer looking, Chelsea took a few quick steps back and grabbed the hand soap dispenser bottle from the top of the counter and took it in with her.

Minutes later Chelsea exited the bathroom and stood between the agents. She raised her arms in expectation of what was to come next. As expected, they patted her down, searching for contraband. When they found none, they put the handcuffs back on her and motioned for her to proceed back to the ticket counter where Williams was finishing up. Seconds after they began walking, Chelsea felt a tug on her arm and looked at the agent that had been standing in the doorway to the bathroom. She looked at him blankly.

"Hold her here a minute. I'll be back," he said, turning to walk back to the bathroom.

At this Chelsea put on the best expression of disappointment that she could muster. The other two agents grunted. Whatever she had tried, her expression testified to her failure, they thought. She hoped they were wrong.

A minute passed and Chelsea began to worry her plan had failed after all. "It shouldn't be taking him that long," she thought. He was doing a thorough search. Finally the agent came out, looking down and shaking his head as if he had caught a child looting the cookie jar.

"That's pretty smart, Miss Matawae," he said smiling. "I almost didn't check the bathroom, did I?" He held his hand up to show the others. "She used hand soap to write 'Help me' on the mirror."

The other agents grunted and shook their heads as well.

Chelsea looked at the paper in his hand. She allowed herself to smile on the inside. It was a paper towel with orange soap smeared all over it.

"Apparently, we're not as dumb as you think we are."

"Apparently, you are," she thought.

The four of them rejoined Williams and Pangani, just as they were finishing up at the ticket desk. Soon they were ushered into a VIP room, usually reserved for passengers with special flight privileges. Chelsea and two of the agents sat down on a sofa. She examined the room. It was not large, but there was certainly enough space to move around in and perhaps even enough space to engage the agents. But handcuffed, four against one, she knew the odds were significantly in their favor. Even if she did somehow get past them, she'd still have to deal with airport security that had no doubt been notified that a prisoner in custody was on location. The pros and cons were painting a very clear picture. She'd have to wait and see if plan A panned out. She settled in and tried not to be distracted by the big screen television, as was everyone else in the room.

Twenty minutes later, every head in the room turned when a Mexican man in a suit walked into the VIP room, flanked by six armed security guards, each with a hand on their weapon. Chelsea smiled outwardly this time, for just a millisecond. This was her cue. It was time for her to put on a show. She dug deep inside, somehow caused her eyes to well up with tears . . . and began weeping. Loud, pitiful, fluid filled sobbing filled the room. She was happy. She was sad. She was saved!

"Oh God, please help me! My God, por favor! Por favor!!! Ayudame! Ayudame!"

All five agents looked at her, incredulous. Williams and Pangani stood and the other agents then followed suit.

"What's this?" Williams asked the Mexican official, raising his voice over Chelsea's moaning still coming from the sofa.

"Sir . . ." the Mexican official began, as he motioned for two of his men to grab Chelsea and remove her from the room, "I'm the Escobedo airport federal liaison. We're going to have to separate you from your prisoner in order to clear up some things."

"What things?" Pangani.

"That woman is in the custody of the British government," said Williams. "Extradition and passport services have already been cleared by Vincent Ochoa of your foreign relations ministry. All documents were filed weeks ago. He was supposed to have called and prepped you for our arrival sometime this week."

"I'm aware of no such phone call but I will be happy to check that. However, we're going to have to validate your credentials before you leave with this prisoner. International law requires that we do so."

"International law? What the hell are you talking about?"

"This is outrageous! I need to be with that prisoner at all times!" Pangani screamed. He began walking towards the door to follow the guards that were escorting Chelsea. He stopped when the remaining security guards pulled their guns and leveled them at him. He turned and looked at Williams who was as dumbfounded as the rest of their group.

"Sir, international law requires that any foreign national that is being detained has certain rights. A claim of sexual deviancy, sodomy or molestation falls under that purview."

"My God man, have you gone mad? What in hell are you talking about?"

"She has accused you of raping her."

All five men simply stood there with their mouths wide open and said nothing for several seconds. The sniper was the first to recover. "How?"

Williams spoke next. "Of course we didn't rape her, but indeed, when could she have . . . ?"

The Mexican official pulled a ziploc bag from inside his jacket and held it up for them to see. "Your prisoner is very resourceful."

Inside was a Tampax applicator - super plus. The pull string had been used to connect it to two strips of toilet paper. On the toilet paper was a very clear message in Spanish written out in bright orange hand soap:

"Help me! These men are not federal agents. They kidnapped me. They raped me! Please tell the police. Please help me!!!"

"She pushed this whole thing up into the place where the tampons came out so it would not be visible. She knew the next person to use the machine would be forced to remove her message first. Very resourceful. And very effective. She now has what equates to a witness that will support her claims. The woman that found this is American."

"Oh no," Williams said.

"Yes, and you know how they are. Arrogant does not quite describe it. She threatened to sue all of Mexico if we don't help this poor woman. I'm not saying I don't believe you. But my hands are tied, gentlemen. Unlike some Mexican agencies, the Transportation Authority takes matters like this very seriously."

"Our plane leaves in thirty minutes."

"You're going to have to wait here until we get in touch with Mr. Ochoa or AFI or someone and they tell us it's okay to let you leave with her."

Pangani began pacing and cursed something under his breath. However, amid the mumbling, clearly distinguishable were two words, ". . . fucking bitch . . ."

Williams and the other agents shook their heads and just sat down and tried to relax. They knew what it meant to be subject to bureaucratic delays. They weren't going anywhere for a while.

Three hours passed before the Mexican official, who still had not given them his name, reappeared at the entrance to the VIP room. He immediately sent away the guards he'd left, which Williams took as promising.

"You may recollect your prisoner, gentlemen. Mr. Ochoa himself was contacted by my superiors and he verified your status as authorized foreign agents."

"Thank you," Williams said, a bit impatiently. "Now what about our flight that we missed?"

"And the bitch? Where is she? Is she secured!" yelled Pangani.

The official cocked his head at the outburst. "You'll be reimbursed for those tickets, of course. Your prisoner is down the hall in our custody. She has been compliant and calm the entire time."

"You're kidding," Williams said. "Very good. When's the next flight out? I'd like to be on it."

"I'm afraid you missed the final flight with a destination at Heathrow that has a layover of less than a day. There is a 4 AM flight, with a short layover in Houston, ending up at Heathrow. I'd be happy to book you on that flight. We'd also be happy to set up a few rooms for you at the Marriott so you can get some sleep until then, unless you'd rather stay here."

"I think some sleep would be brilliant," Williams said, nodding his head.

"Very well then. I apologize for the dela,y gentlemen. Just doing our jobs." He turned and walked out.

"Right gents," Williams said. He blew air out of his mouth and looked at his colleagues, slightly amused. "Let's gather up our clever little prisoner and then get some sleep."

He turned and walked out the doorway behind the Mexican official and looked to his left. Two gates away, exiting another office was Chelsea, surrounded by four mostly overweight Mexican security guards. Williams locked gazes with Chelsea and was puzzled. Her demeanor was beyond nonchalant. Complacent, content she was. Not a care in the world. He knew about her training. He'd read her report. While he waited in the office with the others he had expected to eventually hear the sounds of a conflict, some kind of disruption caused by her attempting to escape. She probably could have overcome them, at least escaped from that office, even handcuffed. But those sounds did not come and there she was walking out of the office as if she had no better place to be.

He decided not to look a gift horse in the mouth. Now all he had to do was get through the next four or five hours without mishap, get her on a plane and hope she hadn't used the time in that room to figure out a way to get them killed somewhere along the way.

The Mexican official arranged for a minivan taxi to come and transport them to the hotel. They waited outside the terminal until it arrived, then the six of them loaded into the taxi. Chelsea was shoved into the middle seat, situated between the same two agents as before. Pangani sat in the back seat with their sniper and Williams sat up front with the driver. The taxi driver pulled off and in Spanish inquired as to their preferences. He wanted to know if he should take the long way, for sightseeing purposes. After Williams' emphatically negative response the driver closed his mouth and focused on the road.

The Crowne Plaza Monterrey, according to the maps Williams perused before they left the airport, was a maximum of twenty minutes away from Escobedo airport. Twenty minutes he'd have to wait before he laid his head down and enjoyed a few hours of much needed sleep. So he sat back in his chair, tried not to be cramped by the minivan's uncomfortable seat and attempted to relax.

Two minutes later, the sound of sirens prevented him from achieving that moment of peace. Behind them lights flashed and police sirens wailed. He looked in his rearview mirror and couldn't help but shake his head in frustration at the sight of three police vehicles coming up fast and pulling in behind them.

"Qué pasó?" Williams asked the driver.

"No sé, señor. I don't know," said the driver, shaking his head.

Everyone in the vehicle except for Chelsea turned to look out the back window.

"They can't want us?" asked one of the agents sitting next to Chelsea.

"Right, why would they?" replied Williams.

"Maybe she left another note somewhere," joked the sniper.

To everyone's surprise, the police cars pulled in behind the minivan, turned off their sirens, remained in that position and followed them for nearly a minute without action.

"Should you pull over?" Williams inquired to the driver, who was now sweating profusely.

"Señor. Es la policía. It's not like in your country."

"He's right," Williams said. "Gentlemen, be at the ready."

"Yessir. Yessir." Those that had them stowed pulled their handguns from their baggage. The two agents sitting next to Chelsea tightened their grip on the pistols they already had sitting in their laps.

Williams returned his gaze to the rearview mirror and waited for something to happen. Another minute passed. And then another. And then five more.

Finally, the sirens were turned on again and the police began flashing their headlights.

"Señor?"

Williams looked at the driver who at that point had sweated through his shirt.

"Pull over."

The driver nodded and turned the wheel. The cruisers pulled over behind the taxi and came to a stop. Again, they sat there for another minute before a lone policeman inside the first police car languidly exited the vehicle. There was no movement from the other two cars parked behind the first vehicle.

"Curiouser and curiouser," Williams said quietly.

He turned in his seat to look over his left shoulder, through the window, to scrutinize the officer walking up to the taxi. His uniform looked legitimate but that meant nothing. Not only were authentic police uniforms readily available on the street in Mexico, but real policemen themselves were well known for taking bribes. Then he noticed something else. The officer was walking slowly. Very, very slowly.

"Out of the vehicle!" he yelled. "Now!"

He turned to reach for the door latch and as he did so, was distracted by movement outside the window. The last thing he saw was the barrel of a Smith and Wesson 9mm pistol. The bullet exploded through the window and pierced his cranium, lurching his body towards the driver, who screamed in terror. The same gunman that had popped into view beside Williams' door turned his weapon towards the agent sitting next to Chelsea and fired a bullet into his head as well.

Another gunman had appeared simultaneous to the first, immediately behind the minivan rear window. He fired four shots in quick succession, two each into the back of the sniper and Pangani's heads, their blood splattering the inside of the van.

The agent to Chelsea's left fired through his window, hitting the man in uniform that everyone had watched approach the vehicle. The bullet hit the man in the chest and sent him flying off his feet and backwards into the street. Immediately after firing his weapon, the agent began to turn to his right, toward Chelsea. She was on him before he completed the movement.

Chelsea raised her arms, cocked her elbow and buried it in the agent's face, crushing him against the interior of the vehicle. She jumped to her feet, crouching so as not to hit her head on the ceiling, pivoted and threw out her left leg. The blow caught him in the head as he was rebounding from her initial strike, knocking him out cold.

Every part of her now energized, Chelsea jerked herself around in a circle, sweeping the inside of the vehicle to identify any new threats. She soon realized the only thing left moving inside the vehicle was the driver. Satisfied she was no longer in danger, she willed her heart to stop banging against her chest. The slow-motion condition that combat engenders quickly dissipated. As her measure of alert dissipated, her ears began to unplug as well and the only sounds left to attend to were those of whimpering — sad, fast breathing that bordered on hyperventilation. The driver sat covered in the other men's blood, crying into his hands. The smell of gunpowder discharge and a sticky, red mist filled the cabin of the large cab.

"Princess."

Chelsea turned to her right and looked out the shattered window at the man who had spoken.

"Are you alright?" he asked.

"I'm fine," Chelsea responded as she wiped drops of the other men's blood from her eyes. "What took you so long, Granton?"

Granton laughed, opened the door and reached his hand in for her to take, which she did as she stepped out.

"Well, I had to find you first of all. I had to wait for Abejundio to enlist enough men to rescue you. Uniforms, paid off some real policia, etc., etc. I was afraid they'd already moved you out of the country until one of his people sighted you at the airport. That was only about half an hour ago."

The nearby sound of a pistol being fired rang out and both turned to see where it had come from. One of Abejundio's soldiers had just walked up to the window beside the agent Chelsea had knocked out and fired a bullet into his head. This, of course, caused the driver to begin bawling even louder. At this, the soldier turned his attention to the front of the van, walked up to the driver's window, raised his gun and aimed at the man.

"No!" Chelsea screamed out at the man.

The soldier dropped his weapon, shrugged and turned around to walk back towards the police cruiser, leaving the driver to continue his wailing.

"We should go," Granton said as he turned to walk. "Quickly."

Chelsea followed him back towards the faux police cruiser. As she passed the back of the minivan, she looked through the window at Pangani's body. The inside of his head was exposed in many places; he looked like roadkill that had been run over many times. For a moment, Chelsea was disturbed by the smile that came to her face as a result of the gruesome sight.

Contrary to what some of her recent choices might indicate, she had never been one to enjoy death, even the death of one who deserved it so. Nonetheless, as she walked, she looked back at his body and smiled again. The pleasure she felt at seeing him decimated in such a way was undeniable. It far outweighed any guilt she might feel. As a matter of fact, she wished there had been a way for her to be the one to have pulled the trigger.

She turned back to make her way toward the police cruiser.

"Granton."

Granton stopped and turned to face her.

"Yes, princess."

Chelsea smacked him as hard as she could with an open palm. The blow whipped his head to the side and when he recovered, his eyes were wide, shocked.

"What the fuck! What are you . . .!" he called out.

Chelsea raised her finger up at him, causing him to flinch.

"That's for pointing a gun at my head." She put her hands on each side of his face. "This is for coming after me and saving me." She then pulled him close, stuck her tongue in his mouth and kissed him hard for a full minute.

When she let him pull away, his mouth was still wide from the surprise. He put his fingers to his lips and touched them where she had kissed him, astounded.

"You are a very complex woman."

He looked down at his clothes and touched them, smiling. "You got blood all over my shirt." He then looked back up at her. "So, does this mean you trust me now?"

"Of course not."

"Hey lovebirds! Necesitamos a get out of here!"

They both turned in the direction of the voice. It was Abejundio calling from the open driver's side door of one of the cars. They walked up to the car and got in.

"Hello, Abejundio."

"Princess."

"Thank you for your help. With everything."

"My pleasure. I hate federales. All kinds, no matter the country. I do have a question though," he said, as he pulled the mock police cruiser into the street, deftly maneuvering around the body of his man who had been shot by the agent in the taxi.

"Please," Chelsea said.

"Something just occurred to me. That tech mine watch you put on her, Granton. I'm an arms dealer. How come I've never heard of the thing? They don't exist, do they?"

"Oh, they exist, my friend," Granton said. "Reicher's very high clearance, very exclusive. They are only used, seldom used even, by British and American agencies."

"Then how'd you get one?"

Granton chuckled and Chelsea smiled.

"That was a Timex. We had an engraver put a Reicher insignia and mock serial number on it in case we encountered a situation just like this one."

"Which was unnecessary. The imbeciles never looked at it anyway," Chelsea said.

CHAPTER 23

My eyes were closed but I was no longer asleep. Whatever instinct it is that causes you to open your eyes as soon as you wake didn't kick in that morning. Or was it afternoon? Or evening even? All my internal clock told me was that it wasn't working.

There were things far off in the reaches of my mind. Painful things. I wondered whether I should allow them the attention they clamored for. And then I told myself not to be so weak. That wasn't me. Accept that she was gone and that it was MY fault. I had to own up to my role in this tragedy. I might even come to value the experience by learning from it.

I'd had a lifetime's worth of lessons thrown at me in one day. "Now, how will I interpret these lessons in the future?" I asked myself. "Because there will be a future. And it has every bit the potential to be as bright as before." That was my unspoken decree, my banner constructed at that moment, though I was still very unsure about so much including where I was. But blind optimism was all I had left. "I will survive this," I told myself. "I will, somehow, overcome and surpass what has happened." I had no idea how I would make it so.

My first step: to open my eyes and accept my world for what it now was. I breathed in deeply, willed myself to open my eyes, and though I had never seen it in such measure before, discovered opulence in effect. It was a hotel room, but none like I had ever seen. A hundred different adjectives scrolled across the word processor in my mind — plush, impressive among them. Luxurious, sumptuous, moneyed. I sat up, looked around and marveled at the luxury that surrounded me.

The bed was so white I thought a flake of my skin on the sheets would be conspicuous. A large comforter fell to my waist, thick like it had been filled with cotton balls. The bed itself was a four poster. Bulbous, wooden poles with illustrations of cherubs etched into the wood rose above me and connected to a canopy for the bed, upon which were more fanciful illustrations of white swans in flight or alighting on a lake. The room itself was very large. The only thing that wasn't white was the carpet. It was off-white. I thought I might be able to take fifteen full paces from the bed to reach the entrance into the bathroom across from me. The rest of the furniture in the room consisted of divans and leather chairs. Not couches, deans. A small kitchen was to my right. A bottle of wine chilled in an ice bowl next to another bowl of fruit on a table next to the kitchen counter. The entire scene, harmonized by the sunlight that shone through the windows to my left and that lit up the room nicely - my own little piece of heaven.

I was surprised by the ringing of a phone. I looked to my right. On a stand next to the bed was an old style phone with a receiver that rested on two prongs that rose up when you retrieved it. The small clock next to it said 5:45 p.m.

"Hello?"

"Nicholas? Good. You're awake."

"Who is this?" My voice sounded gravelly.

"Nicholas, it's me. John Wilkes."

"Oh, yeah, the guy from last night. Sorry."

"It's ok. How you feeling?"

"Ok."

"Take your time."

"Thanks," I said.

"Listen, Nicholas, there's something I need to talk to you about, something I want to show you too, tonight."

"Ok."

"I'll pick you up about twenty three hundred hours, that's eleven o'clock. Meet me in the lobby."

"Yeah, I got it."

"Ok. So, I'll see you then. Until then, get some rest, order room service, whatever you want, ok?"

"Yeah, ok."

"Good. I'll see you tonight then, bye."

I lay back down and looked at the roof of my bed. I'd slept over twelve hours already. I needed some food. I rose, walked to the table and thought that this was the softest carpet my feet had ever experienced. It actually felt great to walk on it barefoot. I picked a plum from the basket and investigated my room while I ate. I walked to the window and looked down onto a garden. It was nearing dusk. I watched a couple walk hand in hand through the pathway that wound through the garden. They looked very happy.

Siphoning my memories of the previous night, I slowly allowed it all to come back to me while I ate. It was too much to have all occurred in one day and one night. My mother dying. Kato dying. The walk home from the station. That was still very fresh in my mind and was for some reason just as traumatic as everything else. Oh, and I guess I couldn't forget Shanay. That was one seriously messed up female. At least she was still alive. Everybody else in my life of late couldn't say that. And Raymond Smalls. I felt the bile rise in my throat when the image of Smalls smiling that contemptuous, triumphant smile at me when I'd finally shot him dead began to make sense. He knew then that even if he didn't manage to kill me he'd won by taking her from me. The most precious resource I had to draw from was gone because he'd ordered it. I'd learned that when there's only one other person in your life that you care for, when they're gone, so is the part of you that loves. Smalls, though not the smartest individual I'd ever met, figured out at least that much before I did. Albeit posthumous, he was to be awarded the trophy. He'd won the match. He'd beaten me and he'd known it when he smiled at me that way.

Everyone I'd known as family or ally was now gone from me. My life had come to an indescribable, irreversible halt. For all intents and purposes, the life I had known for twenty four years was over. And I didn't know where to go from here. Had I been in a more romantic mood, I might have compared myself to the phoenix risen from the ashes, or a comic book character that had his entire family lost in some horrible circumstance, who seeks out revenge and in the process becomes a force for justice. All I could do was hope I might find something to give me purpose and help fill even a little of the void that was left inside me. I didn't want revenge. I didn't even care for justice. Just a reason to keep living.

My thoughts turned to Wilkes. I felt almost as if I was being fattened up before the slaughter. This mystery man, with the hotel rooms and chauffeured limo, was no mere army recruiter. I could see this man brought with him great power just by looking around me. And for the moment, I was blinded by it. Whoever he was, he wanted me bad.

Even more significant was the fact that I was depleted. Whatever it was he wanted from me, not only did I doubt he would leave me much choice on whether or not I gave it to him, but with my mother's death, and everything else that had happened, I felt I no longer had the strength to fight and keep it from him even if I wanted to.

There was one other thing I had known since the moment I woke up in that room and felt that old, strange, premonition. My life would go on, but it would never be the same.

I took a shower and called room service. A burger and potato chips came up twenty minutes later and I watched some TV while I ate. I thought of what I would wear to meet Wilkes. I'd brought no change of clothes. And I didn't relish the idea of a trip to the place that was once my home to get some. A thought occurred to me that I almost dismissed as impossible, but I decided to investigate just in case. And there it was. An entire closet full of brand new, styled clothes. Shirts that fit me perfectly. I generally wore a 32 waist, but the 33's inside the closet fit me better. Inseams perfect. Neck and arm sizes perfect for me. These clothes had been tailored for me, then placed inside this room, probably while I slept. Amazing. I tried on the entire wardrobe. I even liked their style.

Before I knew it, the clock on the bedside table read 10:30. I thought it best to be early. Wilkes did not seem like a man who would appreciate tardiness. I grabbed a key from the table and left the room for the first time, walked to the elevator and took it down to the first floor. The doors opened onto a very large, cosmopolitan-looking lobby with marbled floors. I walked out and found a seat with a view of the entrance, sat and tried to look inconspicuous. I sat for twenty minutes and tried not to guess at what lay ahead for me that night. Then I felt a hand on my shoulder. I looked behind me and saw a man in a very well-tailored black suit. Stereotypical black sunglasses gave him away. And he apparently felt it unnecessary to hide the obvious. Government. He smiled down at me.

"Ready?" he asked.

I rose and followed him to a car waiting on the drive, door still open and engine running. We didn't speak again and I was just fine with that. Though my mind reeled with questions, I thought patience would be most prudent; I'd have my chance to ask them all eventually. I found myself riding through the night, leaving the good side of town and soon ending up back in my neighborhood, which I found puzzling. Why would we be going back that way? My nerves eased some when we left the neighborhood and drove nearly two miles out of it. He pulled in behind a long tractor trailer parked in front of a vacant lot. That was where he stopped.

As soon as we got out of the car, a warning noise sounded along with the sound of latches and air pressure being released. I watched the rear door to the trailer open and begin to fold down. As the door opened, it took a moment for me to see into the trailer, but soon I was exposed to a sight I will never forget. There stood Wilkes, at the top of the ramp, arms outstretched dramatically. Behind him was some of the most sophisticated looking equipment I had ever seen. My eyes had adjusted to the night. I squinted from the excessive bright light that emanated from within. Four men sat in chairs manning large flat panel displays and computer systems the likes of which I had never witnessed before. Wilkes smiled and waved us up.

"Nicholas, come on in."

We walked up and he shook my hand. "Sit down." He motioned me to a stool positioned next to one of the monitors near the entrance. One of the men pushed a button and I watched the ramp close again.

"Ok, now I guess you're wondering exactly what's going on here. Well, this is a mission observation center. We oversee, from this trailer, everything that goes down on an operation at a distant location. Tonight, that operation is in your old neighborhood.

Ok? Alright . . . ." He looked behind him and a man wearing a headset, manning one of the data stations, held up an outstretched hand, signifying five minutes. "We've got a little time. Any questions?"

Did I have questions. "Why am I here?"

"A couple reasons, actually. First of all, and most importantly, because what I saw of you in those store tapes shows me you have some very special talents. A great deal of potential."

"How so?"

"Maybe we'll explore that one together. The other reason is that this operation is linked to your recent situation with the local gangs. We're going to be going in and eliminating key players in your . . . dilemma."

"Eliminating. What'd they do?"

He seemed hesitant to speak, thought about it, then said, "Very bad things."

I laughed a short laugh. I didn't like being patronized. "I guess I should have expected a vague answer. Especially from a spy."

Wilkes smiled, pleased, and looked to the men behind him who were also smiling. The same man that signaled before spoke.

"They're ready sir. Waiting for the go ahead."

Wilkes pointed to a monitor in front of me and leaned down to watch it with me. "Watch your monitor." He turned his head to the others. "Proceed."

"Yessir." The operator pulled his mic down to his mouth. "We have a green light, gentlemen. Repeat, all go. Starting countdown. Coines, go ahead and give me that remote, will ya?"

He pushed a button and a timer appeared onscreen. 15 seconds. The console in front of me came to life. I deduced the image I was looking at was that of a camera mounted atop a moving vehicle. Seconds later, it came to a stop at a curb in front of a house. Four soldiers dressed in black and white camouflage uniforms came from off screen right. I assumed they had exited the rear of the vehicle the camera was perched upon. The soldiers ran to the rear of the house and out of view. At the end of the fifteen seconds, from under the mounted camera, I saw something being fired at the house. The projectile went through a window and into the house. One of the men in the room spoke.

"There goes the toxin."

"It's a paralyzing agent," Wilkes said. "Everyone inside the house will be immobilized." He turned to the controller. "Switch to heads up."

The display changed to a new perspective. A camera that must have been mounted on one of the soldier's headset/breathing apparatus. Another soldier in front of him kicked open the back door and all of them piled in, rifles up and at the ready, aimed in front of them. They cleared the nearby living room and moved back into the kitchen, then went through the awning into the hallway adjoining the bedrooms and bathroom. I couldn't believe what I was seeing. It was like something out of a movie. These were real commandos on a mission that I had somehow instigated.

I watched as two of the men moved down the hallway left of the awning, and with precision positioned themselves on either side of the door, opened it, then aimed and fired into the room with their silenced rifles. They moved into it and reemerged a few seconds later giving the thumbs up. Our soldier, the one wearing the camera, and his comrade, prepared themselves to do the same. Mirroring the other's actions, they opened up the door and looked inside. No one. They cleared the room and still found no one. Just as they emerged from the room, a black man ran from the bathroom in between the positions of the two teams, mouth agape and quivering from sudden exposure to the paralyzing agent. He collided with the wall opposite the exit from the bathroom, and for a moment it looked like he was just standing in place, his body contortioning from side to side. Then I realized that he was held in place, being riddled with an onslaught of bullets fired from opposite sides. Finally, he fell to the ground, his body dilapidated. What looked like hundreds of holes filled the wall he'd stood in front of moments earlier. Through the headset, I saw the soldier raise his hands and make signals to the others and they left the house the way they came. It all took maybe ten seconds, less time than the initial countdown.

"All clear sir. All personnel accounted for . . . and . . . they are ready to disembark."

"Excellent," Wilkes said. He turned to me with a glimmer in his eye. "Exhilarating, isn't it?"

I was still having trouble believing what I had just seen. "What did they do?"

"They're the ones that broke into your house and murdered your mother."

CHAPTER 24

The fall season had arrived. Not a single patch of sunlight broke through the cloud cover. It was as if the sun had been denied access to the world that day. The gray sky showed no signs of relinquishing its hold anytime soon. What started as a light rain was stiffened by the wind that picked it up and caused it to pelt onto my coat. The trees had recently lost their leaves and now those same leaves tumbled through the landscape. I had to pick up my feet periodically to uncover them from underneath the piles that developed around them.

Despite the dreariness brought on by the cold, tedious weather, I could see that this was a beautiful place. Not flat like most cemeteries, this one was hilly and treed. Rabbits and squirrels were visible only yards away from where I stood. There was nature here. I thought that appropriate. Life abundant only a few feet removed from what we all considered the end. An end, at least, on this earthly plane. I believed in God, even then. Though I knew the two were supposed to go hand in hand, I wasn't quite as sure about heaven sometimes. But if there was a heaven, she was surely in it. I could think of no one more deserving.

I stood alone atop one of those hills, overlooking my mother's recently plotted grave. I'd been told that I was no longer to interact with any of the people from my old life. So we parked on the cemetery drive nearby and I sat behind tinted windows and watched the service from inside the car. I'd walked to the hill above the grave and looked down after everyone had finally left. There had been a large turnout. Leslie and all my mother's friends from work had come, my neighbors, the Spanish brothers and their family. Many people I hadn't seen in years showed and they all wept and grieved for her and I was touched, but not surprised, to see there were others who loved her as much as I did. It's funny how much a seven year old can remember. I remembered how my father had looked at her. Even at that age it was noticeable how very much he loved her, just as did all these people. Who wouldn't have?

I looked behind me at the agent standing outside the car, the same agent that picked me up from the hotel lobby a few days before. He had his head down and his mouth was moving silently and I realized that he was praying. Praying for my mother. I suddenly felt an appreciation for this man and was moved by the compassion he showed. I had mistakenly assumed that all these government types were soulless beings but now realized my foolishness. I made a mental note to thank him for it later, then returned my gaze to where Momma lay.

I was right about Wilkes being a recruiter, but not for any agency I had ever heard of. He asked me to join him and I accepted. In a sense it was exactly what my mother had wanted for me. I would complete my education, and then some. I'd have the opportunity to become something more. Much more.

As Wilkes described it, ". . . operative in a super secret program most senators don't know about, Nicholas." I was told I'd be trained to be the elite of the top one percent of all America's secret personnel, as they called it. And now that Wilkes had avenged me, I owed him. Of course, I was sure he had been counting on that. I was beginning to see some of the ironies in life. Although they were two completely different people at enormously different ends of the spectrum, I couldn't help but see the one likeness. Only in my mother's eyes had I seen the faith in my own promise that I now saw in the eyes of this man called Wilkes.

I felt the agent's hand on my shoulder again, signifying it was time to go. I turned, got in the car, and we went to the airport. On the way, I told him I'd seen him praying and that I appreciated it. He merely nodded his head. It was one of the most sincere gestures I'd ever seen. And the last time I ever spoke to him.

We boarded the plane quickly. He flashed a badge and even in that time of high security, we walked *around* the metal detectors and no one dared lift an eyebrow. I wasn't told what our destination was. Only because we took a commercial flight did I eventually learn we were going to an airport near Fresno, California. When we landed, our luggage was removed prior to the rest of the passengers' and was waiting for us along with a chauffeur when we exited the terminal. These people were all about efficiency.

The chauffeur drove fast. It seemed only twenty or so minutes passed before we hit a stretch of road that was heavily wooded on both sides. The trees left shadows on the side of the road we traveled upon and I lost the warmth provided by the ample sunlight that the California sun had bestowed upon me since our arrival. Appropriate metaphor, because that's when I began to worry. Everything was changing so suddenly. I wasn't afraid of what was to come . . . just wary. Mindful that it would be extremely difficult, my next few years. That was the other thing. I'd never been given an exact length of time to expect to be sequestered for my training.

And what if I didn't measure up? That occurred to me too. Wilkes seemed to think of me as some kind of prodigy and I couldn't for the life of me figure why. These people dealt in mass amounts of life and death on a daily basis. Could I operate on their level? No, the question should be, how do I? Because I knew I would have to eventually — measure up that is. Honestly, I just didn't want to look like some kind of fool and in the process make Wilkes look foolish for having so much faith in me.

The race thing occurred to me too. As a result of cultural conditioning, there are certain insecurities that affect even the most intelligent of us. No matter how spectacularly brainy you are, you don't want to reinforce the dumb ass African brute stereotype, especially when you're thrown into a situation where you'll again be the minority. I was fully aware that it was just that, cultural conditioning, but that didn't change the fact that the insecurity was still there. I doubted there would be as many blacks in this program as there were whites. I knew there wouldn't be. It was usually about this point during my ruminations, whenever I started to feel insecure, that I would get angry. "What the hell?" I thought. "I'm smarter than any of these white boys or whoever they got to throw at me! And I'll prove it!"

Men by nature, seldom respect those so dominated by their fear that its presence is perceptible. Insecurity was an anticipant to fear. So I thought it best to quell my insecurities before they even got that far. Then I told myself to stop the unnecessary speculation entirely. Round and round I went. My mind was racing and I had yet to begin day one.

We arrived at a building that I didn't recognize as an actual structure until we were within 50 feet of the place. It was surrounded on all sides by forest. I looked to the top of what I guessed was an eight story building — there was no telling if there were levels below ground — and noticed an entanglement of vines that hung from just over the sides, probably emanating from the ceiling itself. Why would such dense foliage be allowed to grow on the ceiling of the building? Possibly for more concealment, I wondered. Made sense. From a plane, the building would blend in with the rest of the forest. That's when I began to be impressed.

A garage door opened and we pulled into the back of a large underground parking garage. As soon as the agent and I stepped out, the chauffeur locked the doors, put the vehicle in reverse, and was off. I slung my backpack, with the few toiletries and clothes I was allowed to bring with me, over my shoulder and looked at the agent. He motioned to an elevator a few feet in front of us. The elevator door was already open and it stood empty, waiting. I stepped inside and turned around, then put my hand out to hold it for the agent, assuming he would join me. He looked at me inquisitively and I realized he wasn't coming with me, so I let the door close. Then I realized I didn't know what floor to take it to. As I reached for the button that would open the door again, the elevator jolted on its own and I started to ascend.

I guessed at four floors before the doors opened. Standing before me was a woman who looked to be in her late forties. She smiled a pretty smile at me.

"Why hello, Mr. Gambit. Come with me, please."

She turned down a hallway and I followed. At the very end of the hallway, sunlight shone through a window. We walked almost up to that window, then she turned to her right into an office and I followed her in there as well. She walked to an empty desk in front of a wall with a closed door to the right of it, rounded the desk and sat in the chair as if she had done it thousands of times. I looked down at a nameplate on the desk that said Celia Cambridge. She pushed a button on her phone.

"Mr. Wilkes. Mr. Gambit is here, sir."

"Good! Good. Send him in."

"Go on in, sir," she said, smiling up at me.

"Thank you." I opened the door, stepped inside and was immediately met by Wilkes. He reached his hand out to me and we shook.

"Nicholas! Hey, how ya doin?"

"Ok."

"How was the funeral?"

"It was a lot of fun."

"Right, stupid question. Sorry."

"It's alright."

"Why don't you come with me; we'll get you set up in your quarters."

I followed him back through the office. We turned left and walked down the hall to another door that led to a walk across a suspended, enclosed walkway that looked out over the forest beneath us. I saw then that his building was separated from a good portion of the rest of the complex. The walkway itself was arched, designed to give the pedestrian, as they walked towards the complex, a full view of the building's design and architecture. And it was impressive as well. The complex consisted of three constructs built as concentric circles. One circle, then another larger circle surrounding it, then another; a fourth square shaped building enclosed all three. Every structure was at least five stories high. Between each layer, very large trees grew, filling the space between every structure. I wondered how one would make their way from one structure to another without going down to a lower level. I looked more closely and saw that bridges had been constructed connecting each structure. They were nearly invisible, hidden by the foliage that grew up and around them. The view from inside the building would have been profound. All one had to do was walk to a window, any window, and it would seem as if you were surrounded by an ocean of green.

Wilkes saw how affected I was. He said nothing and just allowed it to draw me in. The walkway let out onto the highest floor of the square shaped building and soon we were in the actual training facility. This was when he chose to begin his welcome speech.

"Nicholas, welcome to Noble 13." He waved his hand for effect. "We call it simply . . . The Building."

As he talked, we passed many rooms of various sizes, most of them occupied. In some, instructors stood in front of the class. In others, everyone stood and the students were physically involved in the lesson, what I would soon come to know as "Practical Application." We passed a window which afforded a view of an obstacle course five stories down, situated approximately 50 meters away from the square building.

"Obviously, this is our training facility. You're going to learn to do things here that other people only read about. Munitions, martial arts, common as well as some rare languages; you're going to have classes in history, the arts, foreign policy . . . you name it. If there is the potential that at some point you may need some piece of knowledge, no matter how trivial, we're going to teach it to you here.

"Now, you saw the facility as we came in. There is a method to its design that involves more than just an aesthetic appeal. As you master more skills and become more generally proficient, you move inwards. Your quarters will initially be located on this level on this, the farthest ring. You show us what you can do and over the course of the next few years, you'll move inside to the center, where the best and the brightest reside. The men and women there are every bit as capable at doing limited types of restorative surgery, for example, as they are at killing a man in three moves. My quarters are there as well. To state the obvious, you'll want to be in the inner circle. I have a feeling I'll see you there quite soon."

"Thank you, sir."

"Now . . . " he said, "Nicholas."

My attention had been diverted by a glimpse into a room as we passed. Men flying about the room violently. It was some kind of fight, but I could not see whom they were attacking. And whoever it was, they seemed to be easily overpowering them. A squad of teachers versus a squad of students, I imagined.

"Nicholas."

"Sorry, sir." I returned my attention to Wilkes and we resumed our pace.

"Don't worry, you'll be in there soon enough. Now, as I was saying, you'll become an authority on many subjects."

We reached an elevator and Wilkes pushed a button. It opened for us and we stepped inside.

"You'll have to be, because from now on, Mr. Gambit, everything you do is either going to kill you or keep you alive. No pressure." His timing perfect, he finished just as the doors closed in front of us.

We rode down two levels and the doors opened onto a corridor that was very . . . clean. And very cold. Not the temperature. It was a comfortable 76 degrees. But the obviously intentional dismissal of any color, the artificial, fluorescent lighting and marbled, polished white floors made for a feeling one might get in the isolation ward of the most impersonal hospital in existence. On Christmas Day.

Wilkes stopped at a door, turned to me and handed me a key. "Here's your passkey. Go ahead."

I unlocked the door, turned the handle and pushed. The room was larger than I'd expected, but just as impersonal as the corridor. To my left and ahead of me was a bed with wooden drawers built into it, underneath the mattress. A TV rack was attached to the wall and the monitor hung high, angled down to be viewed from the bed. One medium-sized rectangular window that looked out onto the wooded area was located several feet to the right side of the bed. I looked up. Fluorescent lights. Of course.

"This is going to be your quarters until it's time for you to go," Wilkes said.

"When will that be?"

"When I say you're ready. There's a layout of the building under your bed. Study it. Get some rest. You'll be notified when it's time for the meal. I will see you for a short period tomorrow. Your training starts then. If you ever need anything outside the scope of your training, anything that cannot be dealt with by your primary instructor, whom you will meet tomorrow, you come see me in my office. My door is always open. If I'm not there, Mrs. Cambridge will attend to my getting the message. Outside of that, all I have to say is, welcome aboard son."

"Thank you, sir."

Wilkes nodded his head, turned and closed the door behind him. I threw myself onto the bed. What had I done? The question was pointless. The choice had been made and now I was obligated.

And there was one other statement made by Wilkes that had burned itself into my memory as soon as he'd uttered it.

" . . . every bit as capable at doing limited types of restorative surgery, for example, as they are at killing a man in three moves," he'd said.

The restorative surgery part, no problem. Even knowing how to kill a man in combat, no problem. But actually being asked to do it on someone else's orders . . . problem? Something about that didn't feel right. I had no problem killing a man if it was just. But I had just enrolled myself in secret agent school. I might be asked to do it because it was convenient. I decided it was best to leave further thoughts on the subject until later. I lay down on my new bed and was asleep in minutes.

CHAPTER 25

My first year at The Building passed, in my memory, as if it had been a month. I could truly remember no time in my life when I had more fun. Learning was uplifting for me. It always had been. And six days a week, eighteen hours a day, that was all I did. Only I studied and experienced things most would never have the opportunity, or the time, to devote themselves to truly, as I did.

That first year I began studies in all the things Wilkes had said and more. I trained in gymnastics, exotic fighting styles, anatomy, how to use anatomy in combat. I learned about poisons and their counteragents. I began what was to be the equivalent of a medical degree in some countries. And so on and so on in several other subjects. And there was more to come. There was one goal that I had been instructed to set, and that was to be the best . . . at everything. And I was. After only a year, I was already into the second ring of The Building. Only one ring away from the center. I was told that few had progressed as quickly and demonstrated the proficiency in various subjects that I had. My instructors were almost as pleased with me as was Wilkes. Yet I could not find within me the ability to trust this man who had given me so much. He had killed those men back in my old neighborhood without a second thought. It had even seemed to amuse him. And despite that he had done it for me, I couldn't let it go. It was so . . . sterile; yet it was the most disturbing act of violence I had ever seen — at least up to that point.

The day after my arrival to the complex, Wilkes introduced me to Genai. When you first met him, three things immediately came to mind: short, strong, deadly. The short and strong, you derived from his appearance. Built like a cougar, he was, and that was my occasional nickname for him. A sinewy, powerful-looking torso was accompanied by condensed tree trunk legs. But the deadly part came from the way he would look at you. His eyes searched you out in a way that made the hair on your arms stand up straight. His movements mirrored that of an animal in every way, and the thought occurred to you quite often he just might pounce and tear the flesh from your body as would his namesake. It was almost hypnotic to watch him. But then he spoke. It was a booming, deep and perfect voice that immediately commanded respect. It seemed to be completely neutral, lacking inflection, which made it impossible to guess at an accent. His features were of no help either. Excepting his skin color, which was brownish and lent a hint at some Latin or Middle Eastern background, there was nothing about his appearance to indicate any particular ethnic persuasion.

That first day he'd stood in front of me, then bent down and felt me up from toe to head. Mercifully, he'd avoided my crotch but otherwise investigated every inch of my body, including my eyes, pulling on my eyelids and looking up into the crevice between the eye and outstretched eyelid. Finally, he'd stepped back and nodded his head and made an "Hmmh" sound.

"So?" Wilkes asked, smiling.

"He's well built. A little skinny for his height, but we can change that. Good muscle distribution. Compact torso, long legs, that's good. Handsome boy. I'd be happy to turn him into a killer, sir."

"Good," Wilkes said. "Mr. Gambit, Genai can teach you twenty ways to kill a man with just your pinky finger."

I said nothing. Just nodded my head. It was likely quite clear just how afraid of him I suddenly became.

Genai beckoned with his pinky. "We have much work to do. Come along."

Genai became my primary, my number one instructor and the person I spent most of my time with. He set my schedule every day and therefore organized my other classes around his. Usually, I would wake at 0530. I'd have half an hour to eat breakfast and shower, then would make my way to his dojo/classroom. It was the room I'd looked into the day I arrived. The men being thrown about with ease were some of Genai's students during an exercise. Their task, to kill him. Only him. I'd thought it was several instructors. No. They were told to attack him with everything they had and try and take him out, one man against several. Six of his eight advanced students were sent to the infirmary that day.

His dojo was a very large room with mats placed on the floor. One entire wall of the dojo was glass that looked out onto the forest below. As his dojo was located on the square-shaped, outermost ring of The Building, the view through the window was unrestricted and all you saw for miles was green. Adjacent to that wall was another that was split horizontally in two. The upper half was glass, the lower half drywall. But the view was less picturesque. On the other side was a hallway that was sometimes used by Wilkes for viewing the goings on inside this very important classroom. Many of the rooms where the more integral classes were held were constructed in the same way with a similar observation area.

From 0600 to 1300, I'd train with Genai, one on one. And soon, martial arts became my passion. We studied them all. Aikido, Jeet Kune Do, Okinawan Karate, Bushido, grappling techniques. I learned to use sabres and swords and staffs and many others, but was better at hand to hand conflict. The first six months, he sprained only my wrist, my ankle and caused me to pull a hamstring. He told me that it was his failing as a teacher to have allowed me to be injured so soon. Eventually, I became adept enough to hold my own with him if he restrained himself. And soon after, perhaps to even his surprise, I began to nearly match him in skill.

Often we'd leave The Building for field exercises, where he'd teach simple land navigation or other outdoor survival skills or we'd go to the range and we'd fire M-16s or light machine guns or M-80s or 40 mm auto grenade launchers and so on. I'd learn to build traps to catch game or more importantly, kill an enemy. The forest provided a limited environment for climate training, which required that some days my other classes be suspended so that we could drive to King's Canyon National Park or Death Valley and go into the mountains or Sequoia Groves and spend a week there. He would allow me to take nothing but 7 Meal Ready to Eat packages for foodstuffs and expected me to forage for the rest. I learned to set traps for game, to skin and cook them over a fire that I'd created from scratch. I learned to purify water without using purification pills. I learned how to survive anywhere. Every time I learned something new, my self-confidence soared and I felt it as it was occurring.

There were two ways that Genai demonstrated approval or reproach. When he was displeased there was no outburst; that was not his way. His eyes would lower and his jaws would clench slightly. When he was pleased, he would simply look at you, cock his head ever so slightly, and nod. I sought out his praise with all my being. And I received it more and more as the year progressed. Most everything I learned while at the Noble Complex, I did from Genai. I knew better than to think, despite all the time we spent together, that we had become friends. That was unrealistic and unprovable.

Once, we laid down to rest at the end of a very long day testing survival skills in the Mojave Desert. The temperature had dipped severely and we were wrapping ourselves into our gore-tex sleeping bags inside the tent. It seemed prudent at the time, to know something personal of this man I spent nearly all day, every day with. I'd asked him if he had family. He promptly and almost sweetly, with a smile on his face, told me to shut my fucking jacktrap and never ask another question of that type again.

"There was business. And there was work. And there was family and one's personal life and they were to never be intermingled," he'd said. Still, sometimes I thought he enjoyed the time we spent together as much as I did. That was enough for me.

The rest of my days were spent traversing the building, going from one class to another. Gymnastics, anatomy, recent world history, government structure, reconnaissance techniques. But with each passing day, I became more and more their perfect soldier. Genai noticed. Wilkes noticed as he looked in on me more often. And most importantly, I noticed. Along with my confidence level, my appearance had changed as well.

I stood in front of the window in Genai's dojo that served also as a viewing area and looked at my reflection in the glass. The past year had changed me immensely. I saw myself, for the first time, as a force to be reckoned with, as they saw me.

There was a sleekness to my new form. I scanned upwards and could not prevent in time the smile that materialized on my face, as if I had seen the image for the first time. I was pleased with what I saw. My mother lived still. I saw her in my own face. What in her was an inspired, delicate beauty, was now mine in masculine form. A symmetry of features that conveyed strength, intelligence and intuition, and revealing eyes that told plainly of my thoughts. What I saw wasn't perfect, but was closer than I had ever been to my ideal physical condition.

I pulled myself from the occasional trance I fell into when encountered by my own reflection, turned, and began to stretch. A group of students walked into the room. They were all young. The maximum age might have been in the late twenties. Newbies. Some of Wilkes' recent recruits. Most of them started off training in Genai's late day group classes. Only a select few were trained individually by an instructor of Genai's caliber as I was. Another of Wilkes' choices — one I most definitely would not question and actually appreciated.

Genai had asked me to attend the afternoon class in order to take part in their training. In an unprecedented act of praise, he'd recently told me I was one of his fastest learners ever. And that I was now skilled enough even to instruct.

"You're a killer now, Nicholas. I have seen to that," he'd said. "Soon you'll be able to beat even me. And soon, we will see less of each other as a result. Your training will begin to focus more on the cerebral, rather than the physical aspects of your job. Any man can kill another with his hands. Few can kill with their mind. You now have skills for the one. And now must seek out the mental prowess necessary for the other."

"Genai?" I said, feigning an impressed, serious look.

"Uh?"

I pretended to seriously consider my next question. "Is Wilkes my father, Obi Wan?"

Confusion overtook him momentarily. Then it was the first time I'd seen him laugh uncontrollably. Then he slapped me in the face with his open faced palm, so hard that my neck actually snapped, and walked away. But from behind, I could see his shoulders surging up and down still.

Now he walked up to me as his other students stretched.

"Nicholas?"

I was bent over stretching my hamstrings, sizing up the group. There were five of them. Two of them had a demeanor that caught my eye. From time to time Wilkes recruited FBI agents, cops or other prior service types. These men were always more capable than the "blank slates" he preferred. The two had a "stand up with your back straight" kind of confidence that could also indicate a lot of things. If they were prior service, they could very well be combat experienced. I looked up at Genai, then resumed my stretches.

"I'm ready."

"Very well." He turned to the others. "Gentlemen. I will use this exercise as an opportunity to assess your skills. If you have none, so be it, that's why I'm here. Place no great importance on this, simply do your best. Under no circumstances are you to hold back for any reason. I cannot stress that enough, for that is the only rule to this — that you do not reign in your impulses and instead let them fly freely. Both Mr. Gambit and I will be quite disappointed otherwise."

He continued and I watched the group of men as he spoke. They were looking more unsure of themselves with every word. One man stood and leaned back onto the wall, but not as one who was relaxed and showing it. He was unintentionally publicizing his insecurity, addressing a very normal psychological impulse to provide cover to his backside. Another took half-steps forward then backwards, thoughtlessly, moving yet going nowhere — more nervous energy.

But it was the two I'd noticed earlier that kept my interest. They didn't stray from their positions except to stretch. There was no nervousness to them. As soon as Genai, by speaking my name, had included me in the exercise, their attention had refocused from him onto me and never left. They would periodically, just before our eyes met, avert their gazes. But there was no mistaking it. Their attention was now permanently fixed upon me. Who was this man they'd never seen that Genai referred to as if he was a colleague?

So I kept them in my peripherals and watched them, waiting for it to happen. It only took seconds before it did. They did what they'd been secretly waiting to do since they'd walked into the room. They let their eyes meet. The corners of the larger one's mouth rose faintly and he almost smiled. These two knew each other. There was camaraderie, a familiarity at work. And they were government. Cops were always looser. I knew that from experience back home. These two were very rigid, and extremely sure of themselves too. It was possible they were partners before being recruited, but unlikely. More probable they met after, then were attracted by mutual experience or personal history. Nonetheless, they were now friends and would work as a team, and were likely to both have combat experience.

Friends. The concept was now almost alien to me. Both Wilkes and Genai discouraged fraternization with the other students. After a year there, I only knew a few other students by last name. I didn't care to.

They were one tall, one short. The bigger one looked strong and like he would pack a wallop. I'd do well to make sure he didn't connect. The shorter one, around 5'9", maybe 180, was more a mystery, but therefore made no less dangerous.

Genai finished his spiel and turned to me ceremoniously.

"Mr. Gambit, are you ready?"

"Yessir."

He turned to the group. "Gentlemen, are you ready?"

"Sir."

"Yessir."

"Sir."

"Sir, if I may ask. What exactly is our mission?"

It was the short one. Genai looked at me, smiled and knew that I had recognized the two for what they were already.

"Why gentlemen, your mission is to try and kill Mr. Gambit."

CHAPTER 26

John Wilkes loved to walk along his own private, quiet passageways and spy into the classrooms, dojos and labs and watch his empire being crafted, one inconceivably skilled individual at a time. Hallways like the one he walked in had been constructed all over the Noble complex for that very reason, to give him sole and intimate access into his students' classroom environments. For hours on end, he would traverse the passageways throughout his building and never see another soul in passing, and that was also why he loved them. His secret corridors, his secret building, his oh so secret kingdom.

But today was different. He looked beside him and took in the lovely Selena Garrison. Her stride matched his, and had someone seen them walking, they would not have been able to discern who was leader and who subordinate. He liked that about her. Every bit as capable as any man he'd ever worked with, she was — more so in many cases. Her intense beauty, her femininity and sexuality, they made her doubly effective. And much more dangerous.

A woman like that was infecting. Men were made to bend their wills to women like her; the precedents to be found throughout history. How many times in literature and song had an unwavering, steady resolve been made invertebrate when faced with just the right caress, or just the right silky-voiced suggestion from an irresistible temptress in disguise with her own hidden agenda? Even now as he walked beside her he felt his insides stir.

Every time she'd walked into his office, or the times when they'd come upon each other in the common hallways of The Building and struck up a conversation — usually about a student or some aspect of a particular training evolution — he'd had to fight off the sudden, nearly overwhelming impulse to gather her up in his arms, press his lips and tongue to hers and lose himself in her embrace. Two years is a long time to work with someone you could easily love but cannot allow yourself to have. It was an edict he often repeated to all of his instructors. Some had even taken up using variations of the proclamation for their own purposes. "Work is work. Love is love. And they are never to be intermingled." To be applied even to the exceedingly beautiful ones.

There were larger issues at work now as well. A relationship with Selena would have made what he might need to ask of her more difficult. And nothing could be allowed to stand in the way of him attaining his goals regarding Nicholas.

They walked down his hallway, turning every so often, nearing the destination he'd set for them. She'd felt him studying her. It didn't bother her anymore. She was used to it. It even flattered her somewhat. She turned her head, looked at him and their eyes met. She kept his gaze momentarily, then brushed an imaginary piece of lint from his shoulder just to see the effect it would have on him. He turned his head and looked forward. Anyone who wasn't looking for it, wouldn't have noticed the color that came to his cheek, faint as it was. But she saw it. She made no attempt to hide her smile, but lowered her eyes. It would not do well to seem as if she was bathing in her boss's embarrassment.

"So who is it we're going to see?"

"His name is Nicholas Gambit."

"There must be something to this Nicholas Gambit---," A new line of thought occurred to her and she interrupted herself. "That certainly is a fantastic thing to call yourself . . . Gambit."

"I don't think he chose the name for himself," Wilkes said, amused.

"But someone did. At some point in his family's history, one man chose the word Gambit to represent his clan."

"And get this. He is an African-American," he laughed.

"Ooh, the plot thickens. The word Gambit, usually meaning some kind of ploy or a carefully evaluated strategy. What kind of patriarchal former slave would choose a word meaning a carefully evaluated strategy to replace his given slave name, hmmh?"

"As always, Selena, I bow to your powers for discernment and introspection."

"And as always, I humbly accept all praise due me."

Wilkes laughed out loud.

"And for you to invite me to join you like this, for I have never had the opportunity to walk these hallowed corridors before, and neither have any of the others as far as I know, well, this Mr. Gambit must have some special quality to him or about him. If his name is any indication, there will be much plotting and planning at work."

"Nothing you can't handle, Selena, for you are as crafty as you are lovely."

"Oh, do go on."

"I could go on."

"Well, what's stopping you?"

"Business."

"Of course. It's always back to that with you, isn't it? Then tell me of our Mr. Gambit. Resident degenerate or future protégé?"

"Protégé? Hmh. Doubtful. I think perhaps he hasn't quite decided what to think of me yet."

"Smart guy."

"Yes, he is. Quite that."

"Hmh. How long has he been in?"

"One year. But he is well above average. I'm proud of this one. He'll be moving to the center ring with us soon."

"Really? After only a year? It's not very often I hear you speak so highly of your people."

"Well, this one is exceptional."

"Wow, my heart's all aflutter. Do get me to thy specimen."

"Here we are."

They turned a corner and came up on the window that provided a view into Genai's dojo. A wooden bar that looked as if it was meant to be leaned upon was positioned horizontally just below the large window and extended from the wall. Selena placed her hands upon it and peered into the room.

She knew who he was immediately. His back was turned to them and he was facing the others in the room. But there was no mistaking that this had to be the one whom Wilkes had become so excited about. He was inches away from the glass and she felt almost as if she could reach out and touch his mahogany skin. And though there were many in the room, everyone's attention, including Genai's, was focused on him.

He wore only sweats. They fit him well, but it would have been nice to see his legs, she thought. As her eyes scanned upwards, they encountered a muscular back and upper body. His broad and wide shoulders sloped downwards into large, well sculptured arms. She was curious to see the front of him. But there was no hurry. The perspective provided by this angle was pleasing enough.

Then his head rose as if he'd detected something and he turned and looked her straight in the eyes. She thought she might lose her breath from surprise. He watched her and studied her momentarily, then looked at Wilkes and nodded. Wilkes returned the salutation.

Again, he looked at her and his eyes scanned only her face though it was possible to see almost all of her. But he looked only at her face, searching it. She found herself held in his gaze and she thought he was beautiful. There was an enigmatic, dark contrast to his features. Soft and inviting, sensual and attentive countered by calculating and combative, rugged and dominant. His eyes themselves, open to her suddenly and telling her nothing. A lump formed in her throat and she let it be, for fear he might see her swallow, giving herself away to him.

He nodded to her as well, then backed away, still looking her in the eyes. Finally he turned. She allowed herself to breathe and realized Wilkes had been watching her. She knew she'd been discovered and so chose not to hide her infatuation.

"He's magnificent."

He smiled, turned his head from her and looked through the window. "Just wait."

Suddenly the others crossed the room and attacked him. Her heart jumped and her grasp onto the rail tightened. The first man reached him and threw a punch. It was immediately deflected and the man went flying, his own momentum used against him. Two others, that seemed to be working together, tried to tackle him simultaneously, and everything in the real world lost its meaning to her.

He was suddenly up high in the air and the two assailants tackled nothingness then flew into a wall. He'd jumped. He'd jumped right over them as they came at him and let them pass underneath. He jumped and cleared what must have been a good five feet height and came back down to his feet as if he'd climbed a single stair. There were still three others; and they were closing in. One attacked. The attacker kicked at her protagonist and connected with him just as he'd come down, sending him backwards and onto his back. As if unphased by the blow, he exploited the momentum given him by the kick and rolled, coming up near the others who were just recovering. He kicked one in the head, then came an elbow in a downwards slashing motion that connected with someone's head just as he was standing up, and two of them were sent back to the floor, bloodied. The third was picked up and thrown at the one who'd connected with him and who was now attacking again — and they collided.

Gambit attacked the two of them and hit one in the small of the neck from behind and he fell, unconscious. The other threw up his hands to protect himself from the onslaught that came. A jab to the face, an uppercut, then he was swept, his feet flying out from underneath him. He went horizontal and before he hit the ground was hit in the stomach with a punch that drew from something deep inside the man and flew from the side of his body, leveraged from his waist and the way it swiveled. And that was the end of them all.

She thought she had used the right term earlier. This was indeed, an extraordinary specimen of a man.

"Just look at him Selena. He's perfect. Smart, strong, fast, black. But without any of the failures you usually get with them. He'll always be underestimated because of his color and that's exactly what I need. A prince in pauper's clothing."

She looked at Wilkes momentarily. In another world, his statement would have been incredibly insensitive and unenlightened. She looked back through the glass at Nicholas. His torso looked as if it could have been sculpted; heaving, compact abdominals were clearly visible. Large, squared pectorals jutted outwards and seemed to preside over the rest of his body. He looked like an illustration to her, standing in the middle of the room, breathing heavily, menacingly, men writhing in pain on the floor at his feet. He threw a look back through the glass at the two of them.

A man suddenly jumped to his feet behind him and swung and Selena was sure he would connect. There had been no warning. Without turning, Nicholas ducked, threw an elbow into the man's stomach, causing him to double over; then he whipped his body around, lifted his leg into the air as he turned and caught the man with the heel of his foot as it came around and down, sending him sprawling. Defeated.

"Incredible," she said.

"I thought you might think so. He's your new student."

Wilkes turned and began to walk away. She turned to follow him. As she turned the corner she stole a glance back through the glass. Nicholas was watching her again from inside the room. All the ferociousness that had occupied his body moments earlier was gone and now he looked . . . vulnerable. His mouth was opened slightly and the corners of his eyes and his brow were creased. She felt as if he was calling out to her not to leave. She almost paused and thought she might run back to the window to admire him through it more, but then he slowly began to turn his body, and finally his head turned as well. Their connection was lost.

"In-cre-di-ble. Oh. My," she thought. She caught up with Wilkes and turned to him. "You brought me here just to see my reaction to him, didn't you?"

"You always were two steps ahead of me, Selena."

She laughed a long, hearty laugh. She'd been had and was a little impressed with him for it. "So? Did I pass the test, teacher?"

"You could neither pass nor fail. This was merely about gathering intel to be used for future purposes."

Something was different. The earlier joviality in Wilkes' voice was gone, and suddenly Selena felt reproached somehow for laughing. She'd thought he was resuming the playfulness of their conversation from before. That was not the case. He was dead serious now. And he did not look at her when he spoke. "Could it be jealousy?" she wondered. "No. It couldn't be."

"I see," she said. "Intel to give you an insight into how we will react to each other."

"Precisely. You must remember, Miss Garrison, everything I do is about the good of the program. And everyone within is subject to the decisions I make, even you."

"Of course."

"And no matter the severity, despite the moral implications of what I ask, I expect that everyone do what is necessary to improve the quality of operative that comes out of here."

She said nothing.

"Mr. Gambit may be the best I've ever produced. Nothing will stand in the way of his becoming my perfect operative."

"I understand."

"Good. You'll start with him tomorrow."

"Yessir."

They didn't speak again the entire walk back to the center ring. There was no longer any reason to speak of anything other than business and there was none of that to be had. The buoyant air of the walk to the dojo was far away and gone over the horizon, and what for her had been a relationship approximating a friendship, was now irreparably corrupted. There was no mistaking his tone. The aura of an extremist, a fanatic, had without warning overtaken him — all a result of the mere sight of the two of them watching each other through a glass window. She had never seen it in him before; and now she felt afraid for herself and the one she'd seen inside that room. Wilkes' plan included the two of them together in some strange concoction, and that could not bode well for either of them.

Granted, there was a connection made that she could not explain. Gambit looked right through her and into her and all around her simultaneously. She'd seen what she could only translate as some kind of real pain; it was obvious in him. She found herself wanting to know more and didn't want to have to wait to do it. She knew that because of Wilkes and whatever his plans were, the minute they met they'd been sucked into a convergence of occurrences that would take them down a very dangerous path; and she knew it would likely end sadly for one or both of them. Because of this she had her reservations about even seeing him again. Yet, despite the foreboding components to her dilemma, she knew she had to. She had to see him again. She'd never "yearned" for anything before and had previously thought it a stupid, sentimental thing that women did. Her mother told her once, "Malign something much, and it will always come looking for you." Selena loved her mother, but sometimes she could be a punctilious, inexplicably omnipotent bitch.

CHAPTER 27

I lay on my bed and looked up at the television. I seldom had time to watch any programs so I usually watched CNN or MSNBC to keep up with the Joneses' and be aware of what was going on in the outside world. Outside of the treks I'd made with Genai, I'd not left the Noble Complex once in the year I'd been there. Wilkes did allow the students "Out Passes" four times a year. You were allowed to go in pairs to see a movie or view some other event. He didn't want the students to feel as if they were in jail. He even had a whorehouse set up somewhere that the men were allowed to visit for free. I never chose to leave because there was nothing out there for me. Not that I enjoyed being stuck inside that place, just that it wasn't necessarily any better to leave and be bored somewhere else for four hours. And having sex with a woman that was being paid to do it didn't exactly appeal to me either.

So my free time was spent with news anchors on the twenty-four hour news stations. I'd been told by Wilkes that he'd need to see me and to be ready to go by 1400. It was now 1345. A commercial ended and an anchor appeared.

"Welcome back everyone, I'm Lester Holmes. We have some very disturbing news of what once seemed like nothing more than a shocking one-time occurrence, but now may be turning into a full on trend—a new, increasingly consistent form of robbery.

"Two years ago was the first occurrence of a robbery that just completely appalled Americans everywhere. Jonathan Hagerstrom, a name I'm sure you all know quite well by now, walked into a bank in Marianna, a city in northern Florida, and killed the guard, then mowed down every single one of the tellers, and *then* proceeded to let himself into their drawers and walked out with well over twenty thousand dollars. He killed eight people that day and was caught and killed three days later in Alabama. Apparently, he didn't want to deal with the nuisance of live employees that he would have to keep under control or prevent from pushing the alarm button.

"Last month, same thing. Thieves broke into a restaurant in Long Beach, California, hours after its closing. They discovered a group of employees having a late night birthday party, and killed all but one who did survive his injuries.

"Well, it's happened again, folks. It seems there is yet another copycat robber out there. He's done the same thing, only this time, the only witness left inside was the camera that caught it all on tape. This morning, a man walked into a pawn shop in California and killed both of the clerks, looted the drawer . . . and took what he pleased and left. Apparently, they were both shot with a large weapon, possibly a shotgun. There were some bystanders who were across the street and heard the shots going off and saw the man exit the store. They say he was wearing an overcoat and it looked as if he might be hiding a large weapon underneath it, which leads authorities to think it was a larger gun like a shotgun or perhaps an automatic weapon. The police aren't saying if they have any leads on who this man is, and of course, cannot say whether he will try again. But so far the trail has gone cold. He was wearing a mask so the tape from inside the store will likely be inconclusive, at least regarding his identity, but the authorities do say that typically these men are brought to justice in days and not weeks. The names of the two people who were killed have not been released.

"It is notable that these robberies are just that. They're not an attempt to make some kind of statement. This doesn't seem to be about anything but greed. Let's hope that this doesn't inspire any more copycats in the future. Ok, now let's switch gears and turn our attention to the ongoing effort for peace in the Middle East."

I turned off the television. I wanted to feel sorry for someone but didn't know who.

There was a knock at the door. I stood and Wilkes entered the room.

"Mr. Gambit, let's go."

"Alright sir."

I followed him out. As we walked, I soon noticed we were going to the center ring. I had a couple of classes there, but none in the direction we were headed. Soon we came up on a door and Wilkes opened it and entered, so I followed him in.

There she was. I honestly hadn't thought about her all day. I'd seen the most beautiful girl in history the previous day and I hadn't thought about her since. I don't know why. She stood up from the chair she sat in and moved over to us somewhat stiffly. I didn't know her well enough to translate her body mechanics but I thought it might be . . . reluctance?

She was covered from neck to foot. She wore a snug, knitted turtleneck sweater that was gray and a long skirt with yellow daffodils on it. Something about her conservative outfit didn't seem to fit her, as if she'd been inspired to put up some kind of physical barrier. Still, covered up as she was, signs of voluptuousness shone through with surprising clarity.

"Nicholas, this is Selena Garrison. She'll be working with you closely for quite a while."

"Hi," I said.

"How do you do, Mr. Gambit?"

"I'm good." Boy, I was smooth.

"I'll let you two get started," Wilkes said. He looked at Selena in a way that I didn't understand, then left the room.

"Sit. Please." She motioned for me to take a seat.

I looked around me. It was a very small room. There was space enough for the table and two chairs and perhaps an a/v cart. A chalkboard was built into the wall to my right. Very low tech. Unusual compared to what I'd seen in that complex. I'd half expected all of the center ring rooms to have holographically projected instructors.

"This is very cozy," I said.

"Yes. Like two peas in a pod we are."

She smiled as if we shared a common understanding of the situation. She was wrong because I had no idea what she was thinking. I sat across from her and scanned her face quickly, though there was no need. It had been burned into my memory the day before.

God, she was beautiful. My first guess was Italian. Flawless, bronze skin. Features that walked the line gracefully between beautiful and overindulgent. Though youthful and taut, her face was all soft angles and subtle changes. No breakneck curves or hard turns. Soft looking lips that stopped short of being too full. A small, average looking nose that was just wide enough to give it the appearance of strength. Her eyes were bright and brown and opened to me. Long brown hair that seemed to have natural highlights of gold went down behind her face and framed it perfectly. She was soft and inviting and feminine, yet intelligent and strong.

And while I studied her, she studied me as well. I insecurely wondered if I might be a letdown, in person, from what she'd seen the day before.

"I saw you in practice the other day," she said.

I smiled and could not get rid of it for several seconds. "Yeah, I saw you too."

"I was very impressed. You are . . . skilled."

Again I smiled, this time more slowly. I didn't want her to feel uncomfortable complimenting me.

"Thank you very much. I appreciate it. Uh, so what is it exactly you're going to be teaching me?"

"Well, we'll start off with foreign languages. Then we'll make our way to foreign policy, the American justice system, American politics and government structure, and finally recent history — domestic."

"Sounds like stuff I've already studied in school, regular school."

"Nowhere near the scale that we will. For instance, when we're done you'll be very, very capable in four major languages."

"Only four, huh?"

"If you can handle more I suppose we can go beyond four. Is that what you're telling me, Mr. Confident?"

"Oh, I think that's exactly what I'm saying."

She looked at me and this time I was assured that she was measuring me up. I let her look at me and smiled back and wondered what she was thinking. So I asked.

"What are you thinking?" I think that surprised her. She looked at me, incredulous.

"Why do you behave as if we're familiar? We've just met."

"I'm that way with everyone. At least those whom I decide it wouldn't pay to play the games that people normally play with each other. There are a great number of . . . pleasantries or etiquette, whatever you want to call it, that serve only to reduce the speed at which people get to know each other to a near standstill. It's illogical and inefficient. I want to avoid all that bull and just tell you what's on my mind when it's on my mind, that's all."

I'd made up every single word that had just come out of my mouth. But it sounded pretty so I looked at her as if I'd meant all of it.

"And would hope you'd do the same," I added.

"And what makes you think I don't want to play all those stupid, inefficient games?"

I thought it would be strategically unsound to give up on my plan, that wasn't anything of the sort, so soon. So I decided to turn up the heat rather than retreat.

"The way that you look at me."

She turned her head, snorted, smiled at me, and pretended as if she thought I was mad, but I knew better. I watched her just then, as she'd turned in the chair. I noticed how her breasts pushed against the sweater and the sight of it started my heart beating a little faster and more words pushed themselves out of my mouth.

"And the connection that we've already made somehow. If you look at every man the way that you looked at me yesterday, then every guy you meet must fall in love with you on the spot."

"I am your instructor and you are my student, Mr. Gambit."

"I know that. It doesn't mean we can't be honest with each other, does it?"

She looked down and considered it. "I'm all for honesty. But you must remember your place."

"I wouldn't think of stepping over that line."

"Good. We should start then," she said quickly. "Why don't we begin with Spanish?" She reached down to pull something out of a bag sitting on the floor beside her.

"Ningún problema con mí señorita linda," I said, smiling.

She looked up in surprise. "You speak Spanish."

"What great big powers of deduction you have grandma; yes, I speak quite a bit of it. I had a lot of Spanish friends growing up."

"Hmh. Wilkes told me I'd have to work to keep up with you. How about one of the Orientals, you know any of those?"

I shook my head no.

"Very good."

She stopped and considered something and I was desperate for her to look up at me and speak to me again. When she did speak it was with an honesty and sincerity that I'd previously thought I'd never see again.

"For what it's worth, I do want for us to be . . . friends. Maybe we should get to work. Let's start with the alphabet, shall we, Mr. Gambit."

I understood completely.

Selena became my primary. We spent the next six months inside that tiny room together and it was pure utopia. The enjoyment I'd experienced with Genai: going on treks to the mountain; firing tank killers; learning to disable any man under any circumstances — pure joy for me at the time — paled in comparison to Selena and our talks on how China, not Japan, was poised to be the next most powerful nation, or analyses of Iran's governmental structure (or lack thereof) . . . or even the weather outside. We never took any tests or did any practical app; we just conversed and discussed or argued and it was wonderful.

"Ok, Mr. Gambit, let's talk about fascism."

"Fascism? I thought we were doing recent history today."

"They're on the rise as we speak."

"They?"

"Fascism, nazism, socialism."

"Oh."

"Many of these new regimes call themselves fascists and use Mussolini's orations as doctrine. So, it makes sense to know what that doctrine was, does it not?"

"Absolutely."

"Why do you think it is that this kind of ideology has resurfaced with such ferocity? Totalitarianists have arisen in Spain, Mexico, Russia. And many of these groups have real chances at taking power in their countries. People there seem to believe they may have it figured out this time."

"The poor are still poor and the rich are still rich. Capitalism is as strong as ever worldwide, despite the state of our economy, and that was bound to create some backlash. But capitalism does and always has worked in favor of those who already have money. Don't get me wrong, I'm not knocking it; but it's natural for normal people to dream of a chance to be equals and not starve to death while others live in luxury."

"Ah, now that's the idealist's way of looking at it, isn't it? But I'm here to help you see beyond that."

"What do you mean?" I asked.

Selena stood and walked around the table. I loved to see her like this. She would get so infused with an excitement brought on by the chance to deliver an insight into an issue that normal people would miss completely, that she could no longer be held fixed to her chair. She'd stand and pace that tiny room, going back and forth, back and forth. I'd watch her beautiful face scrunch up and a chill would run through me from the sight of her eyes and how they got so bright when she made a discovery of her own, her need to impart that discovery upon me; it was thrilling to watch. I loved how our exchanges stimulated her mind as well as mine. She'd walk that room and I'd think she was the most gorgeous thing I'd ever seen. I'd marvel at her figure, even through the excessive clothing she always wore. Sometimes I hoped she'd never stop talking and pacing and sticking her head at me with a look of, "Do you see? Do you?"

"Darwinism was one of the contributing philosophies of all of the previously mentioned ism's. And that is why the leaders of these current movements chose past movements that have obviously been proven not to work."

She looked at me as if I should understand it all by then. I didn't.

"Survival of the fittest," she said, stopping beside me. "The strong leading the weak, but for their own hidden purposes."

"So are you saying that the men who are initiating these . . . cells of influence I guess you could call them, are only using these movements that have failed time and time again because they want to usurp power for themselves eventually, that they see them as a means to that end only?"

"Exactly. That is the nature of the beast. The beast being one of these totalitarianistic outlooks."

"Ok, that's not so far-fetched. But am I the only one that is at least open to the possibility that these men could just be misguided and they're mistakingly searching out a way to better the way of life their people are forced to endure? Desperation can make people consider routes of action previously thought unacceptable."

"You poor fool."

She laughed and put her hand on my shoulder and I wanted to lay my head down on it and touch her skin. Instead, I turned and looked at her and rejoiced in seeing her reacting to our closeness too. We looked into each other's eyes for what felt like forever before she removed her hand and went and sat in her chair opposite me. Then she smiled.

"Sometimes you're such a champion for the good in people, Nicholas. Altruism is a lost art."

"Not always," I said.

"Family doesn't count."

"Ok, then what about all the people that volunteer to help others? Peace corps, all that?"

"They're all writing off something, I'll guarantee that."

"Hmh. How can you be so young and yet be so jaded?"

"Ouch."

"I'm sorry, I didn't mean it as an insult."

"I've known since I was very young that I have a capacity for seeing into people. Intimately. And those who are like you and think that everyone has some good in them don't stay that way for very long."

"I think you misunderstand me, Ms. Garrison. I think it would be more accurate to say that I am aware of the capacity for good in *many* people, but not all."

"Do you see that in me?"

I wanted to tell her that I saw perfection in her. "Let me ask you this."

"Hmh."

"Would you give your life for me if the choice had to be made?"

She looked as if I'd just called her momma a whore. She was dumbstruck and had no idea how to proceed. But I'd never planned to allow her to answer the question.

"You see, I would," I said. "Because it would feel like the right thing to do and I don't know that your life, in the long run, won't be more significant somehow than my own. Not because it makes sense, not because I was gonna get anything from it. But that would be my choice. Because I'd want you to live, and if I could give you that gift . . . I just would."

It was the only way I knew how to tell her without really saying it. She didn't move or speak for a very long time. Then, for just a fleeting moment, I thought she might cry and I knew then that she'd gotten the message.

"I think our time's up," she said, without looking at me. "Will I see you . . . uh, same time tomorrow?"

I stood. "Wouldn't miss it for the world."

"Ok. See you then."

We'd barely covered the topic and were still a half hour away from actual quitting time, but I knew that when a woman needed you to leave, you did. I was happy to do it for her and happy that she was affected by me enough so that she needed me to. It was unspoken and obvious that there was a madness at work inside me and it was that I was in love with her. I dreamt of her when I went to sleep and when I sat two feet away from her I dreamt of her still. When I walked out of that room all I could think about was coming back to be near her again. I was lost and I knew it and I didn't care.

CHAPTER 28

"Uh, excuse me, Nicholas?"

I looked up at the instructor standing in front of the classroom. His demeanor suggested he was waiting for something.

"What's our topic today?" he asked.

I hadn't heard a single word he'd said that entire class. My mind was in another far-off realm. It had been a week since I'd told Selena what I'd give for her. We hadn't spoken of it since and I thought that was for the best, but admitting it to her solved nothing for me. I still could not have her and it drove me crazy. Now I wanted, needed to take it further. Logically, I knew it made sense to just let things be — a working relationship that was forbidden to go any further and nothing more. I told myself over and over that it was best to not let it get to me, but that was the hardest thing about it. I couldn't control myself. I couldn't oppress the feelings I had no matter how hard I might try, and those feelings towered over every thought.

It would have been different if I was in love with her and she didn't feel the same. Unrequited love is much easier to handle, I think; a mutual affection that must be endured unsatisfied however — oh, much, much worse. Our feelings were present in everything we did. I saw it when she looked at me. I saw it even more in the way she tried not to let it show. When we touched in the simple little accidental ways that people will when they spend a great deal of time together in close proximity, she'd stop speaking suddenly, and her voice would tremble for just a moment when she began again. There was no mistaking how we felt about each other. That was the problem.

"I'm sorry, sir . . . I'm sorry," I said to him.

"Let's keep our minds on the work at hand, shall we?" he said.

"Of course, sir."

The class was average sized. It was a forensic science course. There were eight others sitting in chairs around me. The instructor stood in front of a white board upon which images were projected. He held a remote in his hand. He rattled off statistics and gave us information that we were responsible to take down on our own. There were no tests in the NC-13 program, just instructors, students, the information that passed between them, and individual sessions where the instructor formulated an opinion of that student and whether he was assimilating the knowledge adequately. What happened to those who didn't perform well enough in these sessions I never knew. One day you'd just notice that one of those that usually attended a certain class along with you wasn't coming anymore. I didn't question it. It wasn't my place.

"Now, gentlemen, we've already covered Pathology and Toxicology, and those of course, are very significant aspects that work in conjunction with the criminalistics of forensic science. But I think you'll find that out in the field, some of the best investigatory steps are utilized right there in the field and not in the lab. It's very likely that you will have access to lab facilities, but . . . I guess what I'm trying to say is that, put simply, you can save yourself a lot of time if you perform adequate, insightful, and knowledgeable investigation on scene. Now I'm giving you the same speech I used to give my students that wanted to be field operatives. You can very often close a case, even a case that seems muddled and complex, right there at the scene of the crime. Here are some examples."

He pushed a button on his remote and the room went dark, then was lit up again by the screen on the wall that came to life. Groans went up throughout the room and I smiled at their reaction. The image depicted the top of someone's head. It looked like it had been drilled through with a jackhammer. The shot had been taken at night, but the flashbulb from the camera lit the grossness well. The photograph was shot at close range and inches above the person's head, or what was left of it. Brain matter and blood lay splattered around the head and on the sidewalk in front of it.

"Now, this guy, the gun was positioned underneath his jaw when it was fired. The bullet traveled into his brain and exited through the crown of his head. Turned out that it was a contract killing. Three men were caught shortly after he was killed. Two of the suspects immediately had guns attributed to them. I say 'attributed' because the idiots tried to dump the weapons and were caught doing it. Now, we know they were all working together. That was established fairly quickly; but ten minutes after the shooting, investigators didn't know which one of the three did it. Whoever actually did the killing was wearing gloves and did manage to ditch those."

"So the next question would be which of the two weapons had been fired recently," suggested one of the other students.

"Well, you're right. But the investigators soon realized that both had been fired recently and both had been wiped clean so no blood splatter. There was a gun battle prior to them actually catching their victim and killing him. So what next, hmh?"

No one spoke up.

"OK. Maybe this will help . . . one of the pistols was a Glock 9mm. The other was a H&K .45."

"The size of the exit wound," I said.

"Thank you, Mr. Gambit. Glad to see you've woken up. He's right. Look at it."

He pointed back at the screen.

"That exit wound would never be that size from a nine. Even from that distance it wouldn't be that size. He would have been just as dead but the investigator wouldn't have been able to put it down on site like he or she did."

"Now, that's simple deduction. I'm gonna get a little more complicated on you," he said. He punched the remote again and six different images came up in boxes on screen, three on the top half and another three below. Each was as gruesome as its predecessor.

"Some very unique types of entrance and exit wounds can be attributed to a few select means of delivery, namely, certain guns that fire certain bullets that make certain kinds of distinct wounds."

He began to rattle off statistics of weapons as the individual photos of the wounds they caused blew up and filled the screen.

"Now this one is interesting. Look at the ring that is caused by the bullet as it entered the victim. This ring is formed because of the way that the round spirals. It's a shredder bullet with the armor piercing tip, that when fired into bare skin literally sauters a ring into the flesh and bone and you get this extraordinary looking wound. I mean, you'd have to be right up close there to notice it, but I think it's amazing. You'll probably never see it; well, it'd be a rare event unless you're the one firing the weapon. It's from a Reicher assault rifle. You've never heard of the company and that's because these days they're solely government contracted. They went into business only six years ago and started selling to the public about four years ago. They did gangbusters business, I mean their stock rose . . . well, a lot shortly thereafter, and then suddenly they went out of business.

"Now what I found out after I began here is that actually they didn't go out of business. They were shut down and contracted by the U.S. government to build weaponry solely for us and the Brits. A lot of the non-standard military stuff that you'll be using out of here is theirs. The modification and accessory capability for their weaponry is astounding. You can do anything with them. Fold em up and carry them around in an unaltered briefcase, almost completely universal scope and silencing modification, etc., and so understandably, their weapons have become very popular with agents that specialize in sniping and close quarters terminations and the like, but you'll never see them used by civilians."

He continued to show the other weapons and the lesson finished after another half hour. I left the room and went to my final class of the day. As soon as I entered and sat down I began to be bothered by something. I prided myself on having a very strong stomach, but it occurred to me that I might be having a delayed reaction to the gruesomeness of the photos.

"Welcome, gentlemen. I trust you all finished the reading I gave you last night."

"Yessir.

"Sir."

"Sir."

"Good," he said.

I was beginning to feel like I might vomit. An uneasiness had crept up on me. I swallowed and shook my head and tried to rid myself of the feeling.

"Today let's talk about homeostasis. Homeostasis is one of the fundamental concepts of modern biology. It's defined as the maintenance of a steady state within a biological system by means of self-regulating mechanisms. The nervous system and endocrine system, together with other regulatory mechanisms that function within cells and coordinate body metabolism, make this possible."

A connection was made that lifted the sickness away somewhat. Something *in* those pictures was causing the disturbance I felt.

"There's a balance at work. And if you can disrupt it, you can utilize what is normally a very stable environment, as a tool with which to kill."

But the photos. Why would the photos be bothering me so much still? I'd seen as bad on the Discovery Channel alone. I even sort of liked that kind of thing. Seeing into the human body was fascinating to me. Gruesome scenes of death were no worse. They were just nameless faces, people I probably would have never known anyway.

"Recent advances in contagion studies have made available a near plethora of new poisons that do exactly that. They turn up the heat, to coin a phrase, and cause the body to heat up to such a degree that organs are cooked and eventually liquefy. Besides the occasional emission of blood through a body cavity, there are no outward signs of what has transpired within the deceased."

People I'd know? Had I recognized someone? Maybe that was it. But how could I? Most of those shots were so close in on the wound that you couldn't see the faces of the victims. Then what was it?! This was becoming frustrating. But it was definitely the photos. Wait. No. It was one photo. That was it. It was just the one photo, the one that the instructor had been so excited about.

I finally closed in on it and I thought someone might have slipped me one of the contagions this instructor was talking about because I began to feel as if *MY* insides were liquefying. That trademark entrance wound that he'd shown-- it was what I'd seen on my mother's forehead the night she was killed. That other instructor had just shown me the kind of weapon that was used to kill my mother.

Images began to appear in my mind and I was suddenly remembering it all. It played back in my mind in slow motion and it was as clear as if it were the day before. I remembered the walk. That long walk . . . home. Home . . . to find her gone away from me. And all the strangers that walked around inside my house as if they belonged in it. And I remembered how they were in the way and I had to make my way through what seemed like a crowd of strangers when I just wanted to get to her. The fake lights. Fake and wrong and artificial light everywhere. And then . . . there she was. I looked at her, then looked up around me and saw the faces filled with pity. Then I looked down at her and tried to touch her but couldn't, and then I cried my eyes out like a child.

I relived the entire event over again and it was as real for me then, as it had been a year and a half before. It hurt the same and it tore at me inside the same, as I sat there in class while the man up front taught us how to kill people with poisons that made their insides heat up and turn into mush.

And then I saw the wound. It was right in front of me as it had been that night and I thought I could reach out and touch it on my mother's forehead. I hadn't thought anything of it at the time. There was no reason for me to. I would have known no better. But now I saw them. Rings. Grooves sautered into her skin and skull. Tiny but clear and all explained to me finally. Finally. Finally.

Now I was remembering my instructor. "Shut down . . . contracted to work solely for the U.S. government . . . used widely by agents for close quarters termination duties . . . "

I hadn't felt right about him from the beginning and this was why. The moment he'd seen me he'd known what I could become if I joined him. This place and the operatives that come out of it are all he's ever cared about. He killed those men back in that house in my neighborhood for no other reason than to get me to come here. But he killed her first. So that I'd be vulnerable. And vengeful.

A wave of anger washed over me; I felt it all the way through. I exploded out of my chair, turned at the exit, and hit the hallway at full speed. I heard my instructor yelling out my name behind me, but soon I was out of earshot. I guessed that no one had ever witnessed someone running in those hallways before because as I shot past them, all the trained killers tensed up and prepared for hell to break loose and wondered if they should follow.

I came up on the bridge in seconds. As I raced across, I half expected the panes of glass that surrounded the walkway to explode outwards as I passed them, my rage manifested.

I reached the end of the bridge, turned the corner, ran the length of the hallway, and burst into the outer office. I never even looked at Mrs. Cambridge and headed straight for his office door.

"Mr. Gambit? Mr. Gambit, he's in a meeting you can't go in there. Mr. Gambit!"

I reached out to turn the doorknob, but my hand was halted by revelation.

"Mr. Gambit?"

"Not yet. I can wait. Get everything I can from him then do it."

"I'm sorry?" she asked, puzzled.

"That's alright," I said. I turned my head and looked at her. "I'll wait."

CHAPTER 29

Chelsea felt more comfortable alone these days. Solitude was pleasant for her. Alone, she needn't concern herself with issues like trust, another's position relative to her own, chain of command, etc. Here in this room, all alone, she could breathe freely. This was her chance to vent.

It was a smallish room with fluorescent light strips in the ceilings and bare, gray walls. But it was large enough to maneuver comfortably and utilize the three man-shaped dummies that stood in front of her, positioned in a small triangle. Behind them was a hundred-pound punching bag that hung from the ceiling.

She stretched for a full ten minutes and went over methods of attack in her mind. She created different body types that each dummy would represent, and consequently developed a plan of attack incorporating likely moves each would make. This was no longer a difficult mental exercise for her. Once that would not have been true. Before her training. Before her metamorphosis. But now, her mind was remade — exceptional and disciplined. She'd done this many times before.

She leapt forward and tore into them. She threw her leg up and hit the first dummy in the head, then whipped around and put an elbow into the second dummy, simultaneously kicking the third in the kidney. She ducked and stepped to the side, evading a phantom left cross and threw a combination of left-right jabs that would have seriously hurt any real opponent.

She stepped back and waited for one to attack. The first dummy, she decided. She took one step forward and lit into it. Body-body-face, body-body-face, body-body-kill, body-body-kill, and stayed with it for several minutes. She practiced ducking and deflecting on her way to the last dummy. She kicked at its knees, then kicked at its kidney, then planted her left foot and drew up her right almost into her stomach and it shot out at the dummy, hitting it square in the chest and sending it flying backwards onto the floor.

She turned her head to the left, located the punching bag and attacked. She ran at it and jumped from four feet away. Her outstretched leg connected with the bag at the heel and sent it up and flying away from her. She landed, and as soon as it came swinging back at her she put her arm up, her forearm pointing straight up like a knife, and let the bag's full swinging weight be deflected from her body as would an opponent's kick or punch or charge at her. She stepped behind the bag so it would swing back at her and as it came, punched at it with all her might and caused it to jerk from the impact. And that's when the real workout began. Jab-jab-uppercut-kick-elbow-kidney shot-combination-kick-straight kick-windmill-roundhouse-jab-hook-hook-jab. And so she went for another half hour.

Obsession was not enough for her. She must be perfect. She must have no equal. There must be no one to capably oppose her, no one to call into question her skills. Too much at stake. Far too much yet left to do. Many who still had to pay for their involvement.

The sweat made its way into her eyes and caused them to burn, but she would not wipe them dry. In combat, the pain would be much worse. She must prepare herself for those moments as much as possible now, so that it would be less bothersome when the time finally came. And she could not wait. Oh, how she dreamed of the time when her parents would be avenged. She desired that power in her country be returned to its rightful owner as well. True, that rightful owner was her, now that both of her parents were gone, but that was secondary. Closure could only be accomplished when those responsible paid for their crimes.

Chelsea stopped and allowed herself a moment to cool down, then walked to a door in the rear of the room and opened it. She stepped inside, reached around the corner and flipped a switch. The room came to life. One by one the lights in the ceiling flashed on, illuminating the cave-like room that had been converted into a crude but adequate shooting range.

Eight stalls had been constructed by hanging wooden dividers to the right of a small table, large slabs of metal placed fifty feet from the tables to receive the rounds at their points of impact.

She stepped up to the table in the first stall and picked up a pistol. She loaded the clip into the weapon and racked the slide into place, chambering the first round. Then she looked down at her target and smiled. Granton told her that he'd left a little surprise for her in the room. She stepped around the table and looked to the right of her first target, into the next stall. Placed on the centers of all the targets were blown-up photos of the men responsible for her parents' deaths and the subsequent toppling of their government. And why? Not for some religious ideology, nor because the people were unhappy under the current ruling system. Avarice. Greed. These were the reasons her father's own officials deposed and murdered her parents. Her country was small, but rich — a small and unimportant little country in Africa that wouldn't raise too many eyebrows around the world, for surrounding regions were known for consistent and almost cyclical coups. But her country was rich enough to make it worth the trouble if anyone did come looking for an explanation. And the money was quite accessible, if the right resources were utilized-resources like the men whose photos were before her now.

Ironic, she thought, that her father had sent her to America to learn skills necessary to fight those who might involve themselves in such a heinous, despicable movement. His intention was to prepare her for when she would ascend the throne so that she would be a versatile ruler ready for the new kinds of threats that the twenty first-century would bring. But he had made the mistake of focusing on external threats and as a result, had been killed by some of his own officials who claimed loyalty to him. She'd not made it home in time to give her father and mother a kiss and tell them that she loved them before the kind of violence he'd sent her away to ultimately come back and combat sprouted up inside their own administration and took their lives.

It was time for payback. She aimed her weapon at the first target and fired. And began to cry. It wasn't weakness, but that she was overcome with pure, unlicensed hatred for these men and what they'd unfairly taken from her. She moved from stall to stall, her rage building with every new face she obliterated. When she reached the last stall, tears streamed down her face uncontrollably and her whole body shook from the pain. Firing a wild shot at the last target, she missed completely; this only made her more distraught. Contradicting her training, she slammed down the weapon onto the table in disgust, then derided herself for not staying focused.

Still crying, she picked up the weapon again and focused on the target. Aiming through her tears, she pulled the trigger. Misfire. She could smell the chamber smoking from the inside. She pulled back the slide and ejected the bullet — hurt, angry, unfulfilled. She placed the pistol on the table of the last stall and when she did so, saw another pistol, ready and waiting, as if her heart, crying out, was sent a sign, there in that room, all alone in so many ways, that justice would not be denied. Chelsea picked up the weapon, loaded the clip, chambered the first with lightning speed, and fired, the hate resurging but now dominated by renewed discipline. She unloaded the entire clip, destroying the photo of her parent's former chief security officer, Maximilian Bergosi. Chelsea wiped the tears from her eyes and walked out.

CHAPTER 30

I'd never felt such an inexorably intense hatred before. Until Selena came along, I'd never been in love either. The two strongest emotions a human being is capable of feeling, and I experienced them at the same time in such massive proportions. Now that was a trip.

From one extreme to the other, that was my daily routine. The time I spent with Selena, soft and happy, and finally content. I'd finally accepted the parameters within which our relationship could function unimpaired. I knew how far I could take things with her and was satisfied with it. As long as I could see her, that was my one pleasure in life. Well, usually that was enough for me.

But the rest of my day was spent lying in wait for someone I deemed thoroughly corrupted. The good of the many versus the good of the few was his rationalization for everything. I saw so far beyond that it made me laugh to hear the phrase. It was the good of his dream versus everything else and there was really no contest. His was the kind of evil often mistaken for pragmatism because it can be made to sound very sensible, which also makes it much more virile and dangerous.

The last six months at the building passed in this way for me. Contemplating Selena's beauty and my love for her, then contemplating ways to bring Wilkes to justice, all the while continuing my own quest for perfection. I wanted to be unstoppable so that when the time came, Wilkes would not be able to protect himself from me.

I was now two years into the program. Compared to most that passed through the program, I'd been there a short amount of time, yet nearly all my classes were satisfactorily completed. So I spent most of my day with either Selena, Genai, or in gymnastics.

"Ok, son. Good, good. Alright, Nicholas, that's good. We're done for the day."

I lowered my feet to the ground and came out of the handstand. I was inside the gym where the gymnastics classes were taught. Tumbling mats covered the floor. Students and their instructors filled the large gym and worked out. We focused on skills to complement my martial arts training. Seldom did we utilize any equipment; instead it was more about balance, basic flips and body contortioning. I'd just completed a set of back flips and been instructed to stop on my hands. It's more difficult than you know.

"Thank you, sir," I said.

Some of the instructors at the building were not military and many of these were not used to such constant formality by some of their students. This was one of them. He looked at me and half smiled, not understanding the change that had overcome me within the past six months. My demeanor . . . well, it had changed considerably.

"You're welcome, Nicholas," he said.

I walked over to a bench and sat down next to my bag. I took off my shirt, retrieved a towel from inside the bag and began to dry off. I looked up as two men who had just finished their session as well came over to the bench and sat next to me.

"Errr," grunted the one to my left. A Marine.

I said nothing. I didn't feel in the mood to exchange pleasantries.

"I don't see how you do it," he said.

I blew out a long breath, attempting to indicate I was not in a talkative way.

"Yeah, man, I gotta admit, I'm impressed. I'd like to know your secret," said the one on the other side of my neighbor.

"What?" I said, finally.

"Well, you spend ninety minutes here doing the most demanding training I have ever seen and then go straight to self defense and train over there with Genai of all people. I hear he's the meanest, most dangerous instructor they've got here. I mean, surely Wilkes can't be that much of a hardass."

"Wilkes." That was all I said. The disgust, I'm sure, was evident. They must've read the look on my face, because they got up quickly and said nothing more to me.

I gathered my bag, headed out the door and into the hallway. My day had been unexceptional until those two had spoken of *him*. And then there he was, right on cue, the object of my obsession. Coming around the curve of the hallway, was Wilkes. I'd done my best to avoid him since my revelation six months prior. And when I was forced to be around him, I utilized every ounce of willpower I could summon just to be civil. He saw me and lifted his head in recognition. His arm rose as if he meant to speak to me. Despite attempts to control it, my face twisted into something less than felicitous and I walked right by him without saying a word or allowing him to. Believe it or not, it was more than just pure disgust which guided me not to speak. I was making a conscious effort to avoid him. I knew that if I was forced to be in his presence for long, I would lose control and I felt that it was not yet time for that. Luckily, he didn't pursue and continued on his way, probably assuming it was a problem with another student or some other petty issue I would best be left to deal with on my own.

I walked into Genai's dojo and emerged two hours later, my face purged of its scowl. I was happy to be going to see Selena. I walked into her room, my hair and forehead still wet. I took a cap from my duffel and put it on, smiling, which was a rare occurrence those days.

"Hi," I said.

"Hello. You're all wet. But you smell good."

"Old Spice. High Endurance. Sport Edition," I winked at her. "I had to take a quick shower; I had blood all over me." I sat.

"What'd you do?" She looked at me and noticed a bruise on my lower cheek. "What'd you do to your face . . . are you okay?" She reached out and touched me. I was pleased that she didn't restrain herself as usual.

"Yeah, I'm fine. I don't know about those other guys."

"So you've been beating up on other students?"

I thought about how to answer that question.

"Yeah, pretty much, yeah that's how I'd describe it."

"And how does Genai feel about you doing that?"

"He thought it was funny. He just shakes his head and chuckles. He thinks it's quite hi-larious when I do that."

She shook her head in admonishment.

"Well, how else are they going to learn?" I asked.

"You, Mister, take advantage of your skill level."

"I'm sorry."

"Are you really?"

"If it makes you not mad at me, then very. Are you?"

"Though I might try, I couldn't stay mad at you even if I wanted to." She said it without looking at me, attempting to portray herself as uninterested.

"Why not?" I asked. I cocked my head and gave her a devilish, questioning look. She looked at me, unimpressed.

"What do you want me to say, because I might love you too much, hmh?"

I was a little hurt by the sarcasm, and she noticed. The disapproval left her face and it was replaced with regret.

"Oh, Nicholas, aren't we friends?"

I was lifted somewhat by the question. "Of course we are."

"And friends can tell each other anything, right?"

"If I tell you everything . . . I just can't, not always," I said. I wanted to give her all of me. Everything about my past, my realization about Wilkes, but I knew I couldn't put her in the position it would force her into.

"I understand that. We both work here, you know?" she said. "I know the pitfalls that a place like this brings with it when it comes to being honest about everything."

"But I do want to be able to tell you everything. Sometimes it actually . . . hurts when I know I can't," I said.

She put her head down and wouldn't look at me in that way that made me desperate to kiss her every time. I had never known anyone to go from aloof and invulnerable to fragile in a matter of a few sentences. And every time it happened, all it did was make me fall harder for her. It was the times that she couldn't match gazes with me that she was the most open. But immediately after, I always felt guilty for the way I took advantage of the fact that I knew how she felt about me. I used her feelings against her. Essentially, I backed her into a corner until she was weakened so, that her true feelings were demonstrated somehow, in some tiny way that only made me feel good.

"I'm sorry, Selena. Forgive me."

She looked up and to my immense surprise, there were tears in her eyes. I rose out of my seat just enough for her eyes to widen at the prospect of my approach.

"No, Nicholas."

She was right. "Nicholas Gambit what you are doing is wrong," I thought. "You can not continue to let this friendship that she wants the two of you to have grow, and then destroy it, at will, with this kind of childish, puppy love idiocy! You are hurting her. Stop it!"

"Friends," I said. "Friends. From here on. I will misbehave no longer, I'm sorry. For really real. Ok?"

She watched me intently for several seconds and searched my face to see that I was sincere. When she was sure that I meant what I'd said, she nodded.

"Ok."

"Ok. Pal," I said.

She reluctantly smiled that brilliant, perfect smile of hers again and I was made more resolute to be good. I decided I couldn't act on my feelings ever again, not like that.

"Buddy," I said.

"You want to get started ol' chum?" she asked.

I nodded my head.

"Ok, my platonic associate," she said, clearly feeling much improved.

"Today's my birthday," I said.

"Really?"

I nodded again.

"Well, what are you going to do?"

"Nothing," I said matter of factly. "I'd almost forgotten myself, to be honest. Besides, I can't leave the building yet."

"Oh. Wilkes is pretty strict, huh?"

"Yeah."

I tried to hide it but the battle was lost. It was in my voice and in my eyes. My death and destruction face retook its ground. Of course, she noticed. She saw right through me and had been, on this issue, for months.

"Why do you hate him so much?"

"Wilkes has psychopath written all over him, Selena," I said, almost yelling. "I don't understand why you don't see that."

"I see more than you know, Nicholas. Nevertheless, I am loyal to him. I have to be. It's best you remember that."

"I'll try not to hold that against you."

"Ok, you know what I don't understand? Why do you hate this life so much? I know the isolation's not great but that'll be over with very soon. You're getting a superb education, training, all free. Wilkes is making you powerful."

"And to do what with it all? That's the million dollar question. And you know, individualism, separatism, it's all being constantly pounded into my head by Genai and Wilkes. Nicholas, you must be expert, distinct, yet blend in with unmatched facility. I've got to be able to survive on my own. I understand why, but lately, I'm just starting to question everyone's motives in regard to me. And yes, lately it's getting to be kind of lonely."

She was watching me more intently than usual and I realized this was the first time I'd told her about my feelings regarding anything other than her.

"You know the weirdest thing is when I was a kid . . . " I chuckled.

"What?"

"I used to love James Bond movies. I used to think that was the life."

"Now you are James Bond."

"Yeah. Now I am. Sure seemed like he was having a lot more fun."

"Nicholas, you don't have to be alone."

Without hesitating, she placed her hand on mine and I wasn't disappointed that it wasn't a romantic gesture. We'd ascended to a new and different, but not less special plateau in our relationship.

"Remember that, ok? Pal?" she said with a smile that warmed me through.

"Yep yep."

"Ok. Hey, you know what? It's your birthday. We should celebrate. I just don't know how. But I'll think of something."

"Yeah? That'd be real nice."

"Yeah, it would." She smiled again.

I was happy with this new place we'd come to.

CHAPTER 31

I slept better than I had in a long time that night. Discontent for so long, this new step Selena and I had taken towards a comfortable, mutual and real friendship, in effect, set my soul at ease. Still I dreamed of her. Of course. I was still every bit as much in love with her as before; but this time, I thought, I might manage to stay satisfied with this new arrangement for a while.

I always dreamed in clichés. In this one we lived at the top of a skyscraper. I was a very popular but only sometimes writer that made millions from the few books I wrote. I guess she didn't have a job other than to please me through intercourse and fellatio and such. We walked around the penthouse atop our skyscraper, always in the nude and spent most of our time in discovery of each other. There were never any arguments, never conflict. Only lovemaking and when we were done with that, we'd hold and caress each other and wait for our desires to rise again anew, then we'd go back to more of the same.

Periodically, we'd be interrupted by a little unnamed Asian woman who apparently was my personal assistant. She'd walk right up to the bed with the two of us occupied with investigating each other's crevices and ask me a business question as if we weren't doing anything that required any privacy whatsoever. She'd tap me on the shoulder or whichever larger body part happened to be up in the air and accessible at the moment and say "Meestah Gambiihht! Meestaah!"

At the height of orgasm, I'd hurl an expletive or two her way and tell her to sell the damn thing, whatever it was, just sell it and leavemebetomywoman! Selena, of course, would find that very gallant of me, profess her love and admiration and tell me that she loved me with all her being, that she belonged to me and that she hoped that I felt I belonged to her as well. Of course I did tell her exactly that. She'd look at me and tears would come to her eyes the way they had earlier that day, but this time she really would cry. She'd sob from being so in love and so happy. My dreams were always like that. Some utopic existence that was completely unattainable and that had they actually come true, I would have immediately been bored all the way through.

I opened my eyes, looked around my quarters and got my bearings. The room was dark. The sun had long since ceased shining through my little rectangular window near the floor. I'd fallen asleep as soon as I put my head on the pillow and was still wearing my clothes. I sat up on the edge of the bed. The dream was still fresh in my mind and I smiled at its absurdity. I turned my head at the sound of a knock at the door. I'd been awakened by the knocking. I stood, walked to the door and opened it, and there she was.

"Hi. Happy birthday."

"Hi," I said. I had to look at her twice to be assured that I wasn't still dreaming. "Uh, come in. Is everything ok?"

"No, you come with me," she said, motioning with her head for me to follow.

"Where? You know we're not supposed to be out right now?"

"Just come on."

She grabbed me by the hand and pulled me out of the room. She turned, and as I came up behind her I saw her legs. Selena's bronze-skinned, toned, wide calved legs. My eyes quickly scanned up the back of her body. She wore a medium sized skirt that tightly contoured her waist and hips, thighs and rear. I'd never seen her in anything like that before. I caught up with her, looked at her beside me and had to will myself not to stare at her chest. She wore a light blue shirt with no sleeves that fit tightly over and exaggerated her breasts. Her hair was up, just as I would have wanted; her lips were glossed and she needed no makeup. Her voluptuousness was in full display. Combined with her perfect beauty, it was almost too much of an assault on the senses.

She saw me looking at her, smiled at me and my head went into a fog. I was at a complete loss for words.

We entered The Building's empty commissary and I followed her to a table with a cloth draped over it that covered something underneath.

"I just got back."

"Uh, from where?" I asked.

She pulled the cloth away from the table and a birthday cake was revealed. Plastic plates, utensils, and cups were set on each side of the table.

"Are you kidding me? You did this for me?"

She nodded her head and stared at me. There was something about her. All of the reservation she'd previously exhibited when it came to our relationship seemed to have evaporated in hours. The smile I saw then was every bit as brilliant as the one I witnessed when we were usually together, but there was something different to it. There was an invitation at work in the way she behaved and looked at me, like she had granted herself permission to let go the bonds that prevented us from being together. But I knew that was a bit far-fetched and had to be nothing more than wishful thinking. The only thing that made sense was that I was seeing the real Selena. We had established that we were going to be real friends so now she felt comfortable being herself with me. She was off duty and this was who she was away from the requirements of her position.

"It's the least I could do," she said. "What about the last two years? What'd you do on your birthday then?

"Nothing."

"Now that's a shame. I guess we'll just have to pack two years worth of fun into tonight."

"Ok," I said abashedly, with an embarrassed smile on my face.

"I really wish you could blush," she said.

I laughed. I liked this new Selena.

I put a forkful of cake into my mouth and washed it down with an entire cup of wine. I doubt there was any mistaking that I was enjoying myself. Selena smiled and replenished my cup with more wine.

"Ummmhh, thank you," I said, as I stuffed myself with more of the cake. I looked up from my plate and noticed Selena studying me. I thought for a moment that she wanted to tell me something, but then she looked away as if to prevent me from asking, so I didn't and returned my attention to my cake.

After I'd had my fill, I pushed the plate away and sighed. She'd been watching me the entire time. I'd look up at times and see her smiling at me, delighted to see me sucking down her gift with such gusto. But other times, that same look that told me she was mindful of something, desiring to tell me something important, was obvious and visible. I decided I should let her tell me when she was ready.

"You . . . are a goddess," I told her.

She put her head back and laughed loudly enough that I thought the sound might reverberate through the entrance to the room, down the halls and wake someone who would come and discover us there when we shouldn't have been.

"It was the least I could do for such a handsome and deserving boy."

I was surprised. She said it with a glint in her eye I'd never witnessed before. There was so much about her that seemed different. And it had come from nowhere so suddenly, it made me pause, but only momentarily. I wasn't about to look a gift horse in the mouth.

"Now, the handsome part I get," I said with a smile. "But deserving?"

"You deserve this. Well, the cake and wine part, at least," she said smiling with her mouth closed, playfully.

"What about the company of an incredibly beautiful woman?"

She leaned towards me, across the table, and smiled. Then she licked her upper lip, slowly, and I felt myself smiling. She was definitely no longer afraid to show her attraction for me.

"That I give willingly. Not because you do or do not deserve it, but because it is mine to give and yours to receive if you wish."

Almost as an afterthought, she smiled. Again, I thought that perhaps there was a cryptic message somewhere in her words.

"Maybe we should change the subject," she said.

"Ok, what do you want to talk about?"

"It's your birthday, you pick."

"So how'd you end up doing this? Here, working in a place like this?"

"You mean teaching?"

"Well, it's not exactly like you're teaching preschoolers here, Selena. How'd you get involved in all this?"

"You won't like my answer."

"Great."

"He came to me directly out of college. I'd been an advanced student. Actually went into and subsequently came out of school two years early. Apparently word that I was "linguistically superior" reached him precisely when he needed someone for the Noble 13 project. And the rest is history."

I nodded my head. "Hmh, yet another vague answer from someone who calls me friend."

She looked hurt and I regretted the statement immediately.

"Now, that's not fair." She refused to look at me again, the same as before in class, only this time there was a tinge of . . . guilt? As if she resembled rather than resented the remark.

"You're right, it's not, I'm sorry."

"You sure say that a lot, Nicholas Gambit. And you haven't exactly been straight with me. You won't even tell me why you hate him so much."

"You know what, let's not talk about him. It'll spoil the mood."

"Oh, we've set a mood already, have we?"

"Yes I think so."

"And what *kind* of mood would that be?"

"Oh, come on. I think you know the answer to that question."

"I promise you I don't. Do enlighten me."

I turned and looked away from her and laughed, contemplating saying the words. But once again the impulse was too strong. And there was no point in deluding myself. Her sitting across from me, so incredibly beautiful and finally accessible; logic, reason, just plain common sense was dispatched like so much worthless refuse and replaced by something else. Mercifully, I can say that it was my heart and not another part of my anatomy that was doing most of the talking.

"Well, one rife with a tension that I could only describe as . . . sexual. And here we are separated by a couple of feet and I look at you and all I can think of is 'Does she know the effect she has on me? Does she know that I think about her when I sleep?' The chronology of my day doesn't revolve around night or day or the sun or the moon or any of that stuff. It's when will I see Selena and after I do, how many hours until I get to see her again.

She watched my eyes, but this time her face told me nothing.

"And I know that we're supposed to just be friends now and I can deal with that and will. And the last thing I want is to make you uncomfortable or unhappy. I want just the opposite, you know?"

She nodded her head slowly.

"And you're thinking 'Wow. That is an attractive man. I mean, he is a really exceptionally good-looking man. And a great body too. What a butt, on that guy. Great butt. Exquisite even'."

She laughed. "Ok, ok, I get the picture. Nicholas, you know that I have feelings too. I just don't know that we can act on our feelings."

"I know. But just for the record, you are totally in love with me though, right?"

She closed her eyes and shook her head slowly, which I thought was weird. It wasn't a no. It was an expression I didn't understand. Then she tilted her head slightly and said so very sadly, "Totally and completely. No matter what happens I want you to remember that."

The solemnity with which she said the words, and my own immaturity, made me think it necessary to intervene before the levity of the situation was upended, so I blew a breath out of my mouth signifying the absurdity of her statement.

"C'mon, do you think I'd ever forget something like that after all I've put us through to get you to say it?"

She tried to smile.

"Yes, I guess you're right."

"Thank you for tonight. You made my year," I said.

"My pleasure. I'll walk you back."

"Ok," I said as I got up from the table.

She took a look.

"You know I wouldn't go so far as to say you have a great butt. It's okay."

"Liar."

She laughed and seemed to be impressed.

We walked back to my quarters silently. We walked side by side, close to one another, and as we walked, moved closer and closer. I could feel myself being drawn to her with every step. I tried to fight it and didn't realize how near we were to each other until, as we approached the door, I felt the back of her left hand touching my right and I had to catch my breath. When we reached the door, I turned to her and looked into her face, mere centimeters from my own. She was vibrant and real and intoxicating.

Her eyes were lowered. She looked as if she might be having trouble with her breathing and I almost laughed out loud. Her eyes closed and then opened slowly, still without looking into my own, showing me that she couldn't; she was affected by my closeness to her. I stepped forward just enough so that she could feel me and see that I was aroused by her. Her eyes fluttered and I was assured that she felt all of me pressing against her. She inhaled quickly, then let out her breath with a soft, quiet moan, to my exultation. I put my hand into her hair and pulled downwards just slightly, in order to watch her head angle up at my command. I felt myself grow again and my own breath became labored. I put that same hand on the nape of her neck, and stroked her there. She put her head back and let the pleasure of it flow through her, then she closed her eyes and I knew . . . she was mine.

I raised my hand and brought it behind her head and pulled her to me softly, until our noses and mouths brushed against each other and I could feel her warm, sweet breath on my face. There was a delicious fragrance to her skin that I'd not noticed before. I grabbed her right hand with my left and interlocked our fingers.

"I know you shouldn't but by God, Selena, I love you completely--I can't help it I try and I try not to let it control me the way it does . . . stop me if you don't feel it too."

She looked me in the eyes for the first time since we'd touched and I saw that she was moved by my words. In her eyes I saw desire and tenderness . . . and sorrow.

"This must be your choice, Nicholas. It must be."

"Do you love me?"

She nodded in that delicate way that women do where they hardly move their heads at all yet you know it's when they mean it the most. But it was when her eyes welled up again that I took her. I reached around her and opened the door. I put my mouth to hers and tasted the lips I'd dreamed about for a year and euphoric clarity about what I needed to do rushed over me. We stepped over the threshold of the room while I closed the door behind me, all without leaving each other. I loved her all the way to the bed, searching out her lips and tongue and dreaming of the moment when I could be inside her.

Suddenly her feet fell out from underneath her and we were on the bed. She pulled herself onto it completely and I straddled her and pulled off my shirt. She ran her hands up my abs and chest then ran her hand along my face and stared at my eyes. Our gazes locked and we just stared at each other for several seconds.

Then I reached down, grabbed the bottom of her shirt and lifted it over her head and arms, and at the sight of her breasts, thought I'd died and gone to heaven. I think she saw my reaction because she smiled and I couldn't help but smile back. Thinking it was best not to overly fixate on them, I instead leaned down and kissed her on the eyelids and then on her nose and then on the lips. She arched up into me and we rolled onto our sides. We lay there, facing each other, for just a moment before I began to work to undo the zipper on her skirt. I sat up on my knees and slid her skirt and panties down and over her feet, then threw them to the side. As soon as I had pulled her clothing off, she'd hurriedly crawled to the foot of the bed. As I had done for her, she progressed to slowly pull down my pants and then my underwear — and bit her lip softly when all of me, fully roused, was revealed to her.

She scooted back on the bed, turned over and lay on her stomach. For a moment, I just stood there and watched her, taking in the image of her from behind. Then I followed her to the bed, reached down and moved her hair to one side. I bent down and kissed and ran my tongue along the back of her neck, then up her cheek and again found her mouth. I pulled away and explored her back with my hands and mouth, making my way down to the curve of her back and then to her gorgeous bottom. I licked and kissed my way down the insides of her thighs — in response her breathing increased loudly and half words escaped her mouth. I made my way to the backs of her knees and finally to her feet which I kissed and massaged with my hands.

She turned over again and looked up at me, and the sight of my beautiful, nude dream girl, open and waiting for me, made my heart beat so quickly I nearly became light headed. She was a vision: very feminine, sexy little feet; toned legs and thighs; perfectly proportioned hips and a flat stomach; large, handsome breasts; and a face that could instill hope in the hopeless, framed by long, brown hair that had come down and fallen around her as if it had been styled for a photo shoot.

This time I moved up her body, and again, as I reached her thighs, her head arched back and she softly called my name. I closed my lips and brushed them up and down against her and felt her wetness on them; again, her back arched and she put her leg around my neck. But I hadn't yet finished exploring her so I continued upwards, kissing her stomach, then exploring the sides of her breasts and then brushing my tongue against her nipples.

Then I found her neck and moved to kiss her there. When I did, the positioning of our bodies caused it to happen. Her mouth went wide and we both cried out from the sensation of me moving just inside her. In an act of pure and admirable will, I pulled out and moved down to between her legs and loved her there with my mouth and tongue, lightly brushing her clitoris with them. Her mouth open wide again and her eyes closed tightly, she cried out, gripped the sheets and spasmed, her head outstretched and bent back. I watched her and reveled as she climaxed.

Her breathing slowed and she looked down her body at me and called me to her, beckoning with both hands. I crawled up her body and put my head beside hers. She wrapped her legs around mine and put her hands on my haunches and pulled me to her, inside her. Again we cried out simultaneously. I put my hands underneath her, at her back and on her bottom and together we pulled and made ourselves into one, again and again.

Her hair and skin smelled like lavender: fragrant, sweet and pungent, soft and feminine. Her hair surrounded my face and filled up nearly all of my vision. I felt her breasts pressed against me firmly and her legs holding me willingly captive. And the middle of us at work all the while. I was immersed. The pleasure of it was nearly unbearable and I climaxed. It had, after all, been two years.

She held on with her legs wrapped around me firmly for several minutes; so we lay there, as one, breathing and recovering and holding each other tightly. I could've stayed that way forever. Any descriptive used to depict happiness is inadequate for what I felt, so I won't try.

Eventually, she released me and I turned over onto my back. She lay down on top of me, her head on my chest. I stroked her back and caressed her face. She ran her hands along my chest and stomach and touched me where I was sensitive still.

"So?" she said.

I suddenly roared and then shook from the laughter. After a minute or two, I finally managed control of myself, but a smile was now permanently etched on my face.

"No, seriously, what'd you think?"

"Uh, well . . . ."

"C'mon, how was it? Scale of one to ten?"

"I'm sorry, ten is far too insufficient. I'm thinking in googolplexes."

She laughed and kissed me.

"Thank you. Though I don't want to, I should go."

"Ok, huh, don't you mean I should go?"

"What?

"Never mind. Remembering ancient history."

She sat up on her side of the bed, turned her back to me and began to dress. She turned her head and looked behind her at me and saw that I was watching her dress. She smiled.

"C'mon, get dressed, you can walk me back."

"Ok," I said.

I sat up, facing away from her, and pulled on my pants, the only article of clothing within reach of the bed.

"I wonder why none of my other birthdays were ever this spectacular?" I asked. "Oh, it must have been the lovemaking with an incredibly beautiful woman, that's what was missing."

I turned to look at her, wanting to see her smile again. Instead, what I got was another of those snapshots in one's life, images that are imprinted, more precisely burned, into one's psyche forever.

Her face was twisted into something malicious and altogether wrong for my girl. Oceans of tears streamed down her face and their mass exodus had suddenly caused the skin around her eyes to puff up into dark bags, a sight I could have never imagined for her. Her hand was raised into the air but was speeding at me in a downwards spiral; and in it was a long, serrated attack knife, that actually gleamed the way you see them do in movies.

I remember how, like you might see in a National Geographic photo or the cover of a magazine like People or Time, only the principal subject, centered in the photo, was clear and everything outside it was blurry and completely out of focus, thus dramatizing the intended object of attention. This was how I saw her then. Or at least that's how I remember it. I also remember that, for just a millisecond, I could not believe my eyes, or perhaps more accurately, my heart would not believe my eyes, and something deep in me told me to trust her. But instinct that had been honed over the course of two years, every single day of those two years, mutinied. Control of my extremities was usurped from my heart by that instinct and it took command in response to the apparent threat on my life.

I ducked underneath her as she plunged at me and fell to my back onto the bed. I caught her knife hand with both of my hands and wrapped them around her wrist, stopping the descent of the blade six inches from my face. She put her other hand on top of the knife and tried to push downwards. For just a millisecond, I looked up into her face and tried to access her eyes, but the woman I'd known and just made love to was inexplicably absent. That woman had disappeared. I pushed back and slowly managed to overpower her, the blade moving further away from me.

Having established control over the wrist holding the blade, I removed my left hand, wound it back towards my right shoulder, clenched my hand into a fist, then simultaneously lowered her wrist with my left and with all my strength backhanded her with my right. The sound of my hand connecting with her beautiful face made me want to be sick. She was catapulted over the foot of the bed and landed on her butt. I got to my feet and she did the same just as quickly, knife still in hand. She put her hand to her face and touched it where I'd hit her. I was clueless and distraught.

"Selena, what are you doing?" I whispered.

I didn't like her answer. She closed her mouth, resolute, and attacked. She held the knife in the manner of one whom has real knowledge of how to use it and that scared me. Incredibly, not because I feared for my own safety, but for hers. The more capable she was, the more possible that I might have to kill her to end the fight.

The knife itself isn't what you defend against; it's the arm that holds it and the body language that betrays where your attacker will strike next. She held the knife in her right hand, and she came at me with a downwards slash from the left side of her body. Again, my focus was on her arm. I put up my forearm and blocked the motion of it, slid my arm down, grabbed her forearm, twisted my waist, stepped back and threw her behind me. She went down, tucked, rolled and turned, back at the ready.

She turned the knife over in her hand and held it blade up instead of sideways as she had, and charged. She lunged at me and I jumped backwards, the blade passing inches before my stomach. Again she struck out at me, and again I evaded. And again. And again. I'd hoped that by avoiding her thus, she'd tire and I could then disarm her easily. But with every new attack, the force behind it matched its predecessor and her face showed no signs of tiring. I decided I was no longer left with any choice. I deflected her attack for the last time and waited for her to try again. When she did, when she got within an arm's length, I let her have it. I twirled and hit her with a vicious whip-kick that impacted with her face and spun her head sickly. She let out a scream of surprise and pain and flew into the wall, dropping the knife to the ground. Moaning, miraculously still conscious, she fell to her butt.

Never taking my eyes from her, I picked up the knife and stood in front of her. I bent down and looked her in the eyes. When I put the knife to her throat, her eyes opened wide and she put her head back against the wall.

"Why?"

"Orders."

"Orders? Whose . . . ?"

Deep cold filled me as the obvious finally became clear. I was betrayed by my own lack of foresight. I expected the voice before it even came.

"Mine."

I removed the knife from Selena's throat, stood and backed away from her. My eyes fixed on a faraway point in the back of the room. I heard the sound of metal hitting the floor and looked down. The knife had fallen from my hand. From the corner of my eye, I saw Selena stand. She gathered her clothes and left.

"You did well."

His voice came from the doorway. My back was turned to him and I saw no reason to look at him.

"What could you possibly be talking about?" I said, more than asked.

"Nicholas, it was a test. An assessment of your skills, as well as a very important lesson that must be learned early in this business. If you survive, you pass. Simple."

Without turning I backed up to the bed, sat down and lowered my head, trying to hide the fact that I'd suddenly lost all the strength in my legs.

"It's a hard thing. But necessary. You'll come to understand, believe me. Betrayal by those you trust is a simple fact of life for us. You must expect it rather than be blindsided by it. Your every choice, every maneuver you make regarding others, must incorporate a general mistrust of their motives. To be honest, Selena was the obvious choice; you should have seen this coming.

"So this is how you choose to share your knowledge?" I asked, still without looking at him.

"This, my boy, as I saw it, was the most effective way to assure that you would never forget this very valuable lesson. Just consider it another lesson learned. I'll see you tomorrow, Mr. Gambit."

"Yes, you will," I said to myself. Then out loud so that he could hear me, "Wilkes. You and I, we have some matters to discuss. And when it's over, you will be held accountable."

There was a long pause and I thought that he might have left already. Then he spoke and I knew that he'd just been deliberating his reply.

"How dramatic of you, Mr. Gambit. Was the trim that good, that she now compels you to take leave of your better judgment?"

I could almost see the warped smile his face must have contorted into. He grunted derisively, then left the room, closing the door behind him.

CHAPTER 32

As I've said before, in combat situations at least, clarity of mind was something I had in generous supply. As if by divine intervention, a crystal clear course of action to deliver me from danger, was usually obvious and accessible. In time, I came to understand it as a complement to, maybe an integral component of, that unusual sense that allowed me to see how someone was going to move before they did it, to prophesize certain events. I *thought* that this was one of those times — explicit, perfect clarity about what I must do. I had been patient long enough. It was time for Wilkes to pay up for his misdeeds.

It was the morning after Selena broke my heart. I walked down the hallway coolly, intent on belying none of my intentions to passers-by. I wanted no one to try and prevent me from obtaining justice.

When I thought about it, I had to admit HE'd played me masterfully. I'd stayed awake all night wondering how long HE'd planned it. I turned a corner. From the beginning perhaps? How many times had he and Selena prepared for that very night? After HE'd left, I looked underneath my rack and found the sheath that must have held the knife Selena used to betray me. Clearly, she didn't have it on her when we made love. HE'd put it there while we were in the commissary and she had plucked it from their hiding place at just the right time, because they'd planned it all.

The conversations they must have had. They'd had to have laughed themselves rotten every time they anticipated the look of pain and betrayal on my face. Perhaps they'd even had sex, excited to intercourse by the fact that they would, together, be responsible for the demise of my capacity to trust anyone ever again.

But mostly, I just felt silly. I marveled at how quickly I'd thrown myself at the opportunity to be humiliated by him. You see, I blamed myself wholly for that fiasco. I turned another corner. It wasn't Wilkes' fault, nor Selena's. Oh, but she was quite the thespian. But no, ultimately the entire turn of events was due to a lack of control over my very own juvenile, reckless desires. HE was right about that part. I still went blind every time I smelled pussy and it would have gotten me killed on a real operation. But that was where his being right stopped. And I wanted to show him how wrong he was in front of everyone.

I made my last turn and came up on a door. I pulled it open and stepped inside into the gymnastics/tumbling area. As usual in the morning, the room was filled with people exercising, working out on the mats. Some were sparring.

I located him immediately, talking to two other men, so I turned to come up behind him. As soon as I reached striking distance I threw a hard jab, right into the middle of his lower back. He crumpled like a beer can that's just been stepped on. His acquaintances were . . . surprised would be an understatement. They just didn't know what to do. I stood at the ready in case they decided to try and defend him. Of course the rest of the room abruptly halted all activity as well. It didn't take him long to recover. He stood with a look on his face that was a comical mixture of pain and surprise. That tends to happen when you've just been bushwhacked.

"Gambit! What are you doing?"

"What, can't take a little of your own medicine, Wilkes? Don't you see? It's a test. If you survive . . . well you know the rest."

I leapt into the air with a full kick and every intention of taking the man's head off. Wilkes ducked and my foot flew over him. As I turned from the kick to face him again, I noticed several of the others in the room circling us, preparing to move in to stop me. Wilkes put his hand out to prevent them from interfering. He turned to me.

"This ends now!" he said.

"You killed her you son of a bitch!" I yelled at the top of my lungs.

"What the fuck are you talking about?"

"I got you all figured out Wilkes."

"Do you now? Well, by all means, please clue me in because I seem to be lost."

"You wanted me bad didn't you? Bad enough to kill. Bad enough to take her from me. You had time. You had time to evaluate me, get somebody over to my house before I got home and then use her death to get my loyalty. I don't know who those people were in that house that night but they weren't the ones that killed her. They couldn't have been. You did it you sick piece of TRASH!"

Yelling, I attacked again with renewed vigor. I threw punches and he deflected them. Jabs missed their mark. Kicks were blocked or simply connected with nothing. Wilkes was more skilled than I'd anticipated; and his skills were quickly emerging as superior to my own. Of course, he was already quite aware of this, and, as we fought, the smallest hint of a smile began to appear on his face. He was smiling at me, in the middle of a fight from which I sought some kind of justice for my mother. What an ass. That was the last thing he should have done.

Another lesson was learned. My gift was less effective when corrupted by intense emotion, as are most things. Wilkes had proven that perfectly with Selena. So, instead of letting him smile at me and make me the more angry and out of control, I shifted gears, calmed myself and let the talent I had guide me. I threw another punch, but this time anticipated the block. I stopped the throw short and instead grabbed his wrist and pulled him to me, then hit him with a one-two to the gut and jaw. I decided to stay close and change my approach completely.

I assumed a boxer's stance and proceeded to challenge his Bruce Lee with my Muhammed Ali. Jab, jab, combination - all connected, to his extreme surprise. I stayed close to allow him no leverage and hit him with a barrage of crosses to his face and close punches to the stomach. He recovered quickly, though he was beginning to bruise, and threw a left to my mouth that connected, then a shoot fighter's kick to my side that hurt. Luckily, that move kept him close and prevented him from backing away in time to keep me at bay. So, undaunted by the pain in my side, I stepped in again and threw another one-two that missed completely. But the uppercut didn't. It caught him square in his jaw and he went down.

He sat down on his butt and looked at me lazily. He put his arm out in front of him and waved, signaling there was to be no more. I had no intentions whatsoever, of allowing him to rise again without being knocked back down. They would have to pull me off of him as far as I was concerned. So I waited.

His eyes began to focus and he looked at me and smiled, which was the last thing I expected him to do. He smiled and looked *pleased,* impressed even.

"I did not kill your mother. But I can help you find out who did."

"Why should I believe you?" I snorted back at him.

"I'll show you." He shook his head. "By God, you are more than I'd hoped for."

He stuck out his hand. I'd been watching his eyes. There was no uncertainty, no concealment behind them as he spoke. I was surprised and confused but I couldn't deny the obvious. He was telling the truth. I took his hand and pulled him to his feet.

We walked to his office. On the way, he further provided evidence of his innocence by muttering to himself under his breath about me and about how they, whoever "they" was, would be impressed with what he'd done with this project and the kind of super soldier he was processing. He talked like we were parts on a Japanese sedan being spat out of a factory. I knew that even Wilkes would not be calmly reviewing, to himself, how spectacularly I'd demonstrated my abilities on the way to an office where it would be just the two of us, if he was indeed guilty of what I'd accused him.

Once in his office, Wilkes pulled my file and sat at his desk. I stood in front of his desk as he perused the file. I quickly became impatient.

"So, then, the only other possibility is that someone else was contracted by some agency to kill her. That type of entrance wound could have only been caused by a Reicher assault rifle."

"Wrong. I'm looking at the autopsy reports I ordered. That weapon does cause that type of wound but not exclusively. From the photographs we determined that unique wound could be caused by three weapons capable of firing that type of round, one of which is the Reicher. The other two are currently, and were at the time of your mother's death, available to the public as an assault weapon."

He turned the file around so I could see it, then sat back in his chair and looked at me triumphantly.

"Oh." That was all I could manage.

"So you see, Nicholas, that little exhibition back there was all for naught."

I was beginning to be damned embarrassed. I'd based the last six months of my life on a hatred for this man, all derived from circumstantial evidence that was now proving to be worthless. Every night I dreamed of confronting him, but didn't. As a matter of fact, I'd even praised myself for instead wisely biding my time. But. All the pieces weren't quite back into place.

"Wait a minute. When did you get that police report?"

"Couple of hours after the murder."

"So those people in that house on fifth owned one of those weapons?"

"Ah."

"Ah? Ah what? You didn't butcher those people just to get me to come here, did you? Because if you did, that's almost as bad as killing my mother for the same reason."

"They were all under suspicion of murder. Not your mother's murder, but another. I had surveillance reports to clearly imply that they did it. We just sort of intervened on the courts behalf, without its knowledge. In the end, justice was done. That's what's important."

"How is it our place to decide . . . you *did* kill them to get me to come here."

"You sure didn't seem to mind that night when you thought it was your mother they had killed."

He was right. I hated it, but it was true. It had never occurred to me to question him about snuffing out those men's lives when it had been on my behalf.

"Yeah, yeah," he said. "I'll see if anything's come up since then in relation to your mother's death."

He threw another file across his desk at me.

"That's your first assignment. Read it and be at the briefing tomorrow. Zero eight."

I was shocked.

"Yes sir."

I took the file and simply left the room.

CHAPTER 33

I studied the dossier again and again though it wasn't necessary. It was a simple matter. I was to follow the man whose picture and address were included in the document, one Victor Passage, for the entire day and report his movements. No reasons were given, no special instructions. Just follow him.

Then I allowed myself some speculation about what exactly had happened with Wilkes. I certainly felt no remorse. Though I'd been mistaken about his role in her death, I still remained completely unapologetic. The mind games, the half-truths — they just weren't my style. Of course, I realized that was a simplistic and unrealistic approach, especially in this business, but there was always more to it with him.

As with most fanatics, he was so good at being unscrupulous and selling it to you as unfortunate yet still necessary, that at times it became difficult to pinpoint exactly where extreme dedication stopped and just plain old-fashioned evil began. But there was no mistaking that evil was laying in wait for when he deemed it useful. Whenever he was forced to commit acts that some might find unethical, he'd feel completely justified. The freedoms endowed by a lack of conscience were undeniable.

And, of course, there were thoughts of Selena. I dared not ask about her, however, in fear that I might expose my feelings again. I had finally begun to realize how adept the man was at manipulating people's emotions. I wasn't ready to go there with him yet, not on that subject.

I was surprised however, at how refreshed I felt as a result of our encounter that morning. I suppose I had finally exorcised a lot of the malevolent energy that had accumulated over the past six months by giving it form — in other words, trying to take Wilkes' head off. And oddly, the two experiences, Selena and the fight with Wilkes, had deposited within me a feeling of self-indulgent and extreme . . . cockiness. For the first time in my life, I really felt like some special kind of badass.

The experience taught me something else too. I learned how dark a place one can live in when they are consumed by hatred and the need for revenge. And I promised myself I would never go there again. Never live like that again.

The next morning, I checked out a black Lincoln, a Reicher pistol, and three clips with ammo. After a short briefing in Wilkes' office I was on my way. He told me nothing more than had been provided in the dossier. There was a particularly steely look to his eyes that told me to ask no questions. Considering this was my very first assignment, I quelled the rebellious impulse to ask anyway. Not that the contest of wills with Wilkes was over, this I saw. We were heading towards some kind of climactic event. There was no way around it. It was becoming more obvious as each day, each conflict arose, that I would not be able to just fall in line and become what he wanted me to. It just wasn't in me to be that way. My mother said it long ago and I hadn't understood at the time. "Righteousness," she'd said. I'd always thought that word painted a picture of arrogance that I didn't want to resemble, as in "righteous indignation." But that wasn't what she'd meant.

I finally understood that to her, it was a way of describing those who have within them an instinctive maneuverability between issues of right and wrong. It was different than simple religious conviction. It was insight that flowed from within and always overcame circumstance, even circumstance that included being a recently graduated super soldier indentured to an unbalanced people killer like Wilkes.

I knew that I wasn't helping the situation any by letting myself be guided by my distaste for the man. Nor was I ignorant of the fact that this person killed other people for a living, and was backed by the U.S. government to do so. And though it didn't make sense to try and fight him and all his resources, I felt that it was something that must come — a confrontation between us. But there would be a time and place for me to further distance myself from Wilkes' fanaticism. This was not it. First, I had a mystery in the form of one Victor Passage to decipher.

I punched the address into the GPS and after three hours on the freeway, found myself in Bel-Air looking at a large, box-shaped Victorian style house painted white with windows that were arranged in fours and covered the entire front of the house.

So as not to be seen, I parked nearly a quarter of a mile away on a street that intersected with another that ran in front of the house. Looking through my windshield, I watched it through a black iron gate that opened up onto a circular driveway that ran in front of the house.

This Victor Passage, whom I knew nothing about except his appearance, apparently had money, and lots of it, or was staying with someone who did. My only instructions were to sit on the house and if he left to tail him; I was to absolutely not, under any circumstances, make contact with him.

"Reconnaissance, report, Nicholas. Reconnaissance, report, nothing more," Wilkes had said.

And so, I sat for hours in front of that house and collected some very important intel, mainly on how many Mercedes-Benzes versus Jaguars drove in front of me.

As is the case with most people when they're bored, the mind wanders into certain areas and subjects. My mind was as disciplined as they came; still, it was no match for my heart. And though I tried and made great effort to keep myself away from it, I couldn't help but think of her.

I hadn't seen Selena in the building since that night. I'd passed by the classroom where we'd spent so much time together and that served, in my memory, as the place where I'd fallen madly for her. Of course she wasn't there. Nor had I seen her anywhere in the hallways or the commissary. Wilkes would have made arrangements for her to be absent until I left the building. Considering that I was on my first field assignment, I expected that wouldn't be too long.

But I'd been kidding myself. Of course I thought of her. I obsessed over her. My feelings for her were inextricably woven into every thought that passed through my feeble, love swollen mind since the night we'd been together. The anger I'd felt initially had finally evaporated, and now two days old, the memory was still every bit as psychotropic as if it happened minutes prior. I couldn't help but wonder if she might be thinking of me, at that moment, as I was thinking about her. Could she? Could she be at her home, wherever that was, feeling confused and hurt? Remembering how perfect it was that night? Maybe hoping we'd have the opportunity to see each other again and achieve some kind of closure?

"Just stop it," I told myself. "Idiot. She used you. It was a game to her. She doesn't want anything to do with you anymore. Sure, the sexual pleasure was probably real, but everything else was just work to her. She sunk your battleship, homie. Face it. You got played, *again*, by the best in probably the whole world. A real professional. You're used to hearing girls talk about how they always get shit on by guys. First chance you get, you go to the hair salon and tell them ladies some of *your* stories. Twenty-six years old and already, oh, what a life you've lead."

But.

I was thinking what anybody would be thinking, "Oh, come on, give it up already. You gotta let her go. Move on with your life." Or, maybe not. That maybe there *was* something there. You see, that's where I got stuck. There were times in that classroom, over the course of that year we spent together. There were things that occurred that night we were together; I guess I was just beginning to have trouble with the idea that they were all manufactured and insincere. And there were so many other things. The way her eyes clouded over completely when we'd come into accidental contact with each other and I felt something from deep inside her call out to me. That day we'd first met in Genai's dojo, she'd looked into me and not at me. The way she couldn't bear to look at me sometimes at all and when she did finally, there were barely discernible tears in her eyes. So many things. So many things that you just don't think could be part of a front like the one she'd perpetrated and I just couldn't get around. Once again, no surprise. Nicholas Gambit. Forever clueless in all things.

Movement extracted my attention and forced it to focus on the task at hand. The black gate was opening, sliding from right to left to allow someone to leave. I removed a pair of binoculars from their case and looked at the front door of the house. It was my target. He closed the door behind him and walked to a black Jeep parked on the drive. He carried a briefcase, but was dressed casually, wearing slacks and a white dress shirt minus a tie. The shirt was unbuttoned even, down to the third button from the top. He was not a very large man. I guessed at 5'8", caucasian and balding, starting from the hair line. He did not look to be exceptionally out of shape, with broad shoulders and a small waist with just a bit of a potbelly.

He pulled out of the driveway and down the street. Due to the many curves to the streets in Bel-Air, I didn't let him get another quarter mile away before I pulled out onto the street behind him, not wanting to lose my visual. I followed him out of Bel-Air and into what the GPS told me was Hollywood, down into the city, then West L.A., and finally to Santa Monica. Eventually, he entered an underground parking garage and entered it. I pulled up in front of the attendant and asked him how you exited the garage. He said there was just the one way out and that was through the front entrance. I thanked him and drove ahead, made a u-turn and pulled the Lincoln into a spot on the street. I got out, punched a button on the GPS that would remember this location, fed the meter and waited for Passage.

A few minutes passed and I began to worry that there perhaps was another exit from the garage after all. I was debating going into the garage to see if I could locate him, when he finally showed. I breathed a sigh of relief, turned my back to him and slyly watched him over my shoulder. I let him get nearly to the end of the block before I began walking. I intended to watch him from across the street, but stayed a good twenty paces behind him. He crossed at the light and I did the same a few seconds later, entering some kind of retail district.

On each side were strip malls, much like the ones back home where we'd had the confrontation with Smalls and his gang. These were much more stylish, and more expensive, of that I was assured. I looked ahead of us and was grateful that the foot traffic along this promenade was light and I could afford to maintain some distance between us without losing him. I looked around, breathed in the ocean air, noticed how good-looking everyone was and realized we were probably only a couple of hundred feet from the beach.

I'd been taught to never just watch a tail, just check up on them. So, every couple of seconds, I casually looked to my right to keep tabs on him and pinpoint his location relative to my own. I didn't want to out or under-pace him. Passage stopped and turned into a video shop, so I looked to my left and did the same, entering a jewelry store. I watched the shop he'd gone into through the window, pulled out a pad of paper and noted the name of it.

Soon, I could no longer see him moving about inside the shop and lost visual contact, but didn't dare cross the street and follow him inside; so I had no choice but to wait. I turned and looked around the store I was in. It was a relatively large jewelry store, and busy. At least nine patrons walked around, looking into glass counters that were raised from the floor. Three employees stood behind these jewelry cases and one woman walked the floor, greeting customers. As soon as I'd entered she'd noticed me.

"May I help you with anything, sir?"

I looked at her and noticed her to be a striking young black lady.

"Uh, no, thank you. Just looking."

"Well, you just let me know if you need anything."

I smiled. "I'll do that. Thank you."

She turned and walked away and I returned my attention to the store across the street until my attention was diverted yet again. A man had walked up on the other side of the window and was now looking in, his eyes flirting about erratically, inarticulately surveying the inside of the store.

When our eyes met, his gaze focused in on me, as if my being there gave him pause, which caused my internal alarm to wail. I stared back at him, already assuming he was up to no good, but of what kind I was still undecided. I'd noticed already that there were a number of vagrants and homeless in the area, despite its affluence. It was possible he was just another of those that roamed the area aimlessly during the day and slept on the concrete sidewalks when the shops shut down at night. But there was more.

You learn in combat, that being in close proximity to an enemy is often preferable to the alternative. You can reach them much sooner if they misbehave; you are the first to recognize their intent and therefore have the opportunity to be the first to react. So I decided not to move from my spot. I quickly scanned him from top to bottom. He returned my stare with bloodshot, dilated eyes. But there was nothing to those eyes; they were vacant, soulless. He wore a dirty, abused trench coat that was tied closed and was weighted down by something, demonstrated by a bulging and what looked like something pulling down on areas where pockets might have been. He held a duffel bag by the straps. The pieces were beginning to fit into the puzzle, but it wasn't until he reached into that bag and pulled out a mask that I remembered the news report and turned to run.

"Get down! Everybody get down!"

I located a counter against the far wall that was constructed slightly differently than the others and made for it, this one built with the lower three feet made of metal. The saleswoman who'd spoken to me stood at it and turned at the sound of my shouting as I ran in her direction. That's when the firing began. Automatic weapons fire rattled off behind me, coming through the window I'd stood at moments earlier.

Most of the people inside, upon hearing my yelling, had seen him and dropped, but others moved too slowly and were felled, flung backwards and into the air by the miniature-missiles being erupted from what sounded as loud as a machine gun.

The woman ran around the counter and threw herself to the ground. I dove over the top of the counter, landed beside her and scooted back against it to use the metal as cover. As the gunman stepped through the now obliterated window, he fired ahead of him into what was left of the glass casing guarding the diamonds and jewels on that wall, completely destroying it and leaving the jewels accessible. He unloaded his entire magazine into the glass and was unmoved by the tormented cries of pain from the people he hit in the process. Screams came from everywhere, inside the store and out.

"What are we going to do?" the saleswoman whispered to me, crying.

I looked over the top of the counter and saw the man reaching into his bag, presumably for another magazine. I only had a few seconds. But that was plenty of time. He was only a few feet away. I lived for this stuff now. I turned to the woman beside me, I suppose with the intention of being perceived as gallant, and nodded my head.

"Excuse me."

I leapt into the air. In one motion I landed in a handstand on the countertop, completed the flip, landed in front of the counter on my feet and at a full run towards the man, causing him to raise his head at me. He'd just pulled the magazine out of the duffel. He inserted the magazine, chambered the first round, raised the weapon and pointed it at me . . . and pulled the trigger. I dropped and rolled, never losing my momentum. The bullets meant for me instead riddled the wall behind me. I came up from the roll and with one hand deflected the weapon upwards and with the other hand slammed the man in the chest plate with an opened palm, sending him staggering backwards but not to the ground. I stepped forward, spun and whipped a left elbow into the man's head, and with my right hand grabbed the weapon from him as he fell. The fact that he was unconscious before he hit the ground was visible in how his head collided with the floor.

I looked around at the dead and injured. Eyes rolled back into their sockets from shock. It looked like someone had violently swung a bucket of red paint, leaving splotches of red covering the inside of the store. People reached out and grasped at nothingness, crying for help. The few who were unhit stood and sort of fell about languorously, unsure of what they should do next.

"My God."

It was the saleswoman, standing now, behind the counter, understandably shaken. She was trembling, surveying the destruction, observing that some of her coworkers now lay sprawled on the floor, lifeless and unmoving. I took a few steps toward her.

"Call the police. Tell them people are down, you're going to need several ambulances." I wanted to stay and help them, but I couldn't allow myself to be found there. And there wasn't much I could do for them in the short period of time I had.

"Ok," she said, still tremulous.

I dropped the weapon and headed for the door.

"Wait. Don't go. I need your help."

"I'm sorry, I can't," I said, without slowing.

"At least tell me your name!" she called.

This time I stopped. I looked back at her and almost said something. I don't know what I would have said and now recall the gesture as pointless. Quickly I regained control of my senses and fled through the door, never looked back in the direction of that shop and didn't stop running until I found my black Lincoln and drove calmly away from there.

CHAPTER 34

"Dammit Nicholas! Nicholas what were you thinking?"

As you can tell, Wilkes was quite angry.

"What was I supposed to do, let him kill all those people?"

"Yes! If necessary! Nicholas, your only interest should be in completing your assignment, nothing more, nothing less. I know it must seem cold. But you must realize that no matter how mundane, how completely irrelevant some of your assignments might seem, they very often are integral parts of much, much larger issues. The big picture Nicholas. And the big picture means hundreds of thousands of people, not . . . ten, or whatever it was."

"I'm sorry," I said.

"Son, I realize you were thinking with your heart and not your head. And I don't blame you for that. From the beginning, part of our intent here has been not to turn men into machines like some agencies do. The notion that emotionless droids are better suited for field work than feeling, thinking men is absurd. I actually value unpredictability."

That was a load of crap. He was angling for something. I didn't know what yet. I did think it odd how much he wanted me on this case with Passage, though. He made it out to be of such importance. So why choose me, a boot? Granted, I may have been the best he had in town, but still.

"And if there is one thing that you have proven to me over and over again, it's that you're no heartless, predictable killer."

He looked at me like he expected me to thank him for being so considerate of my feelings. I thought I'd take this conversation in a direction he wouldn't like, just for kicks.

"Does that mean that you're not going to ask me to term anyone?"

He smiled an arrogant, unsurprised smile.

"Probably not. I have access to other sectors that can handle simple neutralization duties."

"Hmh," I said. "What sector was it that *neutralized* those people back in my neighborhood?"

He laughed.

"Oh, Nicholas. Again you prove my point. You feel guilty about that. And although I value emotions, they must always be kept under control. Lest they get in the way, cloud your thinking, and get you killed. Tell me that doesn't make sense."

"I agree." That I actually did agree with.

"Good---"

"May I make an observation?"

"Of course." He sat down on the edge of his desk, put his hands in his lap and looked up at me, pretending to be interested.

"Not a threat and please do not take it as such. But the emotion and unpredictability you claim to value, take care. Because these two things could be your downfall. Their combination might just cause one to bite the hand that feeds it, so to speak. Like I said, just . . . just a thought."

Controlled rage, or the effort to control one's rage, can be a great deal of fun to watch in action if you pick the right subject. I thought he might spring forward any second and attack. I don't know why I said it, or at least I don't know why I had to say it to him, but I did. The urge was overwhelming. I still couldn't understand it, but I was finding myself more and more at odds with him. And it wasn't just the thing with Selena. Every part of me said not to trust him and it was too powerful to be ignored. I was relatively sure he would not be able to speak without screaming at the top of his lungs, so I decided to redirect our conversation back to the previous topic.

"Even with the incident, I don't believe Victor Passage ever made me as a tail. I'll resume surveillance in the morning if that is acceptable."

"Do," he said, miraculously, without actually opening his mouth.

"Yessir." I stifled a smirk and turned to leave the room.

"Oh, Nicholas, I have something for you." He walked around his desk and picked up a file. "Here's all the information on your mother's death."

My surprise prevented my legs from moving and my mouth from opening momentarily. I gathered myself, then walked back to his desk. I took the file and opened it.

"The man who ordered your mother's death is one Louis Rayes, but you would remember him simply as Ray Ray. Apparently, he did it on Raymond Small's recommendation. Of course, you already took care of him. His power, Ray Ray's that is, has increased at least tenfold since then. It seems that you and your gang war, and consequentially Kato's death and your sudden disappearance made him quite a reputation. He's got more power than a lot of mafia dons. As you'll see in the file, he even purchased himself a personal compound, which incidentally is here in state. It's near Oakland."

"You're kidding," I said.

"I guess he decided about six months ago that due to some serious competition that entered his turf, it would be a good idea for him to move to the West Coast and run his operation from here. I'm sure he has some wildly inadvisable aspirations to move into the local market eventually as well. Now, this compound is heavily guarded. Which means he's going to be hard to get to. You have until morning to do what you have to do. Then I want you back on assignment. Understood?"

"Absolutely, uh, uh, yessir." I was still very surprised at this development.

"Good luck, soldier. Don't get killed. I have plans for you."

That statement provided composure.

"Thanks for the pep talk. Oh, uh, do I need to do a weapons requisition?"

"No, don't worry about it. I'll call down there. He'll be waiting for you."

"Thank you," I said, completely unsure of how to assess this gesture from this man who gave new meaning to "forked tongue pale face," but I could not help but be grateful. "I mean it," I said.

"You got it," he said, genuinely sincere.

You see, that wasn't the problem with Wilkes. He was seldom to appear discompassionate and usually very . . . polite. But from what I hear, so was Jeffrey Dahmer.

I walked back to my quarters and read the file along the way. I should have guessed it then. Smalls would have never had the organizational skills to get into my house, harm her and escape completely unseen the way my mother's murderers had. He would have needed some serious help. And the only help he had at the time was Ray Ray and his people. It all finally made sense.

I changed into black utility fatigues, grabbed my duffel and took the elevator down to W.A.S. — weapons and artillery storage. The elevator door opened into a room that was completely dark except for a strobe light high up in a corner of the room, there for effect more than anything considering it provided virtually no consistent illumination to the room. Among the first few lessons provided after your arrival into Noble was instruction on how to proceed from there.

This first room was where they scanned you. X-ray, heat signature, infrared, metal detecting equipment, any way of detecting whether you were walking into that room and carrying was utilized. And if you didn't have a key card on you that the computers could access and read from a remote scanner embedded somewhere in the walls, with every single one of the weapons you had on your person already written onto it by Rusty when you checked them out, well, I shudder to imagine what would have happened and where your body parts would be disposed of.

I walked in a straight line from the door and after ten paces reached out and felt for the wall. When my hand finally encountered it, I searched for the panel and put my hand on it. A high pitched sound that I always compared to that of a cat's meow resonated from everywhere, signifying my handprint had been recognized by the system. A voice came over the loudspeaker.

"Hi, Nicholas."

"Rusty," I said.

I asked him once, after I'd been in for only a few months, if that was his real name. He'd told me to try and rationalize him working in a place like this and telling people his real name, thus clarifying I was nothing more than another "green" with no knowledge of how things worked in this business.

The wall before me parted in two, sliding open and an entrance into the next chamber was made available. I stepped through. Rusty sat behind a plexi-glass partition and waved at me. Beside the partition was a revolving dumbwaiter that transported the weapons from inside his compartment to the waiting soldiers.

He was an affable, quiet, older gentleman. Not the type that you would expect to work in a place like this. But I'd learned in my two years at The Building to never stereotype anyone based on their profession or appearance. I'd met gruff and muscle-bound men that stood at 6'7" and worked as computer programmers, savants that left the impression of being mentally handicapped but could build a long-range telecommunications device from car parts, and lanky weaklings *I* would hesitate to step into the ring with.

"I heard about your little fight with Wilkes. How come you're still up and walking around? And even being allowed to go off on private missions after sundown? What you got on him?"

That was a good question. And it was one I should have been considering beforehand. Furthermore, it was a question I didn't have an answer for. In most military organizations, attacking a superior officer like that would mean an immediate asswhooping and then major brig time. True, this was no ordinary organization and the decision whether or not to punish me would ultimately have been Wilkes' alone, but surely he didn't intend to just forget all about it.

Apparently, seeing that I was deliberating his question with such distraction, Rusty surmised I would have nothing to do with it and decided to ask another.

"So, are you going to wreak havoc on those who oppress the hopeless and the infirm, to deliver justice onto whosoever might try and combat all that's good and right and just and American?"

"I'm going to kill a drug dealer."

"Cool. What do you need?"

"How much time you got?"

"Ooh, I'm already starting to love it when you come down here, Gambit. There'll be stories to tell tomorrow."

CHAPTER 35

I pulled the 88Occ Honda up to a curb and stopped across the street, making sure I was still within earshot of the two guards posted at the entrance to the compound. The file on Ray Ray provided a general layout of the compound, but I thought it best to know as much about the terrain as time allowed, so I'd already circled the compound twice to get a good look at it from the outside. It was at least a couple of square miles in width and surrounded by a stone wall, which prevented me from getting a good view inside that wall. I could see that trees grew well above the walls and were throughout the estate, which would allow me some cover once I got inside. Night had fallen and that would be helpful as well.

The second time I'd passed by the two, they'd taken notice. Now seeing me for the third time, they were undoubtedly on edge and had stepped out of the warmth of their booth to investigate. One black, one white, they both wore heavy jackets, gloves, and caps to keep their hands and heads warm, causing me, for the first time, to acknowledge the chill to the night. Perhaps it was the Gore-Tex combat vest I wore. But I think it more likely that there was a fire burning inside me that would require more than a brisk California evening to extinguish.

I shut off the motorcycle, pulled out the key, rose off the bike, and faced them.

"Who the fuck is that?" I heard the black one say.

I turned around and reached into the duffel laced onto the seat and pulled out a Reicher assault rifle, a sniper's rifle, and then proceeded to pretend to inspect them. Of course they'd been loaded and chambered before I left. This was all for show. Then, I pulled out a waist holster and clamped it to a belt like, revolving disk I'd already installed on my waist. The disk allowed the holster belt to be rotated, allowing you to change which weapon you had at your preferred shooting hand. The holsters were connected by strong velcro so if you did have to make a change, you could just rotate the belt, remove the holsters with the weapons inside, and replace them facing in the right direction.

"This motherfucker has got to be crazy." The white guard.

I opened a storage compartment of the motorcycle, pulled out an airgun and a pistol and holstered them into the belt on my waist, the airgun to my right, thinking I would need it first. I closed the bag and slung it around my neck and again turned and looked at them. And smiled.

The white guard turned to the other man. "Man, you better radio this in."

"Fuck that! Man, I'll take care of this mufucker if you scared."

"Man, radio it in!"

The black one swore something under his breath and went into the booth and picked up a radio. That was my cue. I wanted him to know I was coming for him. I walked directly towards the entrance, as if I intended to ignore them and admit myself into the compound. The white guard opened his jacket and put his hand on the weapon at his waist and stepped into my path.

"Man, you fucking stay right there or I'll shoot your black ass."

I raised my hands into the air. "Whatever you say, boss. I'm just here to talk to Ray Ray."

The black one stepped out of the booth. "What kind of business you got wit Ray Ray, nigga?"

"Well . . . I came to kill him."

Just as their eyes were going wide, I grabbed the one in front of me and pulled him to me with all my strength, dropped my head and let the crown of it collide with his face. I wrapped my left arm around his neck, holding him up in front of me, and pulled the dart gun from its holster. The black guard had raised his weapon and pointed it at us, but had no clear shot as I'd anticipated. By the time it occurred to him to run, and turned to do so, the knockout dart had already lodged itself between his eyes, quite accidentally. I didn't know what kind of effect such a strong sedative would have on someone when injected directly into the brain, and I'd hoped to be able to avoid having to kill any of Ray Ray's people. I watched him collapse, then fired another dart into his comrade, watching him go unconscious as well. I walked through the entrance into the compound otherwise unmolested.

Ray Ray's compound was very picturesque. It resembled the forest that surrounded The Building, except in smaller detail.

"This to my advantage, the familiar terrain," I thought.

I immediately walked away from the winding drive that led up to the mansion. The mansion itself was not visible from the entrance and, after I entered the gates, I couldn't help but be somewhat impressed with the layout and the privacy it was supposed to afford its resident. Supposed to.

As I'd hoped, large trees and bushes were indeed plentiful and I intended to put them to use. I'd made my way into the woods only about 25 yards from the drive when I heard a car race by. I dropped to my knees and listened as the car came to a screeching halt at the entrance, then I heard the sound of doors opening and shutting. They would be seeing their downed compatriots anytime now. I couldn't see them through the trees but I was surprised by how well the sounds carried back to me.

"Fuuuccckk! You better get me Ray Ray."

A voice came over the radio.

"What!"

"Yo man, what we got here is a fucking breach of security. And he's headed towards the . . . house---"

He was interrupted by Ray Ray's screams before he could finish.

"No shit you fucking Sherlock! Deal with him before he gets here! Fucking idiot!"

"Ok. Ok. Alright, fellas, look it's just one lonesome black bastard, according to what they told me. Find him and kill him aaiight? We'll split up. Jason, you two take the south end, we'll take the north. Make your way clockwise from there."

Good. Valuable intel. Now I knew there were at least four of them in his group; probably more at the house too. I stood and walked forward another hundred yards and stopped. I thought this might be the farthest I could walk without coming into contact with one of the guards circling the place looking for me. Of course, they'd shoot first and ask questions later. I thought it best to take them out of the fight before they had the chance.

I looked above me. Aided by the moonlight, I searched for a tree with branches that looked sturdy enough to support me and my equipment and that would be tall enough to allow a line of vision into the area surrounding the house. There were no such trees in the immediate vicinity. Still searching above me, I walked forward, beginning to feel uncertain about the plan. With every step, I took a chance on encountering one of the guards, and every second my eyes were fixed above me was all the time one of them would need to pop out of nowhere and fire on me. I had to find my tree quickly or give up on the plan.

Once in his dojo, Genai stood me in front of him and grabbed my wrist, pulled it up between us and told me to hold it there. He'd then put his own wrist against mine and told me to close my eyes. This was not an uncommon exercise. We'd done this many times before. The task was to deflect and redirect his arm when he thrust it towards me, by touch alone, using his wrist as a fulcrum, thus teaching a skill that could be used in hand to hand combat. But the lesson that day was different.

"How do you know where my hand is?"

"I can feel it," I said.

"Now what I want you to do, is listen. Your goal in this lesson is to turn off all your other senses and just listen. What should you be listening *for*, Nicholas?"

I struggled with an answer and finally just fessed up.

"I don't know, sir."

"My other arm."

And with this he'd thrown a hook into my side that sent me to my knees. And he'd restrained himself. When I opened my eyes and looked up at him I was strangely comforted by the look on his face that was always there at times like that. No pleasure at seeing me in pain, but no discomfort either. He was doing what he must, the best way he could, to protect me from the violence that would soon become commonplace in my life. His goal was to make me into the best soldier he could and little surprise shots like this would cause me to never forget this lesson. He had to hurt me now, in order to save me in the future. And in a way, I equated that with concern for my personal well-being. I wasn't just another faceless student to him, one of the many. Plus, it was a concrete lesson, not the emotional manipulation Wilkes took part in.

So, in time, I'd been taught to mentally separate my senses and multi-task them. It didn't always work, but when it did it definitely came in handy. I chose to use it now. While I searched the trees with my eyes, I turned off all my other senses except my hearing and amplified it. Every step I took was now heard and not felt; the night was brought alive as I crept towards the house. The sound of twigs and grass crunching underneath was made deafening. Insects that I estimated at ten feet away resonated in my head as if they were buzzing in my ear. A light wind measured as gale force. I picked up the hum of spotlights near the mansion three quarters of a mile away. I listened to my own heartbeat as if through a stethoscope.

The trees. No, not high enough. Another, branches too weak. They passed from the bottom of my vision to the top and then out of sight. For a moment, I was transported to memories of looking up and out the window of my mother's car when I was a child as we drove down a road lined with trees. But these, these were all unacceptable. None would work from this distance from the house. Considering I'd not found one by this point, it was becoming more unlikely that I would at all. I'd have to reconsider the plan and take on any guards as I encountered them on the way, increasing the danger quotient to this operation exponentially.

I dropped to my knees, swiveled on the balls of my feet and pointed my weapon behind me. Sound had been picked up. Footsteps on the ground at my six, approximately 15 yards behind me. I cursed myself for not picking him up sooner. And I cursed again when the bullets tore into the bark of a tree beside me.

I threw myself backwards and into a roll and then was up, sprinting for cover. My assailant yelled as he pursued, stupidly, and fired blindly into the darkness between our two positions, the bullets impacting all over, but seldom close enough to cause any alarm. I stopped on a dime and dove to my right, rolled to my feet, attached myself to the nearest tree, and waited. I would have to do this quickly. His screams would attract the others and they'd likely be there in less than a minute.

I had to admit that the sound emanating from my newest adversary was impressive. It came straight from the diaphragm. The idiot yelled the way you'd expect a recent boot camp graduate to. As soon as the noise reached within a yard of my position, I simply stuck my arm out and let him run into it. He was thrown to the ground by his own impetus. I'd not had a good look at him, nor an estimate of his height. So I just guessed. I guessed pretty good. As he'd fallen, he'd first clutched his throat as if I'd just slit it. Assured that it was a knife I'd stuck out and not just my hand, he writhed along the ground like a worm that had just been cut in half. Without taking his hands from his throat, he furiously searched for a stray vocal cord. I couldn't help but smile and desperately wanted to deliver him from his imagined agony, so I shot him with a knockout dart and finally my poor victim lay quiet and unmoving.

I had seconds before the rest of his crew converged on our location and I had nowhere to go — but up. I truly did not want to get into a running gun battle with these people. I could still succeed, but it'd get bloody and I'd wanted to reserve that for just the one of the group. So I prayed for beneficence and looked up. And there she was, just the tree I'd been looking for.

The first two arrived five seconds after I'd ascended the tree. Luckily, it had a few lower branches and I'd been able to pull myself up after I'd thrown up my bag. As soon as they'd arrived, one of them had turned to speak to another man. This other man I guessed to be the leader who'd taken the orders from Louis Rayes earlier. He'd put his finger to his mouth and motioned to his associate that there might still be danger, that I might still be close, which brought a smile to my face.

Why they waited I still don't understand. I silently and somewhat amusedly watched from mere feet away, my gun pointing straight at them, and hoped they might wait for the rest of their group to come. But I thought it unlikely they'd be that foolish. I was wrong. They were that foolish. Two more men came, hushedly stood over their fallen comrade and tried to rouse him. When I started shooting, all of them fell on their backs with the same looks of immense perplexity — darts sticking out of their chests, pointing up at me indictingly, guilty as charged.

I grabbed my bag, climbed upwards and after a few branches a new vista was discovered. From there I could see all, in every direction. Ray Ray's complete estate was all mine. I reached into the bag, removed the assault rifle, and searched for an appropriate station for it. It was necessary to move again but soon I had the rifle fit snugly between two branches. I tested it for rigidity and was pleased. This would do nicely.

Now, this was no normal Reicher assault rifle. It was part of a two-piece assembly. Centered and at the top of the rifle was a turntable that was fluid in any direction. I retrieved from the bag a Reicher *sniper's* rifle crafted for non-lethal use. I then connected it to the turntable, thus providing the steadiness and balance of a tripod, yet allowing for complete dexterity when aiming—like the machine guns placed in Blackhawk helicopters. I took aim at the front of the house.

Four more men had apparently been ordered to stand guard directly outside the front door. All held their weapons in front of them and smartly surveyed only that approach to the house. I guess it never occurred to them there were more ways into a house other than the front door. They were as prepared for war as could ever be expected of any drug dealer minion types. They made it too easy.

I took aim at the farthest to the right, then slid my aim onto the man to his left, and the same with the other two. I practiced twice and then re-aimed onto the first guard. Within one second, I fired off four direct hits that sent the men to their backs, unconscious. I climbed down the tree, stepped over my now incapacitated former pursuers and walked towards the house. I swiveled my belt again so the pistol would be at my right and reattached the holster so the .45 faced forward. I was no longer interested in the non-lethal approach.

CHAPTER 36

A rapping was heard at the door and Louis Rayes and his right-hand man let loose all the firepower they could muster, disintegrating the door with bullets. They stood atop a balcony and fired over the railing down into the entryway door with their fully automatic weapons. The balcony, three stories high, crossed over the marbled floors of his foyer that nearly spanned the entire lower level, and served as a walkway from the elevator to the hallway that led to his ten room palace.

They ceased fire and listened and prayed they'd hit whomever it was that had knocked on the door and who had apparently taken out his entire security force. They prayed for moaning, screams of suffering and shock. Instead, another rapping at the door. They listened again but didn't fire. The rapping was rapid and shallow. Seconds passed before they discerned the noise as pebbles hitting the door and not a person's knock and then . . . they heard laughter. Laughter that made its way through the now dilapidated entryway and floated through the great hall that was noted among Louis Rayes' greatest achievements. Laughter that extended up to them on that top level, perforated their skin, reached inside them and left them with a chill. Laughter that seemed as if it would never stop, that was bloodthirsty and superior, but sad. And Rayes knew the laughter was meant just for him and he was angered by it. It was not right for him to die like this — a terror-stricken victim of some contractor sent after him by his enemies.

The laughter finally stopped and he'd thought there could be nothing worse than the sound of it until he was assaulted by the silence that followed. He was jittery. Tempted to run into one of the rooms inside his massive house and take cover. But then he or they or it, his pursuer, whatever it was that could laugh in that way, presumably in sick anticipation of carrying out his execution, would eventually find him there cowering like a child.

Rayes himself began to shake with laughter this time. He was so scared that he'd elevated this man, or men, to demon status. He'd killed so many. Watched them die at his hand, with the same horrified looks on their faces that he now wore and it amused him. Even now, probably only moments from his own death, the irony did not escape him. He dreamed of the next life to come. He wondered what it would be like in hell.

"Ray?"

Rayes turned to his second in command, the man he'd put in charge of his personal security, and had no reason or desire to hide his disgust at such an immense failure.

"What."

"What we gon' do, man? He could be coming in through one of the windows on the other side of the building right now. We should try to get outside."

"And do what, motherfucker? Obviously, he's killed everybody out there already. Stupid. You want me to walk right into his hands and what? Turn myself in?"

"I gotta get out of here, Ray. I'm sorry but I got a family to take care of, man. I got a brand new baby, Ray!"

"Man, fuck that ugly ass little rugrat, nigga! You gon' stay right here wit me and protect and serve. You see this guy, you kill him, you heard?"

"I can't, Ray, man, I'm sorry . . . ."

"Nigga, what am I supposed to do then?"

"I'm sorry, man, but . . . I can't do this for you, man," he said. He turned and began walking toward the elevator.

Rayes nodded his head in understanding, then raised his gun. He fired it into the back of the man's head as he walked away and watched him collapse.

The next thing he heard was the sound of clapping. The noise almost caused him to whip around and fire in the direction of the sound but he managed to restrain himself. He knew that if he made a move in that direction he was dead. Instead, he just dropped his gun and stood, unmoving.

Leaning against the door-frame of the entrance onto the balcony, I clapped my hands together and shook my head, smirking.

"Ah, loyalty. Such a fickle, fickle concept, isn't it, Mr. Rayes?"

Rayes turned and fixed his eyes upon me.

"They sent a brother after me? Nigga, ain't you heard? This black on black violence has got to stop."

I smiled. "Hmh. So you have a sense of humor. What about justice? Is that something you can comprehend? Or is it like loyalty, something that just has no place in your life?"

"Babbling mufucker," he said under his breath. "C'mon, man. We both brothers. Why you doing this? I don't even know you, man."

"That's right, you don't know me," I said, as I felt my face mutating, overcome with outrage, as I moved towards him. "You never did know me. Yet at the suggestion of someone you had met days earlier, you decided to kill the only person who ever cared about me."

Facing the man, now cowering against the guardrail, I pushed my whole body at him and breathed down onto him as I spoke.

"Ok, so who was it? Let me do right by it then. Then we'll be up and up, right? Who was it? Did I kill your pops, one your homies what?"

"No," I said, backing away from him slightly. "It was my mother. Does that bring back any memories?"

"Well, uh, let me think . . . ."

"No. Your time is up, my friend. There's a whole bunch of ways for you to die. I'll let you choose one."

I watched Rayes eyes and saw through them. I saw the realization that he was about to die begin to corporealize in his mind. The bravado that came soon after was not unexpected.

"Nigga *fuck* yo momma cause I still don't know who the *fuck* you are."

I leaned in again, but this time put my mouth to the man's ear and whispered, "I am vengeance," and slammed him in the chest with both arms, pushing him over the guardrail.

"No, no!" he cried out, as his whole body flipped in front of me. He made a strange moaning sound as he fell — surprise perhaps — forty feet headfirst onto the marble floor. Maybe it was the noise a man makes when he knows his death is imminent, inevitable, when he can feel it approaching. The sound of Ray Ray's neck snapping as he hit was unmistakable and filled the immense room with its acoustics.

Suddenly, I began to hyperventilate. I was forced to hold onto the rail and stood there trembling. The anguish of my mother's death rushed through me, newly invigorated. It locked up every muscle and set every synapse and nerve in my body ablaze. I felt regret and an immense sorrow accompanied by an almost tangible sensation of former innocence lost. With this act, I was now a cold-blooded murderer, and a question that I'd never posed to myself before fought its way through the confusion. Would God still welcome me through the gates in the end? Or might I no longer be worthy? What if I was now just as worthless as Rayes, Smalls, and all the others?

CHAPTER 37

With Ray Ray's death, all mental and emotional ties to my past life had finally been severed. This act of retribution, so different from anything I could have ever done before Wilkes and his training came along, was yet another strong example of how changed I was. I was no longer an innocent surrounded by wickedness; now I was part of that wickedness — a very lethal part. That scared me because I had always aspired to be better than what I was surrounded by, from the kill zone that was the neighborhood I grew up in, to this new alternate reality that now manipulated me. I'd just wiped out that possibility in a big way. In any case, I knew then for the first time, for I hadn't recognized it to be true until then, that my first life was truly over with, and my second had already begun.

You ever notice how a ride to a destination can seem to take forever, but somehow, following the exact same route, at an equal speed, the return trip seems to abbreviate itself and you're sure it took less time? This was not the case on the ride back to The Building. I'd spent nearly three hours on the freeway going to Louis Rayes compound. It felt as if it took a lifetime to make it home. Home. That that place could ever be home to me struck me as preposterous. But, for the moment, it was all I had. And if that was all I had, then truly, I was all alone in the universe.

Weaving around the few cars that were still on the highway at that time of night, the cold air beat against me on the speeding motorcycle, the pavement rushing underneath me, and this time there was no fire inside me to fight off the physical discomfort. Attempting to draw in the warmth generated by the screaming engine underneath, I leaned in close to the tank of the cycle, never taking my eyes off the horizon ahead of me. I found myself imagining I could drive into that horizon and over the edge of it. I could fall into some undiscovered cosmic abyss and never be seen from or heard of again, and never again be forced to answer to John Wilkes with all his hidden, black expectations of me.

But within moments of my imagined demise, because of it, I was disappointed in myself. Never before, never, had I allowed myself to entertain the prospect of giving up. My instinct for self-preservation was unequaled and I wasn't going to let him affect that part of me. Wait, no. No, it wasn't him this time. I couldn't blame him for this, not this time. No, again, it was my fault. I'd thought that killing Rayes would bring closure, that justice would finally be served in the name of the only truly perfect woman I'd known. And thought that I'd feel some glorious, cleansing, contented feeling wash over me when he was dead by my hand.

But instead — it was amusing really — instead, I'd found only that I was every bit as capable of committing the evil I'd always wanted to fight. Maybe amusing is the wrong word because all efforts to evaluate myself never strayed from similarly gravitied, sullen, wholly dissatisfying conclusions. That was a long ride indeed.

Weary from the ride, I finally pulled into the garage at The Building and checked in with security. After returning the weapons, except for the pistol and ammo I would need in the morning, I took the elevator back to my level. Rusty saw the look on my face and didn't speak a word to me throughout the process of passing the weapons, unloaded, locked back and with the chamber showing clear, to him through the dumbwaiter. Though he seldom took his eyes from the weapons or his computer screen, when he did look up, he watched me and had a knowing look to him that offered compassion, that communicated he had seen many others stand before him after an operation in the same state.

The elevator door opened and I was, after all, glad to be back in The Building, only because it was where I could get to my bed. I crossed the walkway and couldn't have cared less about the view or the splendor of the forest at night or the moon and how it lit the treetops or anything else except getting to my quarters. I made my way through the complex to the center ring, turned the corner and nearly walked right into him.

"Well, well, well, Mr. Gambit."

I should have been expecting him.

"I must say I'm a bit surprised. Not at how easily you infiltrated Louis Rayes' security because, well, I taught you well. Nevertheless, I am impressed. What I am so beside myself about is the fact that you actually killed the man. You went to all that trouble not to kill his men and then you threw him two stories off a balcony. Oh, I'm sorry, four. All these philosophical differences, but when it really comes down to it your and my sense of justice are one and the same."

He cocked his head to one side, apparently to improve his position from which to similarly observe and condescend.

"I feel . . . validated," he said. "I suppose the morality you cling to means nothing when it's you and your life and not some unrelated individual we're talking about."

"He deserved to die," I said, regretting it as soon as the words left my mouth.

"Some would say that it's not your place to decide," he said, laughing heartily now.

I just watched him, speechless.

"Oh, how wonderful. Nicholas, don't worry, I'm just having fun with you. Murder is acceptable, especially when it serves the needs of justice. That's what I've been trying to show you and I think you're finally beginning to see it. I'm proud of you, son. It's our job to make those decisions. Yes, in the course of our work we may take life along the way, but we do it to provide a better life for so many more. Look at the Bible. How many times has life, the lives of innocents even, been sacrificed for the good of others, all in the name of God? That's what we do here, Nicholas. Only I don't profess allegiance to any deity other than the United States of America. And I'd have it no other way and neither should you. I won't sugar-coat it. We do what we must and killing some scumbag mafioso, or well, some murderous drug dealing piece of shit that had it coming anyway is just . . . simply . . . inconsequential," this sticking his face at me for effect. "Think about it. You'll see I'm right, son. Good work tonight."

He nodded, smiled, and turned to walk away, then called to me over his shoulder.

"Bright and early, my boy."

I hated him more than ever at that moment. But much of what he said about me was true. And that made things suddenly more clear than ever. I was beginning to lose my way, and it occurred to me that perhaps it was time I fixed myself. How was another question entirely.

Somehow I managed a full four hours of sleep before rising the next morning. Within another three and a half hours I found myself outside of Victor Passage's house once again, watching the house through the front gate. I sat for several hours as I had before, but this time there was little to think about, not only because my brain was too zombified from lack of sleep and over-thinking everything lately, but because, finally, everything was quite clear. When it came to Wilkes, I would just have to bide my time and find a way to escape this life he'd imposed upon me. Until then, I had to try not to lose too much of myself along the way.

The notion that I still owed him and that plotting to leave the program would be disloyal did occur to me. That notion was fleeting. It would be disloyal, but rightfully so. I owed him nothing any longer. I'd not known what I was getting myself into, and though that was a petty and insubstantial defense in many cases, I felt, I knew, that this was different. I'd never expected that I'd be told by this man that murder and wanton destruction was just as common a tool in this business as any vehicle or computer might be. Now, any or all of that in self-defense? Of course. But just because it made things easier for him and his immensely oblique objectives, no, just . . . simply . . . wrong. No matter what I'd done to Rayes, I just couldn't be a consistent part of that type of evil.

My eyes picked up movement and I surveyed the front of the house with the binoculars. It was Passage. Just as before, he got into his Jeep, waited for the gate to open, then left in the same direction he'd gone before. Just as before, I followed. He came up on a freeway onramp and took it. I followed him up and onto the freeway as well, pulling within a few car lengths of his vehicle. I looked down at the sound of a phone ringing. It was a car phone positioned ahead of the console between the front seats. I picked it up and put it to my ear.

"Hello?" I said.

"Nicholas, this is Wilkes. Now, I want you to listen very carefully. Victor Passage, as of this moment, is under our protection. What that means is that you are to protect him with your own life should it come down to it. Understood?"

"Yessir."

"Now, first chance you get, you are to go to him, identify yourself, and tell him that he is to wait with you until we can get reinforcements to your location. They will take over for you. If necessary, subdue him."

"Understood. I'll call you as soon as we stop . . . ."

I was distracted by an alarming visual picked up by my peripheral vision, a blur through my passenger window. When I'd realized what I was seeing as it passed beside me, my thoughts were suddenly forced in a new direction. What I saw was a speeding van. As it surged forward and ahead of me, a sliding door on the side of the van opened and a man holding an automatic weapon leaned his entire body out, held fast by a length of rope tied to the ceiling of the vehicle. Another car full of men followed directly behind the van, speeding as well.

"Nicholas."

"Oh boy. I'll have to call you back," I said.

I threw the phone to the floor and punched the gas. I pulled up just behind the car full of men, now in the far right lane of the freeway, then jumped two lanes over to the far left lane, and pulled up next to Passage who was in the middle lane. Looking to my right and honking my horn at him, I tried to get his attention. He rolled his eyes and refused to look in my direction, apparently guessing I was some miscreant with nothing better to do than harass him in the middle of the day on the freeway. After a second or two, with a look of pure irritation on his face, Passage did finally turn and look at me. Frantically, I pointed to the men coming up behind us in the van. Passage turned around and looked. I saw his body actually lurch at what he saw. He turned back around, his eyes now filled with terror. He shifted and pulled away, the engine of his Jeep screaming. Finally.

The gunmen, now seeing me as Passage's ally, began firing — on the both of us. I tapped the brakes and tried to put my car directly behind Passage's in order to protect him, and I caught hell for it. Bullets destroyed my rear windshield and it only took the sound of one "phhhttt" streaking by my ear to tell me this was not the best laid of plans. I ducked to my side and did my best to see over the dash of the car, but was unable. My vision seriously diminished, I yanked the steering wheel to the right, swerving out of the lane and away from Passage's jeep and into the far right hand lane again. The van pulled in behind Passage's jeep and continued its assault.

Passage was now swerving back and forth across the four lanes of the freeway. Every few seconds the gunman hanging outside the van would launch a barrage of bullets ahead of the van, in Passage's direction, not yet hitting much. Every time the van got in a position for the man to take good aim, Passage smartly swerved back out of sight. Their strategy had been flawed, but Passage wouldn't be able to avoid them much longer.

But at the moment, I had my own welfare to worry about. The van full of gunmen had followed me over, left Passage to their comrades, and had not let up on their attack.

"Ping. Ping."

It was the sound of bullets hitting my car as they fired out of their windows. It would have been pointless to try and fire back at them. I was going to have to do this another way. So I slowed the Lincoln. I slowed it just enough to let them think that they were going to be able to overcome my car and get beside me, and hoped that I timed the exit coming up on my right appropriately.

I did. Just as they began to swerve to their left in order to pull up beside me, I yanked my steering wheel to the right again, this time careening off of the freeway and onto and up the off ramp. With no time to react and turn, they were forced to continue on the highway. I sped up the ramp and halfway up realized I'd not taken into account a fairly important variable. If the light was green, I might be able to make it across the intersection and onto the on ramp and back onto the freeway and come up behind the terrorists. If it was red and there were cars traveling perpendicular to my path, myself and a whole lot of other people just might end up dead if I didn't hit the brakes immediately.

I had a second to make a decision. I chose to let fate guide me on this one. I punched it and came up on the intersection and my heart fell into a pit that I hadn't encountered since Smalls had walked into that liquor store with his boys that fateful night so long ago. It was red. But I no longer had any choice. Refusing to shut my eyes, I glanced to my right and saw a semi heading for a point of intercept with my Lincoln that would leave me in a hundred pieces all over that road. The pedal already glued to the floor, I pushed harder and watched the semi coming at me as I entered the intersection. Of course I couldn't, but I was sure I could see the semi's driver tense up and his eyes go wide when he saw me, but at this point, his brakes wouldn't change a thing. Either I was dead . . . well, I was probably dead.

I was full on in the intersection when I realized I might make it. And that one moment of uncertainty lasted at least five in my mind's eye. And then, some kind of collision and I was rocketing back down the other side of the ramp. I'd barely felt it. I looked over my shoulder and saw a metal bumper, the Lincoln's metal bumper, being dragged by the semi, hanging from its grill and sparking on the ground. I rejoiced and laughed at myself and spoke out loud.

"You are one crazy son of a bitch, Nicholas Gambit."

I kept my foot on the gas pedal and shot down the ramp. I came up, just as I had hoped, and purely by divine intervention, immediately behind the men I now classified as terrorists, if only for personal justification. My windshield was already shot full of holes so I fired into it with my weapon and let it crumble away completely so that I could have an unrestrained view of my opponents, then fired at their car through their rear window. The first bullet caught one of the unsuspecting terrorists in the back of the head and he slumped forward in his seat. The others in the back seat didn't seem to understand what was wrong with him until they saw the hole in his head. They turned inquisitively to see where the bullet had come from and I fired at them too. They jumped in their seats in surprise, instinctively throwing their hands up in front of their faces, then tried to return fire. I tried to suppress them by sending intermittent rounds at them long enough to get beside them, as they had tried to do to me.

They were in an older car, late eighties or early nineties, and probably stolen. But it was the age of the car that interested me. It meant I could take advantage of the fact that many of the safeguards available in more contemporary automobiles were not available to them. While I glanced towards the rear of the car, I kept my weapon aimed at their windows. Upon finding the plate covering the gas filler, I fired back into the car, hitting another of them sitting in the back seat in the face, and watched him fall over onto his now prostrate friend. I then aimed well underneath the plate, knowing the gas tank itself would be unshielded—and fired. And fired. And fired. And the third was the one that did it.

The car erupted in a series of explosions, starting with the tank itself. The one still living in the back seat, along with the two dead ones beside him, was the first to go. The back of the car went up like it'd just hit a landmine, sending it flying upwards and upending itself, flipping. While in the air, the firestorm caused by the exploding, and apparently full tank of gas, enveloped the rest of the car. This all caused something in the engine well to discharge, sending that part of the car into flames as well, all while in the air. Speeding away, I left the wreckage behind me as it hit the ground upside down.

The explosions and bullets flying caught the attention of most of the motorists and they had wisely pulled off onto the shoulder. This left me now in pursuit of the van that was in pursuit of Passage, whose Jeep was in the middle lane and losing ground quickly to the van. It took me seconds to reach the van and that was when I heard the sirens wailing. I looked behind me and saw that the police had come into the fray. Three highway patrol cars came up behind me. Three of 'em, all at once, which I thought was odd. But I had no time to deal with them. The men in that van were likely not to stop, therefore neither was I.

Suddenly, the back doors of the van opened and a man holding a very LARGE automatic weapon aimed for my head. I slammed my foot onto the brake and barely managed to avoid being made permeable by the bullets, which instead destroyed the hood of my car and caused it to fly open, completely obstructing my view. Unable to see, I had no choice but to pull over onto the shoulder and watched through the window to my right as two of the cops continued in pursuit after the van. The other officer pulled over behind me. I burst out of the car, pissed.

"You Mr. Gambit?" asked the officer.

"Yes. How do you . . . ? Oh. I've got to give it to Wilkes, he is efficient."

"We're supposed to give you any help we can."

"Good. I'm gonna need your cruiser."

"Oh," he said, a little disturbed by the prospect of giving it up, but apparently he'd been highly encouraged to help me because he didn't seem to think he had any choice. "Ok."

He handed his keys over and I rushed to get into the vehicle when I saw something much more to my liking. A half mile away and closing were two more cruisers and another officer, on a motorcycle.

"Wait. I need that!" I said.

"You got it."

Weaving in and out of the throng of cruisers, all in steady pursuit of the van, I made my way to the front of the line and pulled in front of them, then pointed the bike straight for the back of the van. The men in the van showed no signs of giving up just because their situation was hopeless, and I knew that meant Passage was in no less danger. He knew as well as I did that if he stopped and pulled over, they'd just stop behind him, kill him, and try to make some kind of getaway, despite the odds. They had, at least, stopped firing for the moment, and I thought this would be as good a chance as any to take them out before they figured out what to do next.

I pulled within fifteen feet of the van and matched its speed. I fired several shots into the rear doors that opened before and kept my weapon raised and aimed at the same spot the man with the automatic had appeared in. He didn't disappoint me. He opened the door to investigate and I put one between his eyes before he could squeeze off a single shot, then watched him fall back into the van. I holstered my pistol and aimed the bike for the side of the van. As soon as I came around the corner, the man hanging out the sliding door saw me coming and fired in my direction, successfully keeping me at bay and forcing me behind the van again. I decided to try the other side and pulled up on the right of the van and again was sent back to the rear of it by a man hanging his arm outside the passenger window and firing at me. Luckily for me, the velocity at which they were moving made for a bumpy ride, making it difficult to keep a steady aim. And so there I was, stuck at the rear of the van again, making no headway and achieving no more than the cops who wisely stayed a respectable distance behind me.

But one of the rear doors of the van was still open and I quickly came up with an idea. I slowed the bike, put more distance between myself and the van, pulled my weapon again, then throttled the motorcycle. I estimated the appropriate distance, reached it and fired. The bullet tore into the right rear tire and the weapon clicked open, empty. I'd misjudged how many shots I'd fired into the van but I didn't have time to censure myself. The van lurched from the exploding tire, rocking the passengers and knocking the dead gunman in the back through the back door. His body collided with the pavement and I narrowly missed it tumbling at me as I sped toward the van. From my perspective through the ever-nearing open doors, I saw the man in the passenger seat bang his head against the dash and lose his weapon, which fell to the floor and slid behind his seat.

Having never slowed, I first holstered the empty gun, then raised myself off the seat of the motorcycle and let it ram into the back of the van, the momentum throwing me through the door and into the still-moving van. I rolled, managed to quickly get to my feet, simply let loose one of the ropes connecting the man hanging outside the van to the vehicle, and watched him as he was thrown to the concrete from the speeding vehicle and disappeared from sight. I stepped toward the passenger and cracked him in the head with my hand, momentarily disabling him. The driver raised his arm to point his gun at me. I sidestepped behind his seat, grabbed his arm, twisted it, and bent it against my own abdomen, causing him to cry out. I took that weapon from his hand, picked up the other one on the floor and directed a weapon at each man's head.

"Fellas," I said, breathing heavily, " . . . your choice."

CHAPTER 38

"So any special instructions about how to handle these guys?"

The man speaking was a lieutenant named Latimer. He'd been following behind the van in one of the cruisers and had seen the entire event, including the way I'd deposited myself into the van and captured the men inside. He had spent the past ten minutes complimenting me up and down and telling me he'd never seen anything like what I'd just done. He was an effusive man. Not unlikable, I guess. Actually, I was moderately amused by the admiration. The way he reached out to touch me lightly on the arm every so often while he spoke as if to verify for himself that I was of this earth and not some superman. He looked at me with searching eyes, hoping to somehow ferret out whatever secret it was that allowed me to bend rules like gravity and mortality.

Throughout the entire awe-inspired address, I'd reluctantly attempted to show him I was flattered, but eventually I'd begun to tire of the unending affection and he'd noticed. At that point, he must have finally decided that I was in no hurry to part with confidential information and he let it go.

The men from the van were stashed separately into the backs of two cruisers. I'd asked the officers to have them searched for suicide pills, caplets in their mouths or on their persons. Satisfied that they could not avoid interrogation, I pushed that concern to the side. My focus now, was Passage.

He stood along the shoulder of the freeway as we all did. I'd avoided him as soon as we'd pulled over. I'd made my way to the police behind me and asked them to gather my remaining clips of ammo from the Lincoln. But I kept certain that he was never out of my sight. I didn't know how to approach him — friend or foe? And he would have questions, quite a few questions probably, none of which I would have answers for. And Wilkes would certainly prefer me not to try. Though I was becoming more disgusted by the moment with the idea of having to do anything Wilkes told me, I thought it best not to rock the boat just yet, not without good enough reason. My reason was fast on its way.

"Sir?"

It was Latimer. I had been only half listening to him.

"Uh, they'll be taken care of by the agents that are on their way," I responded. "They're going to be replacing me and they'll have instructions for you. I'm guessing they'll be taking them off your hands and you guys will be able to go home."

"Just like that?" he asked.

I watched his face and noticed how his appreciation of me faded and was quickly replaced with aggravation.

"I got a blowed-up Dodge ten miles down the road with I don't know how many sautéed foreigners inside, two more over here sitting inside my patrol cars, who, I might add, were driving a van with enough ordnance inside to level Magic Mountain, and you're telling me that some secret agent that you're affiliated with is gonna come along and take my prisoners away and leave me and mine to do the cleanup? I just love it when federals come into my jurisdiction. I mean, no offense, sir. Hell, if I'm gonna get fucked, might as well get fucked by the best."

"Look, I'm sorry. None of this was my idea. This whole thing . . . it . . . well, it smells. But, I'm not exactly in a position to help anyone out right now, you know?"

"Excuse me, sir?"

I turned to look at another officer walking up behind us. He was speaking to me.

"Sir, uh, this guy over here is asking to talk to you."

"Let him keep on asking," I said, looking over at Passage. He'd already begun walking in our direction.

"Well, he's getting very insistent . . . ."

At that moment Passage broke into a full run at us, surprising the officers that were between him and our position. Latimer pushed at his officer.

"We'll stop him."

"No, no, I'll talk to him. Give me some privacy, will you?"

"Yeah, ok."

The two walked past the now winded Passage who'd traversed forty yards in an impressive sixteen seconds. They turned and watched him near me to see if there would be any action.

"Excuse . . . me . . . sir," he said, panting between every word. I couldn't suppress the smile that came to my face.

"Mr. Passage," I said.

"I'm afraid you have me . . . at a disadvantage, Mr . . . ?"

"Mr. is good enough."

"Right. Ok, well then, sir, I have to go from here."

"No sir. We have people on their way to pick you up. They'll get you where it's safe."

"What people? Who are you? Thank you for all your help, but . . . who are you?"

"I was sent to protect you until reinforcements arrive, and like I said, they're on their way. So, nothing to worry about."

"Ok, you're not answering my questions." He turned around, shook his head, and then suddenly turned on his heels and stepped forward. He stood close to me and looked me in the face. "Nothing to worry about? They're coming to kill me, aren't they?"

"What? You know what? I don't even want to know. I was sent here to protect you and nothing more. You will wait with me until they get here. The end. That's it. Nothing more to discuss."

A desolate, hopeless expression filled his face and I wondered if I should feel sorry for him.

"Then I'm a dead man," he said.

"Sir, why would I be sent to protect you if you're just to be killed anyway? I work with the government, not some terrorist faction."

"Because there are men with direct ties to several government agencies that want something I have, and they don't want these other guys to get it first. And once they do have it they have no choice but to kill me."

I watched him and measured every word that left his mouth. I didn't think he was lying. The words quivered out of his mouth when he spoke and fear caused his eyes to flit even as he tried to hold my gaze with his own.

"I need your help, sir. If you don't help me you'll be a traitor, lackey to a group of treasonous psychopaths. Two government officials have already died."

He saw that he was beginning to earn my attention and that spurred him on.

"Trust me, you do not want that. These guys are all going down sooner or later, and if you're seen as being in on it, you'll go down too. Is that what you want? Devereaux, Wilkes, Constantino, Ahbrahmson, have you ever heard any of those names?"

No, I wasn't surprised either. As soon as he started to name names, I'd expected to hear his. And there it was, plain as day and just begging me, practically declaring it an imperative that I investigate further.

"What about Wilkes?"

"Wilkes, oh yes, he's the worst of them. The ringleader." He put his hand to his mouth and I thought he might fall flat on his back. "My God. My God, you're one of his. You're one of his. My God."

He suddenly began to talk very fast after his epiphany, suspecting he might have only a very short amount of time to convince me not to kill him.

"He wants to kill me because I have evidence that incriminates him. Evidence that shows he masterminded the assassinations of two senators five years ago. Sir, believe me, you do not want to trust this guy. Whatever he's told you, it's all, all of it a lie. He wants to kill me the same way he's killed so many others, all to keep the truth from coming out and to protect a number of crazed, illegal programs and . . . ."

"Hey! Hey! Listen. You know what? No matter how hard I try, I just can't stop myself from hating this guy. So here's your chance. Prove it."

I knew that I was the one taking the chance. But if half of what Passage was saying was true, then I was right about Wilkes. He was out of control.

CHAPTER 39

We took Passage's car to a large warehouse. He had been allowed access by the people he lived with, who owned it. He told me it had been set aside as a hiding place for him in case of emergency. The warehouse itself had been erected in the place of a former government bunker base. Situated between two massive walls of granite rock, the entire facility seemed to be sunken into the ground. Atop the rock walls, and stretching out for what looked like miles, forest had been allowed to grow and appeared to rise above either side of the building.

Passage unlocked the door with a key and entered. I followed him closely. The inside of the warehouse was filled nearly to capacity, mostly with large wooden crates with markings that indicated they contained wooden tables, glass fixtures, and other various pieces of furniture. To our left was a staircase that ran along the wall. At the top of those stairs was a door that served as an alternate exit. It led to another staircase I'd noticed running down the outside of the building. If you turned right at the top of the staircase, you'd find yourself atop a raised walkway that allowed access to a crane. Its purpose must have been to move the large crates inside the building. About half of the lights in the ceiling were lit, and when Passage reached to flip the switch to turn on the rest of the lights, I touched him and shook my head not to. I wanted what little cover the lower light would give me. Not that I was expecting anyone, but just in case. He nodded in understanding, turned, and walked towards the middle of the warehouse.

I stayed close to him, very close. Several times as we moved through the building, he turned his head to the side but stopped himself just before he looked over his shoulder at me, reacting to my nearness to him. It was my intent to keep him on guard, to demonstrate that should a betrayal occur, he would never be out of my reach. His discomfort was, to me, a welcome sight. I wanted him uncertain about what he could expect from me, at least until he gave me reason to relax.

We walked into an area that had been cleared of boxes and debris. It appeared that Passage had spent a night or two in this very spot. A rolled-up sleeping bag lay upright against a crate filled with table chairs, according to its markings. Food provisions, a large thermos, and a space heater sat beside it. In the middle of the clearing was a small TV stand with a television and a VCR atop it. Passage walked up to it, pulled a tape from inside the jacket he wore and inserted it into the VCR. He then turned to me.

"Do you remember about five years ago Senators Don Lumens and Richard Fellowes were assassinated while on a diplomatic mission throughout the Persian Gulf?"

"Little bit before my time."

"Ok, well, it was several years after Desert Storm, couple years before 9-11, they were there trying to maintain relations with the locals, that type of thing. Uh, Don Lumens was chairperson of the Foreign Relations Committee. Don was a very morally ambitious man. He wanted to change the fact that congressional members seldom took on diplomatic duties or involved themselves in foreign affairs unless they were on that committee or there was a war going on. That's why they were in the Gulf."

"Ok, we don't have a lot of time. Let's get to the point. Why kill what I guess would be two relatively respected and liked senators and how is Wilkes involved?"

"You look at the answer every time you look into the mirror. Son, in order to initiate a program such as the one you've obviously been put through, one needs money and some degree of governmental support. Now, of the few officials that Wilkes went to, only two were against it."

"Lumens and Fellowes."

"Exactly. And they threatened to go to the President if he continued to make it so. Technically, besides a number of power-mad senators, private interest groups and other lower government officials who felt they were misunderstood, misrepresented, underutilized . . . whatever, there are no authorized individuals, no true governing bodies, no nothing given governmental permission to build that complex or to train you. All of it's a sham. The NC-13 platform is *not* a congressionally sanctioned program as Wilkes would have everyone believe. The whole thing is against the law. Now, Wilkes may come off as not particularly power hungry, but trust me, that is not the case. And you can't get much more powerful than to have an army of super soldiers at your command."

"Wow. Ok. Why would even one official support him? What do they get out of it?"

"Oh, the world at their fingertips is what he offered. He promised them access to his army. When they needed a 'job' done, he'd take care of it for them. In return, those that could would appropriate funds and basically keep quiet about it. The rest was all private and corporate funding. I mean, really, when you think about it, a few million here, a few million there won't really be missed if the whole thing is hidden correctly and certain people overlook a few transactions, if you know what I mean. It's a bit more complicated than that but you'd be surprised; it's done all the time."

"I take it that's your evidence," I said, pointing at the VCR with the tape inside.

"Right. As you may already know, I'm a journalist."

I didn't, but I saw no reason to correct him.

"I was in Kuwait on special assignment for USA Today when the assassinations occurred. Don Lumens was a good friend. When he got killed, I started checking around. I was able to get the name of one of the men involved in his shooting, and then got to him before the police did. With the help of some other friends of Don's, we managed to get a confession out of him. What he told us was that Wilkes and his associates had contracted members of a Shiite militant group out of Lebanon, called the Ithna Ashariyya, to do the killings.

"But even with the confession it just wasn't enough. There was no one that would believe us. Then suddenly everyone who had helped me started dying. And I knew it wouldn't be long before I was caught and killed myself. So I went into hiding.

"Then I managed to get my hands on this tape. I don't know who made it or even who sent it to me, but it is the only thing that has kept me alive for the past five years. The best I can figure is that a man like Wilkes must make a lot of enemies and one of them saw that I could hurt him. Watch."

He turned on the television and pushed the play button. What appeared was someone's perspective from inside a room, but the perspective was skewed. It seemed to be coming from just underneath this person's head. He sat at a large roundtable with several other men in a room enveloped by windows that allowed a panoramic view of the skyline of a very large city at dusk. It wasn't what you might expect. It typified a boardroom rather than the dark, mysterious rooms of criminals and malcontents of lore.

These men were far from such meager and uninspired professions. No, they were politicians. White bread as white bread ever gets, every single one of them. Of the seven men that I could see clearly in the shot - I guessed there were double that in total - I could not pick out one whose tie clasp would retail at under $150. These men were either very wealthy, or very talented at playing wealthy, as I had heard quite a few politicians are.

Walking around the table, circling it like a vulture in its final descent upon dead or dying prey, was Wilkes. As he spoke, you could see in his eyes, and in his demeanor, that he smelled blood and was desperate to move in for the kill.

"What's he using to tape that?" I asked, curious about how the camera seemed to be shooting from below someone's head, yet remained unnoticed by the others in the room. Passage looked at me, I guessed wondering about my priorities.

"I don't know," he said, cursorily. "Now, I've already fast-forwarded it to the interesting part. Ok, there's Don Lumens right there."

He pointed to a man that was constantly shifting himself around in his chair like he was suffering from a mild case of hemorrhoids.

"As you can see, he doesn't look too comfortable, but he never actually speaks up. He was a smart man. He waited until he was far away from Wilkes to tell him how he really felt about his insane ideas. Of course," he said, lowering his eyes momentarily, " . . . ultimately it didn't really do him any good. Listen up. This is the good part."

"Gentlemen, I couldn't be any more timely. This is what we desperately need right now. Desperately. The CIA is impotent. Bogged down in red tape, misdirected and misled. True covert operations are practically a thing of the past, no matter what pop culture and news magazines might maintain. And that's gonna come back to bite us in the ass."

He stopped, leaned down on the table and surveyed his flock.

"We need this program. And I called you here for a specific reason. Because I knew you could all benefit, in your own way, from this program." He looked across the table at a man with sallow, tired eyes. "Jim. I'm sorry to bring up a painful history, but when your daughter was killed, what was it you told me when the man that did it was allowed to go free because of technicalities, what you wished for?"

"I said that I wished there was a way for me to go beyond the law and see that bag of shit torn apart and sent straight to hell and that I would pay any amount of money to make it so."

Wilkes nodded his head approvingly. "And it got me thinking. If only there was an agency, always operating and standardizing its missions on hard evidence, and believe me there was plenty of it and that man should have been convicted, that could insert itself into situations just like my friend Jim's here, and elicit real justice for the American people."

"Senator Ahbramson," he said, gesturing to a man with slick white hair and dark glasses, "you ran on a platform that called for a crackdown on illegal substance sales in Florida. Yet sales have gone up already. Let's face it, truth is you won't be reelected come 2000. Unless . . . you make good on your promises. Dead drug czars don't do business with anybody."

"They'd be replaced within hours," said Ahbramson.

"Then we'll kill them too. As many as it takes for them to get the idea. Don't you see? I can do this for all of you. That's why I invited you here. And I know that none of you are going to tell me that stopping the flow of drugs into this country is wrong. Hell, yet another of the many, many, many things that is systematically shifting us from most powerful, to most vulnerable.

"We've become nothing more than a group of well-off but complacent idiots ripe for the taking, gentlemen. We need to police ourselves and the world, and I've found the answer. Operatives only you and I would know about and who would not be constrained by the myriad of inflexible, inefficient, and just plain illogical rules that every agency from D.I.A. to my old Alma Mater has to adhere to. Operatives so powerful that they could turn the tide in favor of the right people this time. And all my resources would, in part, be yours. Anything you need done. All you need do is ask. Anything. And most importantly, you'd help America regain its foothold in covert warfare. It sounds extremely cold war-esque, but you'd be a part of regaining the lead when it comes to international affairs."

"Heil Hitler," Passage said without taking his eyes from the monitor, the repulsion in his voice unmistakable.

Wilkes continued.

"Go home and think about it. I know you're all a little hesitant to say anything right now. Take your time and think about it. Of course, everything said tonight is to be kept completely confidential. Gentlemen, it's the right thing to do. We're the greatest country this world has ever known. Thus . . . we're liable. And we're obligated. Obligated to correct all the misdeeds that occur throughout our own land, as well as the rest of the world. It's up to us to rid this country, and this planet, of the cancer that afflicts it. The Noble-13 project will be our means. Our scalpel, laser, radiation therapy, what have you."

Passage reached down and turned the V.C.R off.

"So if your friend Lumens was such a boy scout, then why did Wilkes even think he'd go for it?"

Passage looked at me closed-mouthed. The question that there might have been more to Lumen's relationship with Wilkes than he thought had never occurred to him. But it was pointless to waste time confounding him by maligning the dead, so I changed the subject.

"Must have been in his tie."

"What?"

"The camera. A mini camera. It was on his tie, whoever taped this."

"Oh. So what do you think of all this, sir?"

He'd taken to calling me sir again. He was worried I would just kill him now and take the tape.

"Well, I heard every word. And that's Wilkes alright. The same Wilkes I always knew was there underneath that façade he likes to hide behind."

Passage nodded and smiled. "Everybody wants this tape, as I'm sure you can imagine. Those men today from the Ashariyya, if they can get their hands onto it, they have the only evidence that links them to the assassinations but also have Wilkes' butt in a sling."

"I've read about them. Blackmail is their forte," I said.

"Apparently, subtlety is not," Passage said. "That was unreal what they tried to do today."

"Yeah, I guess they wanted that tape bad. Or you dead, one of the two. Whichever it was, they wanted it done immediately, for them to go after you in that way? That was just plain stupid. Of course you have copies stashed somewhere?"

Passage hesitated. "Yes. No. Not really. There was a fire. All my copies were destroyed." He saw my next question coming and started to nod his head apologetically.

"You had all your copies at one location?"

"I know. It was stupid. I was in a hurry, I guess. I'm not . . . . this isn't my type of thing, Mr . . . ?"

"Gambit."

"Mr. Gambit, I never went through the training that you did. I'm just a regular guy caught up in some very irregular circumstances. I'm just trying to stay alive, you know? At this point, if I thought he'd let me live, I'd just give Wilkes the tape and be done with this whole thing, I swear."

He watched my reaction to his confession. To make him feel better, I let it show that I felt that I could understand the difficulties his life had been filled with the past several years. He saw some of the flinty posturing — probably projected to anyone within visual distance of me since the event on the freeway —

dissipate. And I could see that it made him feel better. There was relief visible in the way he lowered his head.

"I went to the video store yesterday even to make a copy. Some idiot started shooting across the street and I got out of there cause I thought it might have been intended for me or something."

"Yeah, I was there."

"What?"

"I've been assigned to watch you for a couple of days now."

"Really, oh my god!" He grabbed my arms just below my shoulders. I guess he didn't expect me to react the way I did, because he removed his hands after I looked at him like he was crazy.

"You're the guy that saved all those people. Right? You stopped that guy from killing them all."

"Yeah, I guess."

"I knew it," he said. "I knew there was something about you. The minute I started talking to you. I knew you were the only one I could really appeal to. There was something that told me you might listen."

"Still, I'm kind of surprised you're so quick to trust me. I am, as you said, one of Wilkes'. How do you know I'm not here to get the tape for him?"

"I don't. Sir, I'm just so tired of running. I have to trust somebody. Plus, I am really good at reading people. And I get the feeling you're one of the good ones. Righteousness is the closest word that comes to mind. I guess that's all I got right now."

He ejected the tape, handed it to me and watched as I put it into a utility pocket in my pant leg and zipped it up. Righteous, he'd said. Just like momma. Suddenly I liked this guy very much.

"So, what do you think of your esteemed leader now?" he asked.

"You have to have respect for someone in the first place in order to lose it."

"Good, good . . ." he said, with immense satisfaction and relief coming to his face, "then you'll help me?"

I nodded my head, and when I did he literally jumped for joy and rushed at me. I thought for a second that he might kiss me full on the lips. Thankfully, he just put his hands to my shoulders in an appreciative stance.

"Thank you. How ironic. One of Wilkes' own turns against him to bring him down," he said laughing.

The events that took place next occurred suddenly, and spanned only a moment. I heard a sound that I could compare to someone being slapped with an open palm. "Whap!"

Passage's laughter paused and he looked at me in a way that left me wondering if something important had just occurred to him that he must tell me. Instead he sucked in a shallow, rapid breath, swallowed something down his throat, and a mass of white and red and gray, the size of an orange or a peach, viciously separated from his head and flew to the ground a few feet away. It took a millisecond for me to fully comprehend that a bullet had just stillettoed through Passage's cranium and passed from one side of his head through, ejecting itself from the other. Still wearing that same acutely hopeful smile, displaying a feeling of elation and *conclusion* that had eluded him for five very long years, he dropped dead to the ground.

My left leg went limp underneath me and I fell to the ground, surprised and dismayed by the sudden pain that coursed through my entire body. All else overcome by the need to get to adequate cover before another shot was taken, I ignored the increasing pain and crawled behind a crate and put my back to it. Now, almost crying out from the agony, I looked down at my thigh, realized what it was that Passage had seen and had surprised him so. I had been shot. Passage had watched the bullet's impact and my mind's eye had logged his surprised expression even before the pain registered. They'd shot me in the leg and then put a bullet through his head.

CHAPTER 40

"Nicholas! Oh, I am so . . . very . . . disappointed in you my boy. Why didn't you just listen to me, son? We could have accomplished so much together. But this need, this need of yours to be insubordinate I just don't understand. I mean I get that you think you're taking the high ground or something. But the reality is that you're just hiding your inadequacies behind a veil of morality, a very feeble veil at that. You're not some heroic figure. You're a fool!"

The pain was wearing in on me full force now. I desperately wanted to just lie down and give in to it. I looked down at my thigh again and cringed. My utility pants and the flesh in my leg had been ripped open by the bullet and it was bleeding profusely. Searing pain, the sight of my own body torn open, a situation low on hope, the sound of his voice and the contempt within — all made for a complicated, depressing amalgamation. Still, I forced myself to listen. If there was some far-away hope to be wrested from the powers that be, it would come from not losing my wits after being shot. If I was to come out of this somehow, I could not allow myself to focus on the negative element, vast as it was, for even one single moment. I told myself there was one task that I must focus upon. I was going to fight to survive. Screw allowing my death, if that was the way it was to be, to be an easy one. Oh hell no. Not easy. Not that.

So I tried to block out the pain and listen. His voice was coming from well above me and I assumed they were on the walkway. It was more than just Wilkes. I could hear them when they moved by the creaking of the old and no longer sturdy walkway. How I didn't hear them up there before they shot me, I never knew. But I dared not try and sneak a peek at them. The sniper that had so effectively wounded me and killed Passage would already have his sights trained in on my general position, and was likely waiting for me to show myself. So I resigned myself to listening only.

But it occurred to me that was something of note as well. He'd wounded me, the more dangerous of the two, even seriously injured and Wilkes knew that, but ordered the kill shot taken on Passage? Wilkes had something up his sleeve. Whatever his motives, by not ordering me killed first, I'd been given some kind of reprieve. Now it was up to me to take full advantage of his arrogance. I proceeded to remove the belt from my waist and tied it above the wound as tightly as I could, hoping Wilkes and whoever was with him didn't hear the murmurs of pain that escaped through my clenched teeth.

"How could you not see that I was one step ahead of you at every turn?" he called down at me. "Perhaps the fault was my own. I had you figured out after your first six months into the program. I thought you'd come out of it. I thought you'd wise up and liberate yourself of those childish ideas of yours. Of course, that didn't happen. And when I finally realized that I'd given you too much credit, that's when I decided to use your own misguided altruism against you."

What the hell was he talking about?

"And I bet you're surprised, aren't you? You think you're so unpredictable. I assure you it is quite the opposite. I bet you have no idea how I found you here. Of course you don't. Had you simply listened to me, learned from me, instead of resisting me. You'd be able to keep up! Because that's what this business is about. It's about staying ahead of your opponent as well as your ally, for they are very often interchangeable. You must see their actions before they take them. As I saw yours."

Even suffering the intense pain a bullet wound will cause, I was starting to really get sick of his voice. I choked out a quiet chuckle. So that was his plan. He'd stayed his sniper from taking the kill shot so that he could have the pleasure of talking me to death.

"That's why I put you on this, Nicholas. It was a win-win with you. Either you'd do as I told you and perform your duties as well as any other agent I have, or you'd go one better and get close to Passage just because I told you not to, and get him to turn over the tape unwittingly."

But *that* got to me, and it dawned on me that I *was* a fool. How was it that I was so consistently, and more significantly, so easily duped?

"You know it really is too bad. Minus that immense handicap you call a conscience, you are without a doubt, one of my best of all time. Captain, proceed. Bring his body back to the building so that I can view the tape, then destroy it, the body I mean."

"Yes sir."

"Goodbye, Nicholas," Wilkes said.

I listened to the sound of his footsteps as he traversed the walkway, and soon after, the door closing behind him, and thought how fabulously appropriate was the imagery. It was true that from the second I had left with Passage, my life as one of Wilkes' game pieces had ended. Suddenly I was my own man again. And despite the insanity of the circumstances, it felt good, though this freedom might be short-lived were his soldiers successful.

I looked back down at my leg again. The blood was oozing out but it wasn't shooting out, which was good. It meant the femoral artery probably hadn't been torn open. If it had been, I would have bled out in minutes. My body was beginning to reconcile itself to the pain as well. A sharp ache replaced the shooting flames of torment and it provided a very welcome psychological impression of dissipation — still very present, but bearable pain. I knew it was because shock was setting in and that if I didn't get medical attention fairly soon, I could still die. But that was beside the point. The fact was I was beginning to adjust to it and that let me focus on other vital matters at hand. I had some work ahead of me — namely several well trained killing machines, and a future to forge.

I felt that old feeling again and my heart started pumping and my mind started working and maybe things weren't so far beyond hope after all. It came quick, only two years, but it looked like it just might be time to move on to life number three.

I knew that if they were smart, they'd leave the sniper on the walkway. Eventually they would be able to flush me out into view and he could just pick me off, an especially easy target with my new handicap. If they didn't, I just might have a chance of getting out of this place. Knowing they'd start searching near the clearing where Passage's body lay first, I picked myself up and distanced myself from it. I made my way well into the middle of the building, shooting in and out of the small, dark hiding places the crates and boxes provided as well as I could, keeping close to the ground. The pain slowed me but I moved better than I'd expected. The only plan to be made was to wait them out. Let them come to me. It was a comfort, knowing I still had my weapon, and that made the odds narrowly more acceptable.

I thought of something Wilkes had said. "I bet you have no idea how I found you here." If he'd planned this whole thing . . . ? Of course. He'd GPS'd Passage's Jeep some time ago, probably as soon as he'd known he was back in the States, giving him knowledge of where he was at all times. He'd just homed in on us when we weren't where he'd been expecting us. Ah, hindsight is always twenty-twenty. He was right about that. I had been shortsighted. I should have at least suspected that Wilkes had something diabolical planned and that I was expendable if his scheme required it.

So. I had a minimum of three men, from the sound of them on the walkway. After a few minutes of moving clumsily through the warehouse, I thought it safe to sneak a look onto the walkway and did. There was no one there. They'd all moved down onto the floor of the warehouse, which meant the sniper was either out looking for me or posted at the entrance to prevent an easy escape. They'd actually moved him. The one spot in the entire place that allowed for a virtually unobstructed shot anywhere in the building, and they'd moved him from it. Either they were very bold or very stupid. To be on the safe side, I chose the former and decided they wanted to make this fun, considering they outnumbered me and had me trapped inside.

I pulled a silencer from my utes, screwed it onto my pistol, and continued to try and ignore the pain. "Ok, fellas," I thought. "If it's a challenge you crave then you'll have one."

CHAPTER 41

They called him Captain. He was three months in when they began to address him in that way. It was nothing more than a display of affection, as rank did not work that way in The Program.

At first, he'd tried to keep to himself, to involve himself in the others' lives as little as possible. But, as had been the case all his life, people were drawn to him and it seldom took long for them to assign themselves to him, practically begging him to lead them to their glory, to their deaths, what have you. His experience at The Building was no different. The other men looked up to him immediately. He realized that much of the sudden adoration was due to his remarkable good looks. He knew as well as anyone that people seemed to unreasonably interpret attractiveness for merit of greater position. He stood at 6'4" and was as chiseled in body and bone structure as any Polo model. Blue eyes and close-cropped, blond hair served only to complete the illusion.

But much of it was his demeanor. Life had taught him in his twenty-eight years, at the time of joining Wilkes and his new program, to never show a lack of self-assurance, even if in reality it was in short supply. It was a mixture of that appearance of self-confidence and his habit of getting the job done, that caused him to rise above everyone's expectations of him — including Wilkes — and made him a virtual superstar to all the other students. He was unencumbered by concern for the sacrifices that would have to be made. He lacked sympathy. He lacked anxieties. He was a natural born leader. He knew it and upon meeting him, everyone else soon realized it as well.

As soon as he'd graduated, Wilkes paired him with the three other men he now worked with exclusively. They were capable soldiers all, but independently lacking as operatives. Of course Wilkes had the perfect answer. Pairing them with one such as he, who could bring them together as a unit, was inspired. And it worked. Every mission they'd undertaken was successful. His sniper had three confirmed; he had two himself. The others were still virginal but that would soon change, maybe even today. They'd both have a chance to kill this Gambit individual that Wilkes was so perturbed by.

Actually, that was the motivation behind pulling his sniper from the walkway and posting him at the door. He wanted to give the other two a chance at terminating him up close. They were still somewhat unsure of themselves and their close quarters skills, especially Siemaszko, and achieving their first kill would be of immeasurable value psychologically. He felt it was a safe gambit, to use the pun. This traitor had no way out except through the front door. His dilemma was the same as the bear that found itself trapped in a snare, being circled by wolves, and his fate would be the same. Eventually, one of them would take him and relieve him from his misery.

"Where is this guy, Cap'n?" Siemaszko. "Wait a minute, I got a blood trail."

The Captain looked behind him at his sniper standing in front of the doorway, rolled his eyes and shook his head, exasperated. He touched the receiver tucked into his ear.

"Siemaszko, radio silence unless you make contact."

There was a moment's pause before Siemaszko answered, "Yes sir."

Siemaszko was an impulsive brute. Though quite good when simple fighting skills were needed, he frustrated his leader with a complete ineptitude for operations that required precision or subtlety. He lacked patience. He lacked all forms of foresight as far as The Captain was concerned. And if he couldn't somehow bring out of him the skills that were needed to be a part of this type of unit, he would have to have him suspended from the team. What Wilkes did with him after that was of no interest to him. He'd only kept him on this long because he didn't want to be seen as an incomplete squad leader who couldn't cultivate his men instead of recycling them. But if the man continued to perform so inadequately, there'd be no choice left to him.

The Captain had placed himself and his sniper near the entrance. They both lay down in prone positions. He pointed his urban assault rifle, with its shortened barrel, ahead of him and looked over at Waverly, who did the same with his sniper's rifle. They took advantage of the natural cover provided by the enormous crates that were everywhere in the warehouse. He knew Gambit might try to take the easy way out, but he wanted to discourage it; therefore, he and Waverly made no effort to conceal their position, after assuring that if he came their way, they would be able to spot him first. They lay there, never taking their eyes from the small opening in the crates that would bring someone into their line of sight and would have to be taken to reach the doorway.

A loud clicking sound was heard and then what lights were still on in the ceiling flashed off. The interior of the building went completely dark. Gambit had found the fuse box.

"Guess we should have brought our NVG's," the Captain thought. "Interesting ploy, Gambit." Not only did it handicap his pursuers to some degree, but also meant Siemazsko would no longer be able to reliably follow that blood trail he'd encountered. Still, the Captain and Waverly had to wait and hope that Siemazsko and Helms would utilize their training to find and kill him anyway.

A minute passed. And then another. And another. And soon a quarter of an hour was gone with no shots fired. The Captain looked at his watch and then at Waverly, who looked as surprised as he did. Gambit had found a hiding place. That could cause a problem. Seeds of concern began to grow in his mind. He'd expected it to take minutes for Siemazsko and Helms to corner him and finish him off. By now he might be close to finding a way out of the building. He hadn't questioned Wilkes' order to wound him only, but perhaps he'd underestimated his foe by assuming he'd be made helpless by the injury. Surely he couldn't walk?

"Gambit!"

The Captain looked up at the sound of the yelling. It was Siemazsko again. Perhaps he'd finally found him.

"Where are you? Why do you hide like a coward?"

The Captain lowered his head in frustration. Imbecile. He'd likely just killed himself. Indeed, seconds later they heard the nearly inaudible sound of a silenced pistol being fired. A howling sound. Another shot, then all was quiet.

The Captain put his finger to his earpiece.

"Helms, can you get to Siemazsko's position?"

Nothing.

"Helms."

Nothing.

The Captain's day had just gone to shit.

"Helms, come in?"

He looked over at Waverly. He pointed up at the walkway and motioned for him to ascend it and retake the position from which he'd fired before. The experiment had failed embarrassingly. Both Siemazsko and Helms were likely dead. Now he would have to flush out Gambit and let Waverly take the shot. He watched Waverly stand and disappear behind a crate. He'd give him a few minutes to reach it before he'd venture out onto the floor of the warehouse. But. Waverly had to climb those stairs. He put his finger to his earpiece again and whispered.

"Waverly!"

"Sir?"

"You're going to have to wait. As soon as you start climbing those stairs he'll have a clean shot and he'll pick you off."

"Roger that, sir. I'm at the bottom of them now. I was just thinking the same thing. What's the plan?"

"I'm gonna get him to come to me . . . ."

The Captain looked up, interrupted by the lights flashing back on.

"Well, ok," he said in response to the lights. "I'll leave the transmit on my communicator on. As soon as you hear his voice, you get over here and take him out, good to go?"

"Roger that one, sir."

"Don't move until you hear something. He could be anywhere by now."

"Roger."

The Captain decided that it was time to be clever instead of bold. He'd have to think six-dimensionally in order to outsmart this surprisingly ingenuous man that Wilkes hated so much. He cursed Wilkes for ordering them not to kill him first. That decision had cost him two men's lives already, and was now forcing him into a position that required him to put himself at his enemy's mercy. He put the rifle down on the ground, pulled a 10 millimeter pistol from a holster and tucked it into his back waist, then raised his hands into the air. He still had his knife. And it might come in handy, especially if Gambit didn't have his own.

"Gambit!" he called. "Gambit, I'm waiting for you. Wilkes told me all about you. I know there is honor within you. He may not have represented it in exactly that way, but that's how I saw it. But we had a job to do, and that's all it was, at least to me. Just a job. Ok?

"I'm alone. And unarmed. I just want to talk. Gambit, c'mon. By some extreme turn of events you've managed to turn this whole situation into an unfair fight." He said this with a smile and tried to appear sincere and noncombatant.

"And I can see that one way or another you'll either get out of here before I can catch you or you'll kill me first. Neither of those choices seems particularly attractive right now. I want to come up against the best face-to-face first. Gambit. I'm unarmed. All I'm asking for is one chance. You and me. Hand to hand. Whoever wins walks through this door. From what I hear . . . you'll make mincemeat out of me. But I'll take that chance. C'mon. C'mon, answer me."

"I'm here."

The Captain turned and stared at Nicholas, emerging from behind one of the boxes into the open area, limping, holding his weapon in front of him. He came from the same position The Captain had occupied while waiting for Siemazsko and Helms to flush him out.

"So. This is the man that Wilkes has had so much to say about. I half expected you to be ten feet tall."

"Sorry to disappoint you. I seem to be doing a lot of that lately."

The Captain, while speaking, worked to prevent himself from looking in the direction of the walkway. He knew that if he let on that he was waiting for a shot to come, Gambit would notice.

"So, now we fight?"

Nicholas coughed out a very weary, worn out laugh, then looked at the most handsome killing machine he'd ever seen.

"No."

The Captain had no more words. He was surprised by the lack of activity and just stood there.

"I suppose you're waiting on your friend?"

That self-confidence, both the outward and inward kind, that The Captain had always utilized so effectively, was suddenly as alien a concept to him as mercy had always been.

"I'm sorry, he won't be joining us today. It's not his fault. I think his complaint would be back troubles," Nicholas said, nodding his head for effect. "Looked to me like it was broken."

The Captain actually felt his lip quiver and steadied himself. At first, he thought the best he could hope for was to keep himself alive. But quickly, an idea began to materialize. It was ambitious, but considering the circumstances probably his only option. He would *NOT* walk back into The Building defeated, with his entire team dead and his target still at large. He could not be seen as a failure. His first task would be to take Gambit off guard by demonstrating that he was no longer a threat. Then, perhaps that knife would come in handy.

"Believe it or not, Wilkes expressed a genuine sadness about having to kill you. I think he sort of liked you," said The Captain.

"Oh, I plan to show him my appreciation."

The Captain smiled and nodded. "Next to me, he told me you were the best he's ever brought into the program," he said, smiling again slyly.

"Next to you, huh? Well, I wouldn't put too much faith in his estimations of people."

"I guess you're right about that. He told us this would be a piece of cake. He said we'd be in and out of here in three minutes."

"Well, don't you see? He could have easily killed me first instead of Passage and this would have all been over already. This is nothing more than yet another one of his little mind games.

He's playing us both, you every bit as much as me. Don't let him. He doesn't deserve your loyalty."

"I think you're right. He doesn't. But, nevertheless, I have a job to do."

"Why do people keep telling me that?"

"I have a weapon in my back waist."

"Well there's a segway. I know that," Nicholas said, matter of factly. "What are you up to?"

"I'm going to pull it out so that you know I'm not armed."

Nicholas stared at him, curiosity on his face. The Captain did not take this as a no. He reached behind him and slowly pulled out the weapon, facing downwards so as not to spook him, and pulled the trigger, firing a 10 millimeter round into his own leg. He cried out and dropped to his knees. When he was sure he wasn't going to lose consciousness, he threw the weapon as far as he could. It disappeared into the crates, making a clanking noise when it hit the cement floor.

Breathing laboriously, fighting back tears, The Captain struggled to his feet, putting as little pressure as possible on his wounded leg. As he stood, he looked up at a smiling and thoroughly amused Nicholas Gambit, his eyes lit and dazzling. He was completely confounded by the actions of this man who had, not half an hour earlier, happily taken the order to kill him.

Nicholas dropped his head to his chest, lowered his gun, and rocked himself with laughter. The Captain allowed himself to smile as well and watched him until his fit diminished into a chuckle and then finally into just a very wide grin.

"You know, this may be the wrong thing to tell a man in the position you're in right now, but I was totally prepared to just tie you up and leave you here. You didn't have to shoot yourself, partner."

The Captain's smile disappeared.

"I want you to give me the chance to take you in."

"Huh? Ohhhhhh. I see. You still want to fight me. Oh, so . . . now that we're evenly matched, it's, of course, the only honorable thing for me to do. Give you a chance at what . . . killing me, is that it?"

The Captain saw in Nicholas' face the folly of aiming so high, so he redirected his goal.

"The tape," he said.

Nicholas scratched his neck and pretended to consider the proposal.

"Wow. Wilkes is really putting out some special kind of psycho, isn't he? You know what? What's your name?"

"They call me The Captain."

"Ok, well *Captain*, how about we try this? Because if I continue to stand here and talk to you, I'll die. From, incidentally, the gunshot wound I received from your sniper, and from which, I am currently bleeding to death. So how about this, Captain . . ." Nicholas' temper rising, "how about I, out of the kindness of my heart, let you live, and you repay me by not ever coming after me, no matter what Wilkes says; how 'bout that!"

"Then you should kill me."

This seemed to calm Nicholas down.

"But I heard you're not the type that will kill in cold blood. So I guess we're at an impasse."

"I walk out this door and you'll be minutes behind me, won't you?"

"Yes, if I am capable."

"Exactly." Nicholas stepped forward and raised his gun, The Captain turning away and throwing his arms up in front of his face. He fired three times. The first two were calculated, impassive — he lowered the weapon and fired two precise shots into each of his calves, obliterating the tendons he would find necessary for walking. He waited as The Captain collapsed, wailing, and when he did hit the ground, he fired the third with his lip curled, his eyes ablaze — a shot into his left thigh to match the earlier wound in The Captain's other leg, retribution its provocation.

"If you make it out of here . . ." Nicholas said, standing over the man now writhing in agony. ". . . If you make it out of here, I condemn you to live with yourself and the choices you've made. If it's any consolation, that's something we'll share." He started to turn, but stopped himself, an unexpected hint of regret on his face. "Good luck, mister."

Nicholas turned around, limped to where Passage's body lay, and removed the car keys from the man's pocket. He looked at the body for only a moment, knowing he could not allow himself to linger. He had to focus on getting to a hospital. Nicholas, at the time, didn't believe in a great deal of ceremony to honor the dead. But he couldn't help but think that this man deserved better.

"I'll find Wilkes. I'll make him pay," he said. "I hope you're in a better place now."

He placed the keys into a pocket and limped back to the exit. He looked at The Captain, lying in a pool of his own blood. His eyes were fixed, and Nicholas had to look twice to ascertain if he was still alive. Suddenly, he blinked and his eyes focused in on Nicholas, his face twisting into a scowl.

"Kill me."

Nicholas simply ignored him. He was spent. His mind moved at an impossibly slow pace. He felt as if all his strength was seeping out of him from the hole in his thigh, and again, he especially wanted to lie down. But still, his mood was hopeful. For the first time, in what felt like a very long time, he was no longer afraid of what the future held for him. Too weary to let it manifest outwardly, he smiled on the inside. He opened the door and let the sunlight and the cool breeze wash over him, so symbolic that he did smile this time.

He stepped over the threshold and just as his eyes were adjusting, he was whipped around and thrown back against the outside wall of the building by the bullet that tore into his shoulder.

Surprised, whacked by the new, fresh pain, he clutched his shoulder, slid down to a sitting position and looked up. Twenty feet ahead of him, smoke rising from the barrel of the gun he held out in front of him, stood Wilkes — smiling. He lowered his weapon to Nicholas' new position and prepared to fire.

"I didn't think you could survive. I just couldn't believe it. But something told me I had to see for myself. Truly, truly a shame. The best I ever produced."

Before Nicholas had time to think, a bullet ripped into the left side of Wilkes' head and exploded out through the other side. The man crumpled in front of an almost unconscious Nicholas.

Ignoring his mental command not to, his head bowed and he knew he was moments away from blacking out. Somehow he managed to look in the direction the bullet came from, wondering if another bullet meant for him was on its way. Several hundred feet along the cliff, among the tree line, he saw a flash of light, something metal reflecting in the sunlight. "Someone's rifle sight," he thought. He lost consciousness.

Nicholas eyes opened again, awoken by someone moving him. He looked up and stared into a beautiful woman's face. And he couldn't believe his eyes.

"Selena?" he begged, weakly.

"Hi, Nicholas."

She helped him up, wrapped his arm around her, and lugged him to her car. Nicholas was unable to help her much and she was forced to take most of his weight on her back, but she did admirably. She lowered him into the backseat and let him fall back, halfway in. She then went around to the other side, opened the door and got in on her knees, then pulled him in the rest of the way. His head now in her lap, she looked down at him and stroked his forehead.

"I am so sorry for what happened," she said. "I really did care for you. It wasn't an act."

Nicholas opened his mouth, trying to speak, but nothing came out. His eyes fluttered wildly and he passed out again.

"Nicholas?" She touched his neck for a pulse, then jumped in the driver's seat and sped away.

CHAPTER 42

I woke up and though it took a moment for my eyes to focus, I immediately knew I was inside a hospital room. I looked beside me and saw a nurse standing nearby, with her back turned. I reached out and grabbed her arm, startling her. She turned. She'd put her hand over her breast when I'd scared her. She shook herself and looked down at me.

"I'm sorry," I said. "Uhm, where's the woman that brought me in here?"

"Well, hi there, honey. I don't know. You tell us? We been looking for her ever since we finished patching you up. I'll have the doctor come in." She put down the chart she'd been working on and left the room.

"Damn," I said out loud, because I knew. I knew it. I felt it that I wouldn't see her again and that was how she wanted it. I wouldn't have known what I'd say to her if I had. The real shame was that she was the closest thing to being in love that I'd ever experienced. The love of my life a woman I barely knew and that was it. That was all. I was sure I would never see her again and so I just let it be.

I slipped out of the hospital a week later and checked myself into one of those healthcare facilities for the infirm and not the aged, under the name of Schendel. I got it from a doctor's office I'd seen on the taxi ride there. I did a lot of reading. A lot of rehab. A lot of feeling sorry for myself. Not because I was lonely; that was part of my plan. The solitary life meant there was no one about to ask questions. I guess I just regretted how my life had turned out. Yes, I was still quite young. But war was the only thing I'd known for years. That'll make you quite a bit older in spirit, quite a bit faster than most.

Both my leg and my shoulder were nearly a hundred percent in six months. My mother had taken out a life insurance policy some years before she died, so I had some money in an account set aside for me and I paid my bill with that. When all the expenses were finally done for, so was most of my cash. With the near fifteen thousand dollars I had left, I set out across the country and toured for months and tried to forget . . . all of it. Those times were a blur because I never stayed in one place for more than a week. Oklahoma, Mississippi, Kansas, Colorado, New Mexico, Texas. Truth be told, I couldn't give you any interesting regional insights, except that people mostly left you alone if you didn't invite them to do otherwise, the land was generally quite striking, the big cities were smaller than you'd expect . . . and that the girls were pretty and agreeable and not so chaste as the stereotypes might have you believe.

After several months, as the fact that the money would not last forever worked its way more and more into my thoughts, I decided it was time to give myself up and see what happened, because that's how I felt, like a fugitive. Amazingly, almost nothing did happen.

I'd made my way to Florida and that was when I called the FBI. That very same day they came to the hotel I was staying at in Jacksonville. They took the tape and asked me if there were any copies. I told them there most certainly were and that I wouldn't tell them where I had them stashed. This was true. I, of course, had made ten copies the first week I was at the rehab centre, and had sent five to different stores that rented post office boxes throughout the country. The other five went to banks where I'd reserved boxes in their vaults with specific instructions on contacting the authorities if I didn't check in with them every six months. I'd listed all of these boxes with their addresses and phone numbers, memorized the list, then destroyed it. In time, I also identified many of the men on the tape, and memorized their names as well. It wasn't difficult. They were newsmakers and heads of state. Overkill, perhaps, under other circumstances, but I knew that the people on that tape that had joined Wilkes on his crusade of lunacy would see me as a threat when it all came out. And after ascertaining the identities of only a few of the men, it became more evident that they were very powerful men indeed, all of them.

For the most part, what I told the agents seemed to satisfy them. They were very, very polite; very, very appreciative; and that told me they were very, very dumbstruck by the idea of the NC-13 complex having ever existed. Apparently, Wilkes' demise had not caused the program to collapse in on itself, alerting everyone to its existence as I had expected. The U.S. attorney general herself called me and asked me to stay in touch until the appropriate arrests had been made. But besides that, I was a free man.

As far as I could tell, the entire affair was finally concluded. So I decided to make a trip back to my old neighborhood. The night before I left, a man from the C.I.A. visited me at the hotel. We spoke of Wilkes, The Building, its location, and virtually every aspect of my training. Before he left, he told me that I would be registered as dead in order to protect me. And that if I was so inclined, I could go into the WitSec program. I told him no thanks, which is what he expected.

Plus, I knew that he was feeding me a bunch of horseshit. They wanted people to think I was dead, because to them, I was a part of a very big embarrassment and the less the media had to work with, the less they could rake them over the coals about it all.

Then he said something that made the hairs on my neck stand up on end. He said that "my" government might require my services again. I told him to go to hell and kicked him out. It soon occurred to me that they probably wouldn't even shut down the program. They'd just take it over and incorporate it into one of their own satellite agencies. Again, I was made to play the fool. Eventually, I realized I just shouldn't care anymore. Actually, if that was how it ended, all the better for me. No charges being laid meant no one would be coming after me for revenge. "So be it," I thought. "The corrupt being judged by their peers and ethical counterparts." I spent the rest of the night trying to figure out what I was going to do. Maybe go home and finally . . . make good on a promise.

CHAPTER 43

The next morning, I checked out and took a taxi to the airport. When we arrived, I paid the fare, got out, and threw my duffel over my shoulder. I was excited to be going home. I still hadn't figured out how I was going to keep people from recognizing me, or whether I would actually go back to my old neighborhood. But I didn't spend much time thinking about it. I just wanted to be home.

And when I stepped out of the cab, it hit me. I was free. Finally free of it all. Though Wilkes had been dead for some time, I was surrounded by so many bad options that I felt imprisoned, still confined somehow. Before I'd given myself up I'd been a fugitive in many respects. But now, my life was opened up to me again. I was my own man for the first time in a very long time and I could do with my life whatever I pleased. That was infinitely satisfying. My future was what *I* made of it from that point on and I couldn't help but smile at the prospect of it.

I found the ticket counter, showed ID, answered the nice lady's questions, and soon was off towards the terminal. That was when I saw the first one. He was tall and kind of lanky, dressed in a three-piece suit that did not fit him well at all. He stood in front of a magazine counter inside one of the duty-free stores. But what made me notice him was the way he looked in my direction from time to time without ever looking directly at me, and how near to the exit he was.

"One mistake a man that's tailing another will usually make . . ." Genai said to me once, "is to not commit. Because they need an easy egress, they usually stay near the entrance, so that they don't lose you. A good tail will find a spot deep within the shop from which to watch you." So. I had a tail — and a not very talented one at that.

I didn't look at the man more than twice, the second time just to verify my suspicions. He was likely government. I maintained my pace and planned to do nothing until he did. But if he was government, that meant he had at least one other partner somewhere. He'd be around too. It was possible that he was part of some security team placed on me for my own good. But at that point, many things were possible. His motives might not be so benevolent.

Then I saw another. And another. And that's when my internal alarm went off. Starched suits everywhere, conspicuous enough to set me on edge. I counted at least ten of them. One watching me from one flight above, looking down at me over the rail. Ahead of me, I picked out a couple more. Still, I showed nothing outwardly and continued as if I had no idea they were there. I was effectively surrounded, and that meant they could pretty much do as they pleased. Running would just lead to a whole lot of unnecessary exertion. I wanted to let them make their move, get a better idea of exactly who they were, then I'd act accordingly.

It didn't take them long to make that move. Suddenly, a group of them came running at me and I was surrounded by four government-issue handguns pointing at my head. Calmly, I stopped and let them close in on me. I looked around at the men, still quite calmly, and asked them, also very calmly, if I could help them with anything.

"You are to come with us, sir." It was the tall, skinny one.

"Is that right? And who is us?"

"Sir, we are with the U.S. government, which agency in particular is not to be disclosed at this juncture; however, with due authority your presence is required at another location."

I just smiled because I knew that'd be the last thing he'd expect. He squinted his eyes and just managed to keep himself from looking to one of the others for support. Knowing I'd penetrated his self-confidence so easily was very promising. Also, I was a little amused by this guy's knack for making himself sound like a strip mall security guard who'd just been confronted by a real policeman. I couldn't help myself. I'd been good for nearly a year with no real action. I wanted to play so bad.

"So . . . you're new, huh? Ok, I want to see some identification."

Four Department of Defense badges flapped open in unison around my head, causing a slapping sound that reverberated all around us. At that I laughed out loud. After a good thirty seconds of hearty laughter, I composed myself. I was impressed. They were being very patient. So far.

"And if I refuse?"

Each agent cocked his weapon.

"I see," I said.

"Sir . . ." the skinny one said again, now appearing on his face the most subtle hint of irritability, "I have identified myself and what I expect of you. As a U.S. citizen you are lawfully mandated to appear. If you do not come willfully you will be taken by force and I *can* and *will* do so if necessary . . . ."

"Where?" I interrupted. "I want to know where I'm going or I don't go at all."

That did it.

"You will go where I fucking tell you to go! Right now I am the law, sir. And if I say so, these men and I will blow your fucking head off and take you there a decapitated piece a shit, but on time. And if you ask me, that would really be kind of fucked up, especially for you. Nevertheless, one way or another, you will be coming with us. Do I make myself clear? Sir."

His comrades stared at him with wide open mouths and I think they'd discovered a newfound respect for him. I was proud of him too. He'd finally freed himself of that stodgy, government issue reticence that is forced upon all of them at some point or another. But I still wanted to have some fun. My chance was coming, so I played the capitulate.

"After you," I said.

"Very good, sir," he said. He turned, and as he did so, I noticed that his head rode higher on his lanky frame and he looked ahead of him, daring anyone or anything to ever contradict him again. I couldn't help but smile. I'd managed, in less than a minute's time, to bring out the leader in him. He'd been briefed on me, my skills, and had come expecting trouble, that was well apparent. And when he'd so easily convinced me to acquiesce, it was like his first time with a girl all over again. Look out world, here comes tall skinny federal agent guy, that probably had to choose between either his daddy's McDonald's franchise or applying to the intelligence community, and he's on *FIRE* today!

The four men put away their weapons, then formed a perfect square, with me in the center of it, and commenced to march. I snuck a look above me and saw that the agents that had positioned themselves there had disappeared, likely to meet us where the transportation awaited. The others that had been watching the exchange between myself and Ronald McDonald began making their way towards the exits as well, still keeping one eye on me and their compatriots. I gave them a few more seconds to feel confident that they'd tamed me, then threw myself into them.

Lightning fast, I grabbed the two in front of me by their collars and yanked them backwards with all my strength. Because of that stupid square formation they were in, they slammed right into the two behind me, stunning all four, and sending them falling all over each other. I turned, dropped my bag to the floor, and waited for the first one to get to his feet. Again, there was no point in running, the other agents were already on their way to our position and would be there in seconds.

Tall, lanky guy got up first. As he stepped towards me, reaching inside his jacket for his weapon, I took a step forward as well with my left foot. I planted it and let it serve as balance for my right. He never pulled that weapon. I shot the heel of my outstretched right foot into his forearm and crushed it between my foot and his own body. He screamed an unintelligible series of words that sounded kind of like "Fugginshibastard!" and flew into another agent, sending them both backwards, flapping their arms around wildly. I had to move several feet forward to get to the other two and reached them just as they were getting to their feet. One threw a lame duck that I deflected upwards, and because it was available, punched him in the armpit, just to see what it would do to him. He cried out in a way that told me it did hurt pretty good. I pulled on that same arm, brought him in close and kicked him in the stomach. With him now bending over in front of me sideways, I saw his partner reach out over his friend's back and attempt to hit me with a punch. I just threw my head back and avoided it. I dropped to my knees, brought my elbow down on the neck of the one bending over and dropped him. Already on the ground, I threw out my leg and swept it in a high arc and sent his comrade flying onto his back.

I jumped to my feet, ready for more, but very quickly saw that my rebellion was to be extremely short lived. Four semi-prepared agents with the element of surprise on my side, yes. But ten? Not in my wildest dreams. I just stood there and watched as I was surrounded by them all, pointing weapons at my head again.

"Where is it we're going again?" I asked. The next thing I knew, I was falling to the ground, courtesy of a well-placed rifle butt across the back of the head. As I crumpled and began to lose consciousness, I heard the tall, lanky one again.

"That is one determined son of a bitch. Give him the sedative."

My eyes were lead weights. I was conscious long before I could manage to open them. When I finally did, my eyes took forever to get in focus. I felt like I'd just come back from the dentist and he'd administered novocaine through my temple. I became aware of someone else in the room, but for several seconds, he or she remained a slow-motion blur. I was slumped in an easy chair. Slowly, I managed to pull myself up to a normal sitting position and tried to determine where I was. I was surprised by a voice.

"Welcome back to the land of the living, Mr. Gambit. Don't be surprised if you're groggy for a few minutes. I'm told you were given an especially strong anti-stimulant because of the trouble you gave our people."

Finally, the room began to clear and I could make out that it was a bespectacled man wearing a silk tie that speaking to me. He was well into his forties. Slender, both in face and form with a hundred dollar haircut and bright, intelligent eyes. I looked around at his office. A picture of the President on the wall to my right. Photographs of this man's family on his desk. A large, bronzed Eagle Globe and Anchor stood in the corner, but next to it was a well-starched Army uniform that was held up by a cardboard cutout, though it seemed as if it could have stood up just fine on its own. So he was either an ex-Marine or Army or both. According to the nameplate on his desk, I was inside the office of the Under Secretary of Defense for Intelligence. While unconscious, I'd been flown to Arlington, Virginia. I was inside the Pentagon.

"I feel like they gave me two doses," I said. My lips moved laboriously and it came out blubbery. I thought I might need to repeat myself. He smiled.

"All things considered, I couldn't blame them if they did. You, uh, made quite a spectacle of yourself."

"Yeah, like I asked ten of your people to try to force me to come here against my will."

"Well, Mr. Gambit, I asked them to bring you here. And believe me, I would not have gone to the trouble had there not been a very good reason."

"Yeah, I'll bet it's a doozy," I said. I glanced around the room while I spoke. As soon as I'd come to enough to see straight, the nameplate on his desk had me accessing my mental files. "Listen, why don't we get down to business. What exactly is it that you want from me?"

"Alright then. Do you know who I am?"

"Daniel, or Daniyel if you prefer the Hebrew. Last name Henry. Daniel Henry, Under Secretary of Defense for Intelligence. First confirmed by the senate in 2000. Pre-history is somewhat vague, which is why so many people in Washington were surprised by your installation. My own personal research shows ties to one John Wilkes — well, at least that you both graduated from Notre Dame at the same time and were likely friends."

The under secretary was dumbfounded by that last little tidbit. Suddenly I was in solid command of the conversation. I decided I wanted to keep his attention while I had it.

"Yessir," I said. "I assume the reason I'm here is in some way related to that last bit of trivia." I looked him dead in the eyes.

"Actually, you're wrong. Uh, that is not correct."

His acting skills were lacking. He wasn't making me believe it.

"I assumed that was the reason I am here talking to you and not the CIA. or some other pure intelligence agency. That's got to be the most likely answer, you wanting to eliminate a potential danger to yourself and your image, reputation, etc., etc."

While I was speaking, the undersecretary recovered from his surprise and now had a smile on his face.

"You are impressive. No, actually there are a few reasons you're here today. But that other thing . . . with Wilkes. Could you keep that to yourself? I would be extremely, extremely grateful."

"I really have no reason to make an enemy of you."

"Thank you."

"Yet," I said. "Be sure not to give me one."

"Of course," he said. He was annoyed, but waved his hand in front of him to show he was beyond any threats I had to make. "Then, back to business, eh? We had you brought here because we need you to do us a favor."

"A favor."

"Yes, a favor of sorts, for us.

"Who exactly is *us*? You're DOD *AND* DIA. We're at the Pentagon. The CIA and the FBI told me I was free to go. Are we on some kind of spook tour? And a favor? What the hell does that mean?"

"Ok. The *us* in the previous statement signifies a special task force, comprised of elements of the State Department, Defense Intelligence Agency and the FBI/DOJ."

I rolled my eyes. Acronym fatigue.

"The favor is a problem we'd like you to handle for us, for the U.S. government as a whole, that is."

"What, man, you're talking like you want me to stop at the store and pick up some diet."

He laughed. "No, we want you to kill someone . . . for us."

My heart started beating very fast.

"I don't do that." Not incredibly inventive, but it was all I could come up with.

Henry looked down at a dossier on his desk, my dossier, purely for show, and then back up at me.

"That's odd of you to say that. Says here you've done it many times. One Raymond Smalls, one Louis Rayes, John Wilkes and three of his men . . . ."

"So, The Captain survived," I thought.

" . . . at least five confirmed kills during that highway situation of yours . . . ."

"I don't assassinate people," I said.

"You know, I hate that word. Carries so much baggage. Then don't assassinate this person, just do the same as with all those other people."

That caught me off guard. And it took me a moment or two to come up with an appropriate response, but when I did I was quite happy with it.

"Now I realize why you're the *under* secretary," I said. "People probably just don't like you very much."

He brushed off my impertinence yet again. "I don't understand," he said. "Isn't that what you were taught at the Noble-13 complex?"

"Sir, whatever Wilkes told you was probably what he thought you wanted to hear. As a matter of fact, he told me I would never be given an assignment like that."

"I find that hard to believe. Looks like I wasn't the only person he told things they wanted to hear."

"Yeah, exactly. But you know what? I wised up, that's why he's dead. Why'd you come to me for this?"

"Well, to be honest, much of it is just timing. You see, we were going to bring you in anyway because of your connection to Wilkes."

"I don't get it."

"We wanted to know how much Wilkes told you, how much classified information he shared. You are aware that Wilkes was N.S.A?"

I sat back in my chair, a little surprised. "No, I didn't . . . I guess I just always assumed he was less desk jockey and more hands-on kind of lunatic. Unlike you, after he graduated college and was discharged, his trail went cold. So all his field operations training was in the military?"

"Oh, no. He was all over the intelligence community for many years. That's how he developed the contacts that enabled him to start and fund that program you were in. But that's an entirely different and irrelevant story, especially now that he's dead. Uhm, since it was obvious that we would be bringing you in anyway, we were instructed to prep you for this mission when we did. Sometimes the great machine does actually run with some efficiency."

"Yeah, great, whatever . . . there's gotta be more to this than I just happened to be on the way."

"Well, yes, you're right. There are several reasons. Please don't think this false praise, but you sir, are an enigma. Believe it or not, we don't have many black agents, and certainly very few of them have your degree of training. From what I hear, you are one of the best, and I'm talking of all our people."

"Oh, so I'm one of your people now, huh? What does my color have to do with any of this?"

Henry reached into the dossier and pulled out a glossy paper document, face down, and pushed it across to me. "Because this is who we want eliminated."

I picked up the glossy, turned it over and looked at it. At first, I didn't know how to react, but it didn't take long for me to feel very, very offended. It was a photograph of quite possibly the most beautiful brown-skinned creature I had ever seen. The only detraction to which, was that she wasn't smiling, and appeared as if she had never considered the idea. It looked like some kind of staff photo, more similar to a mug shot than any other.

"This is great," I said. "So let me get this straight. First you people tell me I'm dead to the world because really, it makes things easier on you. Then, when I'm finally going home you force me, against my will, to come here so you can try to get me to kill . . ."

I paused, then turned the picture around and showed it to him. I guess my thinking was that the sight of this apparitional vision of beauty, probably his hundredth time seeing her photo, would make him suddenly see the error of his ways.

". . . a black woman. An incredibly beautiful black woman. I spend most of my life trying to get out of a place where murder is a way of life for my people and here you are trying to get me to take the life of something as precious as this? Man, there is no way in hell you're going to get me to do this."

"What's the difference? So this is an ethnic thing?"

Have you ever wanted to kill a bug simply because you felt it wasn't worthy of occupying the same breathing space as you? I got up to leave.

"Look man, find yourself somebody else."

"Mr. Gambit, sit down. Sit down!"

I turned on him, completely unrelenting. The one indignant bone in my body had been seriously compromised and I was not in the mood to be commanded by anyone or anything.

"Mr. Gambit, you will sit down or you will go to jail."

"Then put me in jail, you son of a bitch. I will not kill that woman, not for you, not for anyone else!"

Henry jumped to his feet and yelled right back at me over his desk, his face going red. "This woman is no innocent! She is responsible for the murders of three entire families in the midwest, two men on the east coast, and God knows how many worldwide. She is a terrorist, plain and simple, and whether she's black, white, whatever, one way or another she must be nullified. Now you sit down."

I watched him for several seconds then finally threw myself back into the chair. He did the same, more slowly.

"Ok. Two questions. One — I still don't understand why you want me. Number two — Why is it that she's done all these things that you're saying?"

He took a moment to answer and I realized he was still working to calm himself. The type of screaming match he'd just engaged in must have been an irregularity for him, especially in his own office. That made two government types in one day. Nick Gambit was on a roll.

"Allow me to explain everything and all your questions will be answered summarily. First, frankly, she is one of the best too. Maybe even better than you. I'm not joking. We trained her."

This caused my brow to furrow, but I wanted to let him finish.

"Her father was royalty, a king no less, her mother English. They were monarchs of a funny little East African country stuck between Tanzania and Zambia. It's called Quandry. It was one of the few remaining monarchies still in existence at the time. Her father and the U.S. government were very friendly. In return for access to certain resources, land allocations, those types of things, the king requested one thing in particular — that we train his daughter so that someday she could effectively take over as ruler of their country. That was approximately five years ago. And now we're hoping you can get close to her, which just might give you enough of an edge. She's no fool; she won't give you a chance at an easy sniper shot. When you do it, you're going to have to be close to her. We've learned she distrusts anyone who she hasn't known well for a long period of time or who doesn't owe her in some way. As a black man with your reputation, relevant in its connection with the government, you might have a real chance at acceptance into her group. You, Mr. Gambit, are our best shot at dealing with this woman quietly."

"Why is dealing with her quietly important?"

"Come now, Mr. Gambit, surely Wilkes taught you better than that."

"Shortly after I met Wilkes I learned to evaluate everything he told me for myself before I believed it. What about my second question? What made her go off the deep end?"

"The best we can tell, it's a simple case of revenge. A coup occurred while she was out of the country. Both her parents were killed when it all went down. Three of the king's accountants were the only ones left alive. They were told they would be released upon one condition — they were to transfer all the king's official funds into the coup leader's personal accounts and to make the country's assets ready for the new administration. They were each American citizens and they returned here upon their release. Understandably wanting an environment as low on stress as possible, two of them moved to Nebraska and one to Colorado. Of course they took their families. And when Chelsea Matawae came for them, their families perished with them as well. She also gunned down William Goodacre of Hagerstown, Maryland, and Simon Means of Buffalo, in their respective homes. Those two men were . . ." he flipped through the dossier, ". . . they provided some weapons and certain types of domestic intelligence to the coup leaders. We have reason to believe both were misled about what use their services were being put to. They had no idea they were going to be responsible for all those deaths. But she didn't care.

"We believe she may be targeting several others here in country and at least two more internationally. She's already killed two men in England, was caught the first time she was in North America by a small team of British agents, uh, MI-5, who pursued her for those killings, and . . . they didn't even get out of the country with her before she killed them too."

He laughed.

"You see what we're dealing with here? It's a mess. There's no telling how many more innocents will get caught between her and her targets. And the way she's going, she won't stop until she's killed every coup leader, everyone who follows them and everyone who she might determine helped them.

"Also of note, while still in Africa, she hooked up with a particularly . . . competent mercenary named Peter Granton . . . "

I was hip. Pausing while searching for the right word, then finally settling on competent, meant many things, but none of them was reassuring.

" . . .who will be supplying her with the manpower and assorted weaponry to carry out these acts.

"To be honest," he continued, "I wouldn't give a damn about her or her tiny country if it weren't for the American lives she's taken or has yet to take. Now do you understand why I have gone to such extremes?"

I nodded.

"We would really like to have you on this one, Mr. Gambit. The President himself has shown mild interest in this case. You might even receive his thanks personally."

"Well gee, that'd be swell," I said stone-faced, without looking at him.

He shook his head and smiled, the ill will from earlier now worked out of the room. "Arrogance must be a prerequisite for agents of your caliber. So what do you say?"

I thought about it for a minute.

"I'll find her and stop her but I won't kill her unless I have to."

"Done," he said, nodding. "Thank you. I'd prefer to have her dead, but so long as you can guarantee you'll get her out of my country and she doesn't hurt anybody else. I'll have the intelligence reports sent to your hotel room and $50,000 will be wired into an account we'll set up for you ASAP."

"You mean I get paid?"

"Of course," he said, incredulous. "Unless you'd rather that I didn't—"

"No! No, no, that will . . . uh, be acceptable, just fine. I'll uh, have a list made up of equip I'll need."

"Very well. I'll have my men show you to your hotel. I'll send someone to drop off a complete report and pick up your list in a few hours. Good luck, Mr. Gambit."

We stood and he offered to shake. It occurred to me that this guy was my new employer. The money definitely made him less repulsive, so I returned the shake.

"You said earlier that you were initially bringing me in to ask if Wilkes told me any secrets. Aren't you going to ask?"

"You were clearly surprised when I told you he was N.S.A. If he didn't tell you that, you probably have no more information than what we collected from your instructor."

My heart nearly leapt out of my chest. "My instructor?" I whispered.

"Genai's working with us now."

"Oh . . . Genai. Cool. Can I talk to him?"

"No. Good luck, Mr. Gambit."

"Right. Thanks."

And so, just like that, in a matter of minutes, there I was again — involved in something that was much, much bigger than myself and preparing to put my life in danger without knowing exactly whose side I was on. I had hoped that my life would become simple and that I could finally go home and strive . . . just to be normal. Of course, to the contrary, my life was becoming more complicated by the minute — and by my own doing. I could have said no. And I fully realized that, essentially, I had been contracted to dispose of a woman I had never met, didn't care about, despite what I'd said in Henry's office, and really didn't care to get to know. I guess I just didn't care period.

I was beginning to understand the existence all those countless infamous murderers throughout history experienced; who upon psychological scrutiny, were determined to be lacking any conscience whatsoever — complete, utter indifference. And every day I remained caught up in this environment, I became more like them, which was exactly what Wilkes had wanted. It scared me that I could feel my morality slipping away completely. The moment following my acceptance of the mission, all I could think about was completing said mission, being done with that business, and never looking back.

I shacked up in the hotel room Henry's agents checked me into, ordered room service, spread the file that contained all of the elements that went into Chelsea Matawae's quest for revenge, and mug-upped. Inside the report that had been prepared by some undisclosed agency within the department of justice — probably FBI — was a great deal of conjecture as to what her next move would be. All of their conclusions were painfully obvious and therefore likely to be wrong. This woman, according to her file, was exceedingly intelligent and had a knack for intuitively and creatively accomplishing her goals. Simply put, she found better, faster ways of getting what she wanted. That told me it was likely any profile set up by the analysts who had included their conclusions about her in this report were wrong. At least, that was how I saw it.

They suggested that she was planning on shifting her focus to a relatively small company based out of Ohio, called Mercury Investments, that had struck up a deal with the new administration in Quandry. They thought she was going to try and kill one of the V.P.'s or something ridiculous like that.

After several hours of studying, I eventually came to a conclusion that seemed much more likely. It started out as no great epiphany; but something was nagging at me that I couldn't quite put my finger on. It was likely it wasn't even relevant, but still it stuck with me. Where was the security during this coup where her parents had been killed? A king who would go to the trouble of having his daughter trained in a U.S. government program much like the one I was in, but wouldn't surround his administration with the most capable and prepared security force? Granted, it was an internal coup, but most of his immediate guard remained loyal to him. Yet that entire force had been slaughtered in record time, with apparently no casualties to the invasion force. The king himself had died of bullet wounds to the back, which didn't signify much, until you combined that with another intriguing piece of information — the body of the king's head of security was just . . . absent. Never found. He was assumed dead and not a part of the coup because of his intense loyalty to the king and his family. More than once he had demonstrated his willingness to give his own life in order to protect them. Still, I thought it might be worth checking into. So I called Henry's secretary and asked her to fax me all the information they had on the dead king's head of security. She told me it would take several hours as a number of their key research personnel had gone home for the day. I looked at the clock on the bedside table. I'd been perusing the files since noon, nearly six hours. I told her that'd be fine. I guess even spies have families to go home to.

And of course, one thought leads to another. Families. Henry had pictures of his family in his office. First I thought, "What kind of oddball intelligence executive would keep pictures of his own family up in an office where people like me randomly showed up? He couldn't be that foolish."

Then I remembered some of the facts that had come out when researching Wilkes' background. Henry's entire immediate family had been killed years before in a fire that destroyed their home as well as everyone inside it. Those pictures were probably the only keepsakes he had left. I began to regret how I had spoken to him. We suddenly had something in common. We shared the same kind of loss, though his was on a *much* larger scale. Perhaps I would eventually apologize.

One thought to another. Families. Loved ones. People whom you care about and whom you are important to and that you go home to at the end of the day. I could not think of one single person. Not one. Not even anyone still alive in my past that would welcome me, you know? Grab me up and pull me into their arms and tell me how much they missed me. And all of a sudden a lonesomeness that had been creeping up on me for a few weeks hit me full blast.

I cursed myself for the thousandth time. Mr. Big Tough Macho Superguy is sad because he's all alone. I had to get out of that hotel room. I grabbed my passcard to the room and took the elevator down to the lobby. I decided to ask someone at the front desk to be sure and ring me when the fax came. I was making my way over to it, when I was stopped as forcefully as if a brick wall had been erected in my path in a matter of moments.

From where I stood, I saw the same things you see at any high-class hotel in any big city. People moving about, the sounds they made as they traversed the lobby and talked. Some sitting, pretending to be disinterested in anything but their paper or book or companion. The sound of elevators reaching their floors with a "ding." In front of me, a view of the street that ran in front of the building, visible through the gigantic lobby windows that seemed to go up forever, the traffic on that street and streetlights that shone through the night.

But from my perspective, the resemblance to the hotel that Wilkes had put me up in that fateful day, where he'd sent that agent to pluck me up and deliver me to the first step down the pathway to my new life, was meticulous. I saw myself sitting in that chair all over again, made into an empty vessel by my mother's death, awaiting something, anything to fill me up. Sad and scared. And searching for purpose and truths and vengeance. Oh, that's a dangerous combination.

The visual was just far too much for me. I gave up on the idea of touring the city, made a quick about-face, and went right back up to my room and ordered more room service. Funny, huh? Terrorists, trained killers with orders to eliminate me, drug dealing, gun toting scum — no problem. But hit me with déjà vu that reminds me of how I zigged when I should have zagged and I cower like the NRA after a democrat has taken office. I stayed in that room, ate, watched some television, cleaned my weapon, then thought of Chelsea Matawae and how terrible it must have been for her to lose her entire family, much the way I'd lost my mother.

And we'd both chosen very interesting ways of dealing with our loss. But the fact was, she couldn't be allowed to continue killing indiscriminately. Her pain and the way it affected her had caused her to cross the line into exacting acts of evil, not justice. She had to be stopped. And I'd been elected as the one to make it so.

I finally fell asleep and slept soundly through the night. I was awakened the next morning by the phone. It was the front desk. They had my fax. They had me sign for it when it was brought up to the room and I tipped the bellboy ten bucks on the government's dime. I sat down on the bed, read it, and immediately called Henry's secretary again. After she gave me a couple of numbers, I stayed on the phone for the next couple of hours. Soon, it all finally began to come together and I came up with a plan that was much more efficient than taking the time to become Chelsea Matawae's best friend. My last phone call was back to Henry's office.

"Mr. Gambit?"

"Henry. She's got one last target here in the U.S. then she's probably going back to her country to reclaim the throne. She's spent her time here training and refining her group, and in the process, achieved what she considers revenge."

"Who's this last target she's after?"

"Maximilian Bergosi."

"Bergosi . . . their chief of security? He's dead." He paused and I let him think it out. "Assumed dead. I take it you don't agree?"

"Bergosi's ex-wife and son live here in the U.S., in a New York Suburb. I had your office connect me with the FBI field office there and found out some interesting things. Bergosi's son turned up missing about two months before the coup occurred. The day after the coup, the boy was returned to his mother. It was explained to the authorities that the boy had simply run away and finally decided to come back. I think Bergosi is with them now. And if I figured it out, so did Chelsea. He's her last target before she leaves the country."

"Hmh. How'd you come up with this?"

"It's what I would have done. She and I are very alike. But you already know that. That's why you came to me, isn't it? Let me ask you a question. Do your profilers tell you that I would have resorted to the same kind of insanity had I been given the opportunity?"

There was a moment while he deliberated his answer. I could feel him smiling over the phone. This was the kind of conversation a man like him thoroughly enjoyed.

"Tell me the truth," I said.

"They did mention your similarities. I personally, knowing your record, and knowing you for the short period of time that I have, would say no. Not like her. And I'm not just saying that because I know it's what you want to hear."

I wasn't sure I believed him, but it didn't really matter to me what he thought. I don't even know why I asked.

"But that still doesn't tell us where she's at," he said.

"I find Bergosi, I find her, one way or another."

"What do you need?"

"I need travel arrangements. Mesa City, New York."

"Very well."

"One more thing." The impulse to ask what I was about to came from nowhere. Prior to that moment, I had not even once considered it . . . not consciously. Yet there was a certainty about it. The need to do this was unmistakable. It had all been very unclear, but was suddenly unencumbered. My mind had finally sorted through all the confusion.

"What is it?" he asked.

"I want your people to profile someone based on the information I'm about to give you . . . and then I need you to find this person for me. I don't have much. But you are intelligence. You can do miracles with only a little info, right?"

"Mr. Gambit, I could get someone here to tell me what color boxer briefs you're wearing right now."

I smiled. Likely it was an accident but he was right - I did always wear boxer briefs.

"That's disgusting, Henry. Impressive, but disgusting."

CHAPTER 44

Shortly after my conversation with Henry, a car had been sent for me at the hotel and my driver took me to a heliport in Washington. The plan had been that I would receive the equipment that I'd requested there before an hour's helicopter ride to New York. Surprisingly, the government was rather slow in fulfilling its promises and my gear was stuck behind a wall that apparently was papered with red tape. So, after waiting nearly another day, I called Henry and told him I was going to go ahead to New York and for him to ship everything to my hotel. If I waited for everything to arrive, by the time it did, Bergosi would be John Doe number 650 for the year and Chelsea would be long gone. I boarded the special order copter they sent for me with my duffel bag, a credit card, and my Reicher pistol and ammo. Genai had told me once that mindset, intel, and a capacity for thinking on the run are the most deadly weapons for those dressed lightly for war.

My mindset was established. I wanted to deal with this woman and her team of assassins as quickly as possible so that I could begin to approach some semblance of emotional and intellectual normalcy. My capacity for thinking on the run, according to Under Secretary Henry, was near legendary already. Now my next move was to get the requisite intel. So, as soon as we put down at a helipad in nearby Syracuse, I rented a car with a GPS system and drove to the address belonging to the ex-wife of Maximilian Bergosi that was given to me by the FBI.

Upon touching down, I'd checked with three different rental car companies before I'd found one that had a vehicle with tinted windows and GPS. A luxury rentals company, they'd brought me a 2003 Lexus 400 Coupe. Definitely my style, but not exactly low-profile, as I would have preferred. But I didn't have time to sweat the small stuff. I found the house in a modest, middle-class neighborhood. I drove in front of it once, glancing at it for only a moment, then reconnoitered through the rest of the immediate neighborhood. I parked far enough away to access a visual of the house only through the binoculars I pulled from my duffel. The same car, especially that very recognizable car, might arouse suspicion if it passed in front of that house more than once. The neighbors might not think anything of it, but the other players involved would. Really, my interest wasn't so much in Bergosi himself, but in discriminating anyone else surveilling him.

When I drove through the neighborhood, no one jumped out at me as having an unnatural interest in the house, but that meant nothing. Bergosi was under the impression that everyone thought he was dead. He wouldn't expect anyone to be looking for him. If I were them, knowing that, I would have tagged his car with a GPS long ago and would now just be waiting for him to go on the move. That meant, for all I knew, they could be miles away or watching the house, just as I was. There was one thing alone that I could be sure of if I was right and they were watching him; when he left his house, they would follow. So, I sat.

After an hour, a thought occurred to me and I cursed myself for the thousand and first time. Who goes on a stakeout, where they know they may be holed up for days, and forgets to stop and get munchies? Spy guy Nick Gambit, that's who. In another few hours I would really start to get hungry and if I left, that would be a perfect time for Bergosi to walk out on his lawn to get the paper and have some thug come running up to him and cap him in the face. That would be my luck. Idiot.

Just as I was debating calling Pizza Hut to ask them if they could deliver to the third fire hydrant just west of the corner of Pico and eighth, the man himself popped out of his house, cheery and animated, clutching his son and holding hands with his wife, smiling and happy to be with his family again. I slumped down in my seat as they bounced into her car, backed out of their driveway, and turned down the street. I let them get almost a block away before I started the car. After picking up a visual, thinking I had a good chance of picking up the car again if I did happen to lose it, I even let them get a little further ahead of me.

Distracted as he was by his reunion with his family, this man Bergosi, according to the info I'd received on him, was a consummate professional. There was a reason why the coup leaders had picked him to betray his employers. He was very good at what he did; he and his security force, unseasoned as it was, would likely have still prevented them a successful bid for control of the small country. He was that good. Subconsciously, he'd be searching for a tail. If he picked me up and got spooked, he'd run for dear life, and I might never have this chance again. Plus, I didn't want Chelsea's people to see me tailing him either, which would elicit the same result.

I followed Bergosi and his family to an Italian restaurant in the same lot as an outlet store. I let them park and exit the car before I approached the restaurant. Once they reached the entrance, I pulled into the parking lot and drove around the building, emitting an air of nonchalance that would make anyone disinterested in anything excepting the car. They were being seated when I passed in front of the large window that looked out onto the parking lot and the road that ran in front of the building. I pulled the steering wheel to the left, found a close parking space, and pulled in head first.

Feeling more like a gumshoe than ever, I adjusted my mirrors so I could see through the window and into the restaurant, with clear view of Bergosi's son and wife. My view of Bergosi himself was obstructed mostly by the pillar that he sat behind. But that was of no consequence; I knew where he was.

"Now, where are your pursuers, eh?" I wondered.

I scanned the area and noticed two cars pulling into the parking lot the way that we had come, one driver in each car. The first car parked near the exit. The second car pulled up behind Bergosi's car and studied it quickly, then slowly drove in front of the restaurant, looking through the window. As nonchalant as I had been earlier, he pretended to have no interest in what he saw, but as soon as he was out of their area of vision, gassed the car and pulled up next to his comrade and spoke to him. I watched all of this through my mirrors, never turning to look at them. A tandem.

In case one car lost their target, the other would have circled ahead already, to pick him back up when he came into view. That's why I hadn't noticed anyone following. Very clever.

"Gotcha," I said.

The man in the first car nodded, spoke a few more words in return, then they laughed about something. He nodded again, then pulled away. I turned the key in the ignition, let the engine purr to life, backed out, and followed him. As I pulled away from the restaurant I got a final glimpse of the Bergosis. What he'd done to save his family, I could not judge. I would have acted differently, perhaps, but when posed with such a dilemma, where either choice was horribly deficient in merit, how could I say that his choice was an imperfect one. Could there have been such a thing as a perfect choice under those circumstances?

"Good luck, Mr. Bergosi," I said.

I followed the car to a high-rise brownstone about twenty miles away. The street lacked anything to use for cover, so I was forced to just pull over down the street from the building and watch the man park and get out of his car. He walked to the entrance and knocked. A man opened the door and nodded to him as he entered. He looked around before closing the door and I saw his eyes sweep over the Lexus. I immediately put the car into gear and punched into the computer the name of the hotel I'd been told to check into.

I knew that just because some of their men occupied this building, it was very possible that neither Chelsea, nor Granton were anywhere near there. It wouldn't make sense for them to spend more time than necessary on the premises. They probably rented apartments somewhere close. This meant that if I penetrated the building and she wasn't there, I'd lose my chance at confronting her directly.

But I was beginning to suspect this building served a unique purpose and was integral to her plans. If I was right, destroying the contents within the building would remove almost all of her resources, slowing her down immensely and enabling me to catch up to her later without her leaving a trail of bodies in the interim. Plus, if I followed conventional wisdom it might have required days or even weeks to get eyes on her. I could request wire taps and catch her giving away her location over the phone or have Henry put more tails on her men and catch her that way . . . blah, blah, blah. I had something important to do and didn't want to wait weeks to do it. Either way, if she was there or not, I moved closer to stopping her. As I drove, I formulated a plan. I hoped they wouldn't mind if I crashed the party later.

The equipment I'd requisitioned had arrived in my absence and was waiting inside my room, stuffed inside three sea bags. I picked out what I wanted and geared up. Then I called Henry again and told him to organize a small Cessna and pilot for me and to call me back with a rendezvous point. And that I would also need a layout of the building I'd just reconnoitered. He called me back in twenty minutes and said the fax was waiting for me at the front desk. Never did I tell him what I had in mind, why I needed the plane. He never asked. I was amazed. A guy like him, in his position, knowledge was power. They tended to micromanage every aspect of an operation, yet he'd given me everything I'd asked for without question. Normally, I would have been suspicious of that, but my gut led me in another direction. He trusted me. He knew I would pull this off, and didn't need to concern himself with it. Don't get me wrong. He was still a morally handicapped introvert, but one that I could rely on to not trip me up with a bunch of mind games like Wilkes. By my reckoning, that garnered him a few points in my own private popularity poll.

Along with the pilot, who had introduced himself as Stevenson, I had already made several passes over the top of the brownstone, watching it through binoculars. In thirty minutes we'd seen no one guarding the roof, which was what I'd hoped for. Dusk was fast approaching, and I liked the idea of hitting them just as the sun was going down. There was always a formidable psychological effect to day becoming night, and I wanted to manipulate that effect.
Stevenson turned the plane towards the building yet again and climbed to seven thousand feet. That would result in about a

thirty second freefall. We could have gone higher for a low opening drop of that kind, but I wanted to be in the air and visible to anyone that might be looking, for as short a duration as humanly possible, considering it wasn't yet fully dark. Exiting the plane at a lower altitude, however, would make the Cessna's engines more perceptible. Hearing a single-engine plane flying so close to their building might arouse unwanted suspicion in Granton's people. So I went for the comfortable middle. That meant that as soon as I jumped, I wouldn't have long to let out the line. I stepped up to the door, pulled it open, and let the wind hit me. Stevenson cut the engine and his voice came over the mike in my helmet.

"It's your call, Mr. Gambit. I'll be waiting to hear from you if you walk out of there. If you don't in thirty minutes, I'll have the police here five minutes after that. Son, are you sure you want to do this? Wouldn't it be safer to just call in your people and handle this with numbers?"

He was right, of course. But at that point in my life, impatience ruled everything, though I would have been quick to tell you otherwise. And there was something very important on my mind, something I had to complete, an event that would be like no other in my life and I knew it before it even occurred. It caused in me an impulsive spirit that flirted with utter recklessness.

"I want to get this done now," I said.

I jumped and let the wind take me.

Genai took me on skydiving exercises over the course of a week while at The Building. Seven days jumping out of airplanes. Even then, nearly two years later, it still got to me, the rush, the simultaneous sense of serenity. At the mercy of gravity, yet still so in control of your own destiny. I imagined what it must have looked like from the ground, a figure dressed in an all white jumpsuit and helmet hurtling towards you at 110 miles an hour. But my perspective, the brownstone hurtling towards me at what looked like a thousand miles an hour, reminded me to cease the nonsensical reveling and pull the blasted ripcord.

I did and let myself be wrenched from the freefall. I looked down and waited . . . and waited, waited for my feet to take hold of the nearing rooftop below me. I landed, rolled, and immediately began to pull in the canopy, and before I had it all roped in, released it and let it fall to the ground. I unzipped the upper half of the jumpsuit, reached into the jacket underneath, pulled my Reicher pistol, and surveyed the roof. Once assured I was alone, I dropped down to one knee.

"I'm clear. Over," I said into the mike in my helmet.

"Understood. I'll start my clock now."

"Thank you."

"Good luck."

I think Stevenson was sure he was going to be calling the police in thirty minutes. I thought of how enjoyable it would be to see his reaction when I walked out of this place.

I removed my helmet and jumpsuit completely and threw them to the side. I thought about rolling everything up nicely and stashing it somewhere, but if I had my way, these people would know I was here long before someone discovered my gear lying about on the roof. Underneath the suit was . . . more white clothing. I wore a specialized jacket and pants that held several secret compartments for weapons and other additional gear. The entire outfit was layered with three-inch Kevlar that made me look like Schwarzenegger and would take a forty-five to the chest and leave no marks. I clutched the jacket immediately above my elbow and twisted, engaging a mechanism. A rod slid out from inside my sleeve and protruded from it. That's when I heard the noise.

I had no cover to make my way to, so I sprinted in the direction of the noise, the rooftop access door. Somehow, I made it to the door and against the wall beside it before the rusted out door was finally forced open. A man stepped past the door and into my view, carrying an automatic weapon. Knowing he would turn any second and see me, I had no choice but to attack. Coming from behind the door, I used the metal rod. In a downward slash, I knocked the weapon from his hands, then kicked at his legs. I did this, all very unsure of myself, because I hadn't had time to see if there were others coming up behind him. I cursed myself for the thousand and second time for not closing the door behind him before I attacked.

The kick caught him on the side of his knee and he buckled, but didn't go down. He was a big guy, but held his balance well. I hit him in the face with the pipe again, blood from his broken nose splattering into the air beside him. Somehow, he recovered again. I didn't have time for this; I couldn't allow him to keep me held up in a brawl for much longer. Stunned, seconds away from losing consciousness, but still defiant, the long-haired man stood his ground. He started to raise his hands in front of him in a boxing stance and that's when I leapt into the air. Contorting myself, swinging my leg around in a windmill kick, I connected perfectly and it sent him reeling, rebounding off the side of the roof access well . . . and right over the side of the building, screaming all of the nine stories down. I looked over the side of the building, watched him fall and plainly heard the "smack" from the sound of his body hitting the pavement.

"Well. That's what they call losing the element of surprise," I said to myself.

A few floors down, Chelsea, Granton, and three of their men occupied the room that had been set up as Granton's office. One of those three men stood at the window.

"I don't think we should take him at his house, Chelsea---"

"No," she interrupted. "I want to see him suffer the way my parents did---"

"Fuuuuccccckkkk! Fuckingshitfuckingbloodyshit that was Gunnar!"

Their soldier had thrown himself backwards onto his butt. He turned on his haunches and looked up at them.

"What is your problem, soldier?" queried Granton.

"Gunnar just fell right in front of me sir. Look." He jumped to his feet and pointed out the window towards the ground, where Gunnar's body lay contorted on the street below. The other four gathered around him and looked three flights down. Chelsea turned to Granton, an unspoken message relaying between them. His face wrinkled up as he cogitated.

"No police. No SWAT. This is an attempt at an assassination," he said calmly.

He turned to the others.

"They could have an entire unit up there. Simpson, take the men up to the upper levels and try and hold them off for as long as you can. I'll get the others that are on the lower levels and we'll load up what gear we still have time to take with us."

"Sir."

Simpson and the other two soldiers rushed out of the room.

"They won't be easy to kill," said Chelsea.

"I know. If we get out of here, we'll lose a number of our men. I fear I may have sent Simpson to his death. Chelsea, you should wait for me on the lower level . . ."

She looked at him in protest. He stopped her before she began.

"Ah, ah, listen to me. My only concern is getting you out of here safely. If you wait there for me, I will come for you. But I need you to be there, waiting, so that we can leave as quickly as possible. Those men up there are going to come under some heavy fire, and I'm hoping that will give me the chance at securing some of those weapons that we've worked so hard to get recently. I know that the warrior in you tells you to join the fight. I'm telling you that we will have to retreat, no matter the outcome of this day. This is not a time for bravado."

He pulled her to him and kissed her lightly. Though she had long since given herself to him, he was pleased that she didn't melt into him when he kissed her as every woman before her usually did. There was a rigid property deeply imbedded in her character that matched his own and he would have it no other way.

She detached herself from him and lowered her eyes and nodded her head, then turned to leave the room.

"I will come for you quite soon, and we will leave here together safely, Chelsea."

She spoke as she walked away, without turning to look at him.

"I do not need to be coddled, Granton. Just kill them for me so that we can move past this muddle."

Granton said nothing. He just smiled. That was truly one exceptional woman. He gathered his jacket and weapon and left the room himself, as calmly as if he were taking a leisurely stroll instead of walking into a firefight.

While I was still at the Noble Complex, I'd attended a class called Basic Technologies. There was very little studying to be done in this class. Mostly, the instructor, who I remembered as a very, very odd, sad little man, would parade a seemingly endless number of new weapons technology in front of us.

We'd go, "Ooooh, aaaaah, wooooow, would you look at that?"

He'd briefly explain to us what the weapon did and how, give us a few bits of background info on the contractor if it wasn't Reicher, then would set it to the side and move on to something else. Next to the training sessions with Genai, it was the most enjoyable class I had there. We were like the proverbial kids in candy stores. Sometimes when you learn too much about a weapon — for instance, how to break it down into its one hundred and fifty pieces, and then reassemble those pieces — it takes away all the mystery. There was no danger of this with the pieces he brought in front of us. Very little time was set aside for each individual weapon. So it became an enjoyable though somewhat forgettable experience. Or so I thought at the time.

To this day, there are certain weapons that man demonstrated for us that, to my surprise, I still think about almost every day. There was one especially lethal weapon that I would never be able to forget.

When he brought it in front of us one day, he exhibited something that made him into a stranger to us. A smile. More accurately, it was more of a half-smirking effect. Still, it caused a rising up of certain muscles in his face that had long atrophied and seemed to barely stand the strain of it any longer.

Soon we learned that the inspiration for the thing that wreaked havoc on his face was called a Three Staged Incendiary Propellant Device. Each stage of this awesome weapon alone, completely useless, as with many weapons of mass destruction. A computer center the shape and proportion of a medium-sized organizer. A rounded drum-like magazine that contained up to eighteen vial-like containers that contained a unique combination of the omnipresent substance C-4, in liquid form, and an accelerant that ignited on impact. And finally, a short, seemingly ineffectual metal rod that served as barrel, and ultimately, delivery system for a firestorm constructed in the form of a syringe.

I already had the rod and the first stage out, itching to be reconnected with its brethren. I lifted my right leg off the ground, put my hand at my foot, and engaged another mechanism above my knee inside my pant leg. A pocket inside the pants parted and the smallish computer center was dropped from its perch and slid to a stop just above my ankle. I reached up and inside the Kevlar trouser leg, pulled it out and connected the rod to its catch underneath.

Now, the explosive properties inside the syringes were dormant until the computer center prepared the tip of the syringe with a small igniter. Still, I very carefully reached into a compartment on the outside of my left pant leg and pulled out the metal drum. I then connected it to the rear of the computer center and waited. Two seconds later, a small digital screen on the computer center came alive and the words, "First incendiary armed. Seventeen remain. Proceed," scrolled across the screen. I blew out a sigh of relief, opened the access door and took my first steps into the building.

I'd spent only seconds on the device, but knew that those few seconds were enough for someone to react to the man who'd been knocked over the roof. I'd encounter them sooner than planned. I raised the weapon ahead of me and pointed it down the short staircase to the uppermost floor. I descended the stairs without incident and soon came to another door that let out onto the top floor. First, I put my back against the wall beside the door and listened. Detecting no apparent movement on the other side, I reached for the doorknob. Just as I did, pieces of wood detached themselves from the door and flew away from it in my direction, the unmistakable whistle and "fwiiitttt" sound of bullets passing through was emitted. Surprised, I threw myself back against the wall and watched as bullets tore through the door beside me, and this time plainly heard the repetitive sound of an automatic weapon emptying its magazine at me.

I dropped to my knees and crawled a few feet away from the door, bullets still bursting through, then turned on my back and aimed the IPD ahead of me. First, I moaned loudly, pretending to be hurt so they would near the door, confident their shots had been on target. When I fired, I was unprepared for the hell I unleashed. A fireball enveloped the doorway and unhinged it, sending it backwards, engulfed in flames. It slammed into three men on the other side and carried their dead bodies backwards and into the wall behind them. Too close to the target, the backlash of the explosion threw me backwards, head over heels, until I landed at the bottom of the stairs I'd just descended.

With no time to think, I jumped up, ran to the doorway, threw myself against the wall again, and looked down the hallway. The heat from the flaming door and the cooking flesh underneath was nearly unbearable. I saw no one but heard the groans of other men to the right of the exit. I jumped into the hallway, threw out my arm and the weapon to the right, fired again, and ran in the opposite direction. The resulting explosion was deafening; the back of my head seared from the heat as I ran. I stopped for a millisecond, looked behind me and saw that I'd ripped a giant hole into the hallway, a huge void that now exposed every part of it to the outside.

As I ran I called myself to an assessment. I guessed at two more dead with that second shot. That made six total. Granton was reported to work with a group of men that numbered twenty, including himself. Thirteen more would be lurking around the building looking for me. If they were here, he and Chelsea would likely not involve themselves until absolutely necessary.

It occurred to me suddenly that I might have been hit. I reached around my back and touched an area that was stinging just enough to be noticeable, and recognized the feeling of a crushed metal tip between my fingers. I'd taken rounds from the men in the hallway when I'd run out into it. The body armor had stopped the bullets cold. I turned my head upwards to the heavens and nodded. Carrying the IPD, a light blue haze issuing from inside the barrel, I ran down the hallway, found the entrance to the main stairwell, and entered it.

Surprisingly, I made my way quietly down two flights of stairs without incident and came out on the seventh floor. I began to realize that being alone was working in my favor immensely. They were expecting to encounter a unit, maybe even a squadron of men, and were thus dispersing their men in teams throughout the building to counter the firepower of their presumed attackers. But it was just me and that left a number of sensitive areas unguarded, such as the stairwell.

My perusal of the building's blueprints prior to leaving the hotel awarded me a great deal of vital information and two points of interest. One of them was here, on the seventh floor. When I opened the door, I did so gingerly, then sprang through it and zigzagged into the dark, massive room and nearly collided with a crate of some kind. Those blueprints I'd read, and the architecture of the place that now loomed in front of me, suggested that this building had once been a storage silo of some kind. It had been retrofitted in the seventies, with offices that occupied the uppermost and lower levels of the building. I found myself inside the only part of the building that had been left untouched by the remodel — a chasm like storage room that would be perfect for depositing large amounts of equipment, gear, and explosives. Along the far wall I recognized two freight elevators that, according to the blueprints, accessed a garage on the lowest level and a bomb shelter just below that, my second point of interest.

I knew that Chelsea and Granton were planning an attack on the newly empowered government that now ran her country. They would need a large cache of equipment and weapons in order to do this — likely another of the reasons they'd settled here in America, the twenty-first century's new black market marketplace. Here you could obtain nearly any weapon imaginable and buy it comparably cheap, if you had the money and knew whom to contact. If my assumptions were right, weapons and ordnance filled the crate I'd nearly run into, along with all the others in the room.

I glued myself to the crate and listened. This room would be too valuable to leave unguarded. To my advantage, according to the blueprints, there were six other entrances into the room, and with all the crates, no one location inside with a view of the other entrances. Six different guards would be a lot to commit to this one room under the circumstances, and I'd been lucky when I'd come through one that was unobserved.

I picked out several voices over the hum of what might have been a generator or venting system and tried to put a location on them. They were near the elevators, possibly waiting for a truck to make its way up to them so they could begin loading the crates on board. That meant I didn't have much time. I made my way towards them quietly, using the crates as cover. The inevitable sense of déjà vu that I'd been expecting as soon as I'd seen the room filled with crates hit me, and I wondered how The Captain had made it out alive. I refocused on the men and listened to their nearing voices. I soon realized that it was only two men and that the other voices I'd heard were coming from their radios.

"We're clear, sir. Nothing else. It's like they dropped in, killed Simpson and the others and then left."

The voice of an Englishman came over the radio. I assumed it was the illustrious Peter Granton. That answered an important question. Granton was indeed on the premises. And if he was, she might be as well.

"No, they're still here. Get down to storage and start unloading the equipment. Set up a perimeter when you get down there. He could be anywhere. I'll be with Chelsea."

"Roger."

"Yep, she's here too," I thought. "Apparently, I picked a great time to drop in."

There was only one direction left in the building where she could be. And that was down. Then it occurred to me that he'd said, "He could be anywhere." The conclusion that I was alone was becoming too prominent to dispute. When one of the two men I was hovering near spoke, I realized everyone was beginning to get a grasp of the obvious.

"What if it's just one guy? Or a couple?"

"Can't be. One guy couldn't have done what they said was done up there."

I quietly placed the IPD on the ground, pulled a serrated knife from my vest and peered around the crate I was behind in order to get a clear visual on the two men. Then I just watched them for a few more seconds, waiting, waiting for them to move into just the right positions.

"They're standing too far away from each other," I thought. "Move."

Still, I waited. Finally one of them took a step in the other soldier's direction. It was without purpose. It was nervous energy being released, similar to the students in Genai's dojo. But it was what I was waiting for. Still, I watched and waited until . . .

"Now they're moving," I thought. "Now. Now!"

I ran at them, crossing the few meters quickly. I jumped into the air feet first, holding the knife away from my body so as not to impale myself with it accidentally when I hit the floor. They never saw me coming.

Both of my outstretched legs hit the first soldier squarely. The momentum caused him to impact the second man with almost equal inertia and both were knocked to the ground. I landed inches away from the first man and wasted no time. I got to my knees before either of them could compose themselves, raised my arm and then brought it back down with all my strength, plunging the knife into the back of the first man's neck at the base of his brain stem. He didn't make a sound as his entire body went limp.

All in one motion, I removed the knife and threw it at the second man, who was just then regaining *his* composure. Because of the weird angle of our two positions, or perhaps the speed at which I'd had to target and throw the knife . . . I missed. Well, the knife lodged itself in his shoulder. Not where I'd intended. Shaken, probably in agony, but still very much alive, he stood. I did the same.

He looked to his right, searching for his weapon. I scanned to my left as well and was pleased to see that his rifle was nearly ten feet away - that it must have flown out of his reach when they fell. I could see him thinking he might be able to reach it.

"I wouldn't," I said, shaking my head.

He looked at me. I saw his eyes change. He charged. I let him come. I didn't have time for a martial arts exhibition. And there was a reason I had used the knife. I didn't want any weapons discharging in that room. Not only would it draw attention but in there it could set off any number of explosions. And I wasn't ready for that. Yet.

So I let him charge, knife still protruding from his shoulder. I let him get within a foot, just as he was beginning to lower his head and preparing to lunge at me. That's when I fell to my butt and guided him, in a fashion. I let him tumble on top of me, then put my hands on each side of his head, pulled him in, opened my mouth wide, clamped my teeth down on his nose and bit into it with all the mandible effort I could drum up.

Luckily, his screams were muffled by the closeness of our bodies. He fought and clawed at me and tried to pull away, but I didn't release my hold on him until I was sure he'd be too shocked to continue. Then I pulled my knees in and up into my chest and kicked at him, pushing him off me. He flew backwards and then onto his own back. Clutching at his face, blood rushing between his fingers and down his wrists and his arms, he didn't even look at me when I stood.

He lay there, convulsing, unable to see beyond the terror and shock that washed over him. And had he looked at me, what a sight I must have been. The white of my Kevlar fatigues must have been as bloodstained as was his uniform. I spat out a mouthful of his blood onto the floor beside me. I was surprised by the quantity of it that came out and splattered on the ground noisily.

I walked over to the man and looked at him, waves of crimson spurting from his face. He writhed in intense pain, surrounded in his own blood, and once again, The Captain came back into my thoughts. Here was another person, just like The Captain, and a few others now, destroyed by my choices. My descent into indiscriminate savagery was complete. I'd finally become what Wilkes had always hoped I might.

"C'mon, man, please. Have mercy."

I looked down at him and listened to his gargled words and suddenly didn't feel sorry for him anymore.

"How much mercy did you award those families you helped destroy?" I said, quietly.

His eyes lost all focus and his mouth opened slightly. "I'm sorry. I am sorry."

"Not good enough. I grant you no mercy," I said.

I kicked him. I put my foot into his already nearly severed nose with all my might. He yipped and fell backwards, unconscious.

A voice startled me and I whipped my head around in search of it. It took a moment to realize that the radio mike on the other soldier's shoulder was the source.

"Constantine. Constantine, Constantine, come in."

So that was his name. When he didn't answer, they'd know. I retrieved the IPD, set it atop one of the nearby crates, and flipped open a small cover on the computer center that hid a keypad. I keyed in a ten digit number and 0 for "engage," then waited for the apparatus to emit a whistle that told me it was working. Detaching the velcro holding my jacket together, I pulled out a handgun from inside the vest, walked to the elevator, pushed the button to bring the elevator up, then stopped, thinking. I turned around, walked over to the dead soldier, grabbed his feet, and dragged him into the elevator with me. I pushed "B" and watched the room disappear from sight as the doors closed shut in front of me.

They entered the storage facility quietly, slipping eleven men into the area through four of the facility's five or so entrances. Their new leader's name was Procter. He'd received an immediate, unspoken field upgrade when Simpson had been killed by the intruders, and upon instruction from Granton to occupy the storage facility, had ordered a stealthy ingress. When Constantine had not answered his radio, his anxiety was doubled.

Procter partnered himself with Martinez, divided the others into teams of three, and coordinating their moment of entry, sought to retake the facility. Procter was doing the best he knew how. He was more of a leader than any of the others left, of that even he could be convinced, considering the type of men they were; but that made him no more confident of his abilities in general when commanding men in battle.

He'd not been to this room in some time. It was filled nearly to capacity with crates now, he noticed. That would complicate things. He turned to Martinez and motioned for him to try and get a look over their crate, deeper into the facility. Just as Martinez started to move, Gabriel's voice whispered over his radio.

"Procter. I got something over here, it's a sound, it's a noise or something. Should I check it out?"

He didn't know! How should he know?

"Is it a bomb, mate?" he whispered back.

"It don't sound like no countdown to me."

"Yea, alright, check it out then. But be careful for foock's sake."

Procter's armpits were fast filling to wading pool proportions. He felt his heart beating faster than the time he found himself in Pinckney, having just left the penitentiary three months earlier, when he found that sweet little girl passed out outside a pub. Yeah, she'd been surprisingly submissive for the first hour or so; when he could give her no guarantee that he'd be done with her anytime soon, she'd tried to fight back and that's when he'd been forced to have gone and done it. After he'd had one last go at her.

Yeah, not like this. That had been stirring and diverting and had changed his life forever. This was different. This was out of his control and he knew it. He felt like this was gonna be the end of him.

He looked at Martinez, waiting for Gabriel to answer. Martinez shrugged his shoulders and looked away. What was taking him so long? He tried to fill his lungs with air, but they fought him. He shook his head from side to side, trying to fight off the fog and the lightheadedness.

"Dude, calm down, *mate*," Martinez said scornfully.

"Sod off," he said. "Fookin' spic."

"Procter."

It was Gabriel. Finally.

"Yeah, what you got?"

"It's a gun. It's an odd looking thing, but it's definitely some kind of weapon."

"A gun, huh?"

"Isn't that what he just said?"

Procter threw a look at Martinez that he hoped would register, but the other man just rolled his eyes. He wondered why he picked this ass as his partner. He pulled the mike close to his mouth.

"Team two, check in."

"Nothing, Procter, and we've searched the entire western wall of this place."

"Yeah, same here, Procter. We got the middle half and there's nobody here. Ain't seen nobody, ain't heard nothin 'ceptin that same whistlin' sound. If you and Gabriel got nothin' in your quadrant, I'd say there ain't nobody here no more. "

"Yeah, yeah, maybe so. Alright, team one and two set up a perimeter along the walls and cover as much area as you can. Be sure to cover every entrance except this one I'm at now. *Martinez* will take this one."

"What about the gun?"

"I'm coming your way now, Gabriel."

"Good to go."

Procter was beginning to feel confident that the threat had somehow been neutralized. They might even have gone running when they saw his men coming. Either way, the room was his and now all he had to do was keep it that way until they got out of here. Hopefully Granton or Chelsea would come for them soon and take over. After that, the first thing he would do would be to have Granton put somebody else in charge.

But. After the way he'd handled this situation, Granton might even argue that he was more capable than he gave himself credit for. And perhaps . . . perhaps. He'd been a bit shaky at first, right, but that was a timeless time ago. Minutes even. Now he was a different story. His men . . . *his* men were made confident by the way he directed them. As a matter of fact, he'd been wrong to question his qualities as a leader in the first place. Every man needed an opportunity to let their true nature shine through. Every soldier needed a trial by fire of some kind. This was his. He finally saw it. He could lead. And he would lead. And he'd make Granton proud.

He pulled himself from the glory that was soon to be his and looked at Gabriel approaching him. Gabriel looked up from the weapon he held in his hands, with a look of perplexion covering his face. He held it out to Procter, who took it and turned it over in his hands, inspecting it.

"It beeped once . . . ain't did nothing since," Gabriel said.

"Should we be holding this thing?" Procter asked.

"What else we gonna do with it? There's no timer, no plugs, no wires, so it's not a bomb. There's a trigger. See?" he said, pointing at it. "It's some kind of gun. Must be what the guy was using to do all that damage upstairs."

"Yeah, you're right."

A voice over the radio. It was Coburn, team three. "Wait a minute, we got something here . . . aww, FUCK. It's Lexington. Procter, we found him. He's . . . wait a minute. He's alive but he's out cold."

Procter took a moment to think what this new discovery would mean for their immediate futures. Not that he was surprised. Actually, he'd expected Constantine and Lexington to be dead. They'd found Lexington. Where was Constantine? Maybe Constantine had removed this weapon from the intruder during a fight and then . . . well, then where *were* they?

Another beep caused Procter to retrain his attention on the more immediate concern. He looked at the weapon, held it upright, and peered down into the digital screen.

"Oh, there it goes again," said Gabriel, looking at the IPD having heard the beep as well.

A single word scrolled across the screen and Procter realized his earlier self-congratulatory attitude had been far too premature. There would be no further glory for him, nor the others. The screen read simply . . . "Silent countdown complete. Detonation impending. Goodbye."

"Awww, fook me . . . ."

The implosion ripped through three floors of the brownstone, the force of the explosion sending chunks of debris cometing skyward. Pieces of the building, stone and flesh and asbestos, erupted from the flash of white-hot light that suddenly filled the night and shot out and tore into the buildings across the street. Witnesses on the street below and in the neighboring buildings, who happened to still be in their offices and looking out their windows, would later say that the explosion looked like the night had been torn asunder, ripped apart at its seam, and that daylight was slipping through into where it didn't belong. Many had been forced to put their hands up in front of their faces to keep from being blinded by the unannounced, titanic lightshow occurring before their very eyes.

The sound of massive amounts of ordnance popped and crackled and whistled, heralding the coming of the second massive explosion that occurred next and that left the building moaning and creaking, all foreshadowing the obvious. With nothing to hold it up, the ninth floor and ceiling collapsed in on the building, slammed into the floors below and crumbled all around what was left of the building, most of it still on fire.

CHAPTER 45

After leaving the storage facility, I'd taken the elevator down to the lowest level, the old bomb shelter, pulled the stop button and waited for the explosion to hit. My thinking was that if there were people on the other side of the door, waiting to ambush me upon my exit, they'd certainly be thrown about and generally shaken enough by the explosion to give me a slight advantage if I exited immediately afterwards. The reasoning was flimsy, I know, but I was in a hurry.

I stuck my fingers between the doors and worked to pry them apart. It went slower and with more difficulty than I'd expected, and as they finally began to open enough to get through, it was obvious that any advantage I might have had was lost some minutes ago. So I went to plan B. Instead of opening them only enough to squeeze through, I labored and finally had them open wide enough to allow me and my dead friend to enter the basement.

I picked up the body of the man I'd killed in the storage facility and stood him up in front of me, facing in front of us - my dead human shield. Putting my arms under his pits, my weapon pointing out from in between his arm, I pushed him forward and through the door, where the body collapsed of course. I backed into the interior of the elevator again and listened. But nothing happened. No shots. No sounds of movement. My elaborate ruse had stirred no one to action, it appeared.

I peered around the corner of the mostly open elevator doors. They opened up into a very small hallway that ran a few meters to my left and right and stopped at cement walls. But just across that hallway, and immediate from the elevator doors, was a doorway that led into the shelter. From my vantage, I could see well into the room. Three man-sized dummies, a punching bag, and an entrance into another room. But no one in sight. The room looked empty. Of course that meant nothing, especially when I couldn't see the whole room. I couldn't be sure there was no one standing on the other side to the left or right of the threshold.

I did think it safe to assume that if there were individuals hiding in that first room, there weren't many. I could see most of the room and there weren't a lot of places to hide. I raised my gun, morbidly threw my dead compatriot a thumbs up, stepped over his legs and slowly crept across the hallway and up to the door. I reached the door and first attempted to clear both sides of the inside without stepping in. I saw no one. So I looked in.

Suddenly feet came flying from inside the room, from above the threshold, which caught me completely unprepared for an attack from that direction. They slammed into my chest and sent me to my butt and sliding backwards on the cement floor, back towards the elevator, just missing the soldier's body. I collided into the wall with a thud, but had been at least witting enough to maintain my weapon aimed in front of me as I slid.

That's when I saw her for the first time in the flesh. Chelsea dropped to her feet and leveled her weapon at me. A fraction of a moment passed between us. In the span of that moment, framed by the doorway, I saw her recognize that I was as capable of firing at her as she was at me and that I was also wearing body armor and she'd have to nail a head shot. As quickly as she'd appeared, she then disappeared from sight, wheeling out of the doorway and out of my line of fire. It was time to act.

I jumped to my feet and leapt forward in a sprint. When I reached the doorway I jumped headfirst and dove through the door horizontally. I curled and hit the floor in a roll. I came up, turned, raised my weapon, and was totally caught by surprise by the speed and severity with which she attacked. She was goooood. Using a pipe that she'd apparently procured out of a black hat, she tore into me with efficiency and skill that I thought only I possessed. Using the pipe like a bo staff, she disarmed me immediately then hit me three times in the course of a second and I suddenly couldn't remember my name.

Reflexively, I threw up my hands in front of my face in an inarticulate attempt at protecting myself, molested by the staff that she wielded as comfortably as if it were merely an extension of her arm. In response, she immediately tore into my body. It's funny how the Kevlar suit I wore could stop bullets but did nothing to improve the feeling of being whacked by a blunt object. She hit me with the tip of the staff, the body of it. It twirled around her body and came back at me time and time again, sending me ever backwards, fighting to stay conscious under the onslaught. My eyes began to blur and the blood that trickled down from my temple and the lacerations that were its cause further weakened me.

I cursed myself for, what is it, the thousandth and third time, for having thrown myself into this deadly situation without proper preparation, backup, or adequate intel, despite how I'd convinced myself to the contrary. All because I was in a hurry to move on to another life, another new, more tranquil existence. The way things were looking, it was failing in those very integral details this life, that would prevent me from ascending to the other. I'd been sent to kill her, though it had never been my plan to actually do so, and here I was, about to die by the hands of my own target. Outstanding.

Nearly unconscious now, seeing only a blur where Chelsea stood in front of me, the last of my strength serving to keep me upright, I felt the bottom of a foot condemn me to my fate, ramming into my chest and knocking me off balance, sending me backwards to the ground. Now what happened next, an alternate end to the story only moments away, I'm a little embarrassed to tell. As she approached me, the metal staff poised to be driven through me, two things occurred to me. One: were I to die there, a victim of my own impatience really, that would be it. She'd never know what I felt I was destined to tell her. How I felt I was destined to love her. Two: I was getting my ass handed to me by a girl! At the time, that was just unacceptable.

I turned my head to the side just in time to save myself from being speared through the eye socket. My ear wasn't so lucky and took the brunt of the thrust of Chelsea's staff. I ignored the flash of pain and let my gift take over. Throwing my legs up in a twisting motion that caused my lower body to rise up from the ground, I scissor kicked at Chelsea, which threw her feet out from under her and sent her down and onto her back. Completing the move, my feet replanted underneath me, bringing my torso upright as well. Chelsea was back up quickly as well and attacked again. But this time, I was ready for her. The staff swung out at me. She was too fast to predict where it would connect, so I guessed. I jumped into the air, caged my head between my arms, and let it come. The staff hit me in the ribcage. It hurt, but the pain was no longer of consequence. Upon contact, I wrapped my hand around the staff, lighted, punched the outstretched palm of my other hand into the staff, and twirled. Surprised by the move, the staff was wrenched from Chelsea's hands. I threw it away and turned back to face her.

I expected her to attack and she didn't disappoint. She kicked out at me with a sidekick. I raised my left leg and used it to deflect. She threw a hook that I blocked easily. Then she tried for my hurt ribs: a jab, another hook, another kick at my upper body. No longer angry, I began to be impressed with her. She couldn't have been as strong as me, but you would have never been able to tell.

Recovering, and withstanding her attack more easily now, I went on the offensive and slipped into a form of aikido that Genai had taught me. When she threw a punch or a kick, I let her. Avoiding it at the last second, I'd grab the outstretched arm or leg and throw her, using her own momentum against her. But I made sure to never throw her far, inches even. Her weapon, and my own, which she'd knocked from my hands, were still nearby. I didn't want to allow her time or enough breathing room to get her hands on one of them.

She kicked and threw a right. Standing in front of her, in an angled horse stance, I kicked out hard to deflect her own kick and threw out my own right, palm open, and caught her wrist and pulled her into me with it, then bringing my hand across my body, backhanded her, closed fist. She cried out in pain and surprise. I wheeled around her and threw a jab into her own ribs and watched her head whip back and around. Her mouth opened wide, reacting to the pain. I grabbed her hair and yanked on it, turned her around again to face me, and dropped two rapid jabs into her mouth and nose. Without falling, her hands went to her face involuntarily.

I was tempted to stop, thinking she was finished. Instead, she reached out and slapped me before I could react, and I think perhaps the act was an accidental, impulsive move, because she seemed as surprised by it as I was. I looked at her and slapped her back. That definitely surprised her. I pursed my lips, looked at her again, then punched her as hard as I could. Startled, reeling, exhausted, and finally completely spent, she tumbled backwards into a wall and fell to her knees.

Striking a very feminine, defeated pose, her hands in her lap, she looked up at me with frightened eyes. Frightened eyes that almost made me believe it was over. Frightened eyes that pleaded with me to understand her situation and her loss and her need for revenge. As I had desired only months ago, she just wanted justice, for the murderers of innocents to pay for their deeds. But those frightened eyes disclosed more than just a fear of what I was about to do to her. They were the eyes of someone who would die for her convictions. Defiant, compelling, beautiful, and suddenly very contemptuous. Her hands began to move to the back of her waist and instinctually, I put my hand into my jacket.

"Chelsea," I warned.

With appalling speed, she pulled the hidden knife she'd not had time to go for previously from her waist and threw it, with deadly precision, at my chest. It left her hand and was given a life of its own and once again, I witnessed it coming at me as if time had been slowed; my vision of her and the knife were both in perfect focus while everything else that surrounded the two and filled the rest of my vision was blurred and thus inconsequential.

As she moved, so did I, our actions perfect counterparts. I pulled the backup from the shoulder holster inside my jacket and fired immediately after it left her hand. Sparks erupted as the bullet intercepted the knife and sent it careening, but the bullet continued, its path unaltered. I didn't realize until she looked back at me, the look of defeat on Chelsea's face real this time, that she had a long, severe gash on her cheek. The bullet had grazed her. A surface wound, I remarked to myself. One that would heal well if she took care of it.

"You're going to kill me now," she said.

I looked at her for just a moment before I spoke and really took her in for the first time. Even with her new wound, there was only one other person I'd ever encountered who could match the profound effect the mere sight of her had on me — the way her features showered immediate, inspired wonder upon those who tried to take in all the loveliness. Her beauty was of the sort that it is indisputable that God's hand touched the fusion of two souls that ultimately would give life to one.

"I have come to give you a message," I said. I walked close to her and stood before her, looking down at her. I knelt in front of her, then locked my gaze with hers.

"Look into my eyes, Chelsea. I dare you to find what's left of my soul."

This surprised her, I think. But she did as I asked and we both felt it. A connection.

"Do you recognize what you see? Maybe every time you look into the mirror? Recognize any of the pain? This is what happens when you let revenge consume you the way it has. You're still beautiful on the outside. But if you don't see it, I'm telling you now, it's already made you a monster. Don't let this need for vengeance destroy you."

I removed the slightest expression of compassion that might have slipped into my face and became all business.

"If you don't stop, if you do not end this now and leave this country, I will come for you again. But I won't speak to you, I won't let you know I'm coming. I won't even waste my time. I will find you and I will terminate you."

"You don't know what I've been through. My parents---"

"I do know!" I said, slamming my fist into the wall beside her head, furious with her for even beginning to try and spell out some pitiable excuse. "Believe me, I do know. That is the only reason you're still alive."

"Get away from her."

English accent. The same English accent I'd heard on the radio earlier. Granton. I turned my back, looked behind me, and there he stood at the door, pointing a weapon at me. His face and neck were bloodied, and it looked as if one of his eyes had collided with something fierce, a bluish tone surrounding the already swollen shut eyelid. He had been caught in the explosion but I'd been foolish to think that everyone had been killed.

"Back away," he warned.

I stood and took a couple of steps backwards.

"Drop the weapon."

Again I did as I was told.

"Now, over here," he said, motioning for me to move towards the door. As he moved, he circled me and maneuvered through the dummies as he approached Chelsea, all the while holding his weapon pointed at me. When he reached her, after determining I had no other weapons, he lowered his and inspected her with his eyes. I thought I saw something between them. No. Something he felt for her, but I saw nothing to show it was mutual. He then looked back at me, comfortable that I was no longer a threat because the distance between us measured at least twelve feet.

"You did all this?"

I said nothing. I drew in a deep breath, put my head down, then put my hands on my hips, defeated.

"You're quite a soldier. Too bad we're not on the same side. I could use someone like you . . . your skills.

With my hands now in the right position, I pushed a small button just underneath my jacket, on the waist of my pants. On the right leg of my jumpsuit, close to the rear of my thigh and nearly beneath my buttocks, a flap of fabric fell away into the inside of the leg, exposing my final backup piece — a small nine millimeter six shooter, magnetically fastened to a six by six inch square, polarized metal plate, installed into the leg of the jumpsuit.

"So what do you want to do with him?" he asked, looking at Chelsea. "To be sure, I don't think we have much choice but to kill him."

I watched her. She really gave it some thought before she nodded her head sullenly. "Hurrah, there might be hope for her yet," I thought.

Granton looked back at me. "Sorry, my friend. Indeed, if there's one thing I hate doing, it's wasting potentially valuable resources like yourself. She's the boss, you know?" he said, beginning to raise his weapon.

I nodded a curt, nearly imperceptible nod.

"Someday," I said. I pushed the button again. The magnetic plate reversed its polarity and propelled the weapon inches from my pant leg. I caught the weapon, raised it, and emptied all six bullets into the man who fell against the wall, then to the ground, unceremoniously.

"But not today."

I don't know why I began to whistle. There was no particular tune that came to mind. I just felt . . . finished. Whatever it was that I whistled, it was somber, sleepy. Chelsea tilted her head and looked at me wondrously, like I was some kind of perverse, crazy assassin. Maybe that's why I whistled. Maybe that's what I wanted her to think. I still don't know why, but I whistled for a full two minutes. I completed the tune with a long, monotone sound, like the sound of a flat line on a heart monitor, lowered my head and looked at her through the tops of my eyes.

"Don't ignore my warning. I will come for you again if necessary. However . . . no more mercy. No more second chances. I'll kill you. And then forget you ever existed."

I turned and walked out of the room. I considered the harshness with which I'd spoken to her and knew that anything less might not have worked. For all I knew, it still wouldn't work and she'd go right back to her old ways, defying me to come after her again. But that, if it was to be, was the future. I had something else, much more extant to worry about.

I found the stairwell that Granton must have used, accessible through the small hallway between the room and the elevator, and climbed out into the night and the rubble of the annihilated building. Sirens bellowed from miles away, responding to calls from frantic witnesses.

"Are you alright?"

A man holding a cell phone looked at me, not knowing what to think, and I realized he was reacting to the blood on my uniform and my generally battered and bruised appearance. I ignored him, turned away, and walked down the sidewalk. I reached inside my jacket one last time and pulled out a small walkie from a pocket.

"I need to be picked up."

Stevenson's voice came over the speaker. "Yeah, someone's already on the way for you, Mr. Gambit. Considering you walked out of that mess down there my friend, I guess the mission was successful?"

I contemplated my answer before I spoke. I'd done what I'd come to do, yes, but at what cost to my own sanity — that righteousness my mother had spoken of with such pride? It was then that I remembered the first time she'd talked of it.

"'For the Lord is righteous,'" she'd said to me once. "'He loves righteousness; his countenance beholds the upright.' That's Psalm 11. That's you, boy."

How much of that was left in me after countless encounters with darkness that would always hold me in its clutches, always possess some small part of me? One day, would it, could it, might it envelop me completely? Was there a chance that I might someday become just like Wilkes? Oh, that scared me. I had to get out of this business before that happened. I had to find that part of me that was still pure. I had to find that part of me that could still love unselfishly.

"Time will tell," was all I said.

Of course that wasn't the last time I saw Chelsea. Since before we knew each other, even before either of us knew the other existed, our fates were intertwined. No, we would meet time and time again. I think I knew it even then, as I walked away from that burning building. Our meeting there was just a precursor, an introduction to someone that would play a major role in our respective lives. You see, our stories, Chelsea's and mine, were scarcely beyond their infancy. All I have told you, these three years of my life, that was just the beginning of my second life.

CHAPTER 46

I've always found it amazing, matters of life and death; or, more accurately, matters of my taking life and matters of my causing death. Nonetheless, those kinds of events, exceptional in most people's lives, had become commonplace and unexceptional in my own. And thus, stirred very little excitement in me any longer.

What surprises me so, is how it was other matters, aptly named matters of the heart, which *could* make my heart leap around inside my chest, throwing itself wildly against my sternum, like an animal imprisoned in a cage for the first time. I knew that one was easy to detach from, the other much more difficult, as the former involved people I didn't know, the latter people who'd formed as much an opinion of me as I had them. But that I could do the one with such ease, and the other could be so scary, considering the natures of the two and how one would think it would be the opposite. That is what surprises me so. I guess it was that issues like duty, right and wrong, methodology — all were less permutable, affected in circumstances where I had limited experience with the other individuals involved. They were constants no matter the situation. I could do as was necessary, with perhaps only a tinge or two of regret, ultimately feel satisfaction at a job well done, and my heart, both figurative and literal, was fairly unmoved.

At the moment, not only was my heart racing, but the whole of the inside of my chest was on fire. And with every turn, every red light turned green, every mile marker I passed, the car I drove bringing me closer to my destination, that fire went up a notch. In addition, my brain fogged up every time a street sign came into view, close enough to see but not read, wondering if it might be a street written into the directions I'd been given. The streets that weren't on my list brought out an unintentional sigh of relief. Those that were had just the opposite effect and had me catching my breath in anticipation. Still, I turned and plugged on and looked at the directions Henry had given me and made my way closer to what I suspected would be everlasting heartbreak.

When I finally made the last turn, my whole body screamed at me not to, the potential for disaster so nearly convincing, that I almost obeyed. But as much as I was afraid of how badly things could turn out, I was vigorously motivated by the possibility that something wonderful might occur instead.

I parked and matched the name on the building with that on the paper. Bayview Elementary, 12226 Simon St., Bangor, Maine. I was hit with a nearly overpowering sense of dread. My mouth and throat suddenly became so dry it hurt to swallow. Somehow I forced the feeling to settle into the pit of my stomach and forced myself out of the car. Of course, I just stood there beside the car and looked at the building for another ten minutes. Then I began a frantic game of musical chairs with myself. Back in the car, close the door, hand on keys in ignition, NO!, out of the car, stand beside it again with the door open staring ahead at the building like some kind of indecisive jackass, WAIT!, just go home, this'll never work out, WAIT! . . . Wait . . . wait . . . you know you really have no choice. You must. Idiot.

I closed the door with a final, decisive, conclusive air. I knew what I had to do. There was no altering it, not any longer. I walked through the front doors of the school and pulled the paper Henry had given me from my pocket.

Room 6. 3rd grade. A little girl passed me and waved without smiling. I smiled at her and waved back. It was just after 3:30. School had let out already and only a few children and adults walked the halls. A lady with a pleasant face looked at me as she passed, but seemed to lose interest when I looked back at her and smiled. She probably assumed I was a parent

Room 17. Room 15. Room 13. I looked across the hallway. Room 12 . . . 10 . . . 8 . . . room 6. Without pause, I walked in through the open door and turned my head defiantly towards the front of the class.

The room itself was like any other grade school classroom in America. Banners on the walls imploring students to read everything they could get their hands on. The students' names in bright colors, stenciled, and hung from the ceiling. Little desks filled the room. Gum stuck under the chairs I guessed. Secret messages whittled into the wood by bored little hands. But this room held one special commodity I couldn't help but fixate upon. At the front of the room, facing away from me, erasing the day's lessons from the chalkboard, who I noticed had trimmed a few inches from her beautiful long brown hair, was the one true love of my life.

A whisper was all I could force out. "Still teaching huh, Selena?"

She froze, her hand still raised to the chalkboard. All I desired, at that moment, was to know what she was thinking. She let down the eraser and put her hand to her side. When she finally spoke, she did so without turning.

"Did they send you for me?"

"No one sent me."

"Then why are you here?"

I put my head down and fought back the disappointment that wanted to let itself from my eyes.

"If you need to ask me that, then it was wrong of me to come."

She turned, but I couldn't look at her. I was afraid to. This time, when she spoke, it was a whisper.

"You came for me?"

"I came for you."

"But how can you still . . . but everything I did to you. Nicholas, why would you . . . why?"

The impulse to cry suppressed, I looked up at her and was surprised again by how perfectly beautiful she was. I thought of all the little boys who must have fallen in love for the very first time when they walked into her classroom on the first day of school. It made me smile. Selena saw me smiling and a look of wonderment appeared on her face.

"You tried to tell me, didn't you?" I asked. "That night, in The Building? The clothes you were wearing. The things you said.

The way you were behaving. I knew it wasn't like you. I knew you weren't being yourself."

Her eyes lost their focus and her mouth opened wide. She seemed to want to speak but couldn't find anything to say. Despair, sadness, disappointment. All these things flashed across her face. When she did speak it was bated, breathless.

"It was the only way that I could think of to tell you that Wilkes was forcing me to . . . oh, Nicholas . . . ." She came around her desk, but some fear, some insecurity prevented her from crossing the room. Still, the effect on me was powerful. Finally I could see all of her. She wore the same flowered dress and sweater she'd worn during our sessions together at The Building. My perfect Selena. Only she could simultaneously be elegant, sexy, and demure.

"I was sure you'd figure it out. I was sure you'd understand what I was trying to tell you."

"I was blind, Selena. When it comes to you I always am."

Her lips parted slightly and this time she put her head down.

"I am so sorry, Nicholas. I never thought it would go that far. Or not . . . not, like that."

I could no longer help myself. I moved across the room and stood in front of her. I put my hand on her arm, and when I did she looked up at me with those amazing brown eyes of hers and put the tips of her fingers on my chest.

"Wilkes made it clear, without really saying it, in that way that he did, that if I didn't do what he asked, I'd no longer be of use to him, that I'd be . . . disposable."

I put my hand to her face, touching her bare skin for the first time in so long, and had to close my eyes to contain the excitement feeling her again generated. Again, I was forced to smile. I was lost all over again, and more happy about it than I had ever been happy about anything.

She closed her eyelids slowly and breathed in. When she opened them again the tears that filled them caused me to rejoice. My fate was sealed.

"Well, you showed him, didn't you? Thank you, by the way."

She smiled, then put her head down again.

"I didn't leave the program right away. He wouldn't let me. And I could tell. I could see it in his eyes, how when he would bring you up his face would change. He was planning to hurt you again. When I saw him leave that day, just as he passed me he looked at me and smiled that disgusting grin of his for no reason and I knew what he was going to do. So I went downstairs, checked out a rifle and I followed him. All the agency cars were tagged. If you knew how to get into the database you could locate a car no matter where it went."

"Why'd you leave? The hospital?"

"I couldn't bear to think that you might not forgive me."

"Aw, baby. Babe. Do you know how much time we've missed? I could've forgiven you that and ten times worse."

"But how, Nicholas, what I did to you?" she said, looking up at me now, the tears rolling freely down her cheeks. "The truth is that I wanted to be with you that night. I knew it might be the last time I ever saw you and I knew it was selfish but I wanted you to make love to me. Even though I knew how it would end I still wanted you to make love to me. Selfish and stupid and unfair of me . . . I'm so sorry!"

Her face told me plainly of her shame. She was weeping now, the tears erupting. I pulled her in to my chest and held her tightly.

"You make me weak when you cry," I said, more to myself. "I told you once that I'd give my life for you without reservation, without a second thought. That's still true. It'll always be true, Selena. And it wasn't just then that I had come to that conclusion. And it wasn't so much that I would do it for just anybody, but just for you. You're the only person alive that I would do that for with such faith, such certainty. That was my way of telling you that I gave myself to you. Willingly, happily."

She shook her head a little and looked me in the eyes, I think wondering how it was that I could love her so much.

"I remember how you told me that you fell in love with me the first time you saw me. I think about that all the time."

"Yeah?"

She nodded her head. "You know what I was thinking the first time I saw you?"

"Hmh?"

"Well, it was just . . . it was just that . . ." she closed her eyes and smiled. "I wanted to fuck you so bad."

She had to hold me up to keep me from falling flat on my face from laughing. The surprise and laughter had a welcome, cleansing effect. In one fell swoop, she scrubbed away all the anger, all the disappointment, all the sickness that had taken up residence within me after the events of the past three years. When I finally settled, she looked at me, smiling, and I knew that I was home. Finally.

"But it was those times that we spent together in that classroom," she said, searching my face. "You have no idea the power that you hold over me."

"I dare say that I do, my love."

"So where do we go from here, Mr. Nicholas Gambit?"

"I'm through with that business. I want a different life."

"So, just like that? You and me?"

"I was hoping so."

She smiled. "We're going to have to get a new bed. Mine's just a full."

I smiled back. "I think we can afford it. I've got some money now."

"Is that where that came from?" She reached up and touched my bandaged ear.

"Yeah. I've done enough wrongs to last a lifetime. I want to do something right for a change."

"You hold yourself responsible for too much, Nicholas."

"Do I?"

"Are you always gonna be this melodramatic?"

I laughed. "Probably."

"That's ok." She grabbed her purse, put her arm in mine, walked me through the door, and with the biggest grin I have ever seen on her face, began to speak in an English accent.

"Thy manner, though somewhat perplexing and oft times excessively dramatic, does strike a chord within me, good sir. I think, perhaps, now that I am thy lady, I shall speak like this, hither and thither, and from now on. And when we make love, at the tops of my lungs, I shall scream out things like, 'God save the queen' and 'Bloody good show, good son!'"

Laughing, I said, "Selena, shhh, the children."

"They gotta learn sometime."

NOW

This being my first significant attempt at telling my story, I found myself affected, as I suppose many are when they reminisce, especially when those remembrances have been left dormant for so long. You see, until this point, I never thought about the past - sleeping dogs lie, as it were. And what compelled me to put my experiences to paper, well, that is an impulse that has yet to fully evolve into one my intellect can fully comprehend.

This I know. I have tried to always be honest and true to my memories, and to not let my personal feelings towards an individual color my representation of them. In this, at times, I know I've failed, as with Selena's lack of imperfections; that could not be true of anyone with the one holy exception. Also in my depiction of Wilkes, who perhaps was not quite as evil as I made him seem at times. I must admit there was an irrefutable humanity even to him that did rarely break through to the surface.

And I hope that I have given you an insight into the people and experiences, and loss, that all molded me into the man I was and the man I have become. These three years that I've shown you, long before I became The Black, before Chelsea and I were reunited and fought alongside one another against corrupt governments that arose quietly in the latter part of the first decade of the 21st century, before I lost my beloved Selena, those three years taught me all about the evil that men do, the beauty that we are all capable of, and that place in-between where none of it seems to matter.

And so this telling, as I stated earlier, caused in me an interesting effect. A desire, a yearning even, for a reconnection with my own past. Reliving those experiences, I was suddenly unfulfilled, and was immediately aware of the source of this new

nd unusual discontent. I'd never gone home. My church and my
ouse, which I live in alone, are only fifty miles away from where I
rew up, but I'd never made the trek back to the old neighborhood.
had a number of very good reasons of course. There was the
hurch and my writing, plus I had several books to read and the
ard work, not to mention I had many important programs to
atch each week on the television that a long drive might cause me
) miss. Yeah, an old man's excuses. And I finally realized how
substantial they were after writing this part of my story.

When I drove into my old neighborhood, I'd half expected
1e entire area to have been bulldozed long ago and a community
enter or a mini-mall or a car dealership to have been erected in its
lace. No such luck. It was still the hood. Still where a lot of good
lack people and Latinos and whites were surrounded by the worst
umanity had to offer. The houses and apartment complexes,
hough rebuilt, of course, since I'd lived there, were just the same
1 many ways: raggedy, torn and cheaply constructed. The
hildren that dared play outside, very few of them could afford
cooters or hover boards or holo games and instead, settled for old
chool games like dodge ball or jump rope.

I walked up to the front door of my mother's house and
ound it empty, padlocks on the door and warning signs on all the
vindows screaming at squatters to stay away. In forty years,
mazingly, the place was unchanged. I realized it must have just
eceived a fresh coat of paint by its owners, whoever they were, but
hey'd painted it the same color as it had been when I'd lived there.
t looked the same as the day I'd left, just empty and soulless. As I
eered in through the windows, I wondered how many people had
ived in that house over the years. Then I wondered how many
ad been told of the way my mother had died, whether they would
ave cared. I turned from my house feeling satisfied, I guess. I'd
ot expected to be overcome by the experience. But it was nice to
ee the place again.

I left the house and went searching for Kato's old place and
vhen I found it, was happy to see that there appeared to be a
ribrant and thriving family there. A gorgeous little black girl that
ooked to be seven or eight and her two younger siblings, a boy
nd another girl, all played in their gated yard. They seemed to

have no cares and were unaware that blocks away, after night fell, at least one person would die by someone else's hand. I drove on, preparing to go home, when a notion hit me. I knew it was unlikely that she'd still be there, but I thought it might be worth a try. This was, after all, a day for reliving old memories and seeking out past acquaintances.

I found the neighborhood and searched and searched for her house, uncertain since I had only been there once. Finally, I came upon a street name that I thought I remembered, turned down that street and drove an approximate distance, guessing all the way. But when I saw it, I knew that it was the one. There was no mistaking it. This was Shanay's house. Well, probably someone else's house entirely now, but I wanted to try, just to see. Just to satisfy that odd urge I felt to reconnect with some lost part of that path I'd followed.

Her neighborhood was still the same as I remembered as well. Of course, now it's considered more of a traditional neighborhood, as opposed to contemporary, as it had been when she and I were young. But it's still quiet and the vehicles in the driveways are still all brand new.

I parked in the street and walked up the cement stairwell in the front yard without hesitation. I made my way to the screen door and raised my hand to ring the doorbell but changed my mind and knocked instead. A very little girl with her hair in barrettes suddenly appeared at the screen and looked up at me with big, beautiful brown eyes. There was an innocent gleam to those eyes that I couldn't help but smile at and I let her look at me for nearly a minute without speaking until I realized she expected me to initiate the conversation.

"Hi," I said.

"He-llo. Who are you?"

"My name is Nicholas. What is your name?"

She started to speak, but instead clamped her mouth shut with her hand, looked at me dubiously, then disappeared. I raised my hand to knock again.

"Hello?" An adult's voice this time. A woman's.

"Yes?" I replied.

A person appeared from within the darkness behind the screen, and I knew immediately that it was her.

"Can I help you?"

She didn't recognize me. She looked at me as if I wanted to sell her something, and I couldn't blame her for it, as I was dressed in a suit and tie and wore my overcoat.

"Well. I'm looking for Shanay. My name is Nicholas."

The change that occurred in her eyes was instantaneous. I couldn't know what was going through her mind, but whatever it was, from the look on her face, surprise was a major component. Her mouth had opened just enough to tell me she didn't know what to say so I jumped in.

"I just, uhm . . . I was in the neighborhood."

A long moment passed before she spoke again.

"Do you want to come in?"

"Uh, ok."

She opened the door and watched me intently as I entered, but didn't move. She stood there and looked at me in complete stasis. It wasn't until I looked back at her and smiled that she became functional again. She walked past me and motioned for me to follow her. As I did, I looked at her from behind and found myself not nearly as moved by the sight as I had been forty years prior. She had the hips of a grandmother, visible even, through the long shirt she wore. She had fleshed out quite a bit elsewhere as well, but was not excessively overweight.

We walked into a parlor I had never seen before. On my previous visit, I'd been introduced only to the entryway and her bedroom. Without sitting, she turned on a dime and eyed me, an unassuming, inquisitive look on her face.

"Why are you here? Sit please, I'm sorry."

She was still attractive. Her face was wider, fleshier, but she had that quality certain older women have that tells you they were once formidably attractive.

The little girl had appeared in the entryway to the parlor and was now watching us, her eyes sliding back and forth from one to the other. I smiled at her and she shyly threw one leg in front of the other and smiled back.

"I went and saw my old house today. For the first time in forty years. Actually, this is the first time since I left that I've been able to make myself come anywhere near here."

Shanay nodded in a way that showed she understood somehow. "I really don't know what to say. I almost feel like I should apologize to you for what hap—"

"Oh no no no, that's not why I came, that's not what this is about. I . . . I guess I really don't know why I came. I guess part of it is that much of my past was just so complicated. I've lived hard. I've lived soft. I've defended and protected and preserved life and then turned right around and destroyed it at will. Lord God Jesus has taken me down a truly winding road, loaded with pitfalls and loaded with tests that I haven't always passed. So complicated, all of it. And when I think about it, the only times I can remember that weren't so complex, was the time spent here. My life before it changed so drastically."

"You sound as if you still see yourself as the person who was caught up in all that mess."

"I try not to."

She took a moment to study me. A gentle smile came to her face before she spoke again.

"I have three grandbabies. That's the littlest one," she said, pointing at the little girl who bit her lip upon being included in the adults' conversation.

"They are my life and soul, those kids. I was married to a man for almost thirty years. He died two years ago, God rest him. Every Sunday and Wednesday I sing at my church and four days a week I work at a center for less fortunate children and I love those kids too. That horrible life of meaningless sex and constant mistrust of everyone and . . . self-hate, I gave that up a very long time ago. People change, Nicholas. I did. Haven't you?"

"Yeah. Yeah, I guess I have."

Now that's something. Who'd have guessed that of the two of us, Shanay would become the more functional.

ABOUT THE AUTHOR

After serving in the military, Joe distinguished himself in the private sector, working with detective and contract security firms throughout the United States.

He also writes media scripts, freelances for corporate firms and occasionally works in front of the camera.

Three Lives is his first novel.

Want 5% off the sequel? Want to see what's new with the author and watch "live" video reviews from other readers? Visit WWW.MIDMERC.COM and gain access to it all.